A CORNISH BETROTHAL

Cornwall, 1798. Eighteen months have passed since Midshipman Edmund Melville was declared missing, presumed dead, and Amelia Carew has fallen in love with a young physician, Luke Bohenna. But, on her birthday, Amelia suddenly receives a letter from Edmund announcing his imminent return. When he returns, it is clear that his time away has changed him. Amelia, however, is determined to nurse him back to health and honour his heroic actions in the Navy by renouncing Luke.

NICOLA PRYCE

A CORNISH BETROTHAL

Complete and Unabridged

MAGNA
Leicester

First published in Great Britain in 2020 by
Corvus
An imprint of Atlantic Books Ltd
London

First Ulverscroft Edition
published 2021
by arrangement with
Atlantic Books Ltd
London

A catalogue record for this book is available
from the British Library.

ISBN 978–0–7505–4847–2

Published by
Ulverscroft Limited
Anstey, Leicestershire

Set by Words & Graphics Ltd.
Anstey, Leicestershire
Printed and bound in Great Britain by
TJ Books Ltd., Padstow, Cornwall

This book is printed on acid-free paper

*For my sister, Debbie Snelson,
and our aunt, Dorothy Johnstone-Hogg*

Family Tree

TRURO

TOWN HOUSE, HIGH CROSS

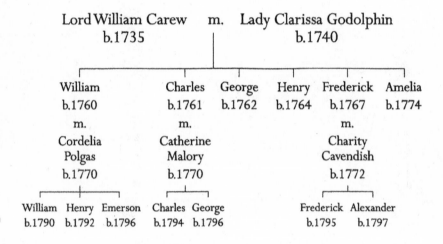

Lord William Carew   m.   Lady Clarissa Godolphin
b.1735   b.1740

William	Charles	George	Henry	Frederick	Amelia
b.1760	b.1761	b.1762	b.1764	b.1767	b.1774
m.	m.			m.	
Cordelia	Catherine			Charity	
Polgas	Malory			Cavendish	
b.1770	b.1770			b.1772	

William	Henry	Emerson	Charles	George		Frederick	Alexander
b.1790	b.1792	b.1796	b.1794	b.1796		b.1795	b.1797

Dr Emerson Polgas   *Physician, brother of*
Cordelia Carew

Seth Mortimer   *Coachman*

Bethany   *Maid*

PERREN PLACE, PYDAR STREET

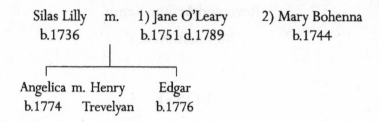

Silas Lilly   m.   1) Jane O'Leary   2) Mary Bohenna
b.1736   b.1751 d.1789   b.1744

Angelica m. Henry   Edgar
b.1774   Trevelyan   b.1776

Luke Bohenna   *Physician*

QUAYSIDE HOUSE

George Fox   *Ship broker / Insurer / Importer*
Elizabeth Fox   *Philanthropist / Ship broker*

QUAYSIDE

Margaret Oakley   *Glovemaker*
Sofia Oakley   *Recently arrived from Portugal*
Joe Oakley   *Twelve-year-old boy*

PENDOWRICK

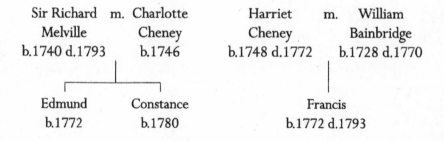

Sir Richard m. Charlotte   Harriet   m.   William
Melville   Cheney   Cheney   Bainbridge
b.1740 d.1793   b.1746   b.1748 d.1772   b.1728 d.1770

Edmund   Constance   Francis
b.1772   b.1780   b.1772 d.1793

Annie Alston   *Housekeeper*

PENDOWRICK RECTORY

Reverend Arthur Kemp

Mr Adam Kemp

FOSSE

POLCARROW

Sir James Polcarrow, MP   *Landowner*

Lady Rosehannon Polcarrow   *Ardent campaigner for women's education*

Admiral Sir Alexander Pendarvis   *Close friend and Amelia's godfather*

Lady Marie Pendarvis   *Advocate for French prisoners*

Come cheer up, my lads! 'tis to glory we steer,
To add something more to this wonderful year;
To honour we call you, not press you like slaves,
For who are so free as the sons of the waves?

CHORUS:
Heart of oak are our ships, heart of oak are our men;
We always are ready, steady, boys, steady!
We'll fight and we'll conquer again and again

'Heart of Oak' by David Garrick

New Shoots

I no longer gaze at the top right-hand drawer of my mahogany dressing table. Six months have passed with Edmund's letters left folded and unread, the blue ribbon tied in a neat bow. I will no longer read them: I do not need to. They are etched on my heart, some days burning so fiercely I can hardly breathe, other days filling me with a sadness that will never go away. Always they leave me with a glow of pride.

This letter, too, must join them: all of them wrapped in their silk pouch, no longer to be cried over.

> *From Admiral Sir Alexander Pendarvis*
> *Office of the Admiralty and Marine Affairs*
> *Whitehall, London*
> *24th July 1796*

My Dearest Goddaughter,

You have charged me with telling you the facts and so I will.

By all accounts, Midshipman Edmund Melville showed unparalleled bravery, distinguishing himself by his actions during the taking of Basse-Terre on Guadeloupe in April proved the turning point in the capture of the island. His action was highly praised by Admiral Sir John Jervis and Lieutenant-General Sir Charles Grey; indeed, both men mention him in their dispatches.

1

Guadeloupe came under British sovereignty and Mid-shipman Edmund Melville resumed his duties aboard HMS Faith. However, yellow fever and dysentery took their toll on the garrison left holding the fort and by late April, only 13 officers and 174 men were left fit for service.

Guadeloupe is an island consisting of two very separate territories. Whereas the more mountainous western half was firmly under British control, the eastern side still contained pockets of French nationals determined to recapture the island. A contingent from the garrison was sent to quell these French nationals but their numbers were low, they were outnumbered, and before long found themselves besieged in Fort Fleur d'Epée.

As no reinforcements were at hand, General Grey gave the order to withdraw the men by sea and it was during the evacuation of the British soldiers that Edmund showed further outstanding courage in the face of peril. His complete disregard for personal safety, his unswerving loyalty to the men in his charge, indeed his absolute determination to go back for the wounded, saved the lives of at least forty men. There is no doubt that he gave his life so that others might live.

My dearest Amelia, in my capacity of Agent to The Transport Board, I have pursued every possible avenue open to me. The representative I sent to Guadeloupe has assured me he left no stone unturned, though I wish it were otherwise. Two British prisoners were captured on that day, and both subsequently died of their wounds. We have their names and Edmund's was not one of them. I can tell you with absolute certainty that Midshipman Edmund Melville is not listed in the prison records of Fort Fleur d'Epée on that day, nor in the weeks and months that followed.

Less than a month after Midshipman Edmund Melville showed such bravery, French forces led by Victor Hughes counter-attacked and secured the eastern half of the island. They took Fort Fleur d'Epée and it is there that our prisoners were held. Lieutenant Melville was not one of them.

Seven men went missing from HMS Faith that day and seven British sailors were confirmed buried. The Fort records are very clear and the numbers tally; one officer, and six sailors. The log sent the following day by Captain Owen states Midshipman Edmund Melville as missing, presumed dead, and I must urge you to take heart from the words written alongside — a truly brave man, deserving of the highest honour.

My dearest Amelia, though it grieves me to speak so plainly, the fighting Edmund encountered was fierce. Two soldiers saw him fall; one was too injured, the other went back to help him but was captured and died later in the fort. Edmund was thrown forward by the force of the cannon and immediately lay lifeless. He did not stir and to this day they believe Edmund Melville died instantly. As a direct result of his brave action, the evacuation was successful. Twenty soldiers were picked up from the water, and another twenty rowed to safety.

What we must conclude from my investigations is that Edmund is at peace, my dearest, and from the depth of my heart I urge you to let him rest. As one who loves you like a father, I urge you to seek your own peace and find new happiness.

Your Devoted Godfather,
Alexander Pendarvis

I was so sure I could never love again. So sure. But nature knows best, sending out her fragile new shoots from what seems like barren wasteland.

★ ★ ★

Be watchful for the emergence of new shoots and protect them against the first sign of frost.

THE LADY HERBALIST

4

1

Town House, Truro
Saturday 30th December 1797, 2 p.m.

'There . . . no, a bit higher. Let me fasten it again.' Bethany's hands trembled as she re-pinned my brooch. 'I'm all fingers and thumbs. Honest, it's like I've never done this before.'

Her eyes caught mine in the mirror. I was wearing my new apricot silk, high-waisted and edged with lace, my hair loosely coiled and threaded with pearls. I looked flushed, almost giddy, my eyes shining like an excited child. She stood back, clasping her hands, and I shook my head at the glittering diamonds. 'No . . . perhaps not.'

She nodded, her smile turning conspiratorial. 'Well, it *is* ye birthday and ye might very well be given a present of some jewellery . . . ' She put Uncle Alex's brooch back into its silk-lined box, pursing her lips. 'You may be given a necklace, or maybe a *ring?*'

'Bethany!'

The clock on the mantelpiece chimed two and Bethany ran to the window, peering down with the same jumpy excitement. The pursed lips were back, the terrible attempt to hide her smile. 'Oh, goodness, he's come early. Perhaps it's on account of seeing to Lady Clarissa's ankle . . . or perhaps he wants a quiet word with Lord Carew?

5

Perhaps he's got something of great importance to ask?'

I joined her at the large sash window, my cheeks flushing. She was worse than Mother — they all were: the maids running up and down the sweeping staircase, singing as they dusted, the footmen smiling as they polished the silver. 'It's only a small birthday gathering,' I whispered, trying not to look too eager.

The day was overcast, a thick blanket of clouds sitting heavily above the town. Men stood hunched against the biting wind, the corner of High Cross almost deserted. Luke was right on time, dressed in his heavy overcoat, his collar pulled up, his hat drawn low over his ears, and I thought my heart would burst. He was smiling up at me, that loving smile that made my whole body flood with warmth.

'Yer mother's foot's done very well under Dr Bohenna's attentive care. His daily visits have made all the difference.' Bethany was as flushed as I was, and well she might be, all of them thinking I had fallen for their ruse. 'I do believe Lady Clarissa will soon be up and able to walk on her broken ankle.'

Luke had not yet knocked on the door and stood smiling up at my window. I leaned against the pane and smiled back. 'I take it Papa has had no more of those *dizzy* turns?'

'None that I know of . . . '

'And Cook's *headaches* have stopped . . . and Seth's *indigestion* is better?'

Bethany had the grace to giggle. 'All better. All thanks to Dr Bohenna.'

6

The footman must have opened the door because Luke picked up his heavy leather case and disappeared under the pillared portico. Across the square, the stones of St Mary's church were growing increasingly grey, the spire now swallowed by the darkening sky.

Our house was set away from the main commerce of the town, one of the few houses to have its own stabling and coach house. Built thirty years ago, Mother had named it 'Town House' mainly as a penance. *Must we go to the Town House?* was her frequent lament. Our country estate, Trenwyn House, was only five miles downriver, but we wintered in Truro like most of society. Neither my farmer father nor my mother — a free-thinking believer in Nature — liked the protocol and gossip of town. *Society can be very trying*, was another frequent saying of theirs and usually I agreed. But not this year. This year had been different. This year I had danced at balls and laughed at plays; I had dressed in my best gowns and attended all the concerts.

'That's a north wind,' I said. 'Those clouds look as if they might bring snow.'

The trees by the church stood bare of leaves, the tips of the branches rustling in the wind. People were hurrying from the market, men pushing barrels or staggering under furze packs; women were carrying heavy baskets, clutching their woollen shawls tightly to their chests. It had snowed before on my birthday, a fine dusting of white powder covering the vast heaps of coal on the quayside and thin layers of ice on the decks of the ships. Perhaps it would snow today, too.

I turned back to the warmth of my bedroom. All the fires in the house were blazing, every room filled with warmth and laughter. I caught a glance in the mirror and hardly recognized myself — I looked like a giddy girl of seventeen, not a mature woman of twenty-five.

Bethany wiped a tear from her eye, her plump cheeks the colour of plums. 'Miss Amelia, ye must know what's meant is meant?'

I smiled at her, warmed by the love in her eyes. Her blush deepened to a fiery red. 'I'll bring your shawl down for ye. Ye might need it . . .'

★ ★ ★

I flew down the stairs as if I had wings. As a child, Frederick had taught me to slide down the banisters and I had taught each of my nephews in turn. *A useful skill*, I had assured them, like climbing trees and making bows and arrows from saplings; like rowing and fishing and cooking marshmallows round an open fire. Like rising with the dawn to gather dew-covered herbs, catching the first call of the songbirds, the air so fresh it cut you to breathe.

The marble floor was gleaming, the mahogany front door polished to a shine. A large parcel rested on the hall table, a footman trying to hide it from my view. The door to my father's study was ajar, the sounds from within too hard to resist, and I peeped into the room. Papa and Luke were standing with their backs to the roaring fire; both were laughing, Father with a glass of brandy in his hands.

'Amelia, dear child, come in.' He coughed, smiling at Luke. 'No need to tell your mother about this.' He held up his glass, finishing it swiftly. 'Doctor's orders, nothing more.'

Luke bowed formally, his eyes setting me alight. He always dressed smartly, always with the same professional decorum, and I loved him all the more for that. His dark jacket and breeches were good quality, his boots polished and shining; never any silver buckles, just a white cravat, neatly folded and pinned with an enamel pin.

'Happy Birthday, Amelia,' he said, and my heart leapt even higher.

There was a time when his smile had been tentative, when he had been too scared to look me in the eye, always glancing down, his natural good manners and shyness at once endearing. But not now. Now, the love in his eyes sent ripples racing through my body: the love of true friendship and complete trust.

'Is that large parcel in the hall from you, Luke?'

He smiled, shaking his head. 'I'm afraid not. My present's in my pocket. Actually, I have two presents for you — and both are in my pocket.'

'Indeed, and what a present it is.' Papa put down his glass. He was wearing his adored red felt cap and woollen housecoat, his strong farmer's frame tied like a parcel in gold braid. 'If you'll excuse me, my dears, I'll be in trouble if I don't get changed. I believe our guests are to arrive any moment.'

We followed Papa to the door, watching him cross the hall and mount the stairs. Luke reached for my hands, pulling me back out of view of the footman. I knew he would. I had been anticipating this stolen moment all morning. He held my hands to his lips. 'You look beautiful, Amelia.' He covered my palm with kisses. 'I'm sorry, I missed that bit . . . I'll just have to start again. Happy Birthday, dearest, dearest Amelia.'

Footsteps hurried across the hall, last-minute instructions echoing up the stairs, and I leaned against Luke's strong chest, his arms closing round me. His lips brushed my hair.

'Who did they send you for this time? We haven't had illness in our house for years, and suddenly we're falling like a pack of cards! Mother's quite outrageous.'

'And my mother. They're in league and thank goodness they are. I think they're scared that if they didn't summon me I'd catch my death of cold standing outside, just hoping for a glimpse of you.'

'Except Mother's foot — that's real. I saw her fall and how painful it was.'

His arms tightened. 'It's mending well. I've forbidden her from climbing any more ladders. Do you think she'll take my advice?'

'Mother, do what she's told? The idea's preposterous.'

He laughed the soft laugh I loved so well. 'Amelia, now we're alone . . . while I have you to myself . . . ' He released his hold, looking deep into my eyes. He seemed hesitant, as if gathering his courage. 'Your father's been extremely kind,

10

he's given me every encouragement . . . both Lord Carew and Lady Clarissa have.' He knelt down, reaching into his jacket and my heart began thumping, jumping, racing so hard I could hardly breathe. In his hands he clasped a smooth walnut box.

His bluest eyes searched mine, full of tenderness and understanding. Deep furrows etched his forehead, eight long years of studying and his patients' suffering leaving their mark. His brown hair was worn short, receding slightly at the temples, his chin was freshly shaven. His cheeks were flushed, a slight tremble in his hand. He was not smiling but looked suddenly nervous. How I loved him. How I adored him.

A sound of scuffling was followed by a breathless shout. 'Aunt Amelia . . . Aunt Amelia . . . Oh, here you are — we've been looking *all* over for you.' My two young nephews beamed with pleasure, their faces flushed from the cold. Their smiles widened. 'Oh, gosh. Good afternoon, Dr Bohenna, I didn't see you down there. Have you dropped something? Only we can help you look for it. We're good at finding things.'

Luke smiled at me, getting up from his knees. 'No, nothing's lost.' Our eyes locked and I wanted to throw myself in his arms.

William and Henry embraced me in turn. 'Happy Birthday, Aunt Amelia . . . we can't wait to give you our present. Are you coming? Everyone's waiting for you in the drawing room.' They slipped their arms around my waist, both growing so fast they almost reached my elbows. 'There's a simply *enormous* present from

11

Captain de la Croix in the hall. What d'you think it could be?'

★   ★   ★

Mother sat on the chaise longue, her bandaged ankle resting on a cushion. Jewels glinted in her green turban, a host of dark eyes bobbing in the feathers above her. Her oriental green gown was threaded with gold, her embroidered shawl sparkling with exotic animals. Papa had somehow been persuaded to swap his favourite corduroy waistcoat for embroidered silk, his felt hat begrudgingly replaced by his grey wig. His smile grew mischievous as he handed Mary Lilly a glass of punch.

'I hope this isn't as strong as your Christmas punch, Lord Carew?' Mary Lilly smiled up at him, her soft Irish lilt full of reproach. She had the same blue eyes as Luke, the same tender smile, and the soft lines on her face showed the same gentle compassion. Her white hair was tied back in a loose bun, her velvet hat matching her blue, silk gown. Dearest Mary, with her plain speaking and her inordinate good judgement, had become Mother's closest friend: they sat on several charity commissions together and were a formidable force for women's education. I loved everything about her.

'Mr Lilly sends his apologies. He'd like to be here, but . . . well, you know how his work takes him away.'

I smiled back, unable to answer. I was being dragged across the room by William and Henry.

12

My sister-in-law held out her arm, embracing me warmly. 'Have we surprised you?' She held the youngest of my nephews in her other arm and he squealed loudly as we embraced.

'You have, Cordelia — a complete surprise. It's so lovely to see you. How's my little Emmy?' I covered the beaming child with kisses. 'Are you staying in Truro? I can't believe you're here.'

Cordelia pulled Emmy back to save my gown from soggy gingerbread. 'The boys wanted to give you their present, and we've such wonderful news. My brother Emerson's coming home . . . it's unexpected and really very wonderful.' She wiped away a tear. 'He's expected any day now. I've brought the children to stay with Mama so we can be here when he arrives.'

My three nephews were smiling, Henry twisting his hands against his chest. 'We haven't met Uncle Emerson yet. He's been away for so long.'

'Indeed he has, Henry.'

So much love, so much happiness. I glanced at Luke and my heart burned. Behind me, I heard the footman cough politely.

'Mrs Elizabeth Fox.'

'Elizabeth!' I rushed to greet my dearest friend. 'I can't believe you're here as well. What a wonderful birthday this is turning out to be.'

Elizabeth stood smiling from under her soft white bonnet. A member of the Society of Friends, she often visited her house in Truro, though their family home and shipping business were in Falmouth. Her cheeks dimpled, her rosebud lips pursing in mock horror. 'As if I wouldn't come on your birthday! Wild horses couldn't drag me away.' Her soft grey gown rustled as I led her to the fire, her simple white collar accentuating her flushed cheeks. She rubbed her hands together, gleefully accepting a large glass of lemonade. 'That wind's from the north — I think it's cold enough to bring snow.'

2

I untied the ribbon on the boys' present. 'It's so we know whether we can come in or not.' William pointed to the piece of wood. 'We found it on the shore and scrubbed it really hard. Then we polished it.' He held it up. 'Henry painted this side . . . *Aunt Amelia is busy* . . . ' He turned the sign over. 'And I did this side because there's an extra word . . . *Aunt Amelia is not busy*. It's for your painting studio.'

I kissed them both. 'Thank you. It's beautiful and very useful. Your lettering's very neat. Thank you so much, I shall use it from now on.'

The boys ran to the table. 'Now shall you open this big present from Captain de la Croix?'

'I wonder what it can be.'

Two years ago Captain Pierre de la Croix had given Frederick his parole after *HMS Circe* captured his ship. He had stayed with us in Trenwyn House while Frederick sorted out his parole papers and we had attempted to teach him cricket — to no avail. He was now in Bodmin with several hundred other French officers and we kept in touch. He was charming, his perfect manners endearing him to everyone. Papa reached for his scissors and I read the attached note aloud.

Dear Miss Carew,
A small gift that cannot in any way repay

15

your kindness or your family's generosity to me. It is not yet complete, but I wanted you to have it for your birthday. Do not set sail quite yet — I have eight more pairs of animals to finish.

My regards to all your family.
I remain, your humble servant,
Pierre de la Croix

I unfolded the brown paper. 'An ark!' I was lost for words. 'He's made me an ark.'

Every plank on the deck was individually crafted, each a slightly different shade, and we gathered round the intricate model, marvelling at the inlaid wood. The hull was round-bellied, sweeping in a delicate curve, with swirls of mother-of-pearl glistening on the bow. 'Look — it's like waves frothing against the side.'

Each exquisite detail drew cries of disbelief. Portholes gave glimpses of animals in individual stables, windows in the cabins showed figurines on chairs. I opened the side door and pulled down the gangplank. 'Look, an elephant . . . a tiger.' Horses followed, then gazelles and sheep and cows, everything carved in the finest detail. 'He must have whittled these . . . and engraved these from bone.'

Papa held up a gleaming white horse. 'And polished them. It must have taken him a very long time. Still, I suppose he has the time. There's a growing market for these French fancies — they command a good price. Prisoners' work is being commissioned by many in London. But this is quite the most splendid of everything I've seen.'

16

Elizabeth shook her head in wonder. 'How is he? Does his note say if he's well?'

'No, but we've only just seen him. Mother and I took him a hamper for Christmas. He has very comfortable lodgings in Bodmin — the proprietor, Mrs Hambley, spoils him quite terribly.'

Elizabeth must be in Truro for shipping business, not just for my birthday. She held up a giraffe. 'I understand the prisoners sell their trinkets in the market — I gather some of them teach fencing and dancing. The people of Bodmin must be getting quite used to having French officers on their streets.'

Papa shrugged his broad shoulders. 'I can't see it as a problem — so long as there's enough food for everyone. Bodmin's in a rich vale — it's not a poor town, and I think that makes all the difference. Here, let me.' He placed the ark on the floor for the boys to examine.

'Well, my present's going to seem very dull in comparison to Captain de la Croix's.' Elizabeth smiled, handing me a parcel. I slipped off the ribbons and held up a pair of soft leather gloves. 'For your herb garden,' she whispered as I reached to kiss her. 'They're to replace your old ones. Try not to get holes in these ones *quite* so soon.'

Our glasses duly refreshed, and the fire newly stoked, Mary Lilly smiled. 'My present's from London. I do hope they're what you're looking for, only I know you need finer tipped brushes for your herb paintings and such.'

I unrolled five finely pointed paintbrushes. 'Oh, Mary, they're perfect. They'll make all the difference. Thank you so much . . . where did you find them?'

Her eyes crinkled along their loving lines. 'I had them made for you, my dear. I said to make them as fine as an eyelash — the proof will be in the painting, but I'm thrilled you like them.'

Liked them? I loved them. They were absolutely perfect. Painting was my passion, especially my herbs. Sometimes the shading in my flowers was too heavy, the veins in the leaves too thick. Often I needed just the illusion of colour, a nuance, the faintest blush.

I had to look away. I remembered another birthday, another gathering of families around the fire. Yet we had not been smiling; we had stared into the flames in stunned silence. The pain was passing now, allowing me to breathe.

Edmund would have wanted this: he would have wanted me to be happy.

Mother ducked expertly as Young Emerson reached up to catch her feathers, handing him some gingerbread instead to feed the animals. He staggered across the carpet to join the others and she swung her foot off the cushion, patting the chaise longue beside her. 'Our present cannot be wrapped, my dear. We've decided to build you a new walled garden — next to the gatehouse at Trenwyn.'

Papa's smile broadened. 'So you can distribute your herbs without everyone *marching across our lawns.*'

'Not that we don't *like* your visiting apothecaries and physicians, my dear.' Mother glanced at Luke, smiling her most endearing smile. 'Of course we do . . . it's just . . . Well, your father thinks they mess up the gravel.'

'Very tedious. No sooner the stones are raked back, another horse and cart comes tearing up the drive. Endless stones scattering everywhere.'

'And sometimes, we're not dressed for company. Your visitors seem rather shocked to see me rowing on the river — or fishing.' She winked at her adoring grandsons. 'And sometimes they get shot with bows and arrows, don't they, boys?'

'Shot and held prisoner, Grandma.'

'Indeed. Though we do let them down eventually.'

Despite the heat from the fire, Cordelia's cheeks went ashen. What Mother knew would strengthen, Cordelia believed would weaken. Far better to keep Cordelia in the dark. 'Down?' she whispered.

Mother shrugged. 'From the treehouse. Oh, don't look like that, my dear — it's not that high. Most of them survive.'

I hugged Papa. Another walled garden and my output could double. My herbs were already distributed all over Cornwall, but demand was outgrowing supply. Now I could fulfil all my orders *and* my promise to supply the new infirmary.

Papa's bear grip tightened. 'You can draw up your exact requirements, my dear — any shape and size you require and as many new gardeners as you need. We'll start building it in the spring.'

Luke had his back to the fire, the love in his eyes making my heart soar like a bird. Dearest Luke, with his shy smile and his sense of honour,

19

his integrity, his complete understanding.

His determination to stand back while I grieved, never demanding anything from me. Always professional, always asking my opinion; discussing tinctures and balms, giving me lists of the herbs he needed, asking whether I could suggest others. He had unlocked my heart so completely, and now it was his forever. His eyes on my eyes, his hand reached into his pocket. 'That only leaves my present.' His voice was almost a whisper, the room growing quiet around us. I would say yes, yes, yes. A thousand times, yes. Outside, the sky was darkening and the shutters would soon be closed; we would draw round the fire and play blind man's buff. My twenty-fifth birthday; the start of my wonderful new life.

It was a letter he drew out, not the small walnut box. He held it in his hand, his eyes burning mine. 'My birthday present is on its way, or rather, I should say on *his* way. This letter is from Mr Burrows of Burrows and Son, the renowned London publishers of botanical prints. Amelia . . . I rescued one of the prints you'd discarded — it wasn't up to *your* standard but to me it looked perfect.' He shrugged his shoulders. 'And it must have looked perfect to Mr Burrows, too.'

He unfolded the letter. 'I shall be venturing down to Somerset and Devon late January and will call on you in early February. I believe Miss Carew has great talent and if this is a discarded painting, then I certainly look forward to seeing her entire collection with a view to publication.'

Tears filled my eyes. 'But, Luke . . .'

'You're not cross with me, are you? Only I knew if I asked, you'd refuse.'

Such a renowned publisher coming to see *my* drawings? I was almost too shocked to speak. 'But, Luke . . . he might not want them . . . they might not be good enough. I'm not ready for them to be seen.'

'You told me you'd nearly finished. That you'd written everything you needed — '

'Yes, I have. I just need to add a few more tinctures — maybe some general health advice from your father's herbal . . . but to have it published? That's too much to hope.'

'Why not let Mr Burrows be the judge?'

'The man will be a damned fool if he doesn't take them all. Damned fool. Damned fine present.' Papa picked Emerson up, throwing him in the air, tickling him as he caught him. 'So, you're to have a famous aunt, are you? What shall we call this book of yours, Amelia?'

Luke handed me the letter. 'That's for Amelia to decide, but my suggestion would be *The Lady Herbalist*.' His voice dropped. 'And I think it should be dedicated to Midshipman Sir Edmund Melville.'

The pain flooded back. Every plant planted, every painting painted; every early morning and every wakeful night spent thinking of Edmund. Luke's generosity of spirit was more than I could bear — to enable me to honour Edmund was the kindness present of all.

Loud knocks echoed from the front door, footsteps hurrying across the hall.

21

'Is someone else coming to surprise me?' I asked, blinking back my tears.

Mother glanced at Mary. 'Mr Lilly, perhaps?'

Mary shook her head. 'I don't believe so. He's away for another week.'

I could hear muffled voices, then the doorman entered, bowing, crossing the room with a letter on his silver tray. 'A letter, m'lady. Straight off the Falmouth Packet.'

Mother's back straightened, her smile vanished. She took a deep breath. Every express brought terror, every letter hurried across the hall bringing the same the same stab of dread. Three sons in the navy, three sons held lovingly in her thoughts every moment of every day. I watched her mouth tighten. 'The poor man must be frozen. Have you offered him some refreshments?'

'Indeed, m'lady. He's been shown down to the kitchen.'

All colour had drained from Mother's face. She looked older, her cheeks ashen. She could hardly hold the letter. 'But it's not for me . . . it's for — '

She glanced in my direction and the room began to spin.

3

Their faces were a distant blur. I could not breathe. 'Some brandy, my dear?'

I shook my head at Papa's proffered glass. *It's not his writing. Not his writing.*

Mother's grip was strong and comforting. 'It's from Portugal,' she said, 'but it seems to have been everywhere — there are so many scribbled directions, I'm surprised it's reached you at all.'

Elizabeth must have helped me to the chaise longue, Cordelia must have gathered up the boys and ushered them quickly through the door. The sudden silence was unnerving, just the thumping of my heart and my head swimming. I looked for Luke. He was facing the fireplace, standing with straight shoulders and a stiff back. Mary Lilly reached for a chair and sat down, staring at her clasped hands.

The writing was faded and almost impossible to read. It was well formed, but it was *not his writing.* The paper was worn, torn at the edges, a crease across the middle, half-obscuring my name. The wax was sealed with a cross inside a heart. 'Shall I open it?' whispered Mother.

'No. I'll open it.'

I slipped the seal and fought to breathe. It *was* his writing, his dearest, dearest writing. I felt giddy, faint, the blood rushing from my head. It was four years since the news of his loss, eighteen months since the confirmation of his

23

death. I had given up all hope. The letter shook in my hands.

'He's alive . . . his writing's very shaky . . . but then it stops. It just stops and another hand takes over. I can't read it — it's in a language I don't understand.'

Elizabeth's arm closed round me. 'Would you prefer to keep your letter private?'

Tears streamed down my cheeks. 'I can't make sense of it.'

She took the letter. 'He's in The Convert of the Sacred Heart, Sao Luis, Brazil. *To Miss Amelia Carew, Town House Truro. August 4th 1796.*' She stopped. 'But that's . . . almost eighteen months ago.'

My heart seized. 'Oh no . . . I didn't see that.'

She cleared her throat. 'The writing's very shaky — it's very hard to read. It says . . . *My beloved Amelia, I'm well, thank the Lord, though this is the first day I've been allowed out of bed to write. I've been given half an hour, and then I shall be placed back in bed by the good nuns who have saved my life. Only half an hour to tell you everything. Yellow fever has me in its grip, such that I can hardly hold the pen, but I will be strong again soon and I will search out the swiftest ship —* '

Elizabeth looked up. 'That's where he stops. The rest of the letter is written in a different hand.' She turned the page. 'There's nothing else in Edmund's writing — it looks like Spanish . . . no, I suppose if it's Brazil, it's probably Portuguese?'

Papa took the letter. 'Who reads Portuguese

24

round here? Elizabeth, have you any ships in from Portugal? In Falmouth we'd find any number of Portuguese speakers, but here, in Truro . . . in January?' He turned to Mother. 'I might have to go to Falmouth to get it read.'

I fought to breathe. I was in a lime-washed room, a huge wooden cross hanging above me. The floor was polished red tiles, a fierce sun slanting through the grilles of the window. They were helping him from an iron bed, gently positioning him at a simple wooden table. Edmund was grasping the pen, trying to stop his hands from shaking. My beloved Edmund, half delirious with fever, reaching for a pen to tell me he was alive.

Every emotion I had tried to bury was flooding back — his smile, the shake of his black curls. His hand slipping into mine — the boy from my childhood who had stolen my heart, the not-so-shy youth who stole kisses as we gathered in the hay. The day he asked me to marry him, standing on the shore of the river below Trenwyn House, kissing the entwined grass ring so tenderly before placing it on my finger. The man I adored, telling me he was still alive. The man I had vowed to love until *death did us part*.

I could hear Mother calling for the globe. My brothers' latest whereabouts were chartered with silver pins, Edmund's last battle marked by a black pin on the distant shores of Guadeloupe. Papa placed it in front of us and Mother spun it round, putting her finger straight on the tiny island.

'Brazil's not directly south . . . it's here . . . a

long way *southwest* of Guadeloupe. Heaven knows how many miles away.'

Elizabeth traced the outline of Brazil. 'It's a vast coastline. Sao Luis isn't marked on here, but I believe it is in the north . . . somewhere in this region. Trade with Sao Luis is a growing business — we've insured several ships from there. Cotton growers, mainly the Maranha Shipping Company. They ship their cotton to London and Liverpool — some of their ships come to Bristol. We cover the trade to Falmouth.'

Luke walked stiffly from the fireplace and knelt by my side. He looked pale, his fingers loosening his white cravat. 'I've heard Portuguese spoken in the seaman's hostel behind the quay. Someone there might read Portuguese — I'll leave you now and search the quays.'

'His writing just stopped. Luke . . . he was so frail . . . ' The words caught in my throat. 'What if he . . . ?'

He handed me his starched white handkerchief. 'We don't know that, Amelia.'

'He was in the middle of a sentence.'

'We must get the letter translated. I'll search the quays. If I'm not successful, your father and I will go to Falmouth.'

He did not take my hand but bowed formally. Any other time, he would have taken my hand and put it to his lips. He would have turned at the door and smiled and I would have gazed back at him. 'Lord Carew, Lady Clarissa, I'll take my leave.'

A thousand knives thrust deep into my heart. I was losing Edmund all over again, the old wounds opening up, the pain so raw I wanted to cry. I should never have stopped believing he was alive. I had abandoned him. I had given up hope when I should have stayed strong.

'Amelia?' Elizabeth's voice drifted through the pain. 'The lady I bought your gloves from had her daughter-in-law with her — she was helping in the shop. You know the leather shop on the quay?'

'Yes,' I managed to murmur.

'I'm sure Mrs Oakley said she had come from Lisbon. She certainly looked Portuguese.' Her heart-shaped smile was not lost on Mother. 'Lady Clarissa, might Amelia and I take a walk to the quayside?'

Papa stood to attention. 'I'll accompany you, my dears. I've been cooped up all day and need to stretch my legs.' His frown deepened as he glanced at the letter. 'It's taken eighteen months to reach here — *eighteen months*.'

★   ★ ★

The cold stung my cheeks and I drew my fur-lined hood over my bonnet, linking arms with Elizabeth, our hands thrust deep into our muffs. The streets looked gloomy in the fading light; lamps were being lit, everyone bending their heads against the wind that funnelled down the cobbles. The market square was deserted, the street sellers packing away their trolleys. Papa strode purposefully in front of us, giving a coin to each ragged child he saw picking through the discarded vegetables strewn on the pavement.

Women were gathering hay blowing from the stables, their heads wrapped in thick woollen shawls. Voices rose from the inns, men stretching out their hands in front of burning fires.

Papa's boots thudded in front of us and we walked in silence, the masts of the ships now looming above us. We turned the bend, entering Quay Street, and I caught the familiar smell of rotting mud at low tide.

Quay Street was the beating heart of Truro; it was where my friend Angelica Trevelyan lived, where Robert and Elizabeth Fox had a branch of their shipping business. It was where the Welsh Fleet brought coal in for the mines and shipped tin out to the smelters; tin, copper, smelted iron — the black blood that flowed through the city. He had survived that day; he had crawled from under the gunfire. He had escaped from the island.

A lamp burned in Mrs Oakley's shop, lighting up the polished wooden counter and the glass-fronted cupboard behind it. Two women were sitting stitching in the lamp's glow, their heads bent; one had grey streaks and wore a white mobcap, the other had thick black hair coiled neatly under a ruby-red bonnet.

'There,' whispered Elizabeth, peering through the tiny leaded panes. 'I'm not wrong, am I? She does look Portuguese.' Like all the Society of Friends, Elizabeth's grey woollen cloak was lined in black satin. She wore no jewellery, no coloured silks, no lace or ribbons, nor did she need to; her beauty shone from within, her kindness and compassion matched only by her extraordinary intellect.

The door opened to the sound of the jangling bell and both women looked up. A flash of anxiety crossed Mrs Oakley's eyes and I withdrew my hands from my muff, showing her how well my new gloves fitted. They curtseyed deeply, Mrs Oakley with a twinge of pain, the younger lady with an air of sadness. 'They fit perfectly,' I assured them. 'Quite the loveliest gloves I have.'

They seemed to curtsey deeper and longer than usual, not daring to glance at Papa, who filled their shop with his great coat and fur hat. Most wives ushered their husbands next door to where Mr Oakley sewed saddle bags and travel cases.

'What an honour, Miss Carew, Lord Carew . . . Mrs Fox.'

The younger woman seemed rather fragile, her skin sallow beneath a crown of jet-black hair, a look of suffering in her dark eyes. Her gown was good quality silk but fraying at the hem, the lace at her sleeves greying. By her glance, I instantly thought her to be a woman who knew sorrow; someone who would understand if I cried in front of her.

Elizabeth smiled. 'Mrs Oakley, I remember you saying your daughter-in-law has recently arrived from Lisbon. May I ask if she can read? Only Miss Carew has a letter of great delicacy that we believe to be in Portuguese.'

She had addressed the elder Mrs Oakley, but the younger woman nodded, her chin rising slightly. 'I am Portuguese. I am educated, and I will gladly read your letter.' Her voice was throaty, thickly accented, but her English was perfect.

29

She did not smile, but held out her hand, taking the letter to the glow of the lamplight. From the corner of the room, the dark eyes of a child stared back at me. He looked poorly nourished with shadows under his eyes, his thin wrists protruding from beneath the sleeves of a fraying jacket.

I gripped Elizabeth's hand. I would not cry. Somehow, at some time, I would visit Edmund's grave in the Convent of the Sacred Heart, and bring back the cross that had hung above him. I would take it to his family seat and lay it next to his father, Sir Richard Melville, fifth baron of Pendowrick Hall. I would collect some earth from his grave and carry it home in a casket.

Elizabeth's hand tightened round mine. The young woman was taking her time, reading the letter carefully. She had extraordinarily high cheekbones, blood-red lips and heavy black brows. She was beautiful; mournful, but beautiful.

'The letter is finished by one of the nuns. Miss Carew, may I suggest you sit down?' She waited while Mrs Oakley drew up a chair for me. 'The man writing the letter did not die . . . he was forcibly taken by Portuguese sailors. Irmã Marie says the Convento do Sagrado Coração de Jesus is frequently raided by ships searching for crew. Their convent is situated close to a beach and ships often anchor there in the sheltered water. The sailors row ashore and capture any man they can find. She says she watched them drag *Senhor Melville* across the sand and throw him into their boat together with the provisions they had plundered. She says they are powerless to stop them — they can only barricade themselves into a locked room and pray the lock holds.'

The room was spinning. I heard the faint jangle of a bell, felt a blast of icy air. Luke stood in his heavy overcoat. 'Oh, I see you've got here first . . . I've just been told a lady in this shop speaks Portuguese. Amelia, are you all right? Lord Carew, please, allow me . . .'

I felt myself lifted in strong arms, heard the distant babble of concerned voices. I could say nothing, do nothing. I was falling — spiralling downwards, a deep, black void opening beneath me.

4

Mother limped across the bedroom, leaning heavily on Bethany's arm. She settled next to me with a wince of pain. 'Good, you have a little more colour. Are you feeling any better?' She lifted my chin and frowned. 'No, I can see you're not. I think we'll use the draught Dr Bohenna prescribed. Bethany, be a dear and run and get it.'

Bethany curtseyed, her eyes wide with fright. I was never ill, I never fainted; I was in a daze, that was all. Four years of imagining how I would fly round the house with wings, how I would laugh and sing, dance with Bethany until we were giddy. Eighteen months ago, Edmund had been alive. But he was weak. He had barely been able to leave his bed.

For the first time in my life, I did not want Mother to sit on my bed. I did not want to hear the slight censure in her tone, or watch the fleeting disapproval in her glance, the tightening of her mouth at the thought of Edmund and his haste to join the navy. She reached for my hand and felt for the pulse racing at my wrist. 'Your father says the convoys leave the West Indies before the hurricane months of August and September, and Elizabeth says the insurance rates double after July; therefore, we believe the ship must have sailed south. Journeys on merchant ships can take a year . . . eighteen months . . . even two years.'

Sobs caught my throat. 'He was so weak.' Mother folded her arms round me, the scent of rose water and lemon lanolin taking me back to my childhood. 'I should have waited longer. I should never have deserted him. I've been dancing at balls . . . laughing . . . singing, and all this time Edmund has been suffering.' I felt as cold as ice.

She tucked away a tear-soaked curl. 'Luke's prescribed you a draught, my dearest.'

Bethany's red-rimmed eyes avoided mine. She must have seen me shiver because she added another log to the already blazing fire. Pulling the eiderdown round me, Mother handed me a glass of amber liquid. 'Drink this, my dear. Would you like Bethany to sleep in your room?'

I shook my head, sipping the fiery liquid.

'In that case, we'll leave the bell by your bed. Ring it the moment you want company.'

She spoke softly, kissing my forehead, but I knew what she was thinking. *He should have discussed joining the navy before he left.* Mother would never forgive Edmund for that, and Frederick would never forgive him for not sending me a keepsake — a token, or a miniature portrait for me to remember him by.

Mother was about to snuff out the candle. 'Let it burn,' I whispered.

She knew my intention full well. 'No, my love, I insist you sleep.' Her abundant grey hair fell about her shoulders, her richly embroidered shawl the work of my hands. Always a red flannel nightdress in winter, a white cotton and lace one in summer. Her bejewelled Chinese slipper sparkled in the candlelight, the bandage on her ankle white against the red nightdress. The colour of blood. Edmund must have crawled away under the cannon fire. He would have been badly injured. He would have been so weak.

'Lady Melville and Constance must be told,' I whispered. 'I must go to them.'

'Hush now . . . try to sleep. Sofia Oakley has kindly offered to write out a translation. She's coming first thing tomorrow and we can send them a copy.'

Bethany helped Mother back to her room and I waited for them to think I was asleep. A red glow flickered in the fireplace and I slipped silently from my bed, opening the top right-hand drawer of my dressing table. The silk pouch felt painfully familiar and I knelt by the fire, taking out his first letter. I knew it by heart but I needed to see his writing.

24, Hanover Square
London
April 20th 1790

My Dearest Amelia,

Four long months in London and already I'm sick for home. I ache for the wind to howl through my casement — for the smell of the moor, the tang of salt in the air. I long for the sound of the cattle, the sheep bleating, the incessant clucking of hens. I miss the chatter of the milkmaids, the first streaks of dawn lighting the purple heather. I miss everything about Pendowrick, but that's nothing to how much I miss you.

Father has introduced us to his business associates and I truly believe his motive for bringing us here is not to put us to work but to show us his true nature — a nature I'm beginning to find not to my liking. Francis and I are paraded round town, following in his wake like wide-eyed puppies. I believe Father finds our country manners amusing and though Francis does his best to please, I find London society shallow and insincere.

Perhaps once we've been truly put to work I might feel better but in the meantime, I will endeavour to learn everything there is to know about spice. Father has given us both a silver nutmeg; it's finely engraved and has space for a whole nutmeg and a small grater. Apparently, we're to take them with us to his gambling parties — to grate fresh nutmeg into our punch.

Are you well, my dearest love? Your seventeenth birthday seems such a long time ago. Even with the spring sunshine, I wish I was back with you, watching the firelight flicker across your face as you open your presents.

You alone are all I live for. I'll do my duty here to Father. I'll obey him as he has so ordered, but on the stroke of my twenty-first birthday, I'll leave London and return like he has promised. We'll be married by your brother and I shall <u>never</u> leave your side. I'll become eccentric like your father and you can wear garlands in your hair and roam barefoot across our pastures like your mother. Pendowrick will be a haven of love and our children's laughter will ring from every room.

Believe me, I'm counting down the days. Until then,

I remain,

Your loving fiancé that adores you,
Edmund

I added another log to the fire, watching the red embers sparkle. I had waited five months for his next letter, racing down the stairs at the sound of each post; twenty whole weeks of wondering what could be stopping him from writing.

24, Hanover Square
London
September 21st 1790

My dearest, true love,

How your letters burn my hands and how I crush them to my lips. Every night when Father finishes ranting, when we nod to the servants to take him to his bed, I take your letters and hold them to my heart. Only then do I feel at peace.

Francis doesn't find it quite so objection-able that Father is a drunken sop, but I find it embarrassing and I long to leave London. I long to breathe our fresh Cornish air and hold you in my arms. Christmas will soon be here. The first day I'm back we shall run to the clifftop where last we kissed. I do nothing but picture it — your hair will be blowing in the wind, your cheeks glowing, and I will fold you in my arms and hold you so tightly that you'll fear I'll never let go.

I love you every moment of every long day, and every chime of every wakeful night. Yesterday, I was reading Hamlet and found the exact words to describe how I feel.

'For where thou art, there is the world itself, And where thou art not, desolation'.

I remain your loving fiancé,
Edmund

I reached for his third letter and the familiar knife stabbed my stomach. Edmund had not come home for Christmas, nor for my eighteenth birthday.

24, Hanover Square
London
February 1st 1791

My dearest, truest love,
I write with shaking hands, my frustration making it hard to hold the quill. Father has no intention of allowing us back this year: not for last Christmas, nor for this summer, and every time I plead with him his rage seems to worsen. I believe he keeps me here to punish Mother — that he plays us like pawns in some revengeful game of his.

Dearest Amelia, Father has debts the likes of which could endanger Pendowrick. The London house is mortgaged and many of the servants have been dismissed. He has all but stopped trading — but that's probably

37

for the best. His foolishness knows no limit. He's paid no insurance and his most recent cargos have been lost at considerable cost to the business. Two shiploads have been spoiled, the spices unusable, and one shipload has sunk. With no insurance.

I believe Father to be very rash — a drunken gambler whose recklessness teeters on the edge of insanity. I've taken over trading and put myself in charge of the next three shipments. Father has been the target of a malevolent fraud. Francis is kinder about Father than I am but I find I cannot respect either. I've collated the damage done by this fraud and it is indeed serious. Francis believes we should bring a court case against the man Father accuses of being fraudulent. He's a servant of the East India Company in Sumatra, who we've since found out is a notorious fraudster. I've written to him demanding he sends the shipment we ordered or we shall take legal action. I just hope that brings resolution.

Please say nothing about this to your family. How are you? I long for your news. Please write, my darling. Please write or I'll imagine you've forgotten all about me. Just a quick letter to act as balm to my aching heart.

I remain your loving fiancé,
Edmund

I could hardly read through my tears. I had written, written and written and received so few replies. Mother was wrong, letters *did* get lost. I could feel my heart rate beginning to slow, a comforting warmth taking hold, and I gathered up the letters, making my way carefully back to bed. Light flickered in the grate, shadows dancing across the ceiling, and I lay listening to the sound of the crackling wood. My bed was soft, the eiderdown warm, and I reached under my pillow like I did every night. Luke's book was where it always lay, the worn cover comfortingly familiar. I held it to my heart, curling round it as my sobs took hold — his father's herbal, the most precious gift Luke had to give me.

★　★　★

Tincture of Valerian Root for the Relief of Nervous Disorders: cut into pieces 6 ounces of wild valerian root, gathered in June and freshly dried. Bruise it by a few strokes in a mortar so that the pieces split but are not powdered and add a quart of strong white wine. Cork the bottle and let it stand for three weeks, shaking it every day, then press it and filter the tincture through paper.
THE LADY HERBALIST

5

Town House, Truro
Sunday 31st December 1797, 11 a.m.

The footman bowed. 'Mrs Sofia Oakley, m'lady.'

Despite walking in the biting cold, Sofia Oakley looked pale beneath her ruby-red bonnet. Her thick black hair was coiled in plaits, a slight frown touched her dark brows. She curtseyed in greeting, her brave smile suddenly filling the room with sadness: it was in the set of her shoulders, the proud but not arrogant tilt to her chin. Her curtsey was demure, elegant, but her downward glance was full of the same sorrow I had noticed the night before.

'Mrs Oakley, how kind of you to come. Won't you sit down?' Mother must have seen her sadness too, the compassion in her voice making the young woman look up. 'I believe you've recently arrived from Portugal? You must find the weather very cold.'

Sofia Oakley nodded. 'A lot colder than I'm used to, Lady Clarissa.' Her cloak was made of Truro's best woollen serge and was rather too small for her, her gown of good quality silk, but faded with several tears carefully mended. The lace on her sleeves looked tired, her shoes scuffed. 'You have a very beautiful room, Lady Clarissa — a very beautiful house.' No smile, but a sweet inflection in her thick foreign accent.

'Have you been to England before? Do, please come and sit by the fire.' Mother nodded to the footman who stepped forward to take Sofia's cloak. 'Come and warm your hands.'

Sofia Oakley sat, demure and elegant, her back straight, her eyes sweeping over the wooden ark before fixing on her clasped hands. I handed her the small brown paper parcel we had tied with ribbon. 'This is for your son, Mrs Oakley. It's gingerbread. We thought he might come with you.'

Her dark eyes filled with tears. 'Thank you, you're very kind. My son has a troublesome cough and I thought it best if he stayed with his grandmother.' She picked up what looked like a brand-new leather bag, opening it quickly. 'I have your letter here, Miss Carew. I have written it out word for word — the Portuguese part, that is.'

Her glance held understanding, the compassion of a woman who knew my heart was hammering. She handed me both letters, and I gave the translated letter to Mother, gazing down at his writing, *My beloved Amelia*. The room was too hot, a terrible weight crushing my chest. His writing swam before my eyes, *I will search out the swiftest ship*. Where was he? Crossing some wide ocean, hauling up sails?

Mother's gold clock chimed in its dome on the mantelpiece. Sofia Oakley was right, it was a beautiful room; two large sash windows at either end letting in the light, a vast marble fireplace in the centre, and a pianoforte in the corner. The pale green wallpaper was striped with gold, the

41

chairs upholstered in matching gold silk. The delicate mahogany furniture had claw feet, a set of family portraits looking down from their ornate frames. Above the fireplace, my four eldest brothers showed off their shot pheasants, Frederick and I playing with dogs by their feet.

'We're very grateful. Amelia, my dear . . . ?'

I came to my senses. 'Yes, Mrs Oakley, we're very grateful.' I picked up the sovereign I had ready. 'For your kindness,' I said, crossing the room to hand it to her.

Her hand shook, her stiff resolve fading as her voice quivered. 'You're too generous. Please, I cannot accept this.'

'I believe you should,' replied Mother softly. 'You are widowed, Mrs Oakley? Forgive me, but I do not think you're used to sewing gloves. Truro is a small town and proud parents like to talk of their sons' successes. Mr Oakley was prosperous, I believe? He was a silk merchant?'

Sofia Oakley took the sovereign, clasping it against her trembling lips. Tears filled her eyes. 'We were prosperous . . . we had a beautiful house, we had servants . . . my children had horses.'

'But not in Portugal?'

'In Mombasa — on the coast of East Africa. I was born there. My father traded in silk — he was Portuguese and mainly traded with Portugal, but when I met and married my English husband, they joined forces and started trading with Britain. They ran a successful business, but life is precarious, fever sweeps through towns leaving families bereft. I buried my parents and

my brother . . . followed by my husband . . . '
She clasped her fist over her mouth. 'Followed
by my two youngest children.'

'I'm so sorry, my dear.'

She squared her shoulders, straightening her
back. 'Thank you, Lady Clarissa. Please forgive
me.'

'You left Mombasa because you were alone?'

She nodded. 'I watched my family die in turn
— first a yellowing in the eyes, then a yellowing
of the skin . . . then purple blotches . . . then the
vile, black vomit. Their cries of pain will never
leave me. I was gripped by the same fever and I
could do nothing. I could barely lift my head and
watched them taken out, one by one. I could not
even bury them. Joe and I were the only ones to
recover and at first I wished we hadn't. I wanted
us all to have died. Then I took root . . . ' She
looked up.

'I believe you mean you took stock?'

'Yes, Miss Carew, I took stock — quite
literally. My son and I were weak, but we were
alive, and I knew we must come to England. My
son needed a family — his family.' She took a
deep breath, bringing out her handkerchief. 'We
had money for the passage and enough silk for
me to sell when we arrived. I knew we would be
able to afford a comfortable house in Truro.'

She stood up, back straight, her chin lifting. 'I
must take my leave. Thank you for your
kindness, Lady Clarissa.' She curtseyed. 'Miss
Carew, I will tell no one about your letter, but I
sincerely hope — I'm sorry, forgive me, I have no
right to meddle in your affairs.'

43

Mother's voice softened, hardly the voice of an earl's daughter who expected to be obeyed. 'Do stay, Mrs Oakley, and let Amelia ring for refreshments.' She nodded and I pulled the velvet bell-pull. 'Won't you take a dish of tea and a slice of Madeira cake?'

Sofia's eyes darted to the ark and I gestured she might like to take a closer look. 'In my country, these would have been carved from ivory,' she said, examining the delicate animals. Her voice turned wistful. 'My son had a horse such as this. We all rode. The sand is so white it dazzles your eyes . . . the sea a rich turquoise. Our silk was the exact turquoise of the sea — just our silk, and no one else's. My husband kept the ingredients of the dye secret. Our silk was so beautiful, it was sought by princes and sultans.'

Mother wiped a tear from her eye. 'Can we help you at all, Mrs Oakley?'

Sofia Oakley stood stiffly, too proud to accept charity. 'Thank you, Lady Clarissa, but I don't think so. Forgive me, but I must get back to my son. He is not well.'

Mother rose to accompany her. 'Of course, but perhaps you may like to visit us again? I have such thirst for knowledge and I would very much like to hear about Mombasa . . . and your family. I have three sons in the navy and I follow their voyages with great interest. Perhaps you could bring your son to enjoy the ark, and you can tell me more . . . about what it's like to live so far away?'

'Thank you, you're very kind. I hope the New

Year sees your family safe and well.'

As they talked I rushed to Mother's desk and reached for her pen and paper.

'Mrs Oakley, may I suggest a tonic for your son's cough? Mr Silo, the apothecary in the High Street, will make it up for you. I'll write down what I suggest — it's usually very effective, but if your son remains ill, please ask Dr Bohenna to visit you . . . and send his account to us.'

A tight band squeezed my chest. Just saying his name made it difficult to breathe.

★   ★   ★

For a troublesome cough. Take frequently a spoonful of barley water, sweetened with oil of newly drawn almonds, and mixed in a spoonful of maiden-hair.

THE LADY HERBALIST

6

I needed to be alone. Pleading the desire for an early night, I sought refuge in my room. The terrible guilt had returned, gnawing my stomach as if it had claws. It was my fault Edmund joined the navy. My fault. I had written so glowingly of the day we spent on board *HMS Circe* with Frederick and Captain Penrose. I had praised them and the ship, emphasizing in no uncertain terms how brave and courageous I thought they were. Edmund was impressionable, I knew that. He must have thought I was telling him to be more like them — to be his own man, to shake off the terrible hold his father had on him.

His letters lay beside me and I picked up the first one he had sent from the ship. His writing was cramped, written in haste.

> *HMS F—*
> *August 4th 1793*

My dearest love,
   I write with shaking hands, the enormity of my decision filling me with sudden fear. You who have three brothers in the navy must understand the desire I have to serve my country. I have been offered a chance I cannot refuse — to escape the confines of London, a city I hate. I'm twenty, entirely my father's puppet, and, for once, I have a chance to be myself.

I've been assured this war will be short-lived — that our tour of duty will be no more than six months. We're to blockade the French ports and I shall return in the New Year with stories to entertain you by the fire.

I write crouched on a tiny bunk, the stench of the bilges and the swell of the waves already making me queasy. We are anchored in Cawsand Bay and sail within the hour; the ferryman who brought me to the ship awaits this letter and will see that it is posted.

Yet my heart beats so. I leave Father with Francis and I see no good arising from their close affection. They are too alike in character. Francis insisted on accompanying me to Plymouth Dock but it soon became apparent he came for his own pleasure, not to see me off. I waited a full two hours for him this morning. He nearly missed my departure but turned up at the quayside just as the ferryman was leaving. He looked disreputable and I felt such anger. He didn't return to the inn last night and laughed at my censure, telling me I was dour, that I lacked manliness and I should become a priest. My last glimpse of England, and my own cousin laughing at me with such scorn!

Forgive my scribbled writing. I waited too long for Francis and Captain Owen is expecting me to report for duty in ten minutes. From now on, my letters will be censored — I won't be able to tell you where I am or

47

with whom we sail. Nor can I tell you the name of my commander-in-chief.

I love you, dearest, dearest Amelia. Think of me when the moon shines brightly. Know that I shall be staring up at the very same moon, aching to be beside you.

I remain,
Your loving fiancé,
Midshipman Edmund, Melville

The fire was dying in the grate and I tightened my dressing gown round me. Wiping my tears, I unfolded his next letter. It was dated four months later.

HMS F—
December 1st 1793

My dearest love,
I can only hope this letter reaches you. I've been told that I must write four letters for every one that arrives and I pray mine are reaching you. I haven't received any letters from you as yet, but I'm informed they can take up to six months to find us.

I'm getting used to life on board. The terrible seasickness has passed, and I find I can embrace my duties with greater relish. I've become used to wiping my fork before I eat and plunging it through the tablecloth to clean between the prongs. And they are right — fourteen inches is quite sufficient for an exhausted Midshipman to sleep in.

I'm now proficient in the bosun's calls and pipes. I know how to call an order — to hoist, to haul, to let go and belay. I can call for attention and pipe still to salute a passing ship. Captain O— is a strict disciplinarian and for that I'm grateful. The Tors like discipline; it stops bullying and keeps a tight ship. I haven't witnessed the brutal punishments I expected to witness, perhaps it's because we're only a small sloop and not a frigate, yet I wonder if Captain O— knows I'm so disliked? I fear my lack of practical skills and future title are held against me. The other midshipmen either are twice my age or have been ship's boys for eight or more years and I've yet to prove my worth — that I'm not some soft-bellied aristocrat who has bought his rank.

I write in the knowledge I can post this letter from the port of L. and it will not be censored. Amelia, I beg you keep this to yourself, but the lock of my sea chest has been forced and each time I return to it, I find something else has been taken. I've lost several shirts, my embroidered waistcoat and two of my silk cravats. A pair of breeches are missing and all the tea and sugar I brought with me has gone. My gold watch, my silver compass and a considerable amount of money have also gone missing. There's a lieutenant I trust and when I told him, he begged me to consider very carefully before I reported it to Captain O— . He left me in no doubt that my complaint would do me more <u>harm</u> than good. Therefore, I must remain silent and hope they'll return my belongings. I believe they're testing me, and if I can only get through this trial of birth, life aboard ship will become more bearable.

I hope this reaches you in time for Christmas. Happy Birthday, my darling. I so wish I were with you. I am three weeks away from my twenty-first birthday and as soon as I have served the minimum term, I shall return and we can be married.

Our ship was in sight of the capture of two French vessels, so I have a small share of prize money to look forward to. Another month, two at the most, and I'll seek to relinquish my position.

I miss you too much and I miss Cornwall so very dreadfully, yet I believe some good has come from this. Serving alongside such courageous men who have so little makes me realize how much I have, and how I took it all for granted. If I must lose some of my possessions to prove I'm worthy of the ship, then I'm prepared to do so.

I love you, my darling Amelia. Perhaps your godfather might find a way of ensuring your letters reach me?

Goodbye, my dearest love,
Edmund

A soft knock, and I hid the letters beneath my bedcover. Mother peered round the door. 'May we talk?'

'Of course, come in.'

I helped her across the room and we sat on my

bed. 'Must you really go, my dearest? Won't a letter suffice?'

I shook my head. 'I have to show them the letter in person. Lady Melville hasn't been strong for some time, and it would be unkind to let Constance bear this news alone.'

She reached for my hand, her tone wavering. 'It's the practicalities that are the problem, my dearest. My foot stops me from accompanying you and your father has an important meeting that he must attend — they're appointing the new Lord Lieutenant and he cannot leave Truro. Perhaps in a week?'

'They have to know as soon as possible. It can't wait a week. Please, Mother . . . I often take the carriage by myself. Seth will take me — there'll be two coachmen, two footmen, and Bethany will be with me at all times. If we leave at first light, I can show Lady Melville and Constance the letter and we'll come straight home. It's six miles there and six miles back. It's a good road and there's been no rain — you've never stopped me going places before.'

Her grey hair shimmered in the candlelight. 'It's whether you're strong enough, that's really my concern.'

I nodded, summoning every ounce of pretence. 'I am strong enough, and I'll be so much happier when they know.'

Her sigh tore my heart. 'Your father will issue the pistols,' she said.

Kissing her cheek, I tried to smile. 'Thank you . . . It's just for the day. We'll come straight home. And we *won't* need pistols.'

51

The clock chimed ten, the candlelight flickering across his cramped writing and I reached for another candle, placing the new wick to the guttering flame. His letter had not reached me for Christmas, nor for my twenty-first birthday: it had taken three months, the next had taken four. I picked up his last letter, written the night before his fateful mission.

HMS F—
March 30th 1794

My dearest love
   How can I describe the beauty of this place? Mango swamps and palm-fringed beaches, the sand so white it's almost blinding. The sea is intensely blue and so clear I can see huge shells on the seafloor and the ripples of the sand. There are brightly coloured fish the like of which I've never seen before — whole shoals of them nibbling the hull as I bend to watch.
   The fleet lays to anchor. No man must sleep on shore and Captain O— is adamant no man must sleep on deck. After the burning heat of day, the dew of the evening falls so heavily and the damp air inevitably brings fever. Yet it is hard to resist the lure of the moonlight. The night air is filled with the heady scent of exotic night-blooms drifting from the land and I sit imagining you're next to me, that we're alone, like the last evening we spent in Pendowrick when the moon

shone so brightly and we watched the sun rise, too much in love to go our separate ways.

Captain O— runs the ship with clockwork precision. At six o'clock, we pipe 'spread awnings' and those on watch hoist the huge canvases to give much needed shade. The fierce rays of this tropical sun burn like fire, shrinking the planking, rendering the pitch soft and sticky. Yet that does not stop the work — each day the decks are swabbed and scrubbed, the brass work polished with brick dust and rags. Then at 11.30 the Watch shouts 'clear deck and up spirits' and the officer of the Watch serves grog — always from an open deck, never, ever, below decks in case of fire.

At 4 p.m. we pipe 'unfurl awnings' and the decks flood with sunshine in time for afternoon grog. The humidity and heat make for such thirst. Captain O— insists on the grog being more diluted than some, but he's right. Salt beef and salt pork can dry your mouth in minutes, yet I'm pleased to say we've parted company with our weevils for a while. The ship has been freshly provisioned and the air of civility among the men is very pleasant. We're surrounded by a constant stream of small craft with wiry-haired, bare-chested men shouting up at us to buy strings of beads and shells. Two weeks ago, I bought you the biggest, most exquisite shell I could see. They tell me when you put it to your ear, you can hear the sea, but I hear nothing <u>but</u> the sea!

My dearest love, I've written everything but what I want to write; that, I must keep to myself. Suffice to say, I do my utmost, just as every other man on this ship is doing his utmost. Captain O— knows he must keep us all busy. No one can admit their fear; we stand and fall as a ship's company and I'm proud to play my part.

But at night, my dearest love, my thoughts return to you. To our walks through the meadows, to the way the ribbons on your bonnet flutter, to your smile. To the way you run so freely along the shore with bare feet. To the trees you taught me to climb. It seems there hasn't been a day or night in my whole life that I haven't held your image in my mind. I hold the exquisite shell to my heart, to my lips, to my heart again, and I ache with longing. One of the Tars has engraved it for you, and I can't wait to give it to you.

The drum is sounding, and I must leave you. Post is being collected from all the ships — yesterday, I spent the whole day writing letters for the men and today we expect to receive new orders. I love you, my dearest Amelia. Love you with every ounce of my being. Soon we shall be together and I shall never leave your side. Never. Not even to go to Truro.

I remain,
Your loving fiancé,
Edmund

7

The wind was bitingly cold, the clouds a blanket of solid grey. With her boots resting on the foot-warmer, her head covered by the hood of her cloak, and her hands tucked firmly in her muff, Bethany looked warm, if not her usual cheerful self. The road was dry, the coach making good progress and I smiled with encouragement, wiping the misty window with my glove. The barren trees in the orchards were giving way to neatly furrowed fields, smoke rising from every chimney, the houses growing poorer as we headed north along the turnpike to Bodmin.

I knew what she was thinking — that they should have a town house in Truro and come for the Christmas season like the rest of us, that they should not bury themselves on the moor in winter. Constance never came to Truro because Lady Melville hardly ever left the house and I had seen neither of them since Uncle Alex had assured me of Edmund's death. The grip on my heart tightened. Eighteenth months was too long an absence, I should have been more attentive, not put my own needs above theirs; stepping back, distancing myself from their pain as my pain began to heal. Now the pain felt raw again. I should never have abandoned Edmund, nor fallen so deeply in love with Luke.

'There's ice on the puddles,' Bethany peered out of the other window, 'and look at those red berries — that's a sign of harsh weather to come. 'Tis no wonder there's no rabbits — they're all burrowed down deep.'

The gradient was growing steeper, the horses slowing as the rich vale gave way beneath us. The trees grew scarcer, the open moorland stretching ahead of us in all its empty vastness. Scattered hawthorns bent like hunched witches, tufts of grass blowing sideways in the icy wind. 'There's ice on the edge of the pond. I forget how barren it is up here — and how sheltered we are in Truro.'

Bethany smiled, but not with pleasure. 'I don't, Miss Amelia. I never forget how cold it is up here. Ye should be back by the fire. Dr Bohenna told me to keep ye warm and . . . '

The knife sliced deeper. 'Don't talk of him, Bethany. Not now.'

She rearranged the travelling rug, spreading it evenly over my knees. Her lips were pursed, her blonde hair curled in two plaits beneath her corduroy bonnet. Her complexion was always ruddy, but her plump cheeks looked drawn, as if she, too, had not slept. 'Seth says he'll stop at the Crossed Keys if ye're cold, so I can get ye to a fire. 'Tis only half an hour to the inn, and an hour to Pendowrick after that. He says as long as we leave Pendowrick by three o'clock.'

It was over three years since I had been to Pendowrick, and never in the winter. The last time I made this journey was to attend Sir

Richard Melville's funeral and the interment of his nephew, Francis Bainbridge. A double loss for the family, yet there had been little grief among the mourners following the coffins.

'Thank you for coming with me,' I whispered.

Bethany rubbed her hands and blew into her gloves. 'Course I'd come with you — like I'll ever leave you.' She looked up and smiled and I caught the fear in her eyes.

★   ★   ★

The familiar treetops of the coombe came into sight and we began winding down the narrow road, the wind lessening as the stone walls of the estate began to line our route. Trees in the orchard became visible through an iron gateway and as we rounded the bend the tops of six tall chimneys stood stark against the overcast sky. The road became cobbled, the horses' hooves louder, the clatter of the wheels announcing our arrival.

Bethany gazed through the gatehouse to the ancient house with its curling Dutch gables and mullion windows. Catching her breath, she pulled her cloak tighter, staring at the pointed arches and the vast Tudor window. I knew she found it foreboding and even I had to take a deep breath. The house looked brooding, sinister, and I tried to suppress the shiver running down my back. Framed by the heavy grey sky, the stone-work looked dark and severe, the only welcoming sign a small plume of smoke drifting from one of the elaborate brick chimneys.

Seth slipped off the driver's seat to the cobbles, the waxed capes on his travelling coat flapping as he crossed his arms and slapped his shoulders. His face was florid, his breath filling the air as he shouted instructions. The second coachman, likewise, rubbed his arms, the footmen stamping their feet and breathing into their gloves. One of them opened the door and pulled down the steps.

'Thank you. I hope you're not too cold?'

'No, Miss Carew — not cold at all,' he said through chattering teeth.

'They'll find you a fire and something to eat.' I glanced up. The door to the house had been thrown open and Constance was running down the path.

'Amelia? My goodness, it *is* you. Quick, let's get you inside.'

She linked her arm through mine, hurrying me down the path and through the heavily studded oak door. She was not dressed for visitors: her black hair fell loosely around her shoulders, her velvet cap looked faded and worn, and I tried to hide my shock. She was dressed like a housekeeper, her thick woollen gown dusty at the hem, her woven shawl frayed at one end.

Her smile vanished. 'What brings you here? What's happened?'

'I didn't tell you I was coming because I knew you'd only worry. I wanted to be with you when I told you . . . '

She stood stock still, her dark eyes piercing mine. 'Told me what?'

'Edmund didn't die that day. Somehow he

58

escaped . . . but he was very ill and taken by a Portuguese trading ship — ' My voice caught at her sudden sob. 'Connie, we don't know if he's still alive . . . but we *do* know he survived the skirmish and escaped from Guadeloupe. That he didn't die.'

Her hand tightened round my elbow. She had grown taller, changing from the willowy girl I remembered to a woman with large, wistful eyes. She was seventeen, the same age I had been when Edmund and I had become betrothed, yet she looked so young. A single log burned in the grate of the huge fireplace and she hurried me past it, twisting up a set of circular stone steps to a tiny room with an equally dismal fire.

'How do you know?' she whispered.

I reached into my bag, handing her the letter. 'This came a few days ago . . . and this is the translation because part of it's written in Portuguese.' I held my hands to the fire, taking off neither my gloves nor my cloak. 'It's dated eighteen months ago . . . and he was very weak. That's all we've got, Connie.'

She looked up, and in that instant I saw Edmund looking at me — his thick shock of black hair, his high cheekbones, his dark eyelashes and heavy brows. I saw the hope in his eyes and my stomach twisted. I had forgotten what he looked like; I had not held his image in my mind for so long, yet there he was: his face in her face — a boy of seventeen, looking up at me, a ring pressing against his lips, my hand pressing against his lips, my lips pressing against his lips.

The pain was unbearable. I had to sit down,

cover my face with my hands.

Another image grew stronger: another man
— the man I now loved, kneeling at my feet,
reaching into his pocket, his blue eyes filled with
tenderness. I saw his familiar deep furrows, his
brown hair worn short, his freshly shaven chin,
and his cheeks slightly flushed. I could not
breathe. Seeing Constance had brought everything back, as if Edmund was there in the room
and if I turned my head I might see him.

Tears splashed Constance's cheeks. 'I can
hardly take this in. He must be alive . . . they
wouldn't have taken him if they thought him too
weak. Voyages take years . . . if he escaped
before, he'll escape again.' She looked too thin,
her slender fingers fumbling to find her
handkerchief. 'I'm sorry, I'm not dressed for
company . . . you must think me very wretched.
I've been sorting the stores — the pickles. We
have so little company that I've become quite a
housekeeper.' She smiled through her tears.
'Mama will be very happy to see you — this
news might be all she needs to get well again.'

'Is it her rheumatism?'

'At first it was just her joints, but she's
developed a persistent cough. She barely eats.
You know how she is — since Edmund's death,
she's lost all joy. Mrs Alston does her best to
tempt her, but Mama won't touch meat
and . . . ' She looked up and Edmund's eyes
pierced mine. 'I can't tell you how wonderful it is
to see you.'

I was back in the spring of 1789, a girl of
sixteen. The sun had shone, the sky intensely

blue, the moor a mass of purple heather and white cattle. As family friends we had been invited to visit Pendowrick. Edmund had been waiting up the lane for our carriage and had jumped down from the wall, running beside our coach, skipping sideways, smiling up at me, and I had pulled down the window, leaning out, holding on to my bonnet, laughing back at him, giddy with happiness. *The exuberance of youth,* Papa had said as Edmund bent double at the gatehouse, too breathless to greet us.

We were so young, yet my heart had been bursting with love. *My beloved is like a roe or a young hart.* We did not need words, both of us thinking with one mind. *Rise up my love, my fair one, and come away.* Edmund had taken me by the hand, whirling me through the ancient house, dipping under the stone arches, smiling down from the minstrels' gallery, and Constance had run behind us, somehow willing to share her adored elder brother with me. She had been eight, a silent girl with hoops and kittens and a small pony called Milor. We were only sixteen, yet I knew our love was real.

Connie wiped her eyes. 'We'll go to Mama now . . . Will you stay the night? Only if you stay we must prepare you a room and something to eat. Your servants must be fed.'

'Please, no fuss. Just a fire and something for them to eat — I don't want to impose on you. We'll leave at three — no later.'

She kept hold of the letters, leading me through a small door and down a narrow corridor into what I knew was the servants' wing. Edmund

61

had never taken me there, even after we returned for a second visit — both of us now seventeen. Our parents could no longer dismiss our love as infatuation and the discussions between them had turned serious.

We had stayed in the east wing, in rooms with dark wooden panelling and carved mullion windows, dining formally in the great hall with its ornate plasterwork and vast Tudor window. Constance had sat beside me, bright-eyed and smiling. *There are five hundred and seventy-six panes of glass* — she had whispered — *I know that because I've counted them all.*

I had smiled back at her, but my heart was breaking. Edmund and I had both smiled, accepting the terms of our engagement with fortitude, if not with relish. What else could we do? Eldest sons of the noble Melville family had to wait until their twenty-first birthday for their allowance and any thought of embarking on marriage. Like all the other heirs to the title and estate, Edmund would prove no exception. After all, four years was not such a long time, he would finish his education in London and learn the family business and frequent visits must suffice. Pendowrick Manor had stood for three hundred years; another four years would pass very quickly.

Constance rested her hand against the heavy oak door. 'Amelia . . . please don't be shocked. Mama's not dressed — in fact, she hardly ever leaves her bed now. Would you give me a minute and I'll prepare her for your visit?'

She knocked loudly, pushing open the studded

arched door. 'Mama,' she whispered, 'Amelia Carew has come to see us.' She turned to me. 'I won't be long.'

She closed the door and I gazed through the small leaded window to the garden below. It was almost unrecognizable from my previous visits. Instead of neat roses and box hedges filled with lavender, hens were pecking at long, woody stalks, scratching in bare patches of earth. An upturned stool lay on its side, an abandoned wooden pail flung beside it. Grass was growing through the gravel paths, the enclosing wall dotted with dark patches of moss. Through the open gate, I saw weeds growing in the cobbled courtyard and the huge barn doors firmly closed.

Constance joined me at the window, her voice echoing my sadness. 'The horses have all gone . . . In fact, we've very few animals left. Most of the servants have gone to Sir Charles Montford's new house and estate — he poached them all and who can blame them?' Her voice caught. 'It's not like how it was, Amelia. We live very simply now . . . ' Tears glistened on her dark lashes. 'That letter brings us such hope. Edmund *must* be alive . . . he *has* to be alive.'

She was too thin, her cheeks sallow, her hair simply dressed, as if she had had no help with the pinning of her clasps. 'Who oversees the estate?'

'Our steward, Mr Elton. He gives Mama an allowance but it's a pittance. The house and estate are entailed to my first-born son. He will inherit the land and title. He'll be the sixth baron, but until he reaches twenty-one, the estate will remain in trust. My husband, *whoever he will be*, and Mr Elton will act in his interest and I'll have no say in the matter whatsoever.' She twisted the tip of her shawl round her finger, bringing it to her mouth. 'We need . . . or rather *I* need, Edmund to come home.'

It was bitterness in her voice, not wistfulness. A definite note of defiance.

'You must have several suitors?'

Her mouth tightened. 'Oh, yes . . . more than you can imagine! They're coming out of the woodwork, scurrying round the house with Mr Elton like swarms of death-watch beetles. Some are from London, some from Devon, and there's one from Wiltshire. There's nothing like a title and an estate to draw them in — and I'm to be bought along with the house.'

'Connie, don't say that.'

'Not speak the truth? There's plenty of new money out there, and plenty wanting to raise their status by marrying the heir to a bankrupt baronetcy, even if they do have to part with a large settlement. Some marry for love, others for *expedience*. When they visit, I pretend I have a headache and that suits them very well. The last person they want to see is *me*.'

'But Connie, you *must* see them. You can't let Mr Elton decide like that. *You* must choose who you marry. You belong to one of the oldest families in Cornwall — you've a pedigree stretching back to Henry VIII . . . their son will bear a noble name.'

She shrugged her shoulders, gazing out of the window to the church just visible beyond the orchard. 'I've been told very little. What I've gleaned is all from listening at doors. I haven't been allowed to see Father's will ... ' She wound the edge of her shawl round her finger, once again drawing it to her mouth. 'When Mr Elton showed Mama the will, I heard her cry out. They had a terrible row. When he left she refused to let me see it. I don't know if it was because Father left us so poor. But there we have it. My son's to inherit the title, and they'll decide who I marry.'

The severity in her voice, the hurt, the twisting of her finger; she was holding back her anger. 'Connie, they can't just discount your wishes.'

'They can, and they *do*. Come, Mama will be ready now.' Her smile was forced, her voice just as tense. 'I'm afraid you'll see an enormous change in her.'

★ ★ ★

The passions have a greater influence on health than most people are aware of. The slow and lasting passions, such as grief and hopeless love, can bring on chronic diseases.
THE LADY HERBALIST

8

Lady Melville sat by the fire with a rug on her lap; the room was stuffy and overcrowded, the furniture too large for the room. A huge bed took up most of the space, heavy curtains swamping the small leaded window. The room was dark, no lanterns lit, just the glow of the fire lighting her pale face, and I curtseyed deeply, hoping the dull light would hide my shock. She seemed twenty years older, as fragile as a sparrow, her cheeks sunken, her hair completely grey.

'Lady Melville, please forgive my unplanned visit.'

Her thin hands plucked at her handkerchief, her eyes glistening with tears. She reached for her Bible and put it to her lips. 'You believe he is still alive?'

Constance pointed to a chair on the other side of the fireplace and I sat down, grateful for some warmth. 'I don't know what to believe.'

'He *is* alive, I know it.' Her words were spoken with such force she started coughing, a fierce racking cough that shook her thin frame. She lay back against the high-back chair, her eyes closed, and in the flicker of the flames, I saw a bluish tinge to her lips. Dark rings circled her eyes, a web of thin red veins on both her cheeks. Bruises covered the back of her hands, a dusky hue to her fingernails. Her grey hair was thinning, bald in patches.

Constance rushed to her side, pouring amber liquid into a glass from a crystal decanter. 'Mama, here, have a sip of mead . . . '

'He *is* alive,' Lady Melville repeated. 'And he *will* come home . . . I just hope I live long enough to see him.' She coughed again, starting to retch, gasping for breath as if she were drowning.

Constance rang a brass bell. 'We need to get you back to bed . . . the shock's too great.' She held up the glass again. 'Mama, please have some more mead, it soothes your cough.'

The door opened and an equally frail woman rushed to Lady Melville's side. 'Lady Melville, let me help you . . . you're not strong enough to be up.' There was panic in her glance, and I recognized her at once: Mrs Alston, Lady Melville's adored housekeeper.

'I'm so sorry — it's my fault. Lady Melville's had a shock — I had no idea she was quite so frail.'

Lady Melville's bony fingers clutched Mrs Alston's wrist. 'He's alive,' she whispered. 'He's coming back. Dearest, dearest Edmund is coming home.'

Mrs Alston's jaw dropped. She knelt by the chair. 'How can that be? Mr Edmund's coming home?'

Tears streamed down her cheeks and I stared into her incredulous eyes. She adored Edmund: she had been his wet nurse, then his nursemaid, staying with Lady Melville as her loyal house-keeper.

'He lived that day, he didn't die. He escaped. We don't know any details except he was a prisoner and he escaped . . . and that eighteen months ago he was in a convent in Brazil. But he was taken from there to serve on a Portuguese vessel. He was very weak, Mrs Alston.'

'But he was alive.' There was such hope in her eyes, such love, and I had to look away, staring out of the window as they helped Lady Melville back to bed.

The room was unfamiliar to me. Constance and her mother must have moved into the servants' quarters to be nearer the kitchens. It was small, cramped, but at least it was warm. A heavy dresser crowded against the wall, a cluttered table crammed beneath the small window. Two clocks were ticking loudly, an assortment of vials and bottles standing neatly on a silver tray. A bottle caught my attention and I hurried over to it, holding it up to the light.

The thick brown glass obscured the contents and I pulled the cork. It was half-empty, a full bottle next to it, and my unease spiralled. I read the label.

J. Reynold, chemist and druggist from Richmond, London, wishes to inform the nobility, gentry and public that all medicines, elixirs and lozenges are prepared and sold on the same terms as in London, under the supervision of Dr Lovelace, renowned physician of St Bartholomew's Hospital, London.

I turned the bottle round, my hands shaking — *Dr Lovelace's Cough Elixir. Two spoonfuls to be taken three times a day.* Behind me, the drapes of the bed drew open and Constance came to my side. 'What's wrong, Amelia?'

I held up the bottle. 'Where did you get this?'

'Mrs Alston bought it from an itinerant doctor. He was on his way to Truro from Bodmin. Amelia, you're frightening me — don't look like that.'

'Connie, this is as good as poison.' Fear made me sound too harsh, but I could not help it.

'He was a doctor . . . he knew exactly what Mama needed.' She looked terrified and I knew I had spoken too fiercely.

'There are imposters out there,' I whispered. 'They are unscrupulous fraudsters who prey on the vulnerable — they tell you what you want to hear . . . but it's all lies. They sell their miracle cures at exorbitant prices and they do such harm. Has Lady Melville lost any teeth?'

'No . . . Oh, Amelia . . . she's been very sick.'

I took Lady Melville's hand, putting her nails to the light. That faint blue tinge. 'Lady Melville, please don't mind me asking this, but have you had stomach cramps, pain and vomiting?' She nodded and I turned to Mrs Alston. 'Mrs Alston, when did you buy this?'

Her knuckles turned white as she gripped her skirt. 'Just the other day. He came to the door . . . he was on his way to Truro . . . he knocked on the door and asked if anyone would benefit from his medicines. He said the dampness of the dell would bring on rheumatism and coughs. He was very pleasant . . . he was so knowledgeable. He was a doctor from London, bringing his remedies to the country. He said country folk needed the same opportunity as those in London.'

I tucked Lady Melville's hand under her counterpane and forced a smile. 'From now on, I beg you — no more of this. You're to take beef broth three times a day . . . You're to have four glasses of port a day and spinach and buttered eggs. I want you to drink as much beer as you can manage. Have you hyssop in the garden? Can you make an infusion?'

Mrs Alston nodded. She looked as pale as Lady Melville, the same dark patches under her eyes, and I took her hand, examining her finger-nails. I held her chin to the light, catching her waxen complexion. 'What are you taking, Mrs Alston?'

Her lips puckered, terror in her eyes. '*Rheumatic Lozenges* and *Cordial Balm of Gilead*. He said it would cure my aches. He was a doctor . . . a real doctor.'

'No, Mrs Alston,' I said, gathering up every vial and bottle I could see, 'he's a horse doctor, a quack, and he's doing untold harm. All this must go . . . every drop.' I opened each bottle, emptying everything on to the fire, throwing the glass bottles into the flames. 'He's undermining the medical profession — making a mockery of *real* doctors.'

Making a mockery of the man I loved.

★ ★ ★

Neither of us had any appetite, staring at the plate of cold ham with no thought of eating it.

70

The door to the kitchen was ajar and we sat listening to the sound of clattering and frantic chopping, anxious voices asking whether there were potatoes in the storeroom. We were in what I knew to be the servants' hall.

'How long have you lived like this?' I whispered.

'A year, maybe more — the servants started to leave so we closed up the east wing. Mama lost interest in everything — she seemed to just give up. She's been hurrying my marriage, but you've brought us such hope. She will be all right, won't she? Amelia, don't look like that. She will live, won't she?'

'Yes, I'm sure she will — given plenty of good food and fresh air. I'll send you some balm for her lips . . . and rub it on to her elbows and heels to stop them from getting sore. These horse doctors are a huge concern. Dr Nankivell puts posters up all over Truro but most people who buy the remedies can't read. I'm sorry, I'm not hungry.'

'Neither am I. Come, I've got something I want to give you . . . something I should have given you before. I was going to bring it to you for Christmas, but I couldn't leave Mama . . . We don't keep the coach horses any more and I had no chaperone.'

'I'm the one at fault, Connie. I should have come long before now . . . I'm so sorry. I've been very preoccupied with the new infirmary. I've been asked to plan their physic garden and supply the plants from Trenwyn . . . it keeps me very busy.'

71

'It's good to keep busy.' She sounded wistful, leading me through a small door and up a set of steep steps that curled in a spiral. 'Who's that doctor your family admire so much? The one whose mother married Silas Lilly?'

I could hardly say his name. 'Dr Bohenna.'

'Will you ask him to visit Mama? Please, Amelia, do your best to persuade him. I'll find the money. Please, ask him to come.'

At the end of a narrow passage she opened a small door, and as I stepped into the minstrels' gallery I felt a sudden, terrible dizziness. I had to stop and breathe. It was as if Edmund was in the room. I could feel him behind me, just as he had stood those eight years before, both of us tiptoeing forward, eavesdropping through the grilles on our parents as they discussed our marriage in the great hall below. Edmund had sounded so sure: *Our parents will agree, I know they will. It's a good match . . . our families have known each other for generations — it's just a matter of sorting out the details.*

He had taken my hand and kissed it softly, placing it against his heart. *Father's going to insist I go to London and I can't disobey. I have to go — but the morning of my twenty-first birthday, I shall come straight back to Cornwall and marry you — so you better be ready.*

Everything was flooding back as if it were yesterday. My parents had agreed to our engagement but I knew they thought Edmund too young — too *impressionable*, Papa had said. The icy air was making me shiver, like the passing of a ghost.

Constance walked swiftly ahead along the heavily beamed landing, the dust sheets draping like shrouds on the furniture around us. She opened the shutters and light filtered onto the portraits beside me. Suddenly they were there — Edmund and Francis staring back at me from their gilded frames. What were they, fifteen, sixteen? Both so alike with their dark black hair curling about their shoulders. Both were wearing fine silk jackets and matching breeches, both the same height and stature, as if one was the mirror of the other. The only difference being that Edmund was holding a violin and Francis a lute — the youths I had known all my life, friends of my brother. Frederick: all of us laughing, growing up together, spending the summer of 1789 without a worry in the world.

The youth I had loved so well. I looked deep into Edmund's eyes and my heart lurched. I had forgotten the gentleness of his smile, the kind, almost lost look in his eyes. His cousin Francis's eyes looked as sharp as they had always been, following me across the room as he had always done, but Edmund's eyes looked vulnerable, even lonely. Was that what Father had meant when he called him impressionable?

'Come, Amelia.' Constance took my hand, pulling me along the dusty wooden corridor with its heavy oak doors in their pointed arches. She opened the end door and a musty dampness stung my nostrils. 'This is Edmund's room,' she whispered. 'Wait and I'll open the shutters — we should have brought a lamp.'

Icy cold penetrated my cloak. Further dust

sheets hung from the furniture like ghosts watching us and I forced myself to breathe. Edmund's face had become suddenly so clear — as if he was watching me looking at his possessions. I could feel his presence in the room and intense pain flooded through me as cruelly as before. Every sore I thought healed seemed to be ripping open. It was his vulnerability I remembered, his gentleness, as if the world was too baffling a place for him and he needed my strength.

Constance pulled back the curtains and diffuse light flooded the room; the brocade drapes hanging round the huge oak bed turned deep burgundy, the tapestries on the walls merging pink and blue. But the mustiness remained, the smell of damp, unbreathed air. Constance pointed to a small ebony box lying on the dust-sheeted table.

'This is what I want to show you. It was sent by the Admiralty — it contains Edmund's possessions from the ship.'

A knot tightened round my heart. 'Is that all there is . . . from his ship? So very little?'

She nodded. 'So very little. I haven't told Mama yet. There's a letter from the Admiralty explaining that they don't have room aboard ship for the possessions of those that die — they just keep their personal belongings. Apparently, they hold an auction and send the money back to the families. There's a list of what was in the trunk and how much everything went for — his Bible was in there, but I have it by my bed. I don't understand why there's so little on the list.' She walked slowly to the box and turned the key.

So little on the list. My heart wrenched. 'Edmund wrote to me . . . he said his possessions were going missing.'

'Missing?'

'Yes . . . from his trunk. But he was advised to say nothing. Oh Connie, Edmund would have been an easy target for malevolence of any sort. He was desperate to be accepted . . . but the truth is . . . some of the men on the ship made his life hell.' Tears pooled in my eyes. 'He should never have joined the navy . . . he wasn't strong enough to overcome any bullying.'

Inside the box a huge shell glinted in the half-light and I lifted it out, taking it to the window. It was the most beautiful shell I had ever seen, and tears blurred my eyes, making it hard to read the inscription: *For where thou art, there is the world itself, and where thou are not, desolation.* 'Oh, Connie!'

Her arms slipped round me. 'Don't cry, Amelia . . . please don't cry. I'm sure he's coming back. He'll come back, and everything will be how it should be.' Her lips quivered, and I held her to me, the pain so intense I thought my heart had burst. 'Your letters to him are in there — and the miniature you sent him. Take the box home with you. Here . . . take it. It's not too heavy.'

I could not speak, but placed the huge shell back inside the casket.

'Amelia,' Connie whispered, 'there's something else I want to show you — in Francis's room.'

9

We wound carefully up another set of stone steps leading to a single room at the top of the ancient Tudor turret, opening the iron-studded door to complete darkness. Constance unbarred the shutters to yet another set of dust sheets hanging like phantoms around us. Our breath filled the air as icy cold took hold.

'Francis could have had a room downstairs but he chose this freezing garret. Edmund said it was because Francis wanted to remind everyone he wasn't really family — that he was an outsider.' Her mouth hardened, the same bitterness I had detected earlier entering her tone. 'Which I think is rather hurtful, considering we always treated him as family.'

She shut the door, taking my hand, leading me across the unpolished floorboards to pull off a dust sheet. 'This is his trunk — it contains all Francis's belongings but Mama wants nothing to do with it. She ordered it up here and locked away the key. She refused to look inside . . . but while she's been so ill, I had the chance to take the key and I've kept it.' Her mouth clamped tight.

'And?'

'Mama keeps everything from me — *everything*.' She reached for a set of keys hanging from her waist and turned the lock. 'I have to tell you something — Father went bankrupt, Amelia, that's why we live so frugally. His business concerns were a shambolic mess. The estate is mortgaged and the London house sold to pay the most pressing of his creditors. Father was a gambler and a womanizer. He was a fraudster and Francis was no better.' She looked up. 'You don't seem shocked?'

I shook my head. 'Edmund told me in his letters. I assumed you knew.'

She reached into the large trunk, pulling out a bundle of papers. 'And I have to tell you something else . . . it's like a flame burning inside me. The truth is, Francis wasn't set upon by thieves on the way *back* from Plymouth . . . he was murdered when he was *in* Plymouth Dock . . . *brutally* murdered by the husband of a woman he'd taken for a . . . well, you know what I mean.' She handed me a pile of papers. 'I'm sorry . . . I shouldn't have just blurted it out like that. I should have warned you. I can see you're shocked. I was shocked too — I still am.'

I held the folded newspaper to the window, reading it carefully. 'It's the account of the trial — of the two men accused of his murder. The woman's husband and brother were convicted and hanged? Connie, what *was* Francis thinking, going after a married woman?'

'Exactly!'

I glanced back at the newspaper. 'In Plymouth Dock as well, *not* on the way back to London?'

Constance's eyes turned to steel, her voice equally hard.

'According to the landlord of the tavern, Francis *extended* his stay. He had booked in for a *further* two nights.'

I felt my cheeks redden. 'Connie, I'm shocked, but I can't say I'm surprised. Edmund wrote to me about Francis and his wild living. He said he was expecting to share a farewell breakfast with him before he boarded his ship, but Francis didn't turn up. Edmund waited on the quayside for almost two hours and Francis nearly didn't come. He was only just in time to see him off. Obviously he'd found more *enjoyable* company.'

'You knew he was so unprincipled?'

'Yes, I knew both your father and Francis were unprincipled. And I knew about your father's financial irregularities. In fact, I knew about their womanizing, but this is quite horrible — the woman's husband and brother beat Francis to death?'

She nodded. 'Yes . . . like I once watched Francis beat a dog to death.'

I stared back in horror. 'No . . . surely not?'

'As God is my witness. I was too late to save the poor thing. I took him to the grooms who released him from his pain. But Francis would have left him to suffer.'

'That's terrible.'

'Yes, it was. But what's more terrible is the lack of compassion I feel for Francis — when I read that report all I could see was the look in that poor dog's eyes.'

A shiver ran down my spine. She had witnessed what I had always felt — a cruelty in Francis that seemed to bring him pleasure. The newspaper shook in my hand.

'The murder happened just behind their house

78

— in a notorious alley.' I held it to the light of the window. 'There were signs of a fight . . . then they dragged him down the lane and left him dangling over a pigpen. The pigs were destined for loading and made short work of him. They found what was left of Francis's body but he'd been . . . well . . . I don't need to read this out. The innkeeper identified him by his jacket and boots . . . '

She reached for another cutting. 'Both men denied it, but the innkeeper gave solid evidence against them. He saw Francis leave with the woman and swore, on oath, that Francis had booked in for another two nights. The husband and brother worked the night shift in the forge, but they must have come back unexpectedly. The pigpen was just behind their house. Here's his testimony.'

I read it aloud. '*Susan Drew was employed to wait on tables. Her work was efficient, and he had no complaints. He says . . . I saw Francis Bainbridge touch her in an inappropriate manner and she did not stop him or act displeased. He was waiting for her when her work finished, and it is my belief that everyone in the inn knew exactly what was intended by the two of them . . .* '

Constance glanced round the room, her mouth hardening. 'Francis was given every opportunity to behave as a gentleman, yet he was murdered for debauchery. It's horrible and I feel sick at the thought of it, but I can't help thinking that it was always going to be like that — one day or another. Father made sure the men were hanged. Do your parents tell you everything, Amelia? Or do they keep things from you?'

'No, they like me to be informed . . . but if it's any consolation, they kept that from me. I had no idea of how Francis died.'

She put the pile of papers back into the trunk and lifted out a small painting wrapped in sacking. 'Poor Aunt Harriet, it's as well she never knew what her son became.'

She unfolded the cloth, handing me the portrait, and I looked into the laughing eyes of Lady Melville's younger sister. A radiant woman smiled back at me, her dark hair spilling in abundance beneath a wide-brimmed hat. Her cheeks were flushed, her full red lips slightly apart; there was a coquettish lift to her chin.

'She was very beautiful. Why don't you take it to your mother? There aren't any other portraits of your aunt here, are there?'

Constance shook her head. 'I can't give it to Mama or she'll know I've taken the key. I'm not allowed up here — or *anywhere*, for that matter. Look . . . there's all sorts of other stuff . . . some books . . . Francis's silver nutmeg grater.' She reached beneath a pile of clothes, drawing her hands back in horror. 'Oh . . . these are his boots — I can barely touch them. I should give all these clothes to Reverend Kemp for charity, but I can't until Mama suggests it.' She folded the clothes, reaching deep into the trunk. 'These must be his father's books. Two of them are in French. I suppose sea captains needed to speak French?'

She pulled out a clutch of leather-clad books,

placing them on the floor beside her, and I pulled one from the pile, opening it with a rush of pleasure. 'The *Botanical Prints of Oriental Spices*, published by Burrows and Burrows . . . Look, Connie, there's an inscription on this first page. *For Harriet, my dearest love. January 6th 1770.*'

'It must have been a present from Uncle William — he must have given it to her before he died.'

My heart burned, my mouth going dry. 'Burrows and Burrows, the renowned London publishers.'

The prints were exquisite: page after page of delicately painted drawings — nutmeg, saffron, cardamom, ginger, cinnamon. I could hardly breathe. Constance took the book from my hands, putting everything back into the trunk. 'I'm so glad I told you about the trial . . . it's been a horrible secret to keep to myself. Come, it's too cold, let's get back to the fire . . . don't forget to bring your casket.'

She shut the door and we returned to the relative warmth of the minstrels' gallery. At the painting of the two youths, she stopped. 'Have you noticed Francis's eyes watch you wherever you are in the room? The painter caught them exactly. Francis was always watching, and Edmund always so loving. Edmund used to save bits of his meal for my kittens. He was as soft as butter, but I don't need to tell you that.'

Edmund's eyes looked back at mine: soft eyes, loving eyes. 'No, you don't.'

Her voice turned bitter. 'Francis drowned them.'

'What?'

'My kittens. He denied it, but I knew it was him. I hated him from then on. I was nine years old and he drowned my kittens. I could never love him, and Mama never liked him. I think she blamed him for killing her beloved sister. Father was right to take him into our family, but Mama always resented him. She didn't shed a single tear when he died and neither did I.'

I stared back at the watchful eyes of Francis Bainbridge. 'Blaming Francis is very unfair. A lot of women die after childbirth . . .'

'Ours has never been a happy house. I don't know how much Edmund told you, but Father and Mama loathed each other. Father spent all his time in London and Mama buried herself here. That's why Edmund loved you so much — you gave him such hope. He just wanted to be happy — we all did. We saw the love and laughter in your family and we were so envious. I still am, Amelia.' Tears welled in her eyes. 'I want that so much. I want to live with shrieks of laughter. I want *real* love . . . I want warmth . . . huge family meals with pies and roast meat . . . and iced cream . . . and . . . I'm so sorry — '

She was sobbing, her body shaking. She had Edmund's same sense of vulnerability and I held her to me, the tears rolling down her cheeks. 'You *can* have all that, Connie, honestly you can. You just have to be very firm in accepting who you choose.'

Her mouth trembled, a fresh burst of tears. 'No, I can't. Believe me, I can't. Mama will see to that.'

'I'm sure that's not right. Lady Melville loves you. She'll want you to be happy. She'll only agree to your marriage if you find someone you can love . . .'

She stared back at me. 'But I love Adam Kemp . . . I love him . . . so very much, and he loves me.'

'Adam Kemp? Reverend Kemp's son?' Connie nodded, hardly able to speak. 'He's come home? Yes, I suppose he must have. Connie, are you sure?'

She reached for her handkerchief. 'I'm *very* sure. He's been back a year now, helping his father with the parish. He's started a school . . . he's such a good man . . . he's honest and upright and everyone loves him.'

'Well then . . . that's wonderful.'

Her back stiffened, her chin lifted. 'Mama's forbidden me to see him. She says he's not good enough for me. *He's a mere curate, the son of a vicar*, and I'm forbidden even to speak his name. So you can see why I need Edmund to come home.'

★   ★   ★

I pulled the blanket over my knees, watching the gathering twilight. The sky was darkening, the horizon lost to a thickening grey mist. We would soon begin our descent from the moor and reach Truro just in time for the church bells to chime five. Bethany remained grim-faced and silent, glaring at the small wooden box on my lap as if it held poison. She must know it contained

Edmund's belongings.

My hands were numb from clasping it so tightly. Through the ebony wood, the carefully inscribed words seemed to burn my hands. *Where thou art not, desolation.* Burning my hands and searing my heart. I should have waited longer, held on to my conviction that Edmund was not dead. I should never have believed Uncle Alex; *never* have loved again.

10

I awoke in tears, my cheeks wet, my heart thumping. I had been doubled-up both from the pain of loss and the pain of running. We were on the moor, my hair streaming against my shoulders, my white muslin gown swirling in the wind. Edmund was running ahead of me, young, lithe, jumping the ditches, looking round, his long black hair a mass of curls under his corduroy hat. The distance between us was growing. I was running to catch him, but I could not reach him. Every time I stopped for breath he seemed further ahead, growing more and more distant.

I had been shouting, urging him to wait, to let me catch up with him, but my words were lost to the wind. He kept turning round, smiling; he was leaving me behind, knowing I could not follow him. Young, strong, looking back at me as I fought to catch my breath, smiling, but not stopping. Not stopping. Not turning back, but leaving me doubled-up and screaming, sobs racking my chest.

I crossed the room, pouring water from the jug, splashing my face with cold water. My heart was thumping, my breathing rapid. I had seen him as plainly as if we had turned back the clocks and had just turned nineteen. They had

85

come down to Cornwall for Christmas — our nineteenth birthdays — and I had been sick with love for him, desperate we had to part again.

Yet, I was right to fear. The feeling of foreboding that would not leave me as I watched their carriage disappear from sight had been well founded: it was to be the last time I saw him. The room was freezing, the fire burnt out and I reached for my dressing gown, wrapping it around me before my tears took hold.

★　★　★

Stay away from the window. I dipped my quill into the silver inkstand as Bethany knocked on the door. I knew it was Bethany, not because it was her distinctive soft tap, but because she had knocked on my door at exactly two o'clock for the last two months. She peered tentatively into the room.

'He's coming,' she whispered, just as she had whispered on every other occasion.

I remained looking down at my writing. 'I'm very busy, Bethany . . . perhaps it's best if you don't disturb me in future. Dr Bohenna is here to see to Mother's foot.' I started writing again, keeping my head bent so she could not see my tears. She shut the door and I covered my face. *Stay away from the window.*

My head was speaking, but my heart would not listen. Rushing to the window, I concealed myself behind the pine shutter and peered tentatively down. A group of people were standing hunched by the church railings, bracing themselves against the icy cold. A woman with a heavy basket was scurrying across the square.

Luke was wearing his overcoat, his familiar warm hat pulled low over his forehead and my ache worsened. I could not see his face, just the bag he was carrying and his well-polished boots, but there was a new stoop to his shoulders, a sadness in the dip of his head. Dearest Luke, just one month later — just one week later, just one day later.

My heart hammered. *If we had been married, everything would be different.*

He glanced up and my heart shattered into a thousand pieces. He looked gaunter, his cheeks strained, his sudden smile full of sadness. I could not bear to see the anguish in his eyes. Luke Bohenna, the man I admired so deeply, who had brought me such joy. The man I now adored. Our eyes locked and by his stiff bow I knew he was holding himself in check.

The miniature portrait I had sent Edmund lay on my desk. I had posed for it with such exuberance, choosing my gown carefully — Edmund's favourite, the one I had been wearing when he had stolen his first kiss. I hardly recognized the girl in the dotted muslin with her scooped neck threaded with lilac ribbon and her straw bonnet trimmed with pink roses. I looked so happy, so young and carefree, my sparkling eyes brimming with love.

A sudden lurch in my stomach, the same twinge of resentment. I had so wanted Edmund to send me a miniature in return. If only he had. If *only he had*. I could have kept his image fresh in my mind and would never have forsaken him — not if I had remembered the vulnerability in his eyes, held his sweet smile to my heart.

Our letters lay intertwined, each an extension of the other. My last letter to him lay open on my desk and I picked it up, reading through blurred eyes. I had encouraged him to join the navy . . . yet why had he not written to tell me of his plans? Why just leave me like that?

Trenwyn House
June 21st 1793

My dearest Edmand,

I hope this letter finds you well, though I suspect that's not the case.

Frederick is home, and I can't begin to tell you how handsome he looks in his new uniform. He is now fully commissioned as Lieutenant — but you already know that because he told me you had dinner together when he was in London. He tells me you look pale, and that London is doing you no favours. You must stay well, my love — we have only six months to wait. Six long months, Edmund, my dearest love. Yet, how am I to endure another six months — especially as you do not write as often as you promised me you would?

Yesterday, we had a tour of Frederick's new ship and I couldn't have been more proud of him. He has joined Captain Penrose on HMS Circe. Captain Penrose has a fierce reputation, but actually, I found him rather shy and really rather endearing.

He's from Truro, and would you believe it, went to Truro Grammar School with Henry Trelawney? Major Trelawney was there, too, and we had a splendid time.

I think you must realize I'm rather in love with Major Trelawney. He is the kindest man I know, but you needn't be too alarmed as he is happily married with three very fine sons. Even so, it might be just as well if you were to hurry home.

Mother has invited Major Trelawney to join her fundraising circle for the new infirmary. He was wearing his red uniform and looked very splendid. But the ship! My goodness, I can't tell you how proud it made me feel. I think, above all, I love the navy best. They are all Cornishmen on Frederick's ship, and the officers were so smart, the Tars standing to attention as we made our way along the scrubbed deck. Everything gleamed — the brass shining in the sun. She's a thirty-four gun, sixth-rate frigate, and I wish you'd seen Frederick's face. He was beaming from ear to ear and allowed us to hold the wheel. I even got to ring the ship's bell. It was a glorious day. Absolutely glorious.

We're to host another concert to raise money for the infirmary. I have two new Beethoven pieces to learn and I'm going to sing 'The Countess's Aria' from The Marriage of Figaro. I know Mozart is your favourite so I'm learning everything I can with you in mind. When we're married, I

89

shall give concerts from the minstrels' gallery which I believe would suit me very well. I'd much prefer it if our guests couldn't watch me while I play.

Six months — however am I going to last six months?

Nothing else changes. Papa is to commission a new rhododendron walk and has drawn up plans for a variety of trees to be planted — mainly oak — and Mother is planning more hothouses and a shrubbery with mirror pieces and shells in the gravel so it shines at night. Dearest love, I can't wait to show you my collection of rose prints. We shall grow more roses at Pendowrick — I shall design a whole new garden with a host of arches and pergolas just like we have in Trenwyn.

Charles has taken up his duties as rector and Papa is thrilled that William is showing an interest informing. My two nephews bring us great joy. Mother is teaching Young William to row and I'm teaching him to climb trees. It's all very splendid, apart from the only thing that matters — you are not here.

Do write, my sweetest love, or I shall go mad with worry. Write and tell me all about your acquisitions of nutmeg and cinnamon. How is trading at the moment? Are you beginning to turn a profit? Please tell me. Please tell me all you do. I don't want to be a silent wife who knows nothing about her husband's affairs. I want to be part of

everything about you. Everything.
Six months. Six long months.
Your ever-loving,
Amelia

This time it was barely a knock. Mother limped across the room with one arm through Bethany's, the other leaning on her Chinese lacquered cane. 'Thank you, my dear,' she said, sitting down at my desk, leaving Bethany in no doubt that she was to close the door behind her.

Her arched eyebrows rose above her straight nose, a glint of iron in her expression as she took my hand. 'Luke has just left. I did ask him to stay but he was extremely reluctant — adamant, in fact. The poor man looks terrible.'

'Mother . . . please . . . '

'Even if Edmund does return, he would expect you to be married by now. You were seventeen when you got engaged — and that's a very long time ago. You've not seen him for *six* years and not many loves can withstand that sort of pressure. He would *not* have expected you to wait so long — you had clear confirmation of his death, and Luke Bohenna deserves — '

'Mother . . . please . . . '

She picked up the miniature portrait. 'Look at you, my love — so very young, in love with the idea of being in love. You were a girl, he was a boy, a mere youth . . . a very charming but idealistic youth who, in our opinion, treated you rather badly.'

'You were seventeen when you became engaged to Papa.'

91

'Yes, but your father was much older — Edmund was too young. It's long been my regret we agreed to your engagement. We should have made you wait to get engaged until after he returned from London. He was clearly not ready for marriage — leaving like that without a backward glance. He has *no hold* over you, Amelia . . . you have no reason to believe your betrothal should be honoured.'

'But I *do* . . . Mother, I promised him . . . '

'I think he's forfeited any promise you might have made. He should have consulted us before joining his ship. If any of your brothers had been in his position I would have *insisted* they discussed it first with the family. His action went against the spirit of your engagement and, as such, I believe you are released from it.'

'Mother, please . . . '

'I know your argument — he was offered the position as a favour to his father . . . an opportunity many young men would jump at, and yes, *had* he been a third or fourth son we would have regarded it as fortuitous, but a man set to inherit a title and estate had no reason to accept the offer. He had a secure future — land, responsibilities, a political career should he so wish. He had *no* reason to become a midship-man. He should have let someone else benefit from the patronage he was offered.'

'Mother, please don't — '

An edge of steel entered her tone. 'He had clear obligations, which he chose to forget.'

'He thought it would only be for a short time . . . '

'Idealistic nonsense . . . believing he could choose to sail round the Mediterranean for six months and come home when it pleased him.'

'Mother . . . please, I was just as angry. When I heard, I was furious . . . really hurt . . . I cried for months, asking myself why he just left like that? But . . . I believe his health was suffering. You remember the Christmas when they came down for my nineteenth birthday and you thought he looked thin and unhappy?'

'When Sir Melville was thinking of sending them to Sumatra? Yes, I remember it well.'

'I told him his father had too strong a hold on him and that he should try to break free from his influence.'

'But he was going to be free of him. He was going to return to Pendowrick and run the estate.'

'Yes, I know, I meant while he was in London but . . . I wrote to him after Frederick showed us round *Circe* and I think he took it wrongly. I as good as sent him to join the navy. He was always in awe of Frederick . . . he wanted to be like Frederick . . . he wanted me to be as proud of him as I was of Frederick. I all but sent him.'

'That cannot be true. My dearest — '

'It is. I made Frederick sound so courageous . . . I told him the ship's company were glorious and brave. We had such a short time to wait but Edmund hated London, he was desperately unhappy, and I made it sound like he should join the navy.' I handed her my letter, my hand shaking.

Her frown deepened, but she shook her head.

'There's no reason to blame yourself — you did *not* tell him to join the navy. You must put this foolish thought aside.'

'I can't, Mother.'

'You have to, my love. Keep this foolish thought in your head and you will retreat back into your world of darkness. You must feel no sense of guilt whatsoever.'

'Mother . . . it's not as easy as that.'

'Yes, my love, it is. Amelia, my dearest child, I cannot stand by and watch you give up a man like Luke Bohenna — a man whom you clearly adore and who adores you in return — for a past, very fleeting engagement.'

'Mother, it wasn't just a fleeting engagement — '

'For a youth who ran away from his obligations? Luke Bohenna is offering you certain happiness. Take a *real* man's love — don't dwell on a past love that was based solely on youthful infatuation . . . and to a man who *may or may not be alive.* Take Luke's love . . . grasp it and stop this terrible guilt. It was Edmund's decision to join that ship. You did *not* send him.'

I had to sound strong. 'If Edmund *is* alive he'll be trying to come home. Merchant ships can be away for years — we both know ships' masters keep their crew locked below in harbours so they can't escape. What if the Portuguese captain is doing that to Edmund?'

'Set a date, Amelia . . . one year from now — only give Luke some hope.'

I could not breathe. 'I can't, Mother. What if Charity gave up on Frederick? What if one of

94

your sons returned to find his loved one with another man? What if Edmund comes back in one year and one day? What would that do to Luke?'

'Just one month later . . . '

'For years I've prayed for Edmund's safe return. What if my prayers are finally to be answered? What if fate brought me that letter as a warning not to make a mistake?'

I could see his ship ploughing the waves, Edmund staring up at the moon, the deck rising and falling beneath his feet. The wind was on his cheek, blowing his black curls from off his face. I could see him suddenly so clearly, looking up at the stars pointing him home to me, and to his beloved Pendowrick.

'Our love was not just a youthful infatuation — it was real, very real. I may no longer be this girl in the painting and Edmund certainly won't be the idealistic youth who left, but our souls have always been, and will always be, united. I *vowed to love him*, Mother, and he vowed to love me. And that vow must hold. I must wait for him to come back . . . ' I would not cry. I must not cry.

She put my portrait on the desk, sighing deeply. 'So the heartache must start again — you will spend your days waiting for Edmund and Luke will retreat into his work and wait for you forever.'

Bethany was waiting at the top of the stairs, her red-rimmed eyes avoiding mine. Mother took her arm and turned. 'Dr Nankivell suggests we should host the next infirmary committee meeting here, on account of my foot. I'll make sure you have a moment alone with Luke.'

The lump in my throat made it too hard to reply.

Bethany's lips quivered. 'Can I bring you something, Miss Amelia? Maybe some buttered eggs or some warm milk?'

I wanted to curl into a tight ball and cry. 'Just some hawthorn tea — no buttered eggs.'

★ ★ ★

Hawthorn heals the heart and lifts the spirit. The pain of loss can be as severe as physical pain. One drop of the tincture to be added to warm water or tea. Alternatively, steep half a teaspoon of crushed dried berries in a cup of hot water, wait ten minutes and sweeten with honey.

THE LADY HERBALIST

11

Town House, Truro
Saturday 13th January 1798, 11 a.m.

I pulled on my new gloves and picked up my basket. Bethany was well wrapped against the wind, almost swamped by her warm woollen cloak and sturdy boots. She tied the ribbons on her hat and took hold of Mother's brimming basket.

'No 'tis not too heavy — though 'tis that full. There's potatoes and turnips . . . and eggs and apples from the gardens in Trenwyn. There's cheese . . . and Lady Clarissa wanted me to bring this honey as well as the whortleberry jam . . . and there's gingerbread for the young lad. You say she's Portuguese, yet she comes from Africa?'

'Yes, she sailed from Mombasa . . . and that's in Africa, but her family were Portuguese. Here, let me take those eggs.' My basket seemed empty by comparison, just two bottles of cough elixir I had prepared for Sofia Oakley's son and Papa's leather gloves which had needed mending for over a year. 'Oh, I nearly forgot . . .'

Rushing back into the sitting room, I picked up the two bone horses I had wrapped in a piece of fine silk and kissed Mother goodbye. I needed to be out in the air though the wind was fierce as we hurried down the busy street. Market day always brought crowds and though it was tempting to avoid the crush, I wanted to thank Sofia Oakley properly and enquire about her son. She had shown such kindness over my letter and I wanted to repay her.

It was surprisingly deserted, only a few carts on the cobbles ahead. The wind was whistling down the river, the rigging jangling on the ships as we hurried along the quayside. We reached the shop and through the window saw Sofia Oakley and her mother-in-law sitting on stools in front of a glowing grate. Pushing open the door, we were grateful for the warmth.

They rose at once, ''Tis that cold, so it is . . . Oh, Miss Carew, what a pleasure . . . ' The elder Mrs Oakley smiled shyly, curt-seying before coming to shut the door.

Sofia Oakley also curtseyed. 'Please, come nearer the fire . . . let me add some more wood . . . '

Though they tried not to, both cast glances at Bethany's heavy basket. I drew out Papa's gloves. 'There's a small tear in the right forefinger. Mother wonders if you could mend them . . . but really, she's sent us with this selection from our kitchen garden in Trenwyn. We're so grateful for your . . . your kindness in going to so much trouble with my letter.'

Sofia Oakley called to Joe to take the basket through to the back. His dark eyes widened in his pale face. He must have been about twelve, wearing the same tight jacket and breeches I had seen him in before. Sofia seemed lost for words. 'Please . . . this is too generous . . . will you thank Lady Clarissa. Such generosity . . . '

'You're welcome to thank her for yourself. I know she would enjoy some company. She meant what she said about you telling her of your travels. I, too, would like to hear . . .'

Mrs Oakley smoothed her apron. 'May I offer you some . . . ?'

'Perhaps just a seat by your fire for a few moments? I can see you're busy with your gloves. You lived in Mombasa — such an exotic-sounding name. Was the journey eventful? Only my brother Frederick would have us all believe the sea is always calm and the sun always shines.'

Her smile broke my heart. 'That's because he's protecting you. Everyone fears the sea — or at least they should.' She drew up another stool and sat by my side.

'Was your journey difficult?'

'Yes.' She picked up her needle, resuming her stitching. 'The ship we came on was an East India ship. Captain Banyan hadn't used his full quota so there was room on board for my silks. He offered me good terms and I checked the ship thoroughly — it seemed sound, the hold was dry and the cargo looked well stored and not going to break free. The crew were from the East Indies but Captain Banyan was from Bristol so I took my chance.'

'A very brave decision.'

'I kept the best of our silk but sold the rest. I had the rolls double-wrapped and sealed in caskets. I brought what I could from the house — my carpets, our clothes, some of my — ' She stopped.

Mrs Oakley put her hand on Sofia's shoulder. 'She bought keepsakes of her lost children — their favourite toys . . . their riding crops — and yet they were all lost.'

Sofia wiped her tears. 'Captain Banyan was impatient to set sail. The winds were favourable — he'd been delayed too long by bad weather and he was anxious to make up time. I'd never sailed before and I found him gruff . . . often unshirted, and I thought him uncouth. But he turned out to be a gentleman of the truest kind.'

'He was good to you?'

'Yes, indeed. He gave us a small berth and did his best to keep us comfortable. There were four other passengers but we kept to ourselves. That was ten months ago, I was newly bereaved and I wanted no company.' She looked up. 'Merchant ships can take a year to reach their intended port — sometimes as much as eighteen months.'

The kindness in her eyes made me catch my breath. In the midst of her misfortune, she was giving me hope.

'At first Joseph flourished, but as the seas grew rougher the quality of the food deteriorated and we both took ill — sometimes for long periods. Then we'd anchor in some palm-fringed bay and small boats would come from nowhere. We'd lean over the ship's side and haggle for fresh provisions, swinging our baskets down for them to be filled. Then we'd dine on pineapples and coconuts and Captain Banyan would make us eat lemons and mangos and freshly cooked fish.'

'That sounds like my brothers. Is this too painful? Only I do love to hear talk of the sea.'

She shook her head. 'We rarely docked — only for repairs. Captain Banyan had been in the British Navy and was wary of marsh fever.' She drew a deep breath. 'I shall never set foot on a ship again. Never.'

'But you arrived safely. Once you've sold your silks you'll be able to — '

She shook her head, her dark brows creasing. Her full red lips looked striking against the pallor of her cheeks. Her beauty was fragile, her dignity extraordinary. 'Our troubles started in Lisbon. The ship was boarded by an officer of the British Navy who examined our cargo. He was very pleasant — charming, in fact — but very stern. He refused to allow us to leave port until the other ships arrived. His ship was on convoy duty. He told Captain Banyan that Spanish privateers had been sighted and all British ships going to England must wait for his escort.'

'He stopped you leaving, Mrs Oakley?'

She frowned, shaking her head. 'I wish he had . . . Captain Banyan insisted on going. One of the passengers was adamant his cargo must get to Bristol. I heard them arguing. He offered Captain Banyan a substantial inducement and further payment once the cargo was sold. The spices were spoiling and would be worthless with further delay. The voyage had already taken too long.'

'So you left *without* a navy escort?'

She gripped her hands together. 'Yes, and exactly what they said would happen did happen. They used false colours, a huge English Jack . . . a series of flags saying they needed to come alongside to give us important mail. I didn't see it, but Joe did. I was in my cabin, packing the last of our things. We were in sight of England — the Isles of Scilly.'

It was the oldest ruse in the book. The moment he knew my brothers were to join the navy, Uncle Alex had sat them down and told them everything to watch for — false colours, the ruse of passing across mail. Never trust a loan ship. Never believe the signals.

'Captain Banyan resisted. He tried to fend them off and they killed him . . . they thrust a sword straight through his heart right in front of Joe. I thought they'd kill us too. They rounded us up and I thought we'd die. I pleaded and pleaded. I was on my knees, begging them not to take the life of my son. I could see England . . . we were so nearly there. I knew enough Spanish to tell them I'd lost everything and that if it was just me I wouldn't mind dying, but they had to save my son.'

My stomach twisted. 'And they let you go?'

'Just the passengers, not the crew. We were forced down a flimsy rope ladder into a rowing boat. Land was visible and the sea was calm. There were four of us — thrown into a rowing boat with nothing but what we were wearing. I don't think anyone has ever rowed so fast.'

'And they took the ship as a prize?'

The dark curls on her brow nodded. 'The ship was called *Isabella* — I only saw that once we were in the boat. They'd covered the name with canvas.'

'But the insurance should still stand. Have you

claimed for your silks?'

She shook her head, her voice a whisper. 'No one can help me, Miss Carew. There is no hope. I have no proof of who I am . . . I left everything on the ship. They held a dagger to my neck . . . I just grabbed Joe and didn't stop to think. When we landed, I went straight to the port authorities and they told me to write to the East India Company.'

'Well, there you are — surely it's all in hand?'

She smiled at my obvious naivety. 'The secretary to the East India Company wrote back. His letter was curt and to the point. I was wasting their time. Did I know how many fabricated claims were made? How many people came forward with false identities? Without proof of who I am, I have no legal way to claim insurance.'

'But can't Mr and Mrs Oakley vouch for you?'

'No one can vouch for me.' She gripped her mother-in-law's hand. 'We met for the first time when I walked through that door. They believe who I am, of course, but they can't vouch for me. According to the authorities, they're part of the hoax. Without the ship's records, there's no proof I was a passenger on that ship, or that I was bringing any silk.'

I rose to leave. 'I'm so sorry to hear this. But all may not be lost. I have a very dear friend who might be able to help. Her husband runs a shipping company and they insure all kinds of ships. May I tell her of your trouble? I believe if anyone can help, she can.'

She cleared her throat. 'Thank you, you're very kind.'

I reached for my basket. There was no need to ask about Joe's health as he had coughed throughout our visit. 'I've brought you two bottles of my elixir. A spoonful every four hours might help soothe Joe's cough.'

Sofia Oakley was on the verge of tears, but she was a proud woman and held tight to her dignity. 'I can't thank you enough . . .'

'And here's a present for you, Joe. Your mother told us you used to ride . . . that you had a horse. Here, please have these . . . ' His thin fingers caressed the polished white horses, his huge brown eyes the mirror of his mother's. He could not speak but held them to his heart.

'What do you say, Joe?' His mother's voice sounded strangled.

'Our horses were white — just like this . . . Thank you, I shall treasure them.'

Sofia Oakley lifted her chin, her extraordinary high cheekbones accentuated by the flickering fire. 'We can't accept them — they're from your ark.'

'I shall write to Captain de la Croix and ask him for two more. He's a dear man and he won't mind one little bit — especially when I tell him why.'

A wistful note crept into her heavy accent. 'You befriend French prisoners . . . you see only goodness in people. Miss Carew, you have a heart that transcends borders and defies the brutality of war. You counteract man's inhumanity to man.' She handed me back the small square of silk the horses had been wrapped in, yet I could see she was enjoying the feel of it.

'The silk is yours . . . please make something from it. And yes, I do believe we must counteract the atrocities of this war. We must treat our prisoners like we would want our loved ones to be treated. My brother captured Captain de la Croix near Guadeloupe . . . where my fiancé . . . where . . . '

'You have not heard any more news?'

'No.' I tried to keep my voice steady. 'I hate this war . . . I hate everything. about it. At first I thought I'd hate Captain de la Croix but he's a good man. But for this war, he'd be our friend and *because of the war*, he is now our friend. Another woman, far, far away may be harbouring . . . caring for . . . my fiancé Edmund, or, heaven forbid, my three brothers. And that makes it even more important to forgive and extend the hand of friendship to those whom we hold captive.'

12

Town House, Truro
Sunday 21st January 1798, 12 p.m.

The green feathers on my velvet bonnet ruffled in the wind, the sky a cloudless blue, the sun glinting on the newly painted railings. Above us, the church bells were ringing, the congregation lingering, enjoying the unexpected change in the weather. Mother nodded to yet another acquaintance and I tucked my hands into my muff, knowing we would be detained even longer. I searched again, the same dread and hope churning my stomach: Luke and Mary Lilly were nowhere to be seen.

Horses clattered across the cobbles and I turned to see a familiar coach draw up outside our house. Uncle Alex swiftly alighted, shaking out the creases of his jacket, glancing around, not entering the house but standing on the steps looking in our direction. Our eyes caught and I knew at once it was me he had come to see.

'Is it? Why, so it is. Look, Amelia, it's your godfather's coach. Forgive me, Mrs Mitchem, Mrs Wendbury . . . I must see to my visitor. Amelia, do you see who it is?'

I stood frozen to the spot, unable to move. As if in a dream, I felt my arm taken, Bethany helping both Mother and I across the square. I had long anticipated such a scene — Uncle Alex

106

arriving in haste and holding out a letter; sometimes he would be frowning, shaking his head and mouthing how sorry he was; other times he would be smiling, tears in his eyes. I had imagined it every possible way: Edmund sitting in the carriage with him; Edmund walking in through the front door; Edmund in the study, waiting for me as I returned home; Edmund running across the vast lawn of Trenwyn House, swinging me in his arms.

A year ago, I would have run to meet Uncle Alex. Before I met Luke, I would have flown across the square, but now I could hardly walk, my legs unstable.

Mother's voice sounded strained. 'It could be any one of them . . . *any* one of them.'

I knew differently. I could feel foreboding deep inside. I knew this day would come. 'No. He was looking at me . . . it's about Edmund — I know it is.'

★ ★ ★

Uncle Alex had his back to the fireplace; the fire was roaring yet I felt as cold as ice. His words were coming and going, one moment loud, the next lost to the pounding in my ears. Behind him, the mantelpiece looked blurred, as if I had painted Uncle Alex but faded out the background. His voice was louder again, coming in snatches.

'It happens more often than it should. Delays on both sides . . . powerless to prevent inaccuracies. Keeping a full account of each prisoner is

fraught with difficulties. These inaccuracies occur
. . . if the source of our information is flawed,
then our lists are flawed. We are dealing with
thousands . . . '

He often did this, swooping into the house, the
first to bring us news. Not swooping like an eagle
— he was too slight and elegant to be a bird of
prey — but more like a swallow, graceful and
charming, his fine bone structure belying his
strength and power. Papa, by comparison, stood
next to him like an ox, broad-shouldered and
ruddy faced, his bushy white eyebrows drawn
deep in consternation.

Uncle Alex frowned back at Papa, his simple
grey wig and travelling clothes as immaculate as
ever but he looked tired, his voice choked with
regret. 'I can only apologize. My information was
incorrect. We believed it to be a trusted source.'

'He's in . . . London? You're telling me he's in
London?'

Wounded in action and knighted for exceptional valour, Admiral Sir Alexander Pendarvis
came stiffly to my side, stretching out his ebony
peg-leg to sit beside me. 'Yes, and I believe he's
quite well. I have two reports from the Admiralty.' He reached in his leather bag. 'The first
report runs to many pages — it's a copy of
Edmund's statement . . . how he crawled to safety
and his subsequent imprisonment in the prison
hulk below Fort Fleur d'Epée in Guadeloupe.'

'No!' I could hardly breathe.

Uncle Alex's frown deepened. 'I'm afraid using
prison hulks is as widespread as it is deplorable.
They use them to protect vulnerable harbours

and forts . . . they fly flags saying prisoners are on board to deter fire. Enemy ships won't attack if there's a chance prisoners are on board.'

'That's terrible . . . do we do the same?' I was in a daze, half-hearing, half-speaking.

'It's not policy but I can't be certain. We use prison hulks, as you know, but out of necessity not to deter fire.' He handed the tightly written pages to Papa. 'I've had this copied for you — Amelia can read it when her shock has lessened.'

The room seemed devoid of air and I fought my dizziness. 'But this is dated *a month* ago . . . Are you telling me he has been back a *whole month* and no one thought to tell me?'

It was more of a sigh than a breath. 'I thought it best to know the outcome of the Admiralty investigation — whether Edmund would be honourably or dishonourably discharged. Amelia, my dear, Edmund was facing the charge of desertion — '

'How dare they think that?'

'They don't, not now. Midshipman Melville was able to give them very precise information and I can state, quite categorically, that there's no stain on his character. The procedure is vital, though it is so distasteful to you. Every day of his disappearance must be accounted for — there's prize money to be considered as well as everything else. A man lost to naval records for such a long period of time must fully account for his absence. Most, I'm afraid, are found to be deserters and they pay the penalty.'

A shiver ran down my spine. 'Of course . . . I understand.'

109

'A two- or three-week delay is nothing after such a long absence.'

His voice was fading again, the roaring fire doing nothing to rid me of my terrible chill. It should not be like this. I should be laughing, kissing him, thanking him for bringing me such good news. I should not be feeling so numb. 'It is if you are in love,' I whispered. 'Three weeks is forever.'

He took my hand but said nothing. He was practically family; Papa was godfather to his son who was married to Charity's sister. He had always been there for us: perhaps not a swallow, maybe more like an elegant reed warbler, forever weaving a strong raft beneath us.

'The truth is, he's been under Admiralty jurisdiction since December the sixteenth.'

'No . . . that can't be true! How could you be so cruel to keep this from me?'

'I've only known for the last three weeks but I believe it's for the best. He was in a terrible state — he was taken to Stonehouse Hospital in Plymouth Dock and was cared for by the naval doctors. On discharge from the hospital he was summoned by the Admiralty and has remained in London for the last three weeks.'

'Did he ask after me? Why didn't he write?'

'I told him not to. Amelia, my dearest, he has been very ill. It's not easy for him . . . nor is it easy for you. The thought of him rushing down to see you . . . to have you meet *before* I could warn you — '

Papa looked up from the closely written pages. 'Quite right; difficult decision, but the right one.

110

Best to get all the official paperwork behind him. I must say, they've been very thorough. *December 16th: Midshipman Edmund Melville saw his chance and jumped from the Portuguese trading ship, the* Santa Theresa, *which was taking salt to Gothenburg, Sweden. The ship had sought shelter in Cork . . .* He jumped from the ship as it was leaving.' His eyes caught mine. 'I must warn you, my dear, this makes for very uncomfortable reading.'

'It does, but to his credit, Midshipman Melville acted by the book. He nearly died from cold, but he made it back to the harbour. He went immediately to the harbour master and requested the navy be informed. The *Santa Theresa*'s passage had been officially logged and the harbour master verified Edmund's evidence. A naval frigate took him to Stonehouse Hospital in Plymouth for an assessment, where they kept him until he was discharged to London.'

'Under arrest?'

'At the time, yes. But he went willingly — he was expecting to see his father and cousin.'

I reeled in horror. 'Oh no! He hadn't heard they'd died? Of course, how could he? Uncle Alex, you *should* have told me he was in London.'

He drew out a letter from the bag and at the sight of the familiar writing, tears filled my eyes. 'The first thing I knew about all this was when Edmund wrote to me — three weeks ago. He asked about you, and how soon he could see you. But he was, quite rightly, highly concerned. He had no idea whether you were married and

111

no longer thought of him and he begged me to be honest. He wanted to know how you were, and whether you were happy. He wrote saying that if you were happily settled, he wouldn't trouble you.'

The letter trembled in my hand. *My only concern is her well-being. If you write that Miss Carew has found new happiness then I will rejoice in her happiness and I shall not return to Cornwall. I will lease Pendowrick Hall and bring my sister and Mother to London to save any embarrassment of feelings.*

Tears blurred the page. Any other time, I would have held it to my lips, to my heart, to my lips again, yet I felt numb, the room fading around me. I should be happy. I should be . . .

Someone was tapping my hand. 'Amelia . . . Amelia? I think you better get her a glass of brandy.' Mother must have used her fan as a stream of cool air brushed my cheeks. 'Alex, Amelia needs more time — she must consider everything very carefully before deciding.'

'Of course, she must take as long as she wants. I've said nothing . . . only at Christmas you led us to believe, or rather, my wife believed — ' He stopped.

'I don't need time,' I whispered. 'Edmund must come home to Pendowrick. Tell him we're waiting for him — all of us. Tell him to hurry, tell him his mother's ill and she needs him urgently.'

Papa took my other hand, his voice choking. 'Amelia, my dearest . . . you must feel under no obligation.'

No *obligation?* The man I had loved so

intently had been reaped with praise for his valour. He had been imprisoned, suffered forced labour on a ship. He had fulfilled every obligation to his king and country and I would just wash my hands of him? How could they think that?

'I loved him, Papa, with all my heart . . . I am engaged to him . . . we are to be married.' My words sounded distant, as if someone else was saying them. 'I've waited so long and prayed so hard for his return. How can you expect otherwise?'

Across the silence. Uncle Alex cleared his throat. 'Then I will write to him. I'll return to Fosse and keep you all informed.'

They stood in the hall, Uncle Alex pulling on his gloves, and I held back, a terrible numbness spreading through me. Uncle Alex had never taken kindly to Edmund: he thought him weak-willed and *sensitive to hurt*. His voice was harsh: 'You must warn her, Clarissa. Men return very changed from war — especially under such circumstances. He's not the youth she fell in love with.'

Mother's voice was strong, edged with anger. 'And she's not the wide-eyed girl he abandoned with such ease. She's studied all Frederick's botany books and has as much knowledge as the best apothecary. She's intuitive and intelligent, her remedies are widely used, and she commands the greatest respect. I cannot bear to think of her giving it all up to bury herself on that moor.'

Uncle Alex's voice dropped to a whisper. 'They're all but ruined — I believe the estate is

113

entailed and until they repay their debts, the income they receive barely covers their costs.'

They smiled as I joined them, Uncle Alex kissing me affectionately before he left. Mother and I stood in silence, watching the carriage until it turned right into King Street and was lost to sight. She drew out her handkerchief, her voice strained.

'You don't need to attend the committee meeting tomorrow, my love. Not if you don't want to.'

In all my imaginings, I had always cried with joy. In the street, in the drawing room, in the carriage, in my herb garden. I would open a letter, or Uncle Alex would be smiling as he walked towards me. Sometimes it was Frederick who brought me the news, sometimes it was my nephews tripping over each other to be the first to give me such happy tidings. Sometimes it would be Edmund himself, standing there, smiling down at me, and I would run into his arms. I would always be crying for joy. Never this numbness.

I wiped my eyes. 'No, I have to see him — ' I could hardly talk. Hardly walk. 'Moses has sent those herbs I asked for, so I'll be in the kitchen making a salve for Lady Melville. Her lips will soon blister, and it's vital she gets some relief.'

★ ★ ★

To make Green Salve: take 4 ounces each of chicken weed, henbane, haymaiden and mallow. Pound the herbs and boil them in salted hog's fat and 2 ounces of almond oil until the herbs soften and discolour. Strain through muslin and cool before sealing.

THE LADY HERBALIST

13

Town House, Truro
Monday 22nd January 1798, 11 a.m.

Dr Nankivell's assistant held his quill in mid-air. 'Yes, I have that down. Members of the committee present are Dr Nankivell — chairman, Lady Clarissa, Lady Polgas, Major Trelawney, Dr Bohenna, Mrs Lilly and Miss Carew.'

The dining table had been cleared, the sun streaming through the window. Dr Nankivell was at the head of the table, his slight frame lost in Papa's huge carving chair. A respectable physician of considerable years, he saw the new infirmary as a vital addition to his work in Truro. Bewigged and bespectacled, with large whiskery sideburns, he wore sober clothes and a resigned expression. 'You all have a copy, ladies and gentlemen? Good, then we'll present our findings in order of this agenda — without too much interruption.' He peered over his glasses at Lady Polgas.

Lady Polgas pursed her lips, a disdainful shrug to her shoulders. 'What needs to be said needs to be said. I was only saying the other day . . . '

'And discussion must be relevant . . . *to the point.*'

Frederick had once likened Lady Polgas to a ship in full sail and she had been known as The Galleon ever since. We had tried to keep it from

116

Cordelia but to no avail; even my nephews knew what we called their grandmother. A deep intake of breath, a wobble of her chins and it was obvious Lady Polgas was not going to let that pass. 'Some of us have more experience to draw on, Dr Nankivell. I, for one, am considered one of the most enlightened — and certainly the most *connected* — members of our society. My family have *influenced* the affairs of Truro for generations. My word, I think you'll find, *holds sway.*'

'Indeed, Lady Polgas, and for that we are very grateful.'

Luke had his back to the sun. I could not see his face, not that I dared cast even the smallest glance. Every other meeting would have seen us suppressing our smiles, trying not to raise our eyebrows. Mary Lilly sat beside him, Mother next to me, and the urge to run from the room was almost overwhelming. He looked tired, shaken, sifting through his papers without looking up. Any other time, he would have slid a bag of bonbons across the table with a conspiratorial wink.

I hardly heard what Dr Nankivell was saying. 'Other banks have offered us more advantageous terms but gambling on shares poses too great a risk for our investment.'

Major Trelawney raised his hand, the red sleeve of his uniform flashing in the sun. A firm favourite in our family, he commanded the respect of everyone in Truro. 'I'm concerned the amount we've put aside as surety will fall short of our requirements. The building costs are

117

escalating — the money left to invest as capital will not meet our future needs.' His brass buttons and gold braid glinted as he handed us each a copy of his accounts. 'The annual subscriptions will only just cover the running costs.'

Lady Polgas held up her copy. 'Is this the list of subscriptions?'

'And our benefactors. The building costs are listed here . . . the annual subscriptions here . . . ranging from one guinea . . . two guineas . . . up to ten guineas. That amounts to two hundred and twenty-four pounds and fourteen pence a year.' A strong, handsome man in his late forties, his abundant dark hair was greying at the temples, tied at his neck in a simple bow. 'The annual subscriptions will cover food, salaries, laundry and so forth, but we need sufficient capital to hold in readiness for upkeep and repairs.'

'I thought we raised more than this — one thousand, nine hundred pounds?' Luke sounded flustered.

'The column below, Dr Bohenna. Six hundred pounds given by anonymous donors, and five hundred and eighty pounds raised through concerts and balls.'

'Of course. Forgive me.' He glanced up, our eyes met, and I could not breathe for the ache in my heart.

Lady Polgas leaned her ample bosom on the table, her smile as false as her sweet tone. 'I'd like a list of all the *anonymous* benefactors, thank you, Major Trelawney.'

Mother raised her eyebrows. 'Whatever for, Georgina?'

A heave of her bosom, a responding rise to her eyebrows, a return to her usual sharpness. 'You may not think it necessary to thank the generosity of those who give so freely, Clarissa, but *I* believe it to be *imperative*. I shall write, *on behalf* of the committee, to each of these generous benefactors and thank them, most graciously, *as is appropriate*.'

Mother glanced at Mary Lilly, who remained looking down at her papers. 'I believe they have already been sufficiently thanked, Georgina.'

'By whom? By someone of little importance outside the sphere of the hospital? These people must be thanked *properly* by someone of influence and *stature* in our community. *Manners are manners*, though many seem to forget.' Her eyes pierced each of us in turn. 'The list, Major Trelawney . . . of those who have donated — what shall we say? — a hundred pounds or more?'

This was about more than the committee: this was about the grandchildren. As Cordelia's mother, Lady Polgas never allowed the feud to go away. *Children left to run wild* was how she viewed the Carew influence. *Ill-disciplined and ill-mannered*, another of her favourite phrases. Apparently, we were too lax with the children, allowing them too much freedom.

A glance of amusement crossed Mother's eyes. 'Anonymous means anonymous, Georgina.'

Major Trelawney tried to hold back the list but Lady Polgas held out her hand, her stare pinning him into submission. One look at the list and her smile vanished, her jowls slackened. She must have seen Mother and Mary Lilly's names on the top. Her mouth tightened. 'Well, yes . . . '

Any other time, I would have enjoyed a sideways glance at Luke. Any other time, he would have held my gaze, the love in his eyes sending my heart racing.

Dr Nankivell returned to the agenda. 'Lady Clarissa, I believe you make several recommendations?'

Mother nodded. 'I showed Mr Wood's plans for the kitchens to my cook and she recommended the kitchens be doubled in size. She says we'll need bigger cauldrons and she strongly recommends they bake bread on the premises. Therefore we'd need separate bread ovens. And the scullery should not be used for slops; she's adamant there must be a separate slop-house with a covered sewer.'

Still reeling from Mother and Mary Lilly's generosity, Lady Polgas could not let that go unanswered. 'Your cook is *adamant*, is she, Clarissa? Is this what you teach my grandsons — to fraternize with servants? To run round like hoodlums — sliding down banisters and playing ridiculous games of herrings? You did not run wild, did you, Dr Nankivell? No, of course you didn't. You studied and were brought up to respect your betters. And I don't suppose you ran riot in that *shop* of yours, did you, Dr Bohenna?'

Luke held her stare. 'I believe the game is called *pilchards*, Lady Polgas.'

Her livid face matched her ruby dress and Dr

Nankivell was quick to intervene, shaking his head at his clerk who looked unsure what to write. He was young, with a mop of blond curls, his jacket sleeves a little short at the wrists. His cheeks flushed as his quill remained poised.

Dr Nankivell glanced down at his list. 'Thank you, Lady Clarissa. Your cook's recommendations will be sent to the architect.' He was our adored physician, present at my birth and those of my brothers, seeing us through our childhood illnesses with his gentle manners and secret bags of jelly drops. 'Mrs Lilly, your brief was . . . ?'

'The washrooms, Dr Nankivell. And I'm an expert in washrooms, so I've no reason to doubt my findings.' She winked at Luke and my heart burned. Mary Lilly, with her dimpled smile and beautiful complexion, her poise and grace. An Irish runaway, a woman who had known poverty and want, now married to the richest industrialist in Truro. Mary Bohenna, working hard with her first husband in his apothecary shop, both dreaming of the day Luke would become a doctor.

She held her report steady, her voice resolute. 'I'd like to see bigger cauldrons, too — if there's to be anything like enough hot water to wash the sheets. And a larger drying room with copper pipes the length and breadth of it, filled with hot water. More importantly, I'd like to see the provision of a room we could call *the first stop*.'

'What a ridiculous name.' Lady Polgas was back on form.

'Well . . . we can hardly call it the *delousing and vermin-catching room*, now, can we? Give

121

the poor souls some dignity. My suggestion is that everyone entering the infirmary should go to *the first stop* and we'll take every stitch of clothing off them to be washed . . . they'll be bathed and tended to, and we'll supply them with fresh clothes while theirs are being laundered. I believe no one should be admitted to our infirmary without going first through *the first stop* — or we'll have scabies and all sorts in the wards.'

Any other time, Luke would be sitting next to me, leaning towards me, touching but not touching. He glanced at me as he spoke. 'I couldn't agree more.' Behind us, the gold clock on the mantelpiece struck the hour and our eyes locked for the full twelve chimes.

Mother nodded to the footman. 'A dish of tea, Dr Nankivell? Or something a little *stronger?*'

Dr Nankivell ran his fingers over his bushy sideburns. 'Indeed, a dish of tea would be splendid, thank you, Lady Clarissa. Dr Bohenna and Miss Carew — will you report your findings together, or take it each in turn?'

Lady Polgas's chins were lost in their folds as she glared down the table. 'I believe *I* am to speak next.'

Dr Nankivell sighed. 'So you are, Lady Polgas; my mistake. Your report is on the choice of matron?'

Lady Polgas peered at her report through screwed-up eyes. 'The matron will be the public face of our infirmary — one to set the standards we require.' She abandoned the page as the writing eluded her without her glasses, raising her voice instead.

'I've drafted the attributes I'm looking for in our matron. She must be well mannered and well bred . . . a strict disciplinarian because the servants will need to be watched. She will hold the keys *at all times* and will keep the domestic accounts *clearly* and *concisely*. She will live above the wards — which she must keep clean and tidy *at all times* — and she will have every other Sunday off. In short, we require a thoroughly respectable woman with the highest credentials and impeccable references. Obviously, I shall have to look *outside* Truro for such a woman. A distressed gentlewoman from Bath or London would be appropriate. Perhaps a governess — '

Mother braved an interruption. 'I believe there might be such a lady in Truro. Ah, thank you . . . ' She smiled at the line of maids bringing in the tea, taking a plate from the tray. 'Some gingerbread, Lady Polgas, Major Trelawney . . . Dr Nankivell? I know you will, Dr Bohenna. I made it myself.'

Luke smiled, but politely refused — Luke who ate gingerbread faster than Mother could make it.

Lady Polgas's first wince had been at the suggestion that someone from Truro might be eligible for the post of matron, her second, more violent wince, was for Mother's baking habits. 'I will advertise the post in the London papers,' she said, shaking her head at the offending biscuits.

Mother tried to conceal her smile. 'The lady's name is Mrs Sofia Oakley. She fits your criteria perfectly — she is a distressed gentlewoman and is highly intelligent. She arrived from Portugal two months ago — she's Portuguese.'

Lady Polgas snorted into her cup, almost spilling her tea. 'A *foreigner*? Have you lost your mind, Clarissa?'

Dr Nankivell nodded to the footman who poured him a large glass of brandy. 'Perhaps, Dr Bohenna and Miss Carew, you should sit together, seeing as yours is a joint report?' He swilled the brandy round the crystal glass. 'You'll join me in a glass, Henry?'

Major Trelawney shot a sideways glance at Lady Polgas. 'Indeed I will. Thank you.'

14

Major Trelawney put down his empty glass, collecting his papers into a neat pile. 'Have my seat, Luke. Please, I insist.'

Luke's voice was almost drowned by the scraping of chairs. 'Are you all right, Amelia?'

I nodded. 'Yes, are you?'

I had been holding back my tears, but now I was in danger of crying. In front of everyone, I was going to cry. I could see him summoning every ounce of his courage, like the first time we had been alone on Christmas Eve and he had spoken words of such comfort. *No one can replace Edmund, Miss Carew. He will always come first. If he returns, your happiness will make me happy.* I gripped my hands beneath the table.

Luke's voice was getting stronger. 'Recent findings from Stonehouse Hospital indicate the importance of good ventilation. So with this in mind, I'd like to see better air-flow through the building.' He looked down at our list. 'I wholeheartedly support the idea of the *first* stop, but I'd like to add another room — the consulting room needs to be separate from the post-mortem room.'

'Agreed.' Dr Nankivell smiled. 'You don't think being up a hill will be enough ventilation? The air will be fresh up there, away from the sewers and smells of the town.'

Luke shook his head. 'I believe we should

125

increase the ventilation. Recent papers show that naval captains who ventilate their ships have a healthier crew and less disease. They position their sails to funnel the wind through the hatches to blow through the lower decks.'

Lady Polgas looked up from examining her fingernails. 'You've been in the navy, have you, Dr Bohenna?'

'No . . .'

'My son, Dr Emerson Polgas, has been a ship's doctor for *ten years* — advising ships' captains to do just that. First-hand knowledge cannot be bettered, don't you think?'

Luke's smile was polite, if a little forced. 'Miss Carew, would you like to mention the dispensary?'

I nodded, smoothing out my papers. 'The plans for the physic garden are perfectly adequate, but I suggest more fruit bushes as the ascorbic properties of soft fruit will benefit the patients.' Luke was too close to me, the room too hot. 'Our real concern is the provision of medicines — for those seen as outpatients. We've studied the reports from The Devon and Exeter Hospital and they show a clear need to distribute medicines from the hospital.'

Days spent sitting at this table, our arms touching as we read the latest research. Side by side, eager, attentive, writing our report with a single mind: his eyes shining with plans for cleaner water, covered sewers, the possibility of adopting the vaccine against smallpox. His passionate belief that poverty and dirt were vectors for disease.

'You were saying?' he prompted.

The list swam in my hands. 'Perhaps, Dr Bohenna, could you . . . ?'

He took the sheet from me. 'The number of patients attending The Devon Hospital has increased — 1,890 goitre and scorbutic disorders, 1,112 dropsies, colic and asthmas, 1,591 rheumatisms, 57 epilepsies and 360 paralytic disorders. Of course, they do have a much bigger hospital but nevertheless, that's a huge provision.' He handed me back the list.

'There's a further 3,115 bruises, fractures and dislocations, and 5,701 for ague, fevers, consumptions, cancers and inflammatory diseases. But it's not the consultations we're concerned about — our fear is controlling the *quality* of the medicines the patients receive.'

I wanted to run from the room. All our plans for his new practice, his desperate desire to be appointed as the infirmary physician: our love flowering from barren wasteland, the tender shoots he had nurtured with such patience. 'The annual subscriptions won't cover the cost of medicines and we believe this is a vital shortcoming. Poorer patients will always seek the cheapest provider.'

'Are you suggesting a hospital apothecary?'

Luke nodded. 'Yes, Dr Nankivell. If our patients turn to rogue practitioners our cure rate will suffer. We must be seen to cure or at least ease our patients' complaints.'

Lady Polgas tapped her stubby fingers. 'Your first husband was an apothecary, was he not, Mrs Lilly? That was your father, Dr Bohenna — is it that you have one of your *friends* in mind?'

127

'No, Lady Polgas. I have no friend in mind.'

Always the same snub, everyone wanting to remind Luke and Mary of their humble beginnings. If not Lady Polgas, then other members of her circle. Fire flamed my cheeks; he did not deserve that. My voice cut across the room. 'Quack doctors have been sighted . . . horse doctors peddling their remedies on the streets. I've recently come across one.'

Dr Nankivell's face fell. 'Where was this, Miss Carew?'

'Up on the moors . . . but I believe he was travelling to Truro.'

Luke drew a deep breath. 'Miss Carew wrote asking me to see the lady in question. She had consumed half a bottle of the peddled elixir.'

'And you have reason to be worried?'

'Every reason.'

'I believe you may speak freely, Dr Bohenna. No names, of course, but if I'm to draft more posters and write to the newspapers, I need evidence that these elixirs are harmful. Rose water doesn't harm. It won't cure, but it does no harm — even the occasional purgative can be beneficial.'

Luke shook his head. 'This was no senna leaf concoction, Dr Nankivell. The lady had extensive bruising on her hands and abdomen and blistering on her lips. There was a fine blue tinge to those lips. She complained of stomach cramps and loss of appetite. Her urine was the colour of mud.'

Lady Polgas flicked open her fan. 'Well, I'm sure! Please remember there are those of us in this — '

Dr Nankivell raised his eyes, clasping his hand as if in prayer. 'You believe it contained mercury?'

'Or lead. I didn't see the colour of the clixir. The label claimed it to be from London — dispensed by a physician called Dr Lovelace from St Bartholomew's Hospital. There was no such doctor by that name while I was there.'

I fought to breathe. 'The mixture was very dark — almost black. I threw it in the fire, along with the bottle.'

Dr Nankivell nodded. 'A wise precaution, Miss Carew.'

'No, it was foolish — I should have kept it for you to test . . . I'm so sorry, I didn't think.' Tears pooled in my eyes. Mercury. Or lead. Edmund should have come home sooner. He had wasted precious time waiting to hear if I was free to love him — three whole weeks' delay. A delay that might have cost his mother her life.

Luke handed me his starched white handkerchief. 'I'm sorry — I didn't mean to shock you. I thought you realized it was likely to be . . . '

'Yes, I did realize. It's just . . . '

Major Trelawney stood stiffly to attention. 'Allow me to help, Miss Carew. You don't look very well — '

The sound of frantic knocking at the front door made him stop. Footsteps were rushing across the hall. A footman opened the door.

'I beg yer pardon, but there's been an accident, Dr Bohenna. You're needed on the wharf. A man's been crushed . . . They want you to come quickly.'

Luke reached for his bag. 'I'm coming. Forgive me, I must go.'

Dr Nankivell began collecting up his papers. 'Of course. I'll follow directly.'

From down the table, Lady Polgas's voice cut like a knife. 'There's still one outstanding matter to discuss: the appointment of the physician in charge of the infirmary.'

Dr Nankivell's eyes followed Luke across the square. 'Indeed. A formality, I believe.'

Lady Polgas's voice was like steel. 'Dr Bohenna is a surgeon as well as a physician, is he? He knows about crush injuries and amputations? He's been *physician-in-charge* of a naval hospital for seven years — on board a ship of the line for three years before that?'

Dr Nankivell fastened the buckle on his bag, pushing his glasses further up his nose. 'No, but he is a first-class doctor of integrity with first-class qualifications behind him.'

Lady Polgas's large bosom rested on the table, her outstretched arm sliding a closely written page along the polished surface. 'This is my son's application for the position of Physician to the Infirmary. His references are extensive: his first — class qualifications, his excellent record of service, his promotions, his recommendations. Let me see, now . . . surgeon's qualifications . . . physician's qualifications . . . first-hand knowledge as physician-in-charge of Port Royal Hospital in Jamaica.'

Dr Nankivell stared at the sheet of paper. 'Your son has returned to Truro?'

Lady Polgas looked like a cat gluttoned with

130

cream. 'He'll be here within the month. A doctor of his experience is exactly what our infirmary needs — but, what's more to the point, he's a man of *considerable social standing.*'

15

We stood under the porch, Major Trelawney wearing his warm cape and black busby, me in my fur-lined cloak and muff. The sky was a brilliant blue, bright sunlight flooding the church tower, glinting on the clock face.

'There now. A breath of fresh air will do you the power of good.' Mother was clearly itching to join us, but she accepted Mary's arm with a stiff smile, nodding to Henry Trelawney as he pointed me forward. Bethany followed in her new Christmas bonnet and matching woollen gloves.

Under Major Trelawney's firm command, the volunteer troops had been mustered and trained. Our towns were safer, the threat of invasion carefully monitored, all thanks to the unassuming man by my side. 'Where shall we go, Miss Carew? Shall we go shopping or shall we go to the library? I'm yours to command.' His smile was as anxious as Mother's had been, concern clouding his handsome face. 'Or to the wharf?'

'Shall we see if Elizabeth Fox is at home?'

He seemed relieved. 'Splendid. Always a pleasure to watch the ships.'

'*Walking is the best exercise for those who are able to bear it and riding for those who are not. When the weather is fair, the open air contributes much to the benefit of exercise.* I'm quoting from my herbal, Major Trelawney. There's a section on how to try to avoid illness.'

He normally walked stiffly, helped by the use of his cane, yet today he seemed to be moving more freely. He answered my unspoken question. 'I must say that willow bark you suggested is certainly helping.'

The sudden good weather had brought everyone out; the streets were busy, people hurrying past. Carriages were rattling along the cobbles, a post coach sounding its horn. We reached the junction of Quay Street and joined a crowd forming behind a wagon laden with barrels. Street vendors staggered behind barrows stacked high with sacks of corn and crates of chickens stood in rows on the roadside. Beside us, a line of carts were piled with potatoes and turnips.

As we streamed through the narrow gap to the wharf, the jostling grew severe. 'Are you all right? I'm sorry about that. Here . . . over here.' Major Trelawney shepherded me through the crowd and we stood watching the ships moored against the quay. Tall pulleys towered above us, loud shouts echoing across the cobbles — it was the height of the tide, every ship disgorging its contents, re-provisioning and re-loading in their strictly allotted time.

Among the crowds, I caught sight of a pretty white bonnet and a plain grey gown. 'There's Mrs Fox and her husband . . . over there by that large schooner.'

Major Trelawney's grip tightened. He steered me round pens crammed with pigs, drawing me swiftly from under the swing of a large pulley. Elizabeth Fox saw us approaching and interrupted her husband with a tap on his arm. He looked up, gave a nod of his head, and returned to the ship's master and the large book balanced on a hogshead between them. Elizabeth ran quickly towards us, her heart-shaped mouth breaking into a dimpled smile.

'How lovely to see you, Amelia . . . Major Trelawney. Are you out for a walk?' She took my arm, weaving us through a pile of sacks, dodging round a pack of mules to the relative quiet of a pie-seller. A strong smell of cabbage wafted from a large cooking pot beside us.

'You're obviously very busy . . . ' A note of anxiety crept in Major Trelawney's voice, as if asking Elizabeth for help. Her eyes sharpened.

'Never too busy for either of you — the cargo's nearly unloaded and with very little damage. We were worried on account of the storms, but the ship put in to Ireland. What would we do without Ireland?'

Major Trelawney shook his head. 'Ireland? Conspirators, the lot of them. We might have forestalled that last invasion, but they'll try again. The French fleet may be scattered, but the threat remains. You'd better check your ship for stowaways.'

'Really, Major Trelawney!'

'No, really, Mrs Fox. The French are determined to invade us through Ireland — there'll be another attempt. It's just a matter of time. Keep a close watch for spies — both Irish and French.'

She nodded, immediately serious. 'I'll have the ship searched. Will you join us for some tea in Harbour House?'

'Another time . . . perhaps I should leave you

134

two together. It was a good meeting, wasn't it, Miss Carew?' He bowed to each of us in turn, no doubt relieved to hand me over to Elizabeth.

She took one look at my tears. 'Luke couldn't save him. He wasn't from our ship, thank the Lord, but there was nothing Luke could do — except give the poor man comfort as he died. They say the rope was frayed. We need to address this . . . all pulleys should use chains. Oh come, my dearest, don't cry.'

We walked along the quayside, Bethany a few steps behind us. Elizabeth's house was the largest in a long row, a vast, red-brick house on three floors with offices below and their living accommodation above. Their main shipping business was in Falmouth where Mr Fox was Consul for the states of America, but they kept a toe-hold in Truro, often visiting the seaman's hostel and soup kitchen Elizabeth had founded. We walked up the wooden stairs, the sign *Fox & Fox Shipping and Insurance Company* glinting in the sunlight. Once in her drawing room, she drew me to the fire.

'Elizabeth, I feel so wretched.'

'Of course you do.'

'My love for Edmund wasn't just a youthful infatuation like Mother thinks — it was *real love*. We always knew what the other was thinking — we'd often say the same thing at the same time.' I sank into a chair, my face in my hands. 'He's in London, waiting to hear if I'm married . . . whether I've waited for him . . . '

Like her starched white bonnet and plain grey dress, the room showed no outward sign of

135

wealth. It was simply furnished with paintings of fully canvased ships sailing across the walls, the pine mantelpiece adorned only by a glass-domed carriage clock and two porcelain figurines. The fire was blazing, yet I felt so cold. She sat by my side. 'What does Luke say?'

'We haven't seen each other to talk, but I know he'll back away . . . Elizabeth, I'm so torn. I should be happy, but I'm scared. I'm so confused . . . '

She smelled of rose water, her soft hands taking mine. 'Of course you are, my love. You're loved by two men, and you love two men. Of course you're scared *and* confused. It's a very difficult state of affairs.'

'But I can't love two men — not how they want me to love them, not how I want to love them.'

She paused, her voice soft. 'For what it's worth, I believe you can love two men. I believe you can love them quite equally, if very differently. I'm certain of that.' Her voice grew stronger. 'But *not at the same time.*'

'What if . . . ?' I could hardly voice my fear.

'What if, when you see Edmund again you don't feel the same love? Or what if you *do* feel the same love?'

I took a deep breath. I knew she would understand.

'Then you must be strong, Amelia. My advice is don't let Edmund *assume* you're going to marry him. Give him time to settle back into Pendowrick but, more importantly, give yourself time to make the right decision.'

'But I'm his fiancée. I've been praying for his return. And would be still. I'd be waiting for him, longing for him — if I hadn't been so completely assured of his death.'

'He's been away a *very* long time and war changes a man.'

I had to tell her. 'Elizabeth . . . I've already given him reason to hope.'

'Oh, Amelia! You didn't tell him about Luke?'

Her sharp intake of breath made my heart race. 'No . . . I couldn't. His mother's very ill. He's returned to England to find his father and cousin dead and the estate in debt — he's in London, waiting for my answer, and I couldn't delay him from coming home any longer.'

She stiffened, a sudden flatness to her voice. 'Why is he waiting for your answer *in London* when his family and estate need him?'

It was hard to breathe, even harder to put my feelings into words. 'My understanding is that if we're not to be together, he'll stay in London. And he hates London. He says he'll move his family up there and he'll lease Pendowrick. Elizabeth, he *can't* do that.'

She grasped my hands. No smile, no laughing eyes, an expression of real gravity. 'Those are not the thoughts of a rational man. Why burden you with that decision?'

'That's why I'm scared. The thought of us being together in Pendowrick is what kept him alive all these years . . . and the thought of being there without me is too wretched for him. It's not that I don't love him. I've never stopped loving him.'

137

'Amelia, it was a very long time ago. You haven't seen him for six years.'

'Wives don't see their husbands yet they don't desert them. What if we'd been married and I'd had his child, like Charity had Frederick's? What if I was already living in Pendowrick? I'd be so happy — '

'But you aren't, and you don't have his child. Listen, my love. It was his decision to join the navy.'

'He should never have gone. He was too gentle for the navy. I wrote begging him to come home but he didn't get my letters — none of them. Instead, he tried even harder to be brave and accepted by the men. Captain Owen's report said Edmund insisted on being part of the landing party and I think it was because he wanted to prove his courage.'

A maid brought in a jug of freshly squeezed lemonade and Elizabeth smiled her thanks. 'Lemons straight off the ship.' She poured me a glass. 'My advice is to give yourself plenty of time. He must understand the situation you're in now.'

I sipped my lemonade. 'Two years ago . . . eighteen months ago, all I wanted to do was to be Edmund's wife and live in Pendowrick.'

'But now you see yourself by Luke's side, helping him in the infirmary and his growing medical practice. Those are two very different lives. That's why you need time — time and courage — and better sleep, by the look of you.'

'I swore an oath — oh, Elizabeth . . . if I'm to live up on the moors, I'll need someone to organize my herbs. I must supply the new infirmary . . . '

'That's far too far ahead. You've plenty of time for all that.'

'What about Sofia Oakley? Mother's going to put her name forward for matron at the infirmary.'

'An excellent choice. She's an intelligent, compassionate woman who's known suffering. I think she'd make an excellent matron.'

I nodded. 'I'll see if I can find her a position in an apothecary shop so she can get references.' I stood up to leave. 'Have you heard from her ship's insurance company?'

She shook her head. 'No, and I must warn you, I think her case is a lost one. I can't vouch for her, nobody can. The East India Company refuses all claimants with no proof of identity — we all do.' Her voice dropped. 'Ships that break from a convoy and sail without naval escort invalidate their terms of insurance. The contracts are very specific. If a ship makes a deviation from the chartered course, or remains too long in port, the insurer can't be held liable for any claims arising from these deviations.'

16

We parted on the quay, Bethany and I heading home in silence. Halfway across the square, my heart leapt. Luke was waiting by the church railings, his face drawn, a deep furrow creasing his forehead. He bowed formally, without his usual smile. His voice was terse, full of despair.

'Abdominal crush injuries with extensive internal bleeding. I was able to give him enough laudanum to ease the pain, but there was nothing else I could do.'

'You eased his pain. That's all he could ask.'

Luke drew me along the railings to the privacy of a large tree. Bethany held back, pretending to examine her shoe, and we stood in awkward silence. He looked drawn, the dusting of freckles on his cheeks and nose more noticeable, the auburn tints to his sideburns accentuating his pallor. I wanted him to hold me, feel his strong arms around me. I wanted him to hurry me inside to the fire, sit me down to listen to his plans on how to prevent accidents on the quayside. Instead, he ran his finger under his starched white cravat, swallowing hard. His voice was soft, hardly above a whisper.

'Amelia . . . we need to talk.'

I followed him to the church porch and we sat on the bench. He reached for my hands, putting them to his lips. His voice was hoarse, choked with emotion. 'Edmund came into your life before me, and as such, I knew he always came first. I've always understood that. From the moment we met, I knew our friendship was . . . that all I could hope for . . . was to comfort you in your loss. Never once did I assume to step into Edmund's shoes.'

A pulse was racing in his neck, his cheeks flushed. 'Time began to heal, and our friendship began to develop. When his death was confirmed . . . when Sir Alex left you in no doubt . . . well, that night I vowed to Edmund — to a man I didn't know but who had loved you so intensely and who'd lost his life fighting for his country — that I would look after you for *him*. That I would love you, honour you and cherish you. I vowed to his departed soul that I'd never seek to replace him in your heart . . . that I'd only seek to lodge beside him, and I would do everything in my power to bring you the happiness *he* would have brought you.'

'Luke . . . stop . . . don't . . . please don't.'

He handed me his large white handkerchief and I pressed it to my face. His mouth tightened, his chest rising and falling. 'Your happiness is all I've ever wanted . . . Edmund's return is a miracle and we must rejoice in that. But I find I cannot. I cannot rejoice in the return of a man I see only as a threat. I feel such fear, such unpardonable jealousy. I can't lose you now . . . '

I could not breathe for the pain, the love in his eyes, the way he was trying to control his voice. I loved him so completely; I loved his compassion, his intellect, his humility. The way his eyes lit up when they smiled, the way they deepened to

141

pools of sorrow. I loved his humour, the way he teased me. The way he adored his mother. The goodness of his soul.

'Luke, I'm so sorry. I never thought this would happen. Never. But put yourself in my place. Or rather, put yourself in Edmund's place. How would you feel if I had deserted *you* . . . if you had lived through hell . . . every day, with only one thought in mind . . . to return home . . . wanting, desperately praying . . . that the woman who had sworn to love you had not turned her back on you but had stayed true?'

He leaned forward, his head in his hands. He was breathing deeply, his shoulders heaving. 'You can be released from your betrothal . . . you were very young . . . I know you loved him, but . . . after so long you are under no obligation. By all means . . . if you find he is still . . . if you find you love him more than me . . . then I will understand . . . I'll back away. I'll come to terms with the fact that I have lost you to a former love . . . and I *will* understand. But this sense of duty . . . Amelia, he is not your husband . . . you did not marry him.'

I could not breathe for the pain. 'Luke, you swore an oath to Edmund's departed soul . . . but what if I swore an oath to *Edmund himself*. Here, in this very church . . . kneeling at the altar. What if we recited wedding vows . . . together . . . kneeling with God as our witness? What if I swore in the sight of God that I would love, honour and obey Edmund Melville until death us did part?'

He gripped his head, his cry tearing my heart. 'You were . . . married?'

142

I could not speak, tears rolling down my cheeks. I had finally spoken the words no one else had ever heard. The weight I had carried — the terrible burden only three other people knew — crushing me, haunting me, dictating my every move.

'He came back to Cornwall . . . Sir Richard relented and they came down for Christmas. He was here for my nineteenth birthday and we thought, well, *I* thought, Edmund was to remain in Cornwall, but it was not to be the case.'

He clutched his head in his hands. 'Amelia . . . just tell me. You were married?'

'In all but legalities. A secret marriage.'

'But how? Why? Who would conduct such a service? You should have told me.' His clenched fist shook against his mouth. 'He made you marry him — but why not wait for your parents? Why did he force you into marriage?'

'He didn't, Luke . . . and it wasn't legally binding . . . we knew that would come later, or rather we hoped it would. It was our fear driving us. And he didn't force me, it was *my* suggestion. We'd not seen each other for two years — it was the Christmas of our nineteenth birthdays. I think they'd been testing us — keeping us apart. Yet when we met again, our love was stronger than ever. We hoped Sir Richard would let Edmund stay in Cornwall, but he just stood by our fireplace and announced his intention to send him to Sumatra — '

'Sumatra?'

'To learn the spice trade at first hand just as Sir Richard had been sent by *his* father. Francis

143

was to go, too. There was a merchant out there who'd defrauded them — shipments and payments had gone astray and Sir Richard wanted Edmund and Francis to get redress — to make new contacts . . . to forge more contracts.'

'So you married in secret?'

'Edmund was petrified of the thought of going to Sumatra — especially with Francis. He had a dream he'd never return — that he'd succumb to some tropical disease and never come back to marry me. Luke, I know this is so hard for you . . . you've been honest with me, and I must be honest with you.'

'Yes . . . please . . . continue.' He swallowed hard, staring down at his feet.

'Edmund only ever wanted to live in Cornwall and make a success of his estate. Being in London was doing him harm. He was over-shadowed by Francis — he believed Sir Richard thought ill of him but he put on a brave face. Then, that Christmas . . . when we should have been so happy . . . Sir Richard announced his plan to my parents *in our house*. It came straight out of the blue, like a death blow to our marriage. My parents were furious but Sir Richard insisted there was time for Edmund and Francis to get back before any wedding.'

'So you decided to take things into your own hands . . . '

I nodded. 'Edmund seemed changed when I saw him . . . somehow lost and more vulnerable. He hated London but he knew it wasn't for ever . . . but at that sudden announcement he became distraught — he told me how being in London

144

scared him and the thought of sailing to Sumatra with Francis petrified him. He always called me his rock. He needed to know I would never desert him.'

'So you decided to marry — in secret . . . '

'Yes. But it wasn't that simple. We were just nineteen, from well-known and respected families, and we only had three days before they were to return to London. No church dignitary would marry us . . . certainly not my brother, though I begged him so hard.'

'So you're not married?'

'We met here, in this porch. My maid was about to leave our employment. She was to marry a butcher and they were our witnesses . . . Luke, it wasn't a real marriage in the eyes of the law, but it was a real marriage to us. We knelt at the altar and repeated our vows with our hands on the Bible . . . and every Sunday since, I've sat staring at the altar, praying for his safe return. Until I met you . . . '

'And now your prayers have been answered — in time to stop you making a terrible mistake. Is that how you see it?' His voice sounded harsh and my heart burned.

'Why else would his letter reach me when it did?'

He grasped my hands, holding them in his — strong, dependable, healing hands.

'Then I must wish you every happiness.'

'Luke, how can you say that? How can I be happy?'

'Because, my darling, my happiness depends on your happiness. And you're quite right. What

145

I see as terrible timing might indeed be divine intervention. Much better to halt anything between us, now, than to have you lying in my arms, longing for another man.'

I could not speak, I could only howl into his starched white handkerchief.

'I'll always be here for you, Amelia. I'll do everything in my power to help you . . . should you require my help as a physician, that is, but we both know . . . that I have to . . . need to . . . distance myself from you for my own well-being as well as for yours. But mainly, for Edmund's. You need time to rediscover your great love. Forgive me, I must go.' He kissed my hand one last time, his voice hoarse, his words wrung from him. I could not breathe; my throat so tight I felt I was suffocating.

Bethany touched my elbow and I looked up. Luke was no longer with me, his thick black coat and wide-brimmed hat lost to the crowd. She gripped my arm and I felt myself guided towards the house. I could hear nothing, see nothing, just fight the agony of heartbreak as the man I loved walked purposefully away.

★ ★ ★

Borage: a heart-centred herb used to aid bravery in difficult times. Roman soldiers are said to have consumed borage wine before going to war. Certainly, tea made from both the leaves and the flowers of borage can be used for those seeking courage.

THE LADY HERBALIST

17

Two whole weeks of standing at the window waiting for a letter, fourteen days of stomach-churning expectation. Mother rustled the pages of her newspaper.

'There's another advertisement warning against rogue practitioners — Dr Nankivell certainly doesn't mince his words. Well, well, look at this — it's The Galleon's announcement. *Lady Polgas is to host a ball to honour the homecoming of her son, Dr Emerson Polgas, who has spent the last ten years serving his king and country.*' She peered over the top of the page. 'A charity ball to raise funds for the infirmary. *Finally*, it seems, Lady Polgas is to raise some money!'

She glanced towards the door. The footman held out a tray, a slight tremble in her hands as she picked up a letter. Her sudden swallow churned my stomach. 'It's not his writing,' she said, as she handed it to me.

It was from Constance, the address smudged as if tears had splashed the ink.

Pendowrick Hall
3th February 1798
My dearest Amelia,
Edmund is home. He arrived four days

147

ago, and my instant joy has turned to the gravest concern. He failed to come down for dinner and I found him lying on his bed. He was delirious, drenched with sweat, and I had to call for a basin of water to sponge his face. He's been given a bottle of quinine by a doctor in the Admiralty and they call his illness Undulating Fever. He told me he has had similar attacks, and not to worry — that it would pass.

Oh Amelia, he's so changed. He's kind and loving and everything that he was, but he's so despondent. He told me he thought we were safe. He knew Father's business was ruined but he believed the estate was financially sound. He arrived two hours after his letter and we didn't have time to prepare. I was frightened to tell him we'd taken to the servants' quarters. He went very quiet and I knew he was appalled. He spent hours at Father's desk reading all the papers. I heard him pacing the floor, then he demanded all the rooms be aired and he sent Mrs Alston to the village for new servants.

He had not known of Father's and Francis's deaths until he arrived in London. The worst is he blames himself for Francis's death. He believes he put Francis in danger. He went straight to Francis's room and I heard the most heart-wrenching sobbing. He said he knew Francis was capable of recklessness and he blames himself entirely. He believes he should have insisted Francis stay in London and not see him off in

Plymouth. He was holding Francis's ring to his heart, sobbing piteously, then he saw me at the door and said Francis's books must be taken to the study and his clothes given to charity — and Aunt Harriet's portrait must be hung next to Mama's.

Mama has made slight progress but Edmund sees only her frailty. He blames himself for her downward spiral of health and it's prompted such remorse in him. He told me he was gullible and naive to join the navy. He can't talk about the navy without a tightening of the mouth and rapid breathing. When he tries to explain, his hands begin to shake.

He must have suffered so much. He has manacle scars on his wrists and has difficulty hearing. The cannon's flash has affected his vision. The doctor in the Admiralty says his hearing will probably never return, but his eyesight may be helped by dulling the light. He has spectacles with darker glass and he says since he's been wearing them his headaches have lessened.

Edmund does nothing but blame himself for leaving but when he talks of you, my heart breaks. I had to tell him you'd visited us in our reduced circumstances and he looked broken, crying out as if in pain. I told him you saved Mama's life — you and Dr Bohenna. He asked after you and I told him how beautiful you were and how kind, and how you understood, and he broke down into such a torrent of tears.

149

He says he's frightened of you seeing him — that he's not the youth he was. He keeps asking me details about you. How you wear your hair, how you smile, whether you might still love him, or at least give him a second chance. Then his hands shake. Always the same shaking when he tries to talk. It's very frightening to watch such a strong man shake so violently.

He told Mama it was wrong to persist with your engagement — that he had little to offer you and he's ashamed of our reduced circumstances. He has prize money due to him but it'll be a while before the estate becomes profitable. Mama said he was being foolish — that he was to go straight to you and tell you everything, and his reply tore my heart.

He said, 'She deserves better. I am only half the man I was.'

Edmund's too ill to travel, yet my hope is that seeing you will remove the terrible anxiety which seems to consume him. I don't ask this lightly, but dearest Amelia, please consider another visit — and soon, if you can.

Your affectionate friend,
Constance

Mother's mouth tightened as she read the letter. 'I'll ask Dr Nankivell to attend to him — undulating fever is very common on return from the Tropics. It's debilitating and unpleasant, but it doesn't seem to threaten life.'

150

'That's not the reason Constance wants me to go.' He was ill. He needed me. *Not the man he was . . . frightened to see me.* All these years he had been ill and alone and to come home to a mortgaged estate, his family in penury. I wanted to run from the room.

She shook her head, pointing to her foot. 'I can't come with you, my love — and neither can your father. He has pressing Militia business, but Dr Nankivell will visit.' Her eyes softened. 'This is no more than we expected. Edmund needs time to get the house and estate in order. Your father will lend him his prize ram and he'll soon get a new flock established. There's a dearth of wool now it's all going for uniforms — the carpet manufacturer is crying out for more wool.'

I knelt by her side, taking her hands. Working hands that liked to gut fish and build treehouses; hands that had taught me to shoot a bow, hold a cricket bat, plant my herb garden. Not hands that stayed in beautiful drawing rooms, avoiding responsibility. 'I must go, Mother, please. I'm twenty-five, I'm a mature woman and Bethany will accompany me — and Seth and the guards. Please let us meet in the privacy of Pendowrick, not under the watchful eyes of everyone in Truro.'

'Your father won't like it. The wind's from the east. It's too cold to travel. But if you must go . . . '

'Thank you . . . We'll set off at first light and we'll be back before dark. Just like last time.'

Her hands gripped mine: frightened hands, holding mine as tightly as I held hers. 'You don't have to marry him,' she said. There it was, back again — the same tone of criticism, the slight hardening of her voice.

I bit my lip and drew a deep breath. 'I'll tell Seth to be ready at first light.'

★ ○ ★ ○ ★

Tincture of Motherwort: an excellent remedy for calming a racing heart caused by the anxiety of loss. Five drops added to a cup of hot water can settle a troubled mind and bring back the restorative balm of untroubled sleep.

THE LADY HERBALIST

152

18

Bodmin Moor
Monday 5th February 1798, 11 a.m.

The carriage was getting colder, our foot-warmers and rugs poor defence against the icy air whistling in at the window. We had watched the sky darken, our anxiety growing as the first flurries of snow began coating the tufts of grass. Now the snow was building, driven horizontally by the biting wind. Bethany wiped the inside of the window.

'It's turning into a blizzard — I can see nothing but white.' Her voice echoed my fear. 'The snow against the window must be at least two inches deep. They won't see to drive . . . '

The coach stopped and Seth knocked on the window, his hat and capes covered with snow. He opened the door to a flurry of flakes, slipping next to me as he shut the door against the howling wind. 'It's not abating — it's getting worse. We've got another two miles to go or we could go two miles back to the inn — two miles either way.' Snow clung to his bushy eyebrows and beard, an inch of white on his huge leather hat.

'What do you think we should do?'

'The inn's at the top of the moor. If we go back, it's open moorland — if we go on, we'll get shelter in the dell. The snow's buildin' an' there'll be rifts — the way's already obscured.

One of us will need to ride ahead to be sure of the road. If we leave the road, we could overturn. I'll unhitch the best horse and John will lead us.'

'Is it safe, Seth?'

'Safer than stayin' here. And safe if we take it slow. I know these moors — lose sight of the road and we could get very lost.'

'Tell the guards to join us in the carriage — they must be frozen.'

'Thank ye, Miss Carew, but I'll need their eyes. They'll ride alongside me. They've good strong coats an' there'll be a fire to warm them when we arrive.' He smiled at Bethany, who attempted a smile back. 'I'm just concerned for yer comfort. We'll get ye there — we have to. There's no turnin' back.'

We inched slowly forward, no milestones, no trees, no rocky outcrops, nothing to show us where we were. Just the driving snow and the whistle in the wind, and the slow rocking of the carriage. At last we heard shouts.

'There's a sign . . . Pendowrick. 'Tis the turning, and just in time.'

Through half-obscured windows we watched Seth walk slowly forward, prodding the snow with a stout stick. His hat and coat were almost indistinguishable against the whiteness, his words lost to the wind. 'Four inches. More in places . . . Stay right behind . . . follow me exactly . . . 'tis a ditch to both sides.'

He led the horses down the lane towards the shelter of some overhanging trees. Drifts were in danger of blocking our progress, the trees' branches heavy above us, but familiar landmarks gradually began to appear — the iron gate to the orchard, the huge stone wall surrounding the estate. We rounded the bend to a vast expanse of white roof, the six tall chimneys lost in the swirling snow.

Bethany folded away the rugs with her gloved hands. 'We'll not get back today — but we've brought nothing with us.'

I tried to sound calm, but my heart was hammering. 'I can borrow a nightdress from Miss Melville. It'll only be for one night.'

★   ★   ★

Constance hurried us to the fire. Her black hair was newly washed and ornately dressed, held in place by a comb of pearls. Her gown was silk, her velvet shawl trimmed with fur, yet she had lost none of her pallor. Behind her smiles, her eyes with their dark lashes looked tired. 'He's in Father's study going through the accounts. He's summoned our attorney, Mr Elton . . . but with all this snow I doubt he'll come. I can't believe you crossed the moor in this blizzard. Your room will soon be ready . . . I've moved back to my old room, but Mama insists on staying where she is. It's warm in there and Mrs Alston hasn't so far to walk.'

'How is Lady Melville?'

She shrugged, tears pooling in her eyes. 'I'd like to say better, but she's very tired today. She really rallied when Edmund arrived. She became quite her old self, but I think all the excitement must have set her back. Her aches have returned

155

and she's not very well.'

A huge log burned in the Tudor fireplace, yet it felt so cold. Above us, the leaded panes in the ancient window formed a black grille against the white snow behind. Constance glanced towards the door. 'I'll arrange for your servants to sleep in the old dairy — I'll ask for fires to be lit in all the rooms . . . we've plenty of food.' She clenched her fist against her chin. 'Shall I take you to him? Only, he won't have heard you arrive.' Again, a furtive glance towards the door. 'Amelia, he doesn't know I wrote to you — did I do right to call for you?'

I could not calm the thudding in my chest. I felt sick with nerves. 'Yes, of course . . . I'll go straight to him — I know where the study is.'

Icy air brushed my cheeks, a cold draught following me down the ancient stone flags — the old screens passage between the great hall and the east wing. We had run down this passage with such abandon, holding hands, laughing, diving under the stone arch so Edmund could press me against the wall and kiss me, far too much in love to care if we were caught.

I wrapped my cloak tighter. The door to the study was open, the room dimly lit. This was my future. My decision. No longer a girl with wings on her feet but a woman who had betrayed a man's love.

Snow was building against the leaded windows, the room in half-darkness. Edmund was sitting at the large desk surrounded by a mound of papers. He had his back to me, and my heart jolted in sudden fear. His familiar long black curls were cut short, a pair of broad shoulders filling every inch of a well-tailored jacket. He was holding a letter to the candlelight, bringing it nearer and further from his eyes, as if having difficulty reading it, and I tried to calm my growing panic.

It looked like a stranger's back. A stranger's shoulders. A stranger's hand reaching for a magnifier. I could not enter but stood silently watching. Glass-fronted bookcases lined the walls, heavy oak furniture where it had stood for hundreds of years. Two high-back chairs sat either side of the fireplace, two knights in armour defending the Melville family crest. Firelight flickered across the ornate plasterwork, portraits of long-deceased relatives looking out from their heavy gold frames.

The stranger ran his hand through his hair and sudden fire burned my heart. The sweep of his hand, the slight toss to his head; if I was right, he would put down the letter and hold his hands against his lips as if in prayer. He would tap his fingers three times, then rest his chin on his interlocked hands. I had watched him do that too many times to count — smiling up at me through his wave of black curls.

One tap. Two taps. Three taps, his chin rested on his interlocked hands and the years stripped away. I stepped forward.

'Connie, this letter was never opened. It's addressed to me — it must have arrived after Father died . . . could you help me with it? I can't make out the writing.' His voice was deeper, hoarser, but the same soft accent I loved so well.

157

He swung round and I stared into the face of the man I had last seen as a girl of nineteen. Weather-beaten, scarred, with dark sideburns and heavy black brows. A man's face, square-chinned, thickly stubbled, a scar disfiguring his upper lip, yet his eyes looked lost — vulnerable eyes, filling with tears. 'Amelia? Amelia?'

He pushed back his chair, falling to his knees, his thick, callused hands reaching for mine. He held them tightly, pressing them against his forehead as if in supplication. 'You've come . . . Oh, Amelia . . . you're here?'

His hands were shaking, tears in his eyes, and I knelt on the cold flagstones, trying to glimpse the joyous youth who had kissed me so passionately. Two huge black pupils tried to focus on my face.

'Use your magnifier,' I whispered.

He reached to his desk and held the brass-handled magnifier to my face, his voice hoarse. 'You're even more beautiful than in my dreams . . . I'm not dreaming, am I? It really is you?'

'Constance wrote telling me that you were too ill to travel . . . and I couldn't wait. I had to come.'

He stood up. 'Your parents are here?' He glanced at the door, sudden panic in his voice.

'No, just my maid — and my two coach drivers, and two guards.'

He ran his hand through his hair, the same shy smile though not the same black curls. 'Then I better watch my step. I presume they're all carrying pistols?'

His familiar gestures, his playful teasing that

my parents were over-protective. The years were stripping back: under the shaking hesitancy, the youth I remembered was beginning to surface.

'Mother would have come only she's broken a bone in her foot. It's mending well but it's left her housebound. She hates it.'

'She must do. Lady Clarissa was never one to sit still. Are your parents well?'

'Very well. My nephews keep Mother busy . . . She's on several charity commissions and Papa's Lord Lieutenant of Cornwall. He's responsible for mustering and equipping all the volunteer forces. My brother William helps — he's Lieutenant of Division — and Charles is now Rector of Feock . . . but you already know that. Frederick's wife, Charity, has just had another baby so I'm now the adoring aunt of seven nephews.'

I was talking too quickly, trying to hide my shock. I must not stare, yet I needed to look at him.

'How splendid. *Seven* nephews. May I take your cloak?'

He must have seen me hesitate, a new strength to his voice. 'Amelia, look at me. Take your time . . . look and you'll see I'm not the youth I was. Every day I write to you, my letters all the same — that I *will not* hold you to our engagement, that you're free of *all* obligations . . . that I'm not the man you deserve. Only I can't bring myself to post them. I crumple them up and throw them on the fire.'

He was standing under the portrait of his father, Sir Richard Melville, fifth baron of Pendowrick, and I stared up at the exact same tilt of his square chin, the same thick black hair, the same heavy brows, and terrible disappointment ripped through me. I could not help it. 'You've grown so like your father. It could be you up there. The likeness is uncanny.'

He stared back at his father. 'In looks, yes. The Melville likeness has always been strong — I've my grandmother to thank for that.' He glanced up at the portrait of a black-haired Spanish beauty with olive skin and dark brooding looks. 'We've her Moorish blood in our veins — but I'm as different from Father as I could ever wish to be.' His prominent Adam's apple caught his cravat. 'I've no desire to be likened to Father.'

'I'm sorry — it was unkind of me.'

He ran his hand through his hair. 'You're not unkind. It's just I shudder at the comparison. In London I saw him for what he really was . . . a brute, a drunkard, a philanderer who put his family in great jeopardy. Amelia . . . I tried to reason with him, but he was too strong for me. He was cruel. I believe he kept me in London to punish Mother.' His touch on my arm was gentle. 'Come and sit by the fire.'

And to punish us, I thought but did not say.

He led me to one of the high-back chairs and slipped to the floor by my feet, hugging his knees in their fine beige trousers. His boots were highly polished, reflecting the firelight, his dark blue jacket and perfectly tailored cream waistcoat doing little to conceal the expanse of his chest. He was every inch a baronet, yet with a weather-beaten complexion and the physique of a sailor.

160

'No doubt you've been given strict orders to return before dusk?' He laughed softly and I slipped down to the rug beside him, side by side, like we used to sit — behind trees, behind bushes, behind hay carts, anywhere so we could hold hands and plan our future. His hand reached out, tentatively taking mine, a rough callused hand, at odds with his fine clothes.

'Do you know it's snowing?' I whispered.

His shoulder was against mine, so achingly familiar and yet the shoulder of a stranger. 'I'm sorry, Amelia, could you speak a little louder — my hearing isn't what it was.'

'It's snowing. More than just a few flakes — there's a blizzard outside! It came from nowhere and we were lucky to get here. The road was all but obscured, and the drifts are mounting — we won't make it back to Truro today.'

'Really?' He laughed again, squeezing my hand. 'A blizzard to the rescue. Only you could arrange that. Only you. May I?' I nodded and he kissed the back of my hand, a terrible ache filling my heart. He had not looked up at the window, not even a glance. He had taken my word for it because he could not see it for himself.

'I thought you were dead, Edmund. Uncle Alex assured me you couldn't be alive. Everyone ... *everything* ... pointed to your death. They *assured* me you had died, and I believed them. I thought you were lying in an unmarked grave — it's been so awful. I've only just got your letter from the convent. It took eighteen months to reach me.'

'The one letter I didn't post. Of all the letters

161

I sent, only that one got through? I must have written ten or more, but I had no means of posting them. I just thrust them at people when I could, praying they would somehow reach you.'

A fine tremor shook the lace at his cuffs, his chest rising and falling, his breathing growing rapid. I glimpsed a band of purple and pulled up his sleeves, sudden revulsion making me gasp. Deep angry scars encircled both wrists.

'Edmund, tell me everything. I need to know *everything*.'

19

His voice was hesitant, more of a whisper. 'The commission on *HMS Faith* was offered to *Francis*, not me. Captain Owen was a friend of his father. I never quarrelled with Francis — you know how much I tried to keep my head down — but when he dismissed the offer so lightly, it triggered in me such anger. He'd been so insistent we went to Sumatra and he was refusing to join the navy? It didn't make sense. Francis's family were all seafaring men — that's what I couldn't understand. I couldn't see why he didn't seize his chance for an honourable solution. Money was tight — there were little enough funds for the family, let alone an allowance for him.'

'Your father didn't insist?'

'No, far from it. They were very close . . . in fact, it made me jealous. Amelia, it won't come as a surprise to you that Father preferred Francis. They constantly belittled me, as if by refusing to join them in their bawdyhouses it made me a lesser man. When I refused to go to Sumatra, Father wouldn't let Francis go on his own and that made Francis furious. He started undermining every suggestion I made — dismissing every trading deal I tried to negotiate, convincing Father they'd be unworkable. I felt very isolated — they were reckless risk-takers where I sought only security.'

He stared into the fire, a pulse racing in his neck, a fine line of sweat forming above his upper lip. Yet he sounded more hurt than bitter.

'Not a night passes without me regretting my decision to join the ship. I should have stood my ground, I should have come down to Cornwall, or found the strength to stay and face them, but I hated the spice trade — the insecurity of it . . . the constant worry of fortunes being lost. All I could think of was to be free from it . . . the chance to earn my own money. And then I got your letter about Frederick — your obvious pride in him, the honour and courage of men fighting to keep our country safe, and it seemed like the answer. That you were somehow pointing me forward, and the lure of prize money suddenly took hold . . . it gave me hope. What if I could accrue enough money to enable us to live *without* Father's allowance?'

An iron grip clasped my heart. I *had* influenced his decision. I could not look at him, nor could I speak.

'I ran from my responsibilities. I see it now as weakness, but at the time I saw it as a chance to escape their endless taunts and innuendoes. I sought honour in place of derision, the constant pulling of strings — Father's idiot puppet, to be paraded and scorned. I thought I was showing strength, that you'd be proud of me. Now I perceive it as terrible weakness.'

I should never have written that letter. He was impressionable and I had planted the idea of glory and honour. I was meant to be his rock, yet I had failed him so terribly.

His frown deepened. 'My life has been spared, Amelia, but not my conscience. I feel such guilt I abandoned Francis. I knew Father's influence was leading him down a path of debauchery, yet I did nothing.'

I forced myself to speak. 'You couldn't do anything. It sounds like he wouldn't have listened.'

'That last night in Plymouth I had the chance to speak without Father being there and yet I didn't. I should have stopped his womanizing.'

He placed another log on the fire and I noticed his nails were bitten, his knuckles scarred. 'In London, I was always going to be Father's puppet, but I thought if I could return with enough prize money we'd be able to start married life free of his control. The idea seemed so simple and it took hold of me. I didn't know the fleet was assembling — that Admiral Jervis had given the captains new orders and we were to be part of Sir Charles Grey's landing force.'

I needed to stay strong. He needed my help, not my remorse. 'I read everything I could. You were catapulted straight into action. Martinique and Guadeloupe asked for British protection because they wanted to keep their slaves. France was to abolish slavery and the plantation owners didn't want to lose their workforce, so they asked for British protection. You went to their aid — to help them keep their slaves enslaved and their tobacco picked.'

His frown deepened. 'When I heard the orders, I felt sickened. It went against all humanity, yet those were our orders. We had to believe that gaining sovereignty over the islands was honourable — vital for our king and country — and I did. At least, that's how I saw it at the time. The plantation owners were French Royalists, and many French Royalists fought in ships alongside us. Their hatred of the new Assembly was enough to make them question their allegiance to France and that made them our allies.'

Firelight flickered across his profile, accentuating a myriad of small scars. Deep lines framed the sides of his mouth, a constant furrow between his black brows. The scar above his lip was reddened and slightly raised; others were hidden beneath his thick, black sideburns. He saw me looking and turned his face to the full glow of the fire.

'Please look, Amelia — look deeply and don't be afraid to show dismay. I'm not the youth you loved.' His voice caught. 'I'd never look in a mirror again if I had the choice.'

A chill flooded my heart, a terrible sense of loss. He was so familiar yet seemed a stranger — the vulnerability in his forced smile, the terrible wanting in his eyes; the way he held up his chin, desperate for me to see him as he now was, knowing I was remembering him as he used to be. He had no laughter lines, no softening round his eyes. All exuberance of youth had gone, just rough, coarse features with skin browned by the sun and pitted with scars. He picked up the poker, tapping it on the hearth in sudden sharp taps. It was the drill of a woodpecker and my heart leapt.

'You never did get it quite right,' I whispered.

'It's much quicker . . . more like this.'

I took the poker, attempting my own wood-pecker drill. We were in the park again, leaning against a large oak tree, the woodpecker drilling above us. Two carefree young lovers, content to while away the afternoon imitating birds.

'Constance gave me the beautiful shell you had engraved. Captain Owen returned it with your private possessions. It's at home with me . . . in Truro.'

'I'm so pleased you like it . . . and I'm so thankful it arrived. I know the real meaning of desolation now — I didn't then.' He cleared his throat. 'Amelia, I wrote you so many letters, but I don't know which ones you received . . . I don't know where to start.'

I had to swallow, hide my resentment. 'Hardly any letters reached me — neither from London nor from the ship.'

'And yet I wrote and wrote. I lived for your letters, Amelia. There was a time when I thought you might have found someone else . . . '

My cheeks started burning, fire scorching my throat. 'You were in the Leeward Islands . . . about to hear new orders . . . you'd just written the men's letters home.'

'My last letter from the ship. Our orders were to evacuate the trapped soldiers in Fort Fleur d'Epée in Guadeloupe.'

'And you volunteered to lead the landing party?'

He breathed deeply, a nervousness to his whisper. 'Yes, I did . . . and I've long since regretted it. The initial conquest went smoothly

— the 6th Regiment of Foot established a garrison and we left them holding the island but soon the soldiers began to sicken — yellow fever and just about every tropical disease took them in a steady stream. We thought the island was secure, but Dockets of freed slaves and French Nationalists still roamed the eastern side. Our troops were weakened, their numbers too low, and the men holding Fort Fleur d'Epée were surrounded and besieged.'

'They were trapped — Uncle Alex sent me the details.'

'The only chance they had to survive was if we could evacuate them from under the noses of the surrounding French.' His hand trembled as he held the poker. 'An advance party was needed to secure the two cannons guarding the harbour . . . and I heard myself volunteer.'

'You saved scores of men, Edmund. You were recommended for bravery.' He prodded the fire with harsh violent stabs. 'Did you want to prove to those who stole from you that you weren't afraid?'

He froze, the poker mid-air. 'I shouldn't have burdened you with that. I'm so sorry.'

'I want to know everything, Edmund. Please don't hide anything from me.'

'We needed to secure the cannons defending the harbour so that our ship could get close enough to evacuate the soldiers. The two cannons were manned — six men on each, and I studied them through my telescope. As they came into focus, I could hardly bear to watch them. Captain Owen called for prayers that night, but I couldn't pray. I stared at those men, knowing I had to kill them. I saw their faces . . . I watched them smoking their pipes and I was petrified.'

A youth unable to kill a chicken, now a man bearing the scars of war.

'Just before dawn we scaled the walls of the battery. *HMS Faith* sailed away — as if she was leaving — and they fell for our ruse. We caught them unprepared. We secured the cannons . . . everything going exactly to plan — but what we didn't know was that another cannon stood out of sight of the ship, positioned to protect the very cannons we were sent to disable. The fighting grew fierce. We just kept loading and firing . . . loading and firing. I'd chosen our best gunners and we returned fire for fire.'

'You saved their lives. Men lived because of your action.'

'But I lost two good men — men whose letters I'd written the night before. It was as if I had iron in my blood. I vowed I wouldn't lose another man. Somehow we held the cannon off long enough for the last boatload of soldiers to get to the ship. There'd been no return of fire for over an hour and I believed we were safe. The first boatload of men left, the second was waiting for me. I was nearly there but a blast caught me and I remember nothing more . . . just my head bursting with bright light. I must have knocked myself out on a boulder. I woke just in time to drag myself behind it. I was drifting in and out of consciousness, but they didn't find me.'

The mother-of-pearl buttons on his waistcoat caught the firelight. 'I should have come forward

169

and demanded my rights as a British midshipman, but I could see them kicking the two fallen men, taking their rings, and every ounce of courage deserted me.'

'It must have been terrifying.'

'By our circumnavigation of the island, I knew small boats lay in a cove nearby — I'd seen a settlement with ships anchored and I thought I stood a chance. In my muddled state, I thought I just needed to skirt the palm-fringed beach and reach those ships. Our forces still held the western island. All I needed to do was get back to them.'

The candle on his desk gutted, a plume of smoke rising from the brass candlestick. The room grew darker. 'They reported the death of six sailors and one officer,' I whispered. 'They were so sure it was you.'

'They must have found my uniform. I stripped it off and threw it to the ground. There were fires all around — castings burning . . . bushes burning. They must have thought I'd been consumed by the flames. Taking off my uniform was the second mistake I made. Without my uniform, I had no proof of who I was. Yet at the time, I couldn't get it off quickly enough. In my muddled state, I thought to pretend to be a merchant. It was incredibly foolish . . . ' He turned to look at me, his huge black pupils seeking reassurance.

'You saved countless men, Edmund . . . you had a head injury. No one can think properly with a head injury.'

'I walked for miles. From the ship, the shore

looked fringed with sand, but there were swamps, tropical forests and mangroves. I was dizzy, blood oozing from my head — yet somehow I forced my way through the dripping branches. When evening fell, I collapsed beneath a banana tree and stared up at the moon. That was my third mistake. I should have known I'd become a feast for insects.'

I caught his wry smile, a flicker of the humour of the youth I had loved so passionately. 'It must have been petrifying.'

'It was — but that was just the first night of being eaten alive. The itch is so powerful, it's impossible not to scratch — then the bites turn to wheals the size and colour of plums. I've the scars to show for them.' He ran his finger beneath his silk necktie. 'When dawn finally broke I saw a track leading into the forest — a waterfall was cascading into a pool of clear blue water and I rushed to it. The water tasted like nothing I've ever tasted — better than the finest claret or brandy. I just cupped it to my mouth and drank — and I bathed my wounds. Do you know they recommend woollen garments for the tropics?'

He smiled again, his hand sweeping through his short hair, the familiar tapping of his fingertips.

'Yes, I do. Frederick told me wool absorbs the sweat — if men are bathed in sweat when the sun goes down it brings on shivers and night fevers.'

His voice softened. 'Connie tells me you grow herbs. She told me you saved Mother's life. Amelia, I can't thank you enough. If Mother had died before I got here . . . ' He tried to control the sudden trembling of his lips. 'I should never have left you. I ran away . . . but I will make amends — I promise, I will make amends.'

He waited for his voice to steady. 'Every single day . . . every single night, I thought only of you. I *had* to survive . . . to see you again . . . to know you were happy and that my actions hadn't caused you despair. As the years passed, I believed there was little hope of you remaining free. I'd been the perpetrator of my own misfortune and I knew I must brave the consequences. I honestly thought I'd lost you — that I *deserved* to lose you. I was foolish and weak. When I read Sir Alexander's letter telling me to hurry back, I could hardly take it in. Amelia, it's more than I deserve — more than I could ever hope. It's like being offered the chance to live again.'

A knock on the door, and Constance entered carrying a huge tray. She peered over it as she stepped sideways through the door. 'Are you in here? Oh, yes . . . here you are — I didn't see you down there. She was wearing a crisp white apron over her silk gown. 'Mrs Alston's prepared a light luncheon for you. Nothing too much as she's roasting meat for later.'

Edmund rose from the floor, towering above me. 'Thank you, Connie. Let me take that from you. You know you really shouldn't be carrying that — you should have sent a servant.'

20

Above us, a row of Melville barons watched in sharp disapproval. Despite the fire, the room smelled musty and damp. Edmund laid the tray on the floor and resumed his place, sitting by my side just as we used to sit sharing a basket of food in the gardens at Trenwyn, or on the stony shore with Frederick and Francis; sometimes we'd be in a rowing boat, sometimes hiding behind a hay-wain when we should have been harvesting.

The cold ham lay barely touched, the bread drying in the heat of the fire. Edmund shook his head as I pointed to the wine.

'I walked all day, eating what I could. The mangos weren't ripe, but the bananas were. A steep track led up through the trees and I could see tobacco plants, so I started up it. I felt certain the plantation owner would be sympathetic, but I was weaker than I thought and I didn't see the line of prisoners until it was too late. They were manacled, chained together, their overseers driving them down the narrow track. I didn't have the strength to run. I could do nothing but cry out as they bound my wrists and pulled me to my feet.'

'The French Nationalists turned on the plantation owners?'

'Yes. They rounded up everyone who'd helped the British — the landed elite, the emigres, the plantation owners — all of them manacled and bleeding from vicious wounds. I could barely keep up with them. I kept stumbling forward, trying to avoid their lashes. That was the beginning of my captivity. Men were needed to repair the batteries to fortify the harbour against another British attack and though I tried to explain who I was — to claim my rights under the terms of warfare — they took no notice. They just forced us into a stinking prison hulk. It was indescribable — the rancid bilges running with rats, the air so foul I could hardly breathe.

'But you must have told them who you were?'

'Each time I told them my rank and ship's name, the beatings got worse. I was never taken to the fort but kept chained in the hulk, driven out by day to labour under the fiercest sun. All of us, rounded up as enemies of the French Republic — plantation owners, merchants, engineers, anyone who'd been in power before the new regime. For twelve months they died around me. Each day the same routine. The guards would unchain the hatch and kick us to see who moved . . . then they'd unlock the manacles of those who didn't and fling them on to a cart. Fifty of us, dwindling to twenty.'

The shaking in his hands was getting worse, his breathing getting faster. 'And every night, we'd take turns to drag our chains to the grille and stare silently up at the moon. It was our only link to home — the same silver light shining on each of our homelands. I lived each day just to watch the moon, hoping you'd be watching it too. And the days when there was no moon, I felt such desolation. As if it was an omen I'd never see you again.'

'I was watching it,' I whispered.

His hands reached for mine — callused hands, holding me softly. 'The French force arrived in their hundreds and the new governor set about his revenge — hanging or guillotining all those who'd helped the British. But we were spared — left to repair the fortifications.'

'You would have stood no chance in the dungeons. At least you were in the harbour.'

'Yes. That's what saved me. I watched every ship that came and went. After a year, I recognized the frequent traders and I was determined to board one. I'd all but given up hope, the repairs were finished, we'd built a vast wall round the fort and I thought we'd be moved to the dungeons. Then a small ship from Brazil arrived bringing, among other goods, the fiery drink, cachaça.'

'Cachaça?'

'A distilled spirit made from fermented sugarcane. It's like drinking fire. Most of the cachaça was destined for the fort but our guards were not above a bit of private bartering.'

Edmund pointed to the portrait of his grandmother, the fiery Spanish beauty whom he had adored. 'I just needed to be in the right place at the right time — to look strong enough for them to want me. Grandmother's Moorish blood acted in my favour. My skin had darkened, my hair as black as any slave's. I knew not to look them in the eyes and the miracle happened — I was swapped for half a bottle of cachaça and

175

forced down the hatch with a dozen other men. We were chained and cramped, but the ship was from São Luís, and I began to hope. Amelia, you cannot imagine that sense of hope.'

'I can, Edmund.' The clock on the desk chimed two. Outside, the snow was building on the mullion windows, the layers of white contrasting against the grey sky.

'Each morning we were allowed on deck for a breath of fresh air. One day, a sail cut loose and I offered to climb the mast. They must have recognized a fellow sailor as one of them handed me a rope and I hauled in that sail with all my strength — desperate to show I knew what to do. After that, I was used as crew and I started to feel well again — the sea air, the smell of the salt. Even the food tasted good. I was so close to freedom, the expectation of escape almost overwhelming.'

'You were heading south-east to Brazil. We traced it on the globe.'

He nodded, drawing a deep breath. 'Across the Caribbean Sea to the South Atlantic. We reached land and turned east, stopping along the coast to collect fresh food. At each stop, prisoners were bartered for provisions and I knew to work harder. My strength had returned . . . I became indispensable as crew and I was never chosen to be sold. We were so close to São Luis and the ships that traded with Britain, but illness struck — yellow fever, caught in the last harbour. All around me men began writhing in pain, vomiting black blood, the appalling stench as their bowels turned to water. I can still hear their cries of pain — when they went silent, we threw them overboard. I began to sicken and I knew it wouldn't be long before I, too, met my watery grave. Sometimes, they don't wait for death . . . they just throw the slaves overboard at the first sign of illness.'

'That's terrible. But you reached the Convent of the Sacred Heart.'

'Yes. I heard a shout and saw white sand glimmering in a turquoise bay — like a glimpse of heaven. We were so close . . . so close. I was forced down the rope ladder — two members of the crew and five slaves, squeezing into a rowing boat — only two of us with enough strength to row. The Master was giving us a chance — the first glimmer of humanity after sixteen months of brutality.' He winced, suddenly clutching his head.

'What is it, Edmund?'

His teeth clenched. 'It passes. There — it's going. But it leaves me with such a headache. I get flashes of intense light, then my vision blurs and nausea takes hold. I'm so *sorry*.'

I helped him into the chair by the fire. 'I've brought my herbs with me . . . I'll bring you something — here, rest here.'

His eyes remained shut; another wince, his scarred hands gripping his head. 'It'll pass. I'm so sorry. Just knowing you're well . . . just seeing you is cure in itself. Amelia, you must see I'm not the man I was. I'm desperate to be well again . . . it's taking its time, I'm not robust. But even if I was well, you must understand you're under no obligation — you *have* to know that.' He gripped his head tighter. 'I can't . . . and I *won't* hold you to our commitment if it's not what you want.'

21

Connie was standing by the fire in the great hall and came swiftly to my side. 'What's wrong? Is he unwell?'

'Yes, a sudden headache — he needs a cold compress . . . I've got something that will help — it's in my medical box.'

'Your maid's taken it to your room. I've ordered some hot water for you . . . there's a privy next door.' She tucked her handkerchief down her bodice. 'Amelia . . . you look rather pale. Are you all right?'

She took my hand, leading me up the stone stairs and across the minstrels' gallery. Love was unconditional; love was not asking the man you loved to say sorry. We were next to the portrait of the two boys holding their instruments; a lifetime ago, Edmund and I had stood on this very spot, laughing, as Edmund showed me how to hold his violin, his hands on mine as he swung the bow. Had he found me equally as changed?

'It gets easier — it's just the first time you see him,' Constance whispered. 'I read his medical report when he was asleep. The blow to his head was very severe . . . the cannon's flash damaged his sight and his hearing. And he suffers terribly from night sweats — ' She stopped as a maid entered with a pile of linen and curtseyed.

'Could you take a bowl of iced water and a soft towel to Sir Edmund in his study?' I managed to ask. The maid curtseyed again and Connie lowered her voice.

'Amelia, is he cross with me?'

'No, of course not.'

Below us, the lavender garden lay blanketed in snow, wheel tracks and footprints criss-crossing the courtyard, smoke rising from the dairy. Maids were bustling round the kitchen door, going in and out of the laundry room, and I forced back my tears. Everywhere were echoes of our happiness — Edmund and I running from Francis, hiding behind swathes of drying sheets in the laundry room, clamping our hands firmly against our mouths to stop us from laughing. We had been so young, so passionately in love.

Connie opened the bedroom door to a blazing fire and the smell of beeswax — a dark room with a diamond-lattice ceiling, the elaborate plasterwork curling like straps around a profusion of leaves and vines. 'This is Mama's room,' she said. 'She's going to move back in soon, so it's been well aired.'

A heavily draped bed stood with an oak chest at its foot and a set of carved steps on one side; the Melville marital bed, each new generation conceived and born beneath those heavy velvet hangings. 'I can't possibly take your mother's room.'

'No . . . honestly . . . you must. She'll move back when you leave — she's quite comfortable where she is.' She saw me staring at the elaborate plasterwork. 'Oak leaves for strength and power . . . vines for eternal love . . . swords for justice . . . and cornucopias for plenty — and, in here, that means *children*. Are you certain he wasn't cross with me?'

'You mean about the tray?' I could not take my eyes off the bed.

She nodded. 'Edmund arrived without notice . . . and within minutes he told me I'd become like a housekeeper and should be stricter with the servants.'

'Guilt often sounds like anger. He feels guilty for leaving us, Connie. He was always protective of you and he's returned to find you in reduced circumstances. If it sounded like anger, I'm sure it was directed towards himself, not to you.'

'He *is* cross with me. He spent yesterday afternoon alone with Mama and I listened at the door. They were discussing Father's will and any suitors who *might* still be interested in me. Apparently, there were *two* wills, but Mr Elton noticed one outdated the other by a day. Mama had it there but she's never shown it to me. Yet she showed it straight to Edmund. I heard her telling him about Adam. She said I had too much freedom and she was pleased he was back because he could keep an eye on me.' Her voice hardened. 'I heard them say I was likely to *disgrace* the family.'

'How could you possibly disgrace the family?'

'Mrs Alston tells her everything . . . or rather exaggerates everything. I've done nothing except talk to Adam after church. I've visited his school *once* . . . and, *once*, I walked up the lane with him. But that's all. I've done nothing improper, yet Edmund looks at me in such a way.'

'He's nearly blind, Connie. He stares because

181

he can't see. He needs time . . . we all need time.'
She was seventeen, not twenty-five. Seventeen. A
lifetime of difference. 'Has Edmund told you
anything about his time on the Portuguese ship?'

She shook her black curls. 'He can't bring
himself to talk about it . . . but the Admiralty
report was in the drawer along with his medical
report and I read that too. He was on the ship
for sixteen months — they traded down the
coast of Brazil, then picked up a cargo of cotton
and sailed to Portugal. There, they loaded a
cargo of salt and set sail for Sweden — apparently Mediterranean salt is very popular in
Gothenburg because it's much stronger. According to the report, Edmund never left the ship.'

'The captain kept them locked below decks for
fear they'd jump ship?'

She smoothed the white cotton nightdress on
the hideous bed-quilt, re-tying the satin bow on
the sleeve. 'Apparently they do that a lot. The
Admiralty questioned Edmund about it for *five*
days — he had to give them details of every port
the ship went to, and what the cargo was. The
ship was called the *Santa Theresa* and it only
called into Cork because of a heavy storm.
Edmund dived from the deck as it was leaving
because it was his only chance to get to England.
Will this nightgown be warm enough, do you
think? There's a bed warmer in the bed.'

The wood panelling in the room was
blackened with age, a row of strait-laced women
frozen in their frames, their tight mouths and
clenched hands mirroring mine. A room full of
heartache. 'Yes, lovely, thank you. Perhaps

Bethany might sleep in here with me?'

'Of course. I'll get some more bedding sent up. Are you shocked I listen at doors and read confidential papers?' She looked fearful, as if I, too, might scold her.

'Not at all.'

'Last night I heard shouting in Edmund's room. He didn't see me, but I could see him pacing up and down, swinging round, no more than five strides at a time. Just pacing and turning, muttering something I couldn't understand. Then he started shouting — horrible angry shouts — and I didn't know what to do. He just kept pacing backwards and forwards, wringing his hands and shaking his head. He was sweating, his hair matted, then he stopped and began crying in great despair — he fell to his knees, pleading for his life. I didn't know what to do.'

'He can't have been awake.'

'His eyes were wide open, but he didn't see me. I helped him back to bed and he went straight to sleep. I stayed for a while and then went back to my room. He said nothing about it this morning, so perhaps he wasn't awake?'

There was no air in the room and I fought to breathe. 'The report mentioned great brutality?'

She nodded, her eyes bright with tears. 'He won't speak of it. He said what he witnessed ate into your soul like a canker, and that once seen it never leaves you. He said that no one should bear witness to such atrocities. Amelia, I'm so glad you've come . . . that we have you. I've always wanted you to be my sister . . . and now — ' She wiped her eyes, her voice breaking. 'Edmund will be all right, won't he? With your love and your kindness, and everything you know about herbs and medicine . . . He will get better, won't he?'

I held her to me, her body taut beneath her heavy shawl. 'I just need a few minutes to freshen up and we'll go and see Lady Melville. Edmund needs time and understanding . . . he needs rest and good food. If you could have a kettle of boiling water sent up to my room, I'll make that draft for his pain.'

I stared into the looking glass. The shock was passing. I needed to stay strong. I needed time, that was all. I had brought my medicine chest and I would make two infusions — willow bark and ginger for Edmund, lemon balm for me.

★　★　★

Lemon balm: an invaluable herb used for settling stomach upsets caused by nervous tension or a broken heart. To make an infusion, seep a handful of dry or fresh leaves in boiling water and leave for five minutes. Strain through muslin. Take after meals, preferably while hot.
THE LADY HERBALIST

22

Pendowrick, Bodmin Moor
Tuesday 6th February 1798, 4 a.m.

Another chime of the clock, another hour spent lying awake. The lavender bags were ineffective against the musty bed hangings: the fire was out, the room icy cold. Bethany's gentle breathing filled the silence and I needed fresher air. I slipped from the bed, opening the door to the corridor. Moonlight flooded through the tiny leaded panes and I stood staring at the huge moon shining on the Dutch gable above me. The vast barn lay bathed in soft silver light, moonlight glinting on the trees in the orchard and the church tower just beyond.

It was almost as bright as day and I breathed deeply, trying to imagine how it could be once again with the barn full of calves, and laughter echoing from the milking parlour. Chickens would scratch the cobbles, geese grazing the orchard, our children running from their nurse to cradle newborn lambs in the warm straw. It was so achingly beautiful, and yet so achingly lonely.

Tiredness had stopped Lady Melville from joining us at dinner: her joints were paining her, yet she dismissed my concern, saying a good night's sleep was all she needed. The three of us had dined formally in the great hall, the crossed swords hanging on the walls above us. Medieval armour had glinted in the firelight, Edmund making every effort to be cheerful but I knew his headache was troubling him and I had filled the awkward silences with talk of my family.

He had sat upright and formal and I had spoken too fast, needing to hide my stab of disappointment. He had used the word *dabble* and that had cut me like a knife. *It's wonderful you dabble in herbs, Amelia. We must enlarge the herb garden here in Pendowrick.* I knew he meant well. Of course he meant well, but 'dabble' had sounded too dismissive a word.

Constance had talked of their father's death — of how Sir Richard had brought Francis's coffin down from Plymouth, and how five days later he had collapsed and died. A dissecting aneurysm, the coroner had said, a swelling in the main artery leading from the heart. Edmund had sat stern-faced and grim, listening in silence as Connie explained that their father's death had only been a matter of time. But though we said nothing, we were all thinking the same: that the stress of Francis's murder had most likely caused a rise in Sir Richard's blood pressure, and the consequent bursting of the artery.

Edmund had fumbled as he tried to cut his meal. He had not drunk his claret. He had sat at the head of the long refectory table with both of us on either side and had barely eaten. I knew what he was thinking — that he should have prevented Francis's death. It had been hard to watch his anguish — his shallow breathing, his constant swallowing, the tremor in his hands. The new maid had cleared away the plates and

186

Edmund had brought out the letter he had been trying to read earlier. He had handed it to Connie with a slight wince.

'How long has this been here?'

Connie had looked surprised. 'I've not seen it before . . . where was it?'

'In the top drawer of Father's desk. Could you read it to me please?'

'I don't have the keys to Father's desk . . . Mama keeps them. Everything that comes gets locked away . . . in your boxes . . . or Father's desk.'

It was good to breathe the air of the corridor. Bethany turned on her chaise longue and resumed her gentle breathing. Last night, I had seen her wipe away her tears and asked her why she was crying.

'Mrs Alston scolded me for crossing myself. But I had to. Honest to God, this house is haunted . . . doors creak with no one behind them . . . footsteps with no one there . . . eyes watching from every corner. The house is restless — surely you can feel it?'

Yes, I could. The house was crying out for love, as surely as its owners.

The letter was from the nephew of the man who had cheated Sir Richard — he was replying to Edmund's demand that they send the shipment. Family illness and deaths had interrupted trading but they had re-established their business and he was honouring their contract. He himself would accompany the ordered shipment and would inform Sir Richard when it arrived in Bristol. Further shipments would follow, as of the new contract.

187

Edmund had gripped the table. 'They're honouring their contract — keeping to the agreement?' He had smiled, reaching out his hand to take mine. 'He's answered the letter I wrote . . . *my order* — the one Francis was so dismissive about? Oh, Amelia . . . Connie, read it again. Perhaps this is the turning point . . . my chance to clear our debts. I can get the estate stocked again. Maybe I should continue to trade? He sounds honest, doesn't he?'

The house was waking, light shining through the kitchen windows; someone was hanging a lamp beside the back door. I turned abruptly. A scream was piercing the silence, echoing across the stillness from the servants' quarters. I knelt on the window seat, staring down at the kitchen. Another scream, louder and longer.

Bethany rushed to my side. 'What's happening?'

'There's a lantern — someone's running along the top corridor.'

'Miss Melville . . . Miss Melville.' We could hear frantic knocking and ran straight to Constance's room. A maid was holding a lamp, her face ashen. 'It's Mrs Alston . . . she's had a fall.' Her eyes were wide with fright. 'She's covered in blood and she's not movin'.'

The door opened and Constance stood pale in the candlelight.

'It's Mrs Alston, Miss Melville — she's had a fall.'

'Where is she?' Connie wrapped her housecoat around her.

'Is she all right?'

'Bottom of the servants' steps.'

'She must be all right if she screamed.'

The maid shook her head. 'No, Miss Carew, 'twas us that screamed. She's not movin'.'

Running along the servants' corridor, we reached the spiralling steps. Halfway down, we could see Mrs Alston sprawled on the flagstones, her arms outstretched, her bony fingers trying to grip the floor. Blood was seeping from her nose and mouth. Seth was leaning over her, shaking her gently. 'Wake up . . . wake up, Mrs Alston.' He looked up. 'She isn't breathing. The maids found her. She's banged her head . . . '

No pulse throbbed at her thin wrist, none at her neck. Her glazed eyes stared sightlessly back at me, the blood at her mouth already congealed. I shook my head. 'She's been dead a while. Feel her . . . she's as cold as stone. She must have tripped and fallen. Connie, I'm so sorry.'

Connie sank to Mrs Alston's side. 'She never rushes . . . she always holds the rail. She's been up and down these stairs since she was thirteen.' She cradled the old woman in her arms, rocking her backwards and forwards. 'She was more than a servant . . . she was our dear friend. She loved us . . . and served us so faithfully. She was my nurse . . . more than my nurse . . . she was like a mother to us.' Tears streamed down her cheeks, her black curls soft around her shoulders.

Mrs Alston was in her nightgown, her velvet housecoat tied at her waist. Her grey hair was loose, thick dark blood oozing through her white nightcap. 'I'm so sorry, Connie.'

The longcase clock in the hall chimed five. 'We need to send for a doctor — to certify her death.

189

I suppose it should be Dr Trefusis?'

'If he can get here. The drifts will be treacherous.'

Seth pointed to the folds of Mrs Alston's nightdress. 'There's a tear in her hem — look, it's ripped. She'd have caught her foot and fallen.'

Constance looked up at the sea of shocked faces crowding around their housekeeper, her tears glistening in the candlelight. 'Mrs Alston must have been coming from my mother's room. She sometimes spends the whole night at her bedside.'

An elderly woman stepped forward. 'We'll lay her on her bed, Miss Melville. We'll wash her an' do the necessary . . . an' ye can come an' see her when she's tidy . . . Perhaps ye'd like some tea brought up?'

'Thank you. Yes, some tea. I'll take it in Lady Melville's room. I need to be there when my mother wakes . . . she'll need to know straight away.'

I helped Constance up the spiral steps, stopping outside the studded oak door. 'Shall I stay with you?'

She wiped her tears, opening the door. 'I don't know how I'm going to tell her. But I'll be all right. They were very close — Mrs Alston could read Mama like a book. She always knew what Mama was thinking . . . and what would make her comfortable.'

I returned down the moonlit corridor yet, almost at once, another scream pierced the silence — a heartbreaking screech, followed by agonized wailing and I ran back, knowing to expect the worst.

Red embers glowed in the fireplace, a lamp burning on the table. 'Mama . . . Mama . . . come back. Please, please . . . come back.' Constance cradled her mother in her arms, but even in the dull light, I saw Lady Melville's ashen hue. Her lips were blue, her arms dangling limp in her daughter's tight embrace. Spittle oozed from Lady Melville's gaping mouth.

She looked warmly dressed, her woollen bed jacket tied with ribbons, her open Bible on the cover next to her. Her hands were white, freezing cold, her eyes staring vacantly across the room. 'Connie, she's gone . . . she's gone.'

I put my arms round Constance's heaving shoulders, the smell of almond oil mixing with the scent of lavender. 'Do you think she died in pain?' she whispered.

'No, I don't . . . she looks at ease.'

'Was it her heart? Dr Bohenna said her heart was weak. He was so kind, but after that terrible tincture . . . I think we all knew she was dying.'

At the mention of his name, I had to walk away. I had to throw a log on the fire, bring some warmth into the freezing room. Behind me, I heard Connie's sharp intake of breath. 'Oh, dear God.' She was standing stock still, staring at the candle. 'She's still here. She's still with us.'

A sudden chill made me shiver. 'Connie, your mother's gone. There's nothing we can do.'

'No . . . she's here . . . she hasn't passed. We must get Reverend Kemp.' Her voice was strangely distant. 'She's here . . . with us, in this room.'

In the flickering light, Lady Melville's cheeks were glistening. She looked to be crying.

'Connie, those are *your* tears, not hers. She's at rest . . . '

There was terror in her eyes. 'No, she's not. She's in this room . . . she's with us. Burn some lavender — she hasn't passed.'

'Connie . . . she looks at peace.'

Her eyes looked wild, her cheeks drained of colour. 'She's not at peace. Look. The flame's blue.'

I stared at the flickering flame with its streak of blue. 'Candles do burn blue.'

'Exactly.'

Bethany stood, wide-eyed with fear. 'Ask them to bring up some lavender,' I said, my heart thumping so fast I could barely breathe. 'And send someone for Reverend Kemp. Tell them to hurry. And get some rosemary — if there isn't any dried, get them to cut some stalks.'

Constance backed away from her mother, reaching for the clock on the table. She opened the back, fumbling with the mechanism to stop it. She was breathing fast, glancing over her shoulder. 'She's here. She's not at peace. Turn that mirror over.' She reached up, lifting the heavy mirror from the wall. 'No! Don't look in it. We mustn't see her.'

'Connie . . . please . . . '

'Do the hand mirror. Don't look in it!'

She stopped the pendulum of the wall clock and the room went eerily quiet. I needed to sit her down, reassure her, give her something for the shock, but her face held such terror. A cold breeze caressed my cheeks, the draught from the door, just an ordinary draught, but her wide eyes

192

and shallow breathing made me rush to the dressing table and I grabbed the hand mirror, turning it over.

'There — I've done it.' My hands were shaking. I was never fanciful. Never. I needed to stay calm. A tray stood on the table and I tried to sound rational. 'The tray's been left — the junket hasn't been tasted . . . Mrs Alston must have come up with the tray, seen your mother was in trouble, and rushed to get help . . . maybe she found Lady Melville dead.'

Constance stared at the flame by her mother's bed. 'I know you think me foolish . . . but those of us who know the house know it speaks for those who can no longer speak. Not in words . . . but in signs. I'm born of this house, born of Melville blood. Men don't see the signs, but we do. Generations of Melville women — *real* Melville women, not those marrying into the family — know and understand every nuance of this house. My aunt taught me the signs, and I will teach your daughters. And I will teach them that the signs are always true.'

A cold shiver ran down my spine 'Connie, please . . .'

'I will teach them that a blue flame at death means your loved one hasn't passed. That they are restless and asking for our help.'

Shouts rang across the courtyard below. 'Someone's going for Reverend Kemp . . .'

Bethany and another maid stood at the door, their cheeks flushed, their chests heaving. 'The lavender, Miss Carew . . . and we've brought some rosemary.'

She handed me the bunches and I dipped them into the fire, waving the pungent smoke into every corner of the room. Lady Melville's Bible lay open on the bedsheets and Constance picked it up, slipping in the ribbon as she closed it. On the bedside table, the candle glowed bright yellow.

'Perhaps Mama was just waiting to say goodbye. No one should die alone . . . perhaps she was just waiting.' She put the Bible down and reached for a hairbrush, brushing her mother's hair, rubbing my green salve on to Lady Melville's blue lips. Tears streamed down her cheeks. 'I always thought I'd be with her when she died. Dr Bohenna was so kind. He told me she was very ill, but I honestly thought she might get better.'

The last of the lavender curled and sparked brightly in the fireplace. 'Oh goodness, Connie . . . Edmund hasn't heard the commotion. He must still be asleep.' I covered my face, fighting my despair. 'Connie, this will break him — I don't think he'll be able to bear this.'

She laid her mother's hands carefully under the eiderdown; her back was stiff, her mouth drawn tight. 'It's no use him crying after the event. He should have thought of that before he abandoned us.' Her words cut like a knife — harsh words, spoken through gritted teeth. 'He chose to join the navy . . . without saying goodbye . . . and his reported death — that's what caused her illness. That's what really killed her. She didn't want to live . . . she suffered years of anxiety . . . *years* of heartbreak when he could

194

have been *here*, giving her years of pleasure. It's no use him crying now.'

I could not move; my heart was racing as I stared back at her furious face. The fire was blazing yet I felt so cold. They were her words, not mine. Her thoughts, not mine. Guilt twisted my stomach — *her thoughts, not mine.*

23

We laid Lady Melville flat, placing a roll of cloth beneath her chin, hiding it beneath the lace of her bed jacket. Constance rearranged her mother's nightcap and added more balm to her lips. 'I'll prepare her properly when I'm dressed.'

'I'll help you,' I whispered. They had gone for Edmund and we could hear him rushing down the corridor. He stood in the doorway, his hair ruffled, dark stubble covering his chin.

'No . . . no.' He ran to the bed, pulling back the covers, reaching for Lady Melville's hands. His cry was hoarse, violent, filling the room with searing pain. 'No . . . no . . . please no.' He clasped his mother's thin hands to his lips, his shoulders heaving beneath his white nightshirt. 'Don't leave us . . . not now . . . not now. Don't leave us.'

He tried to gain control, wiping the tears from his cheeks. 'Someone better go for Mrs Alston. Does she know? The poor woman will be devastated.' He stood up, tucking his mother's hands beneath the cover, bending down to kiss her waxen cheek. 'Mrs Alston will want to prepare Mother for her coffin.' His voice broke. 'The last service of a faithful servant.'

My heart ripped with pain — his beloved nurse; always stopping on his return to pick her a bunch of wild flowers, always stooping for a shell from the beach, or a stone in the shape of a heart. His beloved nurse whom he loved so very dearly.

'Edmund.' He did not hear me. 'Edmund? Mrs Alston's had a fall. We think she rushed out of the room . . . we believe she was running to get help for your mother. She must have been distraught . . . she caught her foot in her hem and fell down the stairs.'

'You've sent for a doctor? I'll go and see her.'

Our silence made him look up, his large black pupils seeking reassurance. I could hardly speak. 'It was a very bad fall . . . she knocked her head. She couldn't call for help . . . she was found this morning by the maids.'

His cry wrenched my heart. 'Not Mrs Alston . . . no. Not her as well?'

Voices rose from the courtyard below, the sound of men stamping snow off their boots, and I caught the steel in Constance's voice.

'I've sent for Reverend Kemp.'

Edmund swung round, fumbling for a handkerchief. 'What? But you're not dressed — none of us are. You can't be seen like this — Amelia certainly can't be seen like this. Intruding on us so early . . . I'm not ready for company . . . I need time to . . .'

Constance was staring at the candle burning by her mother's side and I thought I might faint. The yellow flame was wavering again, a slight flicker of blue. 'Mama needs them. Now.'

'Connie, are you out of your mind?' He stared at her in horror, his trembling hands gripping his handkerchief. People were walking up the spiral steps, footsteps along the corridor. Reverend

Kemp and his son stood at the door, bowing respectfully, both tall and slender, both with high foreheads and kind eyes. They were breathing heavily, their neckties slightly askew.

'I'm so sorry, Sir Edmund, Miss Melville. This is very sad indeed.'

Constance stepped forward. 'Thank you for coming.'

Reverend Kemp's white hair caught the firelight. He was slightly stooped, his movements stiff. Adam Kemp stood shyly in the doorway, the warmth in his hazel eyes exactly how I remembered them. Eight years on, he had the same bright auburn hair and freckled complexion, but maturity suited him. His years of study gave him stature; he looked approachable and kind, and I caught my breath. His furrowed brow reminded me of Luke. His years of study. The kindness in his eyes.

He must have seen the tears welling in my own. 'This is very hard for you, Miss Carew. I'm Adam Kemp — curate for my father.'

'We've met before . . . I remember you.' I could say nothing more. Edmund's frown had deepened.

'If you could wait outside for a moment . . . my sister and Miss Carew are not dressed for visitors . . . this is all very sudden and very raw. If you'll excuse us . . . join us afterwards. Downstairs. When we are ready we can discuss the funeral.'

He held out his arm for Constance, who took it with downcast eyes. She walked demurely by his side — a mouse, turned lion, turned mouse again. It seemed I had a lot to learn about my future sister-in-law. I followed behind them and we parted company, but at the door to her room, I heard Edmund's furious whisper.

'How could you let Adam Kemp see you in your night-clothes like that? Have you no shame?'

★ ★ ★

'I couldn't face this without you,' Edmund whispered as we walked into the great hall. He pulled out my chair and we sat at the long refectory table, Edmund in the heavy oak carving chair, Adam and his father on either side. Constance was next to Reverend Kemp and I sat next to Adam, listening but hardly hearing. Constance had also drawn me aside with the same heartfelt whisper.

Even if the snow cleared, I could not leave them now. I would write to Mother and Seth could send one of the grooms. The wind had dropped, the first glimmers of a watery sun — a single horseman might just get through.

'They'll have it built by this afternoon. There's plenty of oak, but there's some elm too — it's left over from Sir Richard's coffin. Lady Melville ordered extra and told them to put it to one side.'

Edmund nodded. 'I'd like them to use the elm — to match Father's coffin. Mother must have had that in mind.'

'I believe they've also got some of the same grips they used for Sir Richard . . . ' Reverend

Kemp paused. Edmund had risen from his seat and was facing the fire. 'The coffin will be lined with green velvet — just like Sir Richard's, if that's to your taste. We can get the breastplate engraved by tomorrow at the latest.' He glanced at his son, who nodded in agreement.

'Mrs Alston's coffin will be oak. It's going to take some effort to dig her grave because the ground's frozen solid, but it will be done.' His voice was soft, his eyes resting on Constance. 'Miss Melville, are you sure you want the funeral to be the day after tomorrow? You don't want to invite friends, perhaps wait for the snow to melt?'

Constance had been listening quietly and shook her head, her dark hair still loose around her shoulders. 'Mama has very few friends — and certainly none around here. The village people must come, of course, but without Mrs Alston . . .' Tears pooled in her eyes. 'We need to keep everything simple.'

'I'll help find someone to provide food . . . and some beer . . . to do what's needed.' Adam glanced over his shoulder at her brother's back. 'I understand this is very difficult for you.'

Edmund was smartly dressed, his clothes impeccable, but his hair was ruffled, his hands clasping and unclasping by his side. He resumed his place at the head of the table, resting his forehead against his interlocked fingers. 'My sister's right. My mother withdrew from society . . . you know our circumstances . . . you understand how difficult it would be for us to host a lavish funeral on people who . . . who allowed my mother . . .'

Reverend Kemp coughed. 'Of course.'

'So, there's no need to prolong this agony. I'd like the funeral tomorrow.'

A glance passed between father and son; a hesitancy in Reverend Kemp's reply. 'Very well. If you think that isn't too soon.'

'No, I don't. Mother will be laid to rest in Father's tomb?'

Reverend Kemp paused, his quill poised above the notes he was taking. He had a fine bone structure, bushy white eyebrows and long tapering fingers. He seemed to be choosing his words carefully. 'When we have to use a tomb again — within a fairly short period of time — it is sometimes necessary to remove the old coffin . . . only the coffin, mind you . . . in order to allow enough space for the new one.'

Constance covered her face with her hands, leaning forward on her elbows. 'Remove Father's coffin?'

Adam Kemp's eyes filled with pain. He was so like Luke it hurt to breathe. 'Usually just the lid but if the sides haven't rotted down sufficiently, then they'll have to be taken out . . . very carefully, of course. New earth will be placed over your father's bones and a layer of rushes — and rosemary or anything else you'd like to put in. I'll see to it personally. The lid will be replaced, and the tomb will only be re-opened when we place your mother's coffin inside. The old coffin pieces will be burned, and the ashes placed back into the tomb. I'll supervise the whole proceedings.'

Edmund pressed his fingers against his temples,

his hands trembling. 'That seems very straightforward. But we need to decide what wood to use for my mother's coffin. My preference is elm. Do the carpenters have sufficient elm?'

He looked up in the ensuing silence, glancing at me with obvious confusion and I saw the fright in his eyes — a wounded, scared man who did not know what he had said wrong. I gripped my hands under the table, trying to breathe. It was as if I was suffocating — as if nails were banging into my coffin, clamping the coffin lid shut.

I somehow rose, leaning on the table, staring back into Reverend Kemp's compassionate eyes. 'Thank you, Reverend Kemp . . . Mr Kemp . . . you've been very kind . . . and very attentive. Elm would be perfect . . . thank you.'

24

Constance laid her mother's maroon silk gown, a pair of her satin shoes, and a simple velvet cap on the bed. 'That will look perfect, won't it?' she said, reaching for a large pair of scissors. 'I think this is probably the only way, don't you?'

We had washed and dried Lady Melville's stiff body, dressing her thin grey hair, smoothing balm on her blue lips, and I nodded, smiling my encouragement. The fire was blazing, the clocks still silent, the only sound the snapping of Constance's large scissors.

'It's more difficult than I thought,' Connie whispered, and I leaned forward, holding the material taut. The back cut, she hesitated. 'How are we going to do this? Perhaps, if you lift Mama's arm, I can slip this sleeve on first. Can you bend it? Oh, good . . . ' We were wearing starched white aprons, our sleeves tucked to our elbows. 'Now this arm . . . can you manage?'

We were both too scared to use force; Lady Melville's cold body seemed too fragile to handle. The gown swamped her, the maroon suddenly too dark against her white face. 'Perhaps we should roll her . . . first to you, then to me . . . only it'll make it easier to tuck all this fabric under her? She's as light as a sparrow — I don't want to break any bones.'

The same awful thought had crossed my mind. 'Maybe we should place the shroud under

203

her at the same time?' I unfolded the stiff white linen, the scent of almond oil mixing with rose water and lanolin. The procedure was new to both of us and taking much longer than we had expected.

'We can tuck these sprigs of rosemary into the folds of her gown. I wish we had flowers . . . but these lavender bags will be perfect. I had no idea when I made them that I'd be using them for this.' Her voice caught. 'Shall I leave her hands as if in prayer?' Hours of loving kindness, the last, most precious gift a daughter could give her mother. 'Oh, Amelia! Her jaw's dropping. Quick, pass me the rolled towel. We still need it. What if I tuck it under this lace? No one will see it, will they?'

'No. No one will see. That's perfect . . . she looks very peaceful.'

Connie stood back to survey our work. 'She looks too waxen — she needs a dab of rouge. There. And now the cap. Can you hold her head while I slip it under?'

The cap strings tied, and her hair tidied, Lady Melville looked elegant and at peace. 'The signs aren't always bad,' Connie whispered, smoothing the pillow. 'Sometimes they foretell of fortune . . . sometimes they speak of great happiness. Like the swallows nesting against the east window this year.' She smiled up at me.

'Whole generations can pass without any swallows nesting against the east window but last year we had *three* nests. And each nest had two sets of fledglings. The nests are still intact and that foretells *great* happiness. The swallows came back just like Edmund came back. I should have recognized the sign . . . that he'd come back, and we'd all be happy again.'

She sounded suddenly bitter, not happy at all, and my chest tightened. 'Connie, please don't be angry with Edmund. He's angry enough with himself.'

She picked up Lady Melville's Bible. 'I find it very hard not to be cross with him when he speaks so harshly to me.'

'Connie, try not to be . . . '

'I know I mustn't be. I hate being so cross . . . but I can't help it.' The lion had entered her voice again.

'Edmund sounds harsh, but he's in a lot more pain than he wants us to know. He's really struggling . . . he's forgetting things and putting on a brave face.'

'I know, and soon everyone else will know that, too. Reverend Kemp was obviously shocked but neither of them will say anything. And you're right — of course, you're right. It's just that I've looked after Mama every single day since Edmund left — eight very painful years since he left for London . . . and, all that time, Mama's only ever thought of him. Only of Edmund — I just didn't count . . . and I didn't mind because I, too, adored him. But what I find really hard is that within minutes of his return, they shut the door on me. They discussed the way I dressed, my demeanour, my relationship with the servants . . . and that most of my suitors would now withdraw because their sons could no longer expect the title. It was very hurtful.'

205

'Connie . . . they didn't mean it unkindly . . . '

She shook her head, looking down at her mother. 'I was listening at the door. What I heard was unkind and I can't pretend otherwise. And I'm not speaking ill of the dead, I'm just telling you how I feel.'

I slipped my hand through her arm. 'Then you must tell Edmund. You were always so close — tell him how you feel.'

'I don't know if that's possible. I was nine when he left for London . . . he was seventeen. I hardly count that last Christmas — that awful time when Father said he was going to send them both to Sumatra — I hardly spoke to him. He had eyes and thoughts only for you.'

A knife sliced my heart. 'It was a very difficult visit . . . he wasn't himself.'

'And he's not himself now. I've adored Edmund all my life, and yet I see it now as nothing but childish adoration for an elder brother. We're both so changed. He thinks me his adoring younger sister, but I have suffered too. He must understand I've shouldered rather a lot of responsibility for someone so young.' She opened the Bible at the ribbon, glancing down at a marked passage. 'Oh, this is rather apt.

'*Anyone who loves their brother and sister lives in the light, and there is nothing to make them stumble. But anyone who hates a brother and sister is in the darkness and walks in the darkness. St John.*'

She closed the Bible, placing it carefully in her mother's hands. 'Mama loved her sister — she and Aunt Harriet were very close. She must have known she was dying and would soon be with Aunt Harriet. You know Mama blamed Francis for her death . . . she could never bring herself to forgive him?'

'That was rather unkind. You can't blame a child for his mother dying in childbirth.'

'Mama nursed Aunt Harriet for three weeks before she died. She never spoke of it as I believe it was too painful.' She stopped, suddenly staring at the bedside table. 'Oh, goodness — Mama's box. Quick, I need her keys . . . ' She rushed across the room, opening the top drawer of the dressing table, searching between the contents. 'Here they are.'

Dashing back, she slid open the bottom drawer of the heavy oak wardrobe and lifted out a small wooden box. 'She hid it beneath this blanket. Mama put everything of importance in here. I've watched her lock it so many times, but she never let me see what was inside.' The inlaid box had a brass keyhole and Constance chose the biggest of the three keys.

'Connie — shouldn't you . . . wait?'

Her cheeks were flushed, sudden fear in her eyes. She glanced at the door, her fingers fumbling with the lock. 'No. That's just the point. I need to open it while there's just the two of us. Woman to woman. We're the guardians of this house. We keep its secrets. The men may own the bricks and mortar, but we women own its heart and soul.'

The lock clicked and she opened the lid, lifting out a pile of letters, and I ran to her, kneeling beside her as she laid them on the floor.

'It's her letters from Edmund . . . and these are from Father. Goodness, what's this?' She picked up a folded page, smoothing out the stiff creases. 'It's been torn out of a ledger . . . It looks like it's from a church registry.'

I stared down at the meticulous writing. 'It's a registry of births.'

Only half the page was written on, each entry recorded in the same neat handwriting. Along the top was: *Name of infant, Date of birth, Mother, Father, Address.* Only half a page of entries, then the names stopped. 'The first is dated 1755, the last 1772.' We stared at the last entry.

Francis Selwyn Bainbridge, Born September 25th 1772 Mother: Harriet Elizabeth Bainbridge. Father: unknown. Pendowrick Hall.

Constance drew a sharp breath. 'Father *unknown?*'

In clear, concise writing, Harriet Bainbridge's secret was staring straight at us. 'Your mother must have torn it out to protect her sister's reputation.'

'When Uncle William died Aunt Harriet came down from London to have the baby. It was the most natural thing to do — poor Aunt Harriet was only twenty-three. Mama was bereft when she died and took Francis in as family. Edmund was born three months later. But not to know the father?'

'Your uncle must have died well before . . . or else he would be named on the register.'

'I don't know the exact date of his death. He was buried in London and we've never visited his grave. I can understand how petrified Mama must have been of any scandal.'

Across the room, the candle on Lady Melville's bedside flickered strong and warm, the comforting yellow flame of a church candle. 'Mama wanted this kept secret, Amelia, so we must honour her wishes. Here . . . it has to go.'

She thrust the page into the blazing fire, the edges quickly catching, the names curling and twisting before succumbing to the flames. 'Promise me you'll never speak of it, Amelia?'

'Speak of what?' Edmund stood in the doorway.

Constance froze, staring at the black coils disappearing to ash in the grate. 'It was nothing.'

Edmund stepped forward, shutting the door behind him. 'That's not true, Connie. You've just burned something.' There was authority in his voice, a sense of command.

Constance turned to face him, staring straight into his eyes. 'It was a letter . . . an unsent letter to Father. It was a very unhappy letter and it upset me to read it.'

To lie so blatantly and for me to just stand there. I could feel my cheeks burning and I turned to hide my sudden panic. Edmund's voice softened. 'What was it about?'

This time there was no hesitation. 'Mama was asking Father for money.'

Firelight flickered across Edmund's face. He looked strained, a sudden hardening of his mouth. 'I think there was more to it than that. You're protecting someone, aren't you? Is it me you're protecting, Connie?' His chest rose and

209

fell, the tremble back in his hands; there was vulnerability in his glance, a look of real pain. 'What was the letter about?'

Constance squared her shoulders, a flicker of defiance before she lowered her eyes. 'If you must know, Mama was begging Father not to allow you to join the ship.' Her cheeks flushed as she took a sideways step to hide Lady Melville's open box.

I was part of her lie, hiding the truth from Edmund. But why say that? How could she be so unkind? By the conviction in her voice, I knew Lady Melville must have sent such letters — begging her husband to let Edmund return to Pendowrick, but why hurt him like that?

Edmund's shoulders stooped. Crossing the room, he bent to kiss Lady Melville's cold cheek. 'I wish you had sent that letter, Mother. You were right: I should never have gone.' His voice was hoarse, tears in his eyes as he fought his quivering lips. 'Mother looks so much younger . . . she looks at peace.' A tear rolled down his cheek. 'Rest in peace, dearest Mother. Please find it in your heart to forgive me.'

I knew I must go to him. I stood by his side, his forced smile bringing tears to my eyes. 'Have you done everything you need to do?' he said softly. 'Only they've got her coffin downstairs and I can ask them to bring it up. It's very heavy but there are six of us. We'll carry her down the grand staircase and leave her to rest in the parlour. I'll set up an overnight vigil — the servants and estate workers will want to pay their last respects.'

He stood back, blowing his nose, straightening his shoulders. 'Mrs Alston's coffin will lie by her side. Reverend Kemp says we'll bury Mother first, then we'll lay Mrs Alston to rest at three o'clock tomorrow — as long as Dr Trefusis has signed the death certificates.'

Constance stayed firmly in front of her mother's box. 'Yes, we have. I'll sew the shroud up when we close the coffin lid. I've had a note from DrTrefusis to say he'll be here this afternoon. He's going to walk through the snow.'

'That's very good of him. I'll get the coffin now.' At the door Edmund paused, turning round as if in afterthought. 'What else is in Mother's box, Connie?'

Constance's cheeks drained of all colour. 'Only your letters to Mama . . . and a few from Father.'

'Then, maybe I should take them?' His quiet authority filled the room. It was not a question but a command and a cold hand clamped my heart. Constance stared back at him, trying to shrug it off, but he held out his hand, walking towards her. 'The box, please, Connie.'

★ ★ ★

Bethany poured hot water into the basin, glancing nervously over her shoulder. Her usually plump red cheeks looked pale, her mobcap in need of pressing. She had been lent a clean apron, but her hair looked untidy, her dress crumpled. Both of us were grateful for an early night.

211

'Were you looking for a special remedy?' I asked as I dipped my hands into the basin.

She drew a sharp breath, her eyes widening. 'No, Miss Amelia. I've not touched your herbal.'

I gripped the basin. I would have to give it back to Luke. I must not keep it. 'Then one of the maids must have been tidying up — it's been moved.'

Bethany clamped her fist against her mouth, her eyes like saucers. 'Honest to God, Miss Amelia . . . things moving when they shouldn't . . . doors opening . . . eyes watching all the time . . . and the thought of them two coffins.'

I splashed my face, dabbing my cheeks with the towel. 'Bethany, no one's watching.'

Even as I said it, I could feel their eyes boring into my back — rows of Melville women with their suffocating white ruffs and tight smiles, their hooded eyes and thin white hands gripping their prayer books. Each of them trapped in their elaborate wooden frames, each with their own hidden wooden boxes — the keepers of secrets, the guardians of the house. Well, I was one of them now with my promise to Constance that I would keep her aunt's secret.

'All old houses creak. It's just the floorboards and the wind blowing the doors shut.' My throat was so tight I could hardly swallow. Why had Constance been so hurtful? Why punish Edmund when he was already punishing himself?

'Miss Carew . . . they say Sir Edmund never sleeps in his bed. They say he don't close his curtains at night . . . that he sleeps on the floor beneath his open window . . . that he pleads all

212

night for his life . . . and in the morning he cowers under his blanket till he knows he's safe.'

My chest tightened. 'Bethany, that's enough. I'll not have you repeat servant gossip.'

My curt rebuke must have stung her. I should never have spoken so sharply. She looked struck, tears in her eyes. 'I'm sorry — I thought ye might like to know. 'Twasn't easy sayin' it because I knew 'twould make ye upset.'

I looked back at the portraits, each of them staring back at me with their knowing looks — the guardians of the house with their secretive eyes, hidden signs and sayings. Had they, too, leaned clutching the basin like this, their hearts breaking?

Bring back the swallows, I pleaded to them through silent eyes. *Please, please. Bring back the swallows.*

25

Pendowrick Church, Bodmin Moor
Wednesday 7th February 1798, 3 p.m.

Ahoar frost clung to the trees spiking the branches above us. The church bell was tolling, the north wind stinging my cheeks. No longer in the shelter of the church, it bit suddenly deeper, ruffling the fur on my hood. Constance gripped her heavy black cloak, her cheeks red with cold, and we bent our heads against the icy wind.

The path was too treacherous to carry the coffins so they had pulled them from the house on wooden sledges. Adam had chosen the five strongest men and we stood watching them lift Lady Melville's coffin from the sledge onto their shoulders. Effort racked their faces, the muscles in their arms shaking. Until this point we had not been able to see the open tomb but now it stood gaping in front of us, a scaffold of steps on one side, a makeshift wooden ramp on the other. At her sudden intake of breath, I slipped my hand from my muff, taking hold of Constance's arm.

'Do you think Lady Clarissa would mind if I came back to Truro with you?' she whispered.

My heart lifted. The tension between Edmund and Constance had been building all day — not in words, but in their averted glances and terse, if polite, nods and shrugs. 'No, of course not,

Mother would love you to come ... and so would I.'

The coffin steady, Edmund nodded to Reverend Kemp and we began following them up the churchyard, the snow crunching beneath my borrowed boots. A narrow path had been cleared and we snaked in a long line, the bank of snow obscuring the names on the graves on either side. From beneath his large black hat, Adam Kemp glanced at Constance and I gripped her arm, more for support than for comfort. The love in his eyes tore my heart, a surge of emptiness flooding through me.

All night I had lain awake. Love was selfless. Love was compassionate. Love was loving the whole man. Love was taking the good with the bad. *In sickness and in health. Until death do us part.* Love was being loyal to your oath, not stepping away when you were needed most. Love was understanding another's needs, being strong for them. Love was not abandoning a man who no longer looked at you with the same devotion, who could no longer laugh, and who lay awake each night tormented by his private demons.

Very few had been invited to attend the service, merely the house and estate servants and a handful from the village. Reverend Kemp was treading carefully, leaning heavily on his stout stick. Adam was just behind him, carrying the large church Bible; the rest of the small congregation fell in step behind them, all of us hunching against the wind. We followed the elm coffin with its elaborate brass handles to the higher ground where generations of the Melville

215

family had been laid to rest. Huge stone tombs began to line our way, some with iron railings, some with names of infants, many with second or third wives — each successive Lady Melville recorded by a portrait in the house and an inscription on a tomb under her husband's name.

A lifetime ago, Edmund and I had walked, hand in hand, through these graves, Edmund laughing at the tales attached to each of his forbears; we had seemed so far from death we hardly saw them as tombs, but now death felt horribly close. Constance hesitated, glancing across at two headstones half-covered in snow and set slightly apart from the rest. Mother and son, lying side by side: *Harriet Mary Bainbridge nee Cheyne 1748–1772 May she Rest in Peace*, and *Francis Selwyn Bainbridge 1772–1793 God rest his soul.*

'No one will hear her secret from me,' I whispered.

She drew her cloak tighter, her eyes watering in the wind. 'Edmund didn't allow me to read the letters.'

Once again, it seemed I must come between them. 'That's understandable, Connie — they're his letters to his mother.'

She clasped her hood as it caught the breeze. 'Not *his* letters — Father's letters to Mother. Edmund burned them — he said they were too full of malice and it was far better I didn't read them. Now we're about to condemn Mama to lie in eternal unrest in the arms of the husband she hated and she'll never be free of him.'

The ground around the tomb was muddied

with imprints of huge boots and signs of a recent heap of earth. Adam directed the coffin bearers to the foot of the wooden ramp and began securing three heavy straps around the coffin. He pulled them tightly. A dank stench rose from the tomb, catching me off guard. The rest of the mourners shuffled into a circle behind us, some bringing out handkerchiefs, others shifting to stand upwind of the tomb. Bethany was among them. *Eternal unrest.* She, too, had sensed the unrest in the house.

The straps in place, Edmund, Seth and another man mounted the steps on the opposite side of the tomb and began pulling on the leather, hauling the coffin up the wooden ramp, Adam's soft instructions keeping them in time. 'And pull. And pull.' The coffin was heavy, and more men were needed. 'You two — take the straps behind the others. Ready on my command.'

Two men stepped forward, gripping the straps, and Lady Melville's coffin slid slowly up the side of the tomb. Halfway to the top, another two men climbed the steps to help take the weight — ten men in all, gripping the heavy ropes that straddled the open tomb, all of them gritting their teeth to allow Lady Melville a slow and dignified descent into the gaping tomb. Constance gripped her cloak and I searched Edmund's face. He stood upright and proud, his mouth held tight, a stoical tilt to his chin, and I knew I must show the same courage.

The straps and ropes gently lowered into the grave, the men bowed, stepping carefully away to join the circle of mourners. Once again, Adam looked at Constance, his white bands blown by the wind. With one hand holding his hat, he held out the other, helping her up the makeshift wooden steps and I followed as Constance's gloved hand gripped mine. Fresh earth had been placed above her father's bones, a layer of sweet-smelling rushes, but the strench of death lingered. On the ground below, Reverend Kemp's words blew in the wind. *Earth to earth, ashes to ashes, dust to dust. In sure and certain hope of the Resurrection into eternal life.*

Bethany handed me the two baskets of herbs I had spent the morning gathering. I could find only a few and had dried them by the fire — snow-dusted stalks with just the faintest fragrance. Others had been gleaned from wardrobes or found hanging in closets — rosemary for remembrance, lavender for peace, lemon balm and thyme for healing. Taking each bunch in turn, Constance threw them on to her mother's coffin and I reached into the basket, handing her the dish of dried rose petals I had taken from my room.

'And rose petals for love,' Connie said, a tear rolling down her cheek.

'Amen.' Reverend Kemp gently shut the Bible and we stood in silence, Edmund's eyes pooling with tears. I slipped to his side, putting my arm through his. A fine tremor shook his sleeve, he seemed uncertain what to do, and I drew him closer, leading the way down the trampled path to the second sledge bearing Mrs Alston's coffin.

'It's taken them all day to dig Mrs Alston's grave — they had to thaw the ground with hot embers.' He took a deep intake of breath, steadying his voice. 'There's something rather awful about a frozen grave. I wish it was otherwise. I wish it were spring or summer so I could send her to rest with the flowers she loved so much.'

No birdsong, no cattle lowing in the field beside us, no sound of sheep, just the icy wind and the fine white snow blowing across the frozen moor. I knew I must think of summer, of the smell of honeysuckle in the hedgerows, of the lambs that would be born. Of the calves we would raise, the laughter of our children. The house needed love, that was all. Edmund needed love. The swallows *would* return, I would plant a rose garden like the one at Trenwyn House and I would fill every room with bowls of rose petals.

'We'll make sure there are always flowers on Mrs Alston's grave . . . and shells and heart-shaped pebbles . . . and everything else you used to run home to give her.'

He gripped my arm. 'I couldn't do this without you. I love you, Amelia. I don't deserve you . . . but I love you so very desperately. I promise I *will* get better and I'll make you so proud of me.' He stopped, the long snake of mourners stopping behind us. His hat was drawn low, dark circles shadowing his eyes. The injury above his lip looked brutal in the daylight, his long sideburns hardly disguising the pitted red scars disfiguring his cheeks. A deep furrow lodged between his heavy black brows, a tightness round his mouth. A face with no laughter lines, no softening round the eyes. He seemed to be struggling to find the right words.

219

'What is it?' I whispered.

His chest rose and fell, his breathing faster. His hands began shaking, a look of panic in his face. 'I can't keep you against your will . . . You're free to go. I can't and won't hold you to our engagement.'

My throat was dry, my words a whisper. Deep in my chest, my heart burst into a thousand fragments. 'I know. It will be my choice to stay.'

'You look cold, Amelia. It's far too cold. We need to go in. We must get you to a fire.' His hand pressed against his forehead. 'We shouldn't be out here in this weather.'

A knot twisted my stomach and I fought my tears. 'Edmund . . . we're here to bury Mrs Alston — we're here because it's her funeral . . . do you remember?'

He looked round at the watching faces, a flash of sudden panic. 'Mrs Alston . . . yes, of course . . . Amelia, please help me . . . I don't know what to do.'

I took his arm. He was so vulnerable, Constance was wrong to be angry. She must never let him hear what the servants were saying — that his beloved Mrs Alston had thrown herself down the stairs because she had bought the tincture from the rogue peddler. 'Come, stay by my side. I'll tell you what to say.'

He must never know that if he had come home just one month sooner, neither of them might have died.

26

I left Edmund in his study, a cold towel pressed against his forehead. His headache had become blinding, a terrible nausea making it difficult for him to lift his head. He was asleep, a blanket keeping him warm, and I slipped on my cloak, opening the heavy back door.

The huge moon bathed the courtyard in silver light. The wind had dropped, the steady sound of icicles dripping from the eaves. A brazier was burning, lanterns hanging either side of the open barn doors. Instructions from the kitchen echoed across the well-trodden snow, a fiddler playing, the sound of voices drifting from inside the barn. Seth knocked out his pipe and came to my side.

'The wind's dropped, Miss Carew. It's gettin' warmer. I reckon we should leave tomorrow — leave too late an' the roads will be awash. The snow will melt to a quagmire. We need to leave while the snow's firm enough to take the wheels.'

'Will the drifts be clear?' As a child, I would have crossed every finger and tried to cross my toes.

He must have heard the hope in my voice. 'I'll get you home, Miss Amelia. I've had men workin' on the dell — they've taken horses up an' down all day and so long as we use the brakes, I reckon we'll make it to the top. Once atop, there's every chance of gettin' back safe — if we take it slow. The post's through from

221

Bodmin to Truro so it's just the first two miles to watch. I'd rather go while the snow's firm — or we'll have to wait.'

'My parents have been told?'

He nodded. 'They know ye're safe. John rode the mare through the snow. He's back now — that's how I know about the post gettin' through.' He was hardly wrapped up against the weather, his head uncovered, his short grey hair bright in the moonlight, his smile lighting his face, and I had to turn away. He was my parents' coachman. He would stay with them and I would no longer have him by my side.

From the age of two, he had taken me wherever I wanted to go: letting me take the reins up and down the long drive, stopping to build bonfires, eating imaginary food off bark plates. He had helped me run away more times than I could remember. Sometimes Frederick and I would kidnap him; often we would use his coach as our ship. Latterly, he would load it up with my herbs and take them all over Cornwall.

He pointed to the open barn door. 'Miss Melville's done her mother proud — her and Reverend Kemp. She wanted to say goodbye properly . . . with a proper wake as befitting the custom of the house. Reverend Kemp's roasted her a huge ham an' the biggest goose I've ever seen. Said it was his oldest gander — said the bugger had been biting him!' He laughed. 'Well, the bugger bit him once too often, an' we're to benefit. Are ye to join us, Miss Amelia?'

There was tenderness in his voice, a touch of sadness; a burly man, with the softest of hearts and I put out my arm like I had done at countless harvest suppers. 'Will you be my escort?'

'Would be my honour, Miss Carew.'

A long trestle table had been laid, lamps burning from hooks, the white linen tablecloth overlaid with trails of ivy. Knives and forks were set, three large earthenware bowls overflowing with boiled potatoes and parsnips. There must have been twenty-five or more crammed along the benches, sitting in solemn reverence as Reverend Kemp held up his knife to slice the huge roast goose. Fat splashed on to his apron and he looked at Adam, indicating to stop playing his fiddle and help me to my seat.

Adam had taken off his heavy black coat and was wearing a fine tweed waistcoat, his sleeves rolled to the elbow, his cleric bands swapped for a white cravat. His red hair was ruffled, swaying in time to the lament he was playing. He saw me and nodded, putting down his fiddle, leading me to the head of the table. 'Will Sir Edmund be joining us?'

'I'm afraid not. His headache has worsened.'

Eyes turned, everyone rising to their feet in respectful silence. I smiled back at them, raising my voice. 'I'm afraid Sir Edmund isn't well enough to join us, but he wants you all to enjoy the evening. Please, sit . . . I believe we have Reverend Kemp to thank for this funeral feast?'

He stood to say grace and as the Amen echoed to the rafters, a woman in a white apron started handing out bread from a huge basket. Another woman was refilling cups from a pewter jug and

I had to look twice. Constance came to my side, putting down the jug, smiling to the man next to me as he shifted down the bench to make room.

'Edmund wouldn't permit me to feed everyone in the house, so I arranged for our funeral dinner to be in the barn. I won't send people away hungry. They've worked very hard for us and they deserve to be thanked.' She spoke so quietly, I could hardly hear her.

'Of course,' I whispered back.

'I wanted to tell you, but I didn't want Edmund to forbid it. I know he'll be cross, but I'm prepared to shoulder his displeasure.'

She got up to help serve the goose, but Adam put his hand on her shoulder. 'I'll help Father. You sit down — you must be tired.' His smile lit his face, the warmth of his affection burning his eyes. Lanterns hung from the heavy oak beams, two cats watching us from the top of a stack of straw. Behind us, horses nuzzled bags of hay in their wooden stalls, everyone rosy-cheeked from the biting wind, ready to do justice to the golden-crusted goose and the huge loin of ham.

'Reverend Kemp likes cooking,' Constance said, watching the old man place slice after slice onto a silver platter. 'He's been a widower for twenty years — Adam likes to cook, too. He made the bread.'

The affection between the two men was obvious. Adam started handing round the goose, laughing with the men as he served them, asking the blacksmith to carve the ham, another to follow him with the boiled potatoes. Halfway down the bench, Bethany made room for Seth, smiling as his great bulk squeezed beside her. 'Is Adam the only son?'

Constance's eyes had never left him. 'Yes. That's why he came back from Oxford. He was offered another living, but his heart's here. He won't leave his father . . . and his school is doing well. It's getting a very good reputation.'

'I remember him telling me he liked collecting minerals.'

She nodded, looking up at Adam who stood behind us. 'You have a very fine collection of minerals, don't you, Adam? Come . . . it's your turn to sit down. I'll take round the next platter.'

She was wearing a black silk gown with long sleeves. Flushed like the rest of us, she looked poised and dignified, yet gracious and charitable, and my respect for her deepened. So, too, my respect for the cook. I thought I would only eat sparingly but just one bite and I knew I would finish my plate. There was much appreciation in the faces around me, such companionship and friendship, everyone raising their glasses to commemorate the lives of their mistress and the formidable woman who had run the house with clockwork precision — Mrs Alston, beloved and feared in equal measure.

When the last of the apple pie had been cleared away, Adam reached for his fiddle and began playing a hymn. At once, a man's rich voice started singing, others joining in, their voices growing stronger, rising in volume. The barn's rafters formed an arch above us as grand as any church and my heart swelled with sudden, inexplicable certainty. The swallows *would* come back to the east window. There *would* be happiness again in the house. Happiness and love.

No one sang like that in our church, but as the drinks were refilled and the benches pushed back, the volume increased. Reverend Kemp had brought a handful of hymn books, but everyone knew the words, their voices soaring, echoing round the oak rafters; each one of us happy and sad at the same time; each singing hymns for those we had lost, and for those we could never bear to lose.

A movement by the door made me turn round. Edmund was standing in the shadows watching us. He stood back, quickly hiding from sight and I knew I must go to him.

'Who organized this?' His voice sounded strangled.

'Constance didn't want anyone to go hungry. She was worried she wouldn't be able to manage without Annie . . . and you forbade her the house.'

'Only because I didn't want to put any extra strain on my servants who are without their housekeeper. How have they managed a funeral feast?'

'Reverend Kemp offered to help . . . he likes cooking — he and Adam both do. They roasted the meats in the vicarage and brought them over.' My mouth was dry, a terrible pounding in my chest.

'On the same sledge we carried Mother and Mrs Alston to their graves?' He sounded distant, his hat pulled low, his black coat concealing him in the darkness.

I stood watching the gathering through his eyes — Adam and Constance at one end of the long table, Reverend Kemp in his splattered apron at the other. Adam had put down his fiddle and was singing Psalm 23, Constance standing by his side, their voices rising in perfect harmony, two rows of tearful eyes watching them. 'You were in such pain, Edmund . . . you were feeling sick . . . so I greeted them for you. Constance never intended — '

He grasped his head between his hands. 'I should be at the head of that table. I should be there, thanking everyone for their help . . . not cowering in the shadows, too frightened to step forward.' He gripped his shoulders as if hugging himself. 'But I can't . . . I want to be there, I want it so badly, but my body won't let me. I see their faces and I freeze. I lose my words — my whole reason. I just freeze . . . you've noticed it, I know you have.' He looked up, his huge black pupils lost in the darkness.

'Come with me now,' I whispered. 'Come and join them for a few minutes. I'll be right beside you. I'll hold your arm. Just thank them for coming and then wish them all goodnight.'

Sweat glimmered on his upper lip, sheer panic in his voice. 'I can't, Mel. I can't. I thought I could, but I can't . . . Please don't make me.' His tremor was back, his hands trembling against his face.

'Then we'll go back to the house and sit by the fire. Or would you prefer to retire to your room?' I reached for my cloak, which I had left hanging at the door.

'I just need to breathe the night air.' He gripped my hand and we stood in the moonlight, the singing drifting through the open door behind us. He seemed to grow calmer. 'I'm sorry you had to witness that.'

'I'll help you, Edmund.'

'You have no idea how much just having you here means to me. I can't imagine how I would have got through all this without you.' He looked up at the huge moon shining above us. 'My one symbol of hope . . . a constant beacon telling me not to give up. It's our moon, Mel . . . I promise I'll do everything I can to get better . . . to make you proud of me again.'

Three years of staring up at the moon, hoping and praying for his safe return, six months of turning from it because it was too painful even to even glimpse it: a whole year of sending out new shoots, feeling renewal and happiness through the love for another man. It felt like treachery, the worse kind of disloyalty.

'I can't stay, Edmund. I need to go home. Seth wants us to leave before the roads become impassable — he's just told me the conditions would be best tomorrow. He'd like to leave before the snow melts.'

'Of course, I can't keep you, though I want you to stay more than anything.' He took off his hat, pulling me slowly towards him, his jacket against my cloak. Resting his forehead against the top of my head, he breathed in the lilac essence I used in my hair. 'Mel, would Lady Clarissa mind if Constance came back with you to Truro?'

I felt uncomfortable in his arms, a sudden rise in my heartbeat. 'No, of course not, Mother would be delighted to have her visit . . . but don't you need her here?'

He breathed deeply, smelling my hair. 'I think it best, under the circumstances. We must separate her from that man.'

A cold shard pierced my heart, he was using my pet name yet there was such authority in his voice. 'But, is it really so terrible? Constance is seventeen and Adam is kind and respectable . . . I believe she really does love him . . . and you always said how much you admired him. Surely you can allow her to marry for love?'

His lips began brushing my hair, tentative at first then growing firmer. 'Of course, she must marry for love. But not Adam Kemp. I do like him, I've always liked him, but Mother was adamant she didn't want Constance to marry him.'

'Edmund . . . we were seventeen when we got engaged. I know it's young but . . . ' My heart was pounding, a twist in my stomach.

His voice softened, his breath on my face. 'It's not her age, Mel. Constance is the sister of a baronet and whoever she marries must enhance our family not disgrace it. I have to honour Mother's wishes. I must do *something* right. I've failed her in just about everything else.'

Rough cheeks, bristles where there had never been bristles, sideburns where there had always been smooth skin; no longer the youth I loved but a mature man with a man's needs. His kisses were strengthening, growing more urgent.

'Edmund . . . you never failed your mother.'

'I did, Mel. I failed her in just about everything I did. Dr Trefusis said her heart weakened but we all know I caused her death — she died of a broken heart, of years of uncertainty and sorrow. I should have come sooner — just one month earlier and she wouldn't have needed that potion. That's the truth I have to live with.' His voice was hoarse, filled with remorse. 'And what if the rumours are true? What if our dearest Mrs Alston threw herself down the stairs because she thought she was responsible? Because no matter how innocently, she was the one who bought the poison and gave it to Mama? That's what they're saying.'

The cold shard pierced me again. Constance had no reason to tell him. 'It was an accident, Edmund. Mrs Alston was distressed . . . she was in a terrible panic. She caught her foot and tripped. She fell down the stairs and knocked her head. She was old and frail and she took such a blow. It was an accident.'

His breathing became heavier. 'Either way, I should have been here with her, and I need to make amends — for Connie's sake, at least. She's borne the burden of an impoverished house for too long. She wears aprons and carries trays — she fraternizes more with servants than her own class. She meets no one, at least no one of any worth.' His lips pressed against my forehead. 'It's unfair, Mel; Connie needs to spread her wings. She needs to go to concerts and be introduced to suitable young men. Mama

230

spoke of it. She was very concerned that Connie's childhood infatuation with Adam Kemp might lead her to do something foolish.'

My cheeks, he was kissing my cheeks. He would soon reach my lips. He was so physical, so strong, almost too fierce. I felt no responding desire, just a flash of terror.

'It would be a pleasure to have her — Mother would love her to come and stay. We both would.'

'I'll come to Truro and visit you. I need to see a doctor — Connie seemed very taken with that Dr Bohenna, should I see him, do you think?'

His lips were hovering over mine, slightly apart, the unfamiliar scent of tobacco on his breath. He lifted my chin, pulling my face to his. 'No . . . not Dr Bohenna . . . Dr Nankivell has always been our doctor . . . and Cordelia's brother's coming back — he's been in the navy. He'll know everything there is to know about tropical diseases.'

His lips remained open, poised, edging closer. 'Back there . . . in the barn — do you remember the day we were in the hayloft and Francis came looking for us? We didn't hear him climb the ladder and he caught us in the hay? Do you remember?'

His breath was pungent. I should not feel like this. I should be thrilling at his touch, wanting him to kiss me. 'Yes, I remember.' Under his satin waistcoat and breeches, I felt the muscles of a sailor — hard tight muscles full of power. His lips brushed mine and I tried not to recoil.

'We'll go back there. When I'm better, we'll go

231

back to the hayloft — just like before. Poor Francis.'

'Why poor Francis?'

His arms tightened, squeezing me to him. 'He was in love with you. Everyone was in love with you and yet you chose me. I can't tell you how that made me feel. It was like having wings . . . like I could conquer the world. The most beautiful, intelligent girl in the whole of Cornwall — in the whole world — choosing *me* when you could have chosen anyone.'

The singing was reaching new heights, the brazier almost burnt out: the snow was glistening, a steady drip from the eaves; an enchanted night, yet I forced back my tears, turning my face from him.

'Don't cry, my love, please don't cry.' His whisper was urgent, full of tenderness. 'I've frightened you . . . I'm so sorry . . . it's too early — I've been a clumsy fool. It's just I love you so much, and I've waited so long. I *will* get better and I'll make you so proud of me. When that shipment arrives I'll have the means to pay off our debts and I'll give you everything I've ever promised you. That order was *my* order, Mel. *My shipment.*'

I stared across the moonlit cobbles, tears stinging my eyes. His arms tightened round me. 'Everything will be as it should be — I'll trade in spice again. I'll make us a fortune and we'll fill this house with laughter, just like we said we would.'

★ ★ ★

The door to the kitchen was ajar and I peered slowly round the door, desperate not to be seen with such red-rimmed eyes. Large stone jars, china tureens and jelly moulds stood in long rows on the shelves, a huge dresser at one end, a hearth with copper pans hanging from large hooks at the other. Plates piled high on the scrubbed pine table, the carcass of the goose stripped clean. The maids would soon be in to wash the dishes but for the moment, there was no one there and I seized my chance. A large kettle steamed on the griddle and I reached for a cloth, taking the handle in both hands.

I had turned from him, rejected his kiss.

He thought I could not see his tears as he walked slowly up to his room. He had tried to conceal his hurt with words of hope and promise, wishing me goodnight, but I had seen the desolation in his eyes, and at the turn of the stairs I had watched him reach for his handkerchief and bury his head in his hands.

★ ★ ★

Rose petals calm the nerves, relieve insomnia, and can be used to overcome the physical fatigue of grief. Place half an ounce of rose petals in warm water and allow to steep for five minutes. Do not oversweeten as the flavour is mild.

THE LADY HERBALIST

27

No wind, clear skies, even a glimpse of the sun, and Seth was anxious to set off. Bethany rearranged the rugs on our knees and I pulled up the carriage window, waving to Edmund who stood watching us leave. Awkwardness lodged between us, his sudden shyness adding to the strange formality of our departure. He stood stiff-backed and stoical, telling us his darkened glasses protected his eyes from the glare of the snow, but I believed he was hiding his tears and felt torn with remorse.

Eight men were to walk at our side, two men per wheel, ready to apply the heavy brakes to stop the coach from rolling backwards. Frost had settled on the drifts, the ground crisp, the men's boots crunching the snow and I crossed my fingers, glancing up at the heavily laden branches hanging above us. I was desperate to leave, and so was Constance. I could see it in the way she did not look back, her abrupt farewell to her brother as she took her seat in the coach.

We pulled forward, starting slowly up the steep hill. The night had brought more frost; there was no sign of a melt, no ice on the road, just a firm grip beneath the wheels. The carriage stopped at the top and Seth shouted.

'Thank you . . . that'll do. We'll be all right from here. No need to come any further.'

The white moor glistened in the strengthening sun and we settled back, wrapped in our cloaks, the hot coals keeping our feet warm. A series of tracks showed carriages had already passed, and our progress became steady; no melt, no quagmires, no drifts, just the intensely blue sky and the vast snow-covered moor sparkling in the sun. Constance drew a deep breath.

'His glasses come from Venice. They wear them there because the sunlight on the lagoon is so bright it hurts their eyes, but I think on days like this we could all do with a pair.'

Seth did not stop but kept up a slow pace, the rhythmical jolting lulling Bethany to sleep. Constance opened her embroidered purse and brought out a letter. 'Edmund gave me this to give to your mother. He wants her to find me a suitable husband.'

I smiled in what I hoped looked like encouragement. 'Mother's very good at that sort of thing. A lot of her friends ask her for introductions. Edmund says he wants you to go to concerts and maybe a few balls.'

She put the letter away, her mouth tightening. 'So soon? Am I not allowed to grieve? I'm sorry, Amelia, it's just my brother has very decided opinions.'

This time my smile was heartfelt. 'I don't want to go anywhere either and Mother certainly won't make you.'

The hours passed, each of us lost to our own thoughts. I had turned from his kiss, shown him coldness, not love, and now he would be alone in that austere house, left to grieve by himself. It seemed so cruel. He did not deserve that. The carriage began its slow descent, a row of tall chimneys showing red against the bright blue sky.

I had never been so glad to see the rooftops of Truro.

★ ★ ★

Mother could read me like a book and I knew not to look at her. I avoided Papa's gaze, too, embracing them back, rushing Constance to the fire, telling them everything about the journey — the two deaths, the funerals and the feast; telling them nothing about how my heart was breaking. Papa stood in his beloved felt hat, his large farmer's hands grasping Connie's. 'My dear Miss Melville, your misfortune is indeed our gain. You must stay as long as you like.'

Mother put down her new lorgnettes, a slight shake to her head. She refolded Edmund's letter. 'You're in mourning, for goodness' sake. Concerts and balls can wait . . . and so can any thought of marriage. He suggests new gowns, would you consider some new mourning gowns, my dearest? Only, Amelia has one she can lend you . . . ?' She looked up at Connie's tentative nod. 'Excellent, we shall arrange that. And shall we learn to speak Italian, only there's an Italian Count in town and he's offering to give me lessons?'

Papa beamed with pleasure. 'And I can

236

explain my new breeding programme to you, my dear. Those moors of yours are all very well in the summer, but in the winter?' He shook his head. 'Sheep have to be hardy up there, don't they? Poor creatures buried up there in all that snow.'

Mother was wearing her bright red Chinese gown. It flowed long and loose, the huge sleeves hanging down either side of her. Her hair was softly coiled, her turban glinting with coloured glass. 'Do you like baking, Constance? I do hope you do.'

Light streamed through the huge sash windows, the black-and-white marble floor glinting in the sun. Everywhere light and air, and love, my unconventional parents wrapping Constance in their warm affection. I had to excuse myself, run upstairs to my room.

I knew Mother would follow. She limped across the floor, standing behind me as I stared into my dressing table mirror. 'I'm glad you brought Constance back with you.'

'She wanted to come. She asked if she could come first, then Edmund asked me if we wouldn't mind having her to stay.' She was looking at the faded red leather cover of Luke's father's herbal and I knew I must answer her unspoken question. 'I'm going to give it back to Luke. I can't keep it now.'

'Mr Burrows, the publisher, left his card yesterday. He's staying at the Red Lion. Now you're back, I'll send him word that you can see him.'

I shook my head. 'I can't go through with it, Mother. Not now.'

'You can, my dear, and you must.' Her voice took on the tone of my childhood, kind but firm. 'What if he likes them and *does* want to publish them? Luke can't give it to me as a present — not now . . . anyway . . . I've decided against it. I don't want my prints to be published.'

Her mouth tightened, her chin dipping as her eyes searched my face. 'You have to show them to him, Amelia. He's made a long journey and it would be an appalling lack of manners to turn him away. If he wants to publish them, then you must accept graciously.'

Tears stung my eyes. 'Mother, that was all before. It's different now . . . and it's not what I want.'

'Amelia, you must go ahead — not just for Luke but for all the physicians and apothecaries who will use your paintings to distinguish one herb from another. Let alone all the women and mothers of children who will read every word and follow your recipes. And if you won't do it for them, then you must simply do it to show everyone what a woman is capable of doing. Don't hide your light . . . let it shine.'

'You haven't asked me anything about Edmund,' I whispered.

'I don't need to, my love. It's in your eyes, your brave smile, the falseness of your laughter.'

'I just need more time.'

Her voice softened, her hand on my shoulder. 'To do the right thing? To marry him because you *believe* you must?'

'I don't *believe* I must . . . I just *must*.

Mother, Edmund's come back a broken man — he's suffered unimaginable hardship. He's thrown into blind panics . . . he gets confused, he can't sleep at night for terrors. The man I love is still there . . . shaking and vulnerable. He freezes in company . . . he forgets where he is. He's been the subject of great brutality and he needs help to know he's safe . . . that he's loved. That everything he's gone through has ended. Only his love for me kept him going . . . and now he needs me more than ever.'

'Of course he does, and you must help him recover, but you don't have to marry him.'

'What if it was Frederick? What if Frederick returned broken and vulnerable and Charity decided he wasn't the man he had been . . . that she no longer loved him? Can you imagine how Frederick would feel? You think it was just a youthful infatuation, but it wasn't. I loved Edmund with all my heart and he loved me. I vowed to love him and you don't just abandon a man because his suffering has changed him . . . you love him *because* his suffering has changed him, and he needs your help.'

She held my gaze in the mirror, her hand tightening on my shoulder. 'My dearest, you think I don't understand but I do. It is the suffering to come that worries me — the inevitable years of pain. Years of watching the light leave your eyes and your laughter become stilted.'

'I love him. I'll always love him.'

'I know, my love. That's what I mean. But it's Edmund you're planning to marry.'

Pain ripped through me. 'Don't . . . please

239

don't. I was talking about Edmund — you know I was.'

She took the faded book from my hand, opening the page to Luke's father's cramped writing, his remedies and wise advice written sideways against the printed words, other pages inserted, stuck in with glue. 'I shall send word to Mr Burrows that you are free to see him tomorrow at eleven, and to save you any embarrassment with Luke, your father and I will pay any publishing expenses. But you must have your work published for Luke's sake.'

In the silence. I fought to breathe. Already I felt different, a terrible loneliness nestling in my heart. Sun was streaming through the huge casement window, the sky outside a glorious blue, but all joy had left me. In a moment the gold clock on my mantelpiece would chime two o'clock — every day from now on, I would have to endure the sound of the clock chiming two.

It began to strike, and I looked away. Mother reached for her handkerchief, her voice breaking. 'My foot has almost healed. I have just one more appointment and then I believe I can remove these heavy bandages. Luke won't come to the house again unless you invite him.'

The door closed behind her and I threw myself on my bed. The whole way back from Pendowrick I had tried to shake off the gnawing in my stomach. Still it gnawed me, just as I know it had gnawed at Constance. I could not name it before, but now I could.

It was resentment I was feeling: resentment holding me back.

Edmund had not apologized for rushing to join the ship, nor had he asked me to forgive his haste. He had excused his behaviour as weak and foolish and I had been too afraid to say what I really felt. I should have spoken out, cleared the air between us. He had only six months to wait — only *six* months before we could be married. No matter how controlling his father had been, he should have waited those six months.

28

Town House, Truro
Friday 9th February 1798, 11 a.m.

A good night's sleep showed in Constance's face; the shadows under her eyes had lifted, her newly washed hair dancing in curls around her shoulders. Mother had lent her a dark burgundy shawl and black pearl-drop earrings which swung as she talked. 'That must be him now,' she said, peering out of the window.

A gentleman in a heavy overcoat and tall hat was hurrying across the cobbles. Mother put down her pen, getting up from her writing desk. 'And right on time, too.'

Mr Burrows stood at the door, handing his hat and cane to the footman. His wig was grey, his thin face flushed. He had taken off his overcoat and stood in smart tweed breeches and jacket, a buttoned-up woollen waistcoat and a carefully pinned cravat. A pair of round glasses perched halfway down his nose, the eyes above them hardly frightening at all.

Mother, dressed in a conventional silk morning gown and demure headdress, smiled elegantly back at him. Introductions dispensed with she said, 'It's very kind of you to come. How do you find Truro?'

'Very handsome ... there are some fine buildings. And I've been very well looked after in the Red Lion.' His tone matched his clothes, educated and respectful, even a touch shy.

'Splendid. My daughter has laid out her drawings on the table by the window. We thought the light would be best there.'

He went straight to my paintings and I could barely breathe, my heart pounding as he drew out a magnifying glass. He said nothing but slowly examined each drawing in turn, holding them to the window with fixed concentration. A frown creased his brow and Constance handed me a glass of lemonade. I could not drink it.

'Are you familiar with any of the books we publish, Miss Carew?' he said at last.

'Yes, I am. By pure chance, we've just recently come across *The Botanical Prints of Oriental Spices* that you published some time ago. Didn't we, Constance?'

He looked up. '*The Botanical Prints of Oriental Spices?*'

Constance nodded. 'Yes, I believe you were commissioned by my uncle.'

His frown cleared. 'Miss *Melville*? How remiss of me not to recognize the name. I remember your father and I was very sorry to hear of his death.'

'You knew my father?'

'Yes. It was Sir Richard who commissioned the work, not your uncle — the prints of oriental spices were collected and published at your father's request. I remember it very well — indeed, it was my first day at work and no one forgets their first day. My father compiled the book and I had just joined the firm.'

243

He glanced out of the window. 'I delivered the book on a snowy day not unlike the weather we're having now. February, it was — because I joined the firm on my seventeenth birthday. I remember rushing through the snow desperate not to slip. Sir Richard was thrilled with the book and so was Mrs Bainbridge. They were going to the theatre and I think I made them late but they were enthralled with it — just as I hope you will be with yours, Miss Carew.'

He smiled at my sudden intake of breath, looking over his glasses to Mother. 'I have rarely seen such accurate and exquisite drawings, Lady Clarissa. I propose we publish full-colour plates of all twenty. The writing will be interspersed between the sheets and I propose we interlace a fine layer of paper between each of the prints to protect them. I envisage a print run of five hundred. Do you have a title in mind for your work, Miss Carew?'

I stared at him, barely able to speak. 'I thought perhaps we might call it *The Lady Herbalist*.'

'Yes, I like that. I think that captures the essence of the book. I'll need your manuscript and all your descriptions . . . the usage and your remedies, and so on.' He seemed reluctant to leave the table, his eyes not leaving my drawings as a new tension entered his voice. 'Have you asked any other publishers to consider these drawings, Lady Clarissa?'

Mother shook her head. 'No, you are the first to see them, Mr Burrows. If you could send us your exact proposal and the sum you have in mind, my husband and I will give it careful consideration. Though I have to warn you my daughter's drawings are already attracting *considerable attention* and we would prefer to print *more* than five hundred.'

'Indeed, Lady Clarissa. I'm sure you're right. I'll send my proposal to start with a run of a thousand.' He straightened, turning to me. 'Miss Carew, may I congratulate you . . . seldom have I seen such exquisite work. It would be my honour to place your drawings where they can be seen and admired.' His eyes darted to the table again as if reluctant to leave.

'Splendid,' said Mother, 'we await your proposal.' She smiled her most enchanting smile. 'Now, how about some refreshment, Mr Burrows? Would you like a cup of hot chocolate?'

Mr Burrows backed slowly to the door, bowing stiffly. 'Thank you, but no. Another time, Lady Clarissa. I have work to do — my proposal will follow shortly.' Excitement shone in his eyes. 'Believe me; I see a great future for this book.'

I hardly saw him leave. Never in a million years had I expected anyone to publish my prints. I turned to see Constance sit down: just one glance at her face and I rushed to her side.

'Connie . . . are you all right?' She looked ill, as if she might faint. 'Connie, what can I get you?'

'I'm so happy for you . . . I think I'm just a bit hot.'

Mother opened the sash window and Connie breathed the cool air. 'What is it?' I whispered.

She waited for Mother to cross the room to pull the bell rope. 'You heard what he said

245

— Father and Aunt Harriet were together in London. They were going to the theatre.'

'She lived in London ... she was his sister-in-law.'

'But they were *together* — going to the theatre *together*. Amelia, none of us knows when my uncle died — not the exact date. We just assumed it was after Francis was conceived, but it must have been well before. Otherwise the register wouldn't say *father unknown*.'

I sat next to her. 'Oh, my goodness, Connie.'

Her eyes were wide with shock, the colour still drained from her face. 'But he wasn't *unknown*, was he? They all knew who the father was.'

'Connie ... '

'Father commissioned that book — it was his writing in the front. You saw it ... *For Harriet, my dearest love*. Now I think about it, the writing looked familiar ... Amelia, they were lovers — while Mama was down in Cornwall they were in London. Mama miscarried her first child and that's how he treated her?'

Mother held out a glass of lemonade. 'Has the air helped, my dear? No, obviously not. You still look rather unwell.' She pulled down the sash. 'Perhaps you should lie down for a while? You look very shaken.'

'A sudden giddiness, that's all, Lady Clarissa, but the air's helped. Would you mind very much if Amelia and I took a short walk round the square? I'm so sorry to cause you such concern.'

A firm believer in fresh air and exercise, Mother nodded. 'Of course not. A brisk walk always does one good.' Her eyes followed us to the door. 'Wrap up warmly, though — the sun may be shining but there is still ice in that wind.'

* * *

There was no one bv the church railings and we linked arms, crossing the square to the privacy of the side entrance and the stone seat in the porch. 'We're out of sight — lean forward, put your head between your knees. Take some deep breaths.'

Constance held her bonnet and bent forward, her head on her knees. 'It's passing. I feel better now. They were lovers, I know they were — Mama's own sister. No wonder Mama hated Francis — that marked passage in her Bible was about her sister. Amelia, just imagine being betrayed by the people you love the most. That must be why she hated Father — she couldn't find it in her heart to forgive them.'

'Maybe Sir Richard only paid for the book . . . ' Even as I said it, I knew Constance must be right.

'It was Father's writing. Why didn't I see it before? And Mother must have known. She removed the page from the register to protect us — not her sister.' She straightened, taking a deep breath. 'Francis was our half-brother. That's why he looked so like us. We shared *all four grandparents*.'

Guilt sliced my heart. Edmund must have found out too — of course he could not wait another six months. He wanted to get away from them. He'd discovered the truth and could not tell me. No wonder he was envious of the close relationship Francis had with his father. He had taken all he could of their mocking taunts: Francis, the son of the woman Sir Richard adored, Edmund the son of a woman he barely tolerated.

'It makes sense now. The signs are never wrong.' Constance stared into the distance, her eyes widening. 'The night Francis died, I heard the water in the parlour.'

'Connie . . . there's no water in the parlour.'

'There was. And it's not *in* the parlour, it's under the floor. A leat runs under the house — a brick tunnel used in Tudor times to flush the garderobes. It's still there but it's dry. That night, I heard it in full stream.'

A shiver ran down my spine. 'It must have been raining very hard.'

'No, it was a hot day when I heard the water. They say you hear it when a son of the house dies in violent circumstances. It's since the Civil War. The house was being searched by Parliamentarians — the heir of Pendowrick was hiding in the tunnel and he nearly escaped. The soldiers were leaving, but one of them had been sweet-talking a maid and she glanced down at the flagstones. They found him and dragged him off. Days later, he was hung, drawn and quartered.'

Her mouth tightened. 'When Edmund's letter arrived and we knew he was safe, I was so relieved. After the water, I was convinced he was dead. But then I decided the water I heard must have been for Francis because he'd been brought up as a son of the house. But it makes sense now because he *was a son*.' She caught her breath. 'Those crows are watching us — they're just like Francis and Father.'

Two crows were inching towards us, huge black birds with piercing eyes. Their feathers shimmered in the sun, strong, powerful, and I fought my fear. Connie's quiet conviction, her belief that the sound of water made sense; she was living with ghosts, her world inhabited by signs and omens. No wonder Edmund thought she should get away from the house.

Her voice was cold. 'Francis was no brother to me. He once dunked me in a horse trough just to ruin my new shoes. I tried to dry them but Mama was furious. She said I had ruined them with no thought to the cost, and I was too scared to tell her what he had done. And Francis just watched . . . with that sly smirk of his. He's no brother to me.'

We needed time before we returned to the house and sat watching people hurrying down the High Street towards the quay. Eventually, I spoke. 'The ships must be arriving. Do you feel strong enough to go down to the wharf? We could see if Elizabeth is at home?'

Connie got to her feet, her head high as she walked defiantly past the watching crows. 'Yes, I'm all right now. It's just good to know the truth. Do you mean Elizabeth Fox? I'd love to see her. We can tell her your wonderful news. Wasn't your mother marvellous? *One thousand* copies. And they're to pay *you*. I can hardly take it in.'

Mother was looking out of the window and we waved as we passed, pointing in the direction of the wharf so she knew where we were going. Constance looked stronger, the colour back in her cheeks and we walked in step, joining the steady stream of people heading down Quay Street. The tide would be in, the water high — the same river that curved in a bay below my herb garden in Trenwyn House.

A sudden weight crushed my chest. Someone would have to oversee the growing and distribution of my herbs. All deliveries to the apothecaries must be maintained; I *had* to keep my promise to supply the new infirmary. Panic ripped through me, a sense of betrayal. I did not *dabble* in herbs — I lived and breathed them. Edmund must understand that. Every herb had been planted for him, each painted with only him in mind, my heart in every brushstroke, but what if he did not approve of the book? What if he did not let me continue?

I had to stop, pretend to admire a bonnet in a shop window. 'That's very pretty,' I said, trying to fight my sudden panic.

I hardly saw the woman leaving the shop and almost bumped into her. She had extraordinarily high cheekbones and blood-red lips, her thick black hair coiled beneath her ruby-red bonnet.

'I'm so sorry — Oh, it's you, Miss Carew. Good morning,' she said in her thick Portuguese accent.

'Mrs Oakley . . . what a lovely coincidence. May I introduce my friend, Miss Melville?'

She curtseyed deeply. She was wearing the

same silk gown she had worn before, but the cuffs of her sleeves had been replaced with fresh white lace. Her heavy cloak seemed to swamp her, but her eyes looked bright, her olive complexion less sallow. She seemed suddenly shy. 'I'm just delivering some gloves . . . '

'Are you well? How is Joe?'

Her smile faded, a sudden frown across her high forehead. 'My son's still troubled by his cough. It's a bit better, but sometimes it can be quite severe.' She twisted her gloved hands. 'Though your tincture brings him great relief.'

She turned quickly, her frown deepening to concern. Joe was hurtling down the street, weaving his way between the groups of people. He was running fast, cap in hand, and he doubled up when he reached us. Trying to catch his breath, I heard a wheeze in his gasp, saw a blueness to his lips.

'Mama . . . I've just . . . ' He gulped for air, his small chest rising and falling.

'Take your time, Joe. Steady your breathing. Only speak when you're ready.'

Joseph Oakley's huge eyes stared at his mother. He looked gaunt and thin, a definite blue tinge to his lips. 'I've just seen Mr Daniel . . . as plain as anything.' He gulped for air. 'He was walking down the quayside . . . and I tried to follow . . . but he was walking too fast . . . I couldn't keep up . . . and I lost him in the crowd.' His voice was rasping, his words coming in snatches. 'Honest to God . . . it was him, plain as day.'

He threw his arms back, his chin held high,

fighting for breath. His heavy jacket seemed to restrict him, his woollen scarf too tight. Sofia Oakley pulled away his scarf, hurrying to undo his buttons.

'Purse your lips as if you're going to whistle,' I said quickly. 'Make an 'O', like this. Force your breath in slowly through your lips. Don't gasp, just force your breath slowly in and out. Does that help?' He nodded. 'Good. Don't try to talk.'

Sofia Oakley watched her son's lips change from blue to pink and tears welled in her eyes. She loosened his collar. 'You saw Mr Daniel? Joe, are you certain? Mr Philip Daniel was getting off a ship . . . here, in Truro? Perhaps he's trying to find us?'

Joe shook his head. 'Not getting off the ship, though I suspect he might have . . . he was walking along the quayside. Honest . . . as plain as anything. Only his beard was clean shaven and he looked . . . you know . . . richer.' He drew a wheezy breath. 'His clothes were fancier — not like the old ones he wore on the ship.'

'Who is Mr Daniel?' I asked.

'A passenger with us — he was already on the ship when we embarked. We joined him in Mombasa.'

'He must be looking for you. Did you give him your address in Truro?'

'No . . . we hardly spoke. He kept himself to himself. Sometimes he helped sail the ship but he never ate with us. Maybe he got our address from the East India Company — or the insurance company?' Tears filled her eyes. 'No, that can't be. If he was getting off a ship, he's probably come from Falmouth.'

'Was he in the rowing boat with you — or was he one of the men they kept on the ship?'

'Neither — he stayed behind in Lisbon. He had a fierce argument with Captain Banyan, his spices were spoiling and he was adamant we had to leave. The shipment was already late because we'd suffered terrible storms and he was under pressure to fulfil his contract. It was because of him we sailed but he stayed in Lisbon. He never came back to the ship.'

'He stayed behind, yet his spices remained on the ship? Why would he do that?'

She reached for her handkerchief, giving it to Joe. 'Captain Banyan said Mr Daniel sent a message to sail without him — that he was staying behind to broker more deals.'

Joe's huge black eyes blinked back at her. 'I lost him in Prince's Street. He was carrying a large bag and walking very fast.'

I felt suddenly hopeful. 'Whatever his actions, it's wonderful he's in Truro. It's just what you need, Mrs Oakley. He'll be able to verify who you are . . . he can sign an affidavit swearing to your presence on the ship, then you can claim your insurance and . . . well . . . Mr Daniel knew about your silks, didn't he? He must have seen them in the hold?'

Sofia Oakley nodded. 'He will know me, and he'll certainly be able to verify my cargo of silks . . . but don't you see? I mustn't raise my hopes.'

'Why not?' He's the one man who can identify you. He can tell the insurance company you are who you say you are.'

'But Mrs Fox explained it very clearly — ships that sail *without* an escort fall foul of their contracts and that stops the insurance being valid. She doesn't know if it is the case . . . she was just telling me what usually happens. So the truth is, even if we do find Mr Philip Daniel there's very little chance the cargo will be insured.'

Constance had been silent, her brows creased in concentration. 'Amelia, I recognize that name — where have I heard it before?' She tapped her mouth with her gloved hand. 'Wait, I remember — Edmund's letter . . . the letter about his shipment.' The colour drained from her face. 'It was signed by *Philip Daniel*.'

My heart jolted. 'Mrs Oakley, you said Mr Philip Daniel was a spice merchant?'

'Yes . . . from Sumatra. His spices were spoiling and he was insistent he got them to Bristol.' She took hold of her son's hand. 'I'm so sorry, but I better get Joe out of this cold air. Forgive me if I leave you — I must get Joe warm. Good day, Miss Carew, Miss Melville.'

She curtseyed and we stood staring after her. *There's very little chance the cargo will be insured.* Unease was turning to dread: this was Edmund's shipment, all his hopes pinned on securing a good sale, his pride, his ability to free his family's estate from debt. Even his belief in himself.

'Oh, Connie . . . ' I whispered. 'We need to speak to Elizabeth.'

29

Elizabeth Fox closed the door to her drawing room, ushering us straight to the fireside.

'Yes, I did tell Mrs Oakley it was most likely to be the case. I explained ships that sail without a navy escort — we call them *runners* — jeopardize their insurance the moment they deviate from the agreed terms of their contract. This war is making the seas very treacherous, though some ports are considered safer than others, and certain routes are deemed less hazardous.'

'What if ships have been delayed by bad weather?'

'*Unnecessary* delays and *unwarranted* deviation will invalidate the insurance. The ship's master agrees the route and appropriate time scale before the ship sets sail but there's always an allowance for having to shelter from storms.'

Despite the heat from the fire, I felt chilled to the bone. Constance seemed calmer, as though she had never expected Edmund's shipment to arrive. 'So why didn't Captain Banyan wait to be escorted?'

Elizabeth clasped her hands as if in prayer. 'From what Mrs Oakley told me, I understand there was a fierce argument. Philip Daniel offered to pay Captain Banyan a substantial amount of money. I can only imagine that neither of them had sailed those waters for a couple of years and after the miles they'd covered England must have seemed very close. They might have dismissed the warnings as scaremongering.'

'But they should have listened to our navy!' Constance's voice was fierce, the steel back in her eyes.

'Indeed they should. But the spices were spoiling — they may have rotted. The delays Mrs Oakley spoke of might have already negated the insurance.'

She sounded cautious but there was something in her tone. 'Elizabeth . . . what aren't you saying?'

'I don't want to raise your hopes, my dear.'

'Please do . . . please give us every hope. Sofia Oakley's future depends on this shipment . . . and Elizabeth, Edmund needs this shipment too . . . ' I glanced at Constance. 'You must have heard the rumours of the family's financial difficulties?'

Elizabeth nodded, her heart-shape lips pursing. 'Yes . . . I have. But I have to say, if this is Edmund's shipment — and I believe it is — then his claim for insurance might prove difficult.'

'Because there was no escort?'

Her white bonnet framed her troubled face. She shrugged her shoulders. 'Not entirely. I have grave misgivings about this case. Why didn't Mr Daniel return to the ship? Was it really to broker new deals, or was it because he knew the ship was likely to be seized by the enemy?'

Constance gripped my arm. 'Philip Daniel paid Captain Banyan to endanger the ship but remained behind because he knew it would be taken?'

Elizabeth ushered us to some chairs and we

256

sat stiffly, waiting as she chose her words.

'I think it very likely that we'll find Philip Daniel negotiated *further* insurance in Lisbon — an expensive but valid insurance for the cargo to sail without an escort.' She reached for the newspaper on the table. 'Since the Dutch ceded ownership of Ceylon, the supply of spices has increased. Prices have fluctuated and I imagine Philip Daniel was anxious to catch the Christmas market.'

She turned the pages of the newspaper, running her finger down the print. '*Cinnamon — 12 shillings a pound, Nutmeg — 33 shillings, Black Ginger £3.5.* Here's more . . . *Cinnamon — 30 bales in lots at 12 shillings per pound.*' She looked up. 'Last year, we were insuring cinnamon at 15 shillings a pound.'

'Surely, if the spices were spoiling he wouldn't get new insurance?'

Elizabeth sighed. 'Not everyone has your goodness, Miss Melville. Merchants can be very underhand. What I'm saying is that he may have re-insured the cargo — and the insurance would cover being lost at sea, or taken as a prize by an enemy ship.'

'He was prepared to send a ship's crew into danger — a ship with a woman and child onboard?' It was too awful to consider. 'Edmund would never want his debt cleared through such disregard for human life.'

Elizabeth saw my revulsion and her eyes filled with love. 'It was Captain Banyan who sailed his ship into danger, *his* decision. I can only imagine he thought the reward worth the danger. But for

257

Mr Daniel to remain in Lisbon seems both cowardly and suspicious. I may be wrong: the cargo may have remained uninsured, in which case neither Sir Edmund nor Mrs Oakley can expect any money. Only time will tell. Shall I ring for refreshments?'

Shouts were drifting up from the wharf, carts rumbling across the cobbles. Our hot chocolate finished, Constance stood staring down at the huge cranes lifting sacks from out of the ships' holds.

Elizabeth's voice dropped, her hand squeezed mine.

'You looked strained, Amelia. How is Sir Edmund?' She glanced at Constance. 'We're to leave for Falmouth soon. I can't decide whether to stay for Lady Polgas's ball or not — though I think not.' Her eyes held mine. 'Dr Polgas is expected home very soon. You know what they're saying?'

'That he's to apply for the position of physician at the new infirmary? Yes, Lady Polgas has made that very clear.'

'I'm worried about you, my love.' Tears stung her eyes. 'Write to me if you don't want to talk.'

'He's a broken man,' I whispered. 'He's confused and troubled . . . he's vulnerable and he's ill. Severe headaches leave him disoriented and that makes him scared. His sight is bad and his hearing is difficult.' I reached for my handkerchief, drawing a deep breath. 'He loves me, Elizabeth . . . and he needs me so much. I can't abandon him. It would break him completely.'

She smiled, grasping my hand. 'I understand,

really I do. Does he know about Luke?'

I shook my head, glancing at Connie. 'Neither of them do . . . and I want it to stay that way.'

She took a deep breath. 'There's love, and there's duty, and there's also pity. Promise me you won't rush this decision?'

'And there's also a vow I cannot break,' I whispered.

She shook her head and I rose to go, kissing her soft cheek. She did not understand, no one understood. They did not know him as I knew him. He was gentle, he was kind. He was loving and loyal. He was no match for his father, the navy or the brutalities of war. I had sworn to love him. I was his rock. I had to hold fast to my promise.

30

We stopped outside our house. 'Connie, you go on in. Tell Mother I'm going to visit Mrs Lilly and I'll be very quick.'

Mary's house was just round the corner in Pydar Street, a large ancient house with thick cob walls and mullion windows and five tall chimneys towering above a new slate roof. The iron gutters and downpipes had been newly replaced and the front door recently painted. The brass knocker gleamed in the sunshine and I breathed deeply to steady myself. Luke would not be there, he would be in the rooms he hired behind the library.

The footman opened the door to the familiar beamed ceiling and gleaming flagstones. The smell of beeswax filled the air and I crossed the hall, passing the grand wooden staircase, and waited to be announced.

Mary Lilly stood by the fire, her hands stretching out in welcome. 'Amelia, my dearest. Your mother has just sent word. It's wonderful news — quite wonderful. And to think Mr Burrows is to pay to Dublish your book. Oh, my dearest. I am so thrilled for you.'

I loved her soft Irish lilt, her beautiful white hair, her blue eyes that could shine with such mischief. She had Luke's smile, the same lines of compassion across her brow, and I forced myself to return her smile.

A lump caught my throat. 'I've come to ask you if I may dedicate my book to Luke's father? I've changed a few of his remedies . . . and I've added others. I've brought them up to date . . . I've dispensed with the ones that don't work, but mostly they're all his . . . and I'd like his name to be remembered.'

Tears pooled in her eyes. 'We would consider that a very great honour. Thank you. Luke's not here, or he would thank you himself.'

I forced back my tears. 'Mary, I can't see Luke . . . not yet. Give me a little time. How is he?'

Her elegant shoulders shrugged beneath her embroidered shawl. 'All that honour and stiff resolution may fool others, but it doesn't fool his mother. It hides a broken man, my love. This isn't easy for either of you, and I don't underestimate the pain you're both in. It grieves me so badly to witness your terrible heartache — both of you lost souls. But your happiness is all Luke wants, and I want that, too — and you know how I think that should be resolved!'

A painting of Mr Lilly's first wife hung on the wall behind her, together with portraits of his daughter, Angelica, and his son, Edgar. They were all so dear to me and I fought the wave of emptiness threatening to engulf me. My heart ached, knowing this would have to be my last visit — it was too painful to come again.

'Mary, could you ask . . . could I please engage Dr Bohenna to see Joseph Oakley in the glove shop on Quay Street? Please ask him to send his account to me, only Mrs Oakley has no money . . . she's from Portugal.'

'I know very well who she is, my love.' Her voice was soft, making the ache worse. 'And I know Mr Joseph Oakley. I'm sorry to hear he's ill.'

'Not, *Mr* Oakley — his grandson, young Joe. He wheezes when he coughs and his lips turn blue. It's not a rattling cough — and there's no bark to it. There's no hoop, but his breathing sounds rasping and I'd like Luke to see him.'

She glanced at the longcase clock with its elaborate dial of painted ships. 'I'll tell Luke the moment he comes home — that is, *if* he comes home. If he doesn't, I'll send word. Rest assured, Luke will treat the boy for you.'

Three other paintings adorned the wall: roses from the rose garden in Trenywn House, my last birthday present to her. I had painted them at Luke's request and I could not help but look at them. Her hand slipped through my arm. 'He's to leave Truro, my love. He says he has to go back to Falmouth.'

'He can't! Mary, he has to stay. He can't leave . . . what about the infirmary?'

Her hand tightened. 'He says he needs to go where he can no longer look for you — not be in places that constantly remind him of you. I wish he'd just come out and tell you how he really feels . . . Honestly, my love, he worships the ground you walk on. He'll never be free from the love he bears you, but oh no, it's all about Sir Edmund being your first and true love. I want to shake him, my dear. He needs to fight for you, not back away like some defeated wrestler.'

A sob caught in my throat and her arms folded

round me. She held me to her. 'I'm so sorry, I spoke out of turn . . . Do what you have to do my love, and leave Luke in my care. Perhaps he's right; perhaps Sir Edmund *does* have prior claim to your heart. Forgive a doting mother and leave Luke to me. I'll see he comes to no harm.'

I walked back hardly knowing where I was. The door to our house flew open, and my two nephews hurtled towards me. 'Aunt Amelia . . . Aunt Amelia . . . you're here *at last*. We've been waiting simply ages.'

They held up two small wooden ships. 'Uncle Emerson is back. Look what he's brought us. See these sails? They've got tiny ropes that you can pull.' My hands were grabbed and they dragged me towards the house. 'Mama cried when he arrived. Honest, you think she'd be happy, but all she could do was cry!'

'People cry when they're happy, William.'

He seemed relieved. 'Is that why you're crying?'

Henry smiled up at me. 'We've been playing wiv the ark . . . wiv Miss Melville.'

'We've been using our ships as a naval escort. Grampa suggested that.'

Mother stood smiling in the hall, her large white apron tied tightly round her. In her hand she held a letter. 'I've just received this recipe from *Il Professor*. It's for *biscotti di Saronno*,' she said, stumbling slightly with the pronunciation. 'We need *mandorle* — that's almonds, I believe. Oh, and you'll like this, boys . . . we're going to need sugar and lemon.'

Through the open door, Papa and Connie

were arranging the bone animals in pairs on the gangplank. 'Of course, some say piglets should be weaned at twenty-one days, but I say twenty-eight days at the earliest. What do you say, Miss Melville?'

Connie paused. 'I've never considered it before . . . What if there's a discrepancy in size, Lord Carew? Could you wean the fattest piglets at twenty-one days and leave the smallest piglets for another week?'

'My dear, how very sensible.'

I turned at the sound of knocking on the front door. The footman took a note from the errand boy and handed it to Mother. Her eyebrows rose, a slight tightening of her mouth.

'Edmund is in town.' She glanced at the letter again. 'He's staying at the Red Lion and begs to be remembered to us.'

I caught my breath. 'He's come to town? So soon? He must have followed us straight here.' I tried to hide my sudden fear. Mother was watching me carefully and I knew I must smile. 'That's very good news . . . he must be feeling better. I'm glad he's come.'

'Splendid, then I shall invite him to join us for dinner tomorrow.' She put the letter down on the silver dish. 'Now, boys, how about we make a start on these *biscotti di Saronno* for Uncle Emerson?'

* * *

The clock chimed eleven and I stared down at the stack of numbered pages. The fire was crackling, shadows dancing on the ceiling above. Lighting another candle, I drew my shawl closer, dipping my pen into the ink. There was still so much I needed to include.

Childhood wheezing: if there is tightness in the chest, pain, trouble sleeping caused by shortness of breath, coughing, wheezing or a whistling sound when exhaling. If the condition be more severe after exertion, or is exacerbated by chilled air, then my advice is to seek the assistance of a physician, or apothecary, who will very likely prescribe tincture of opium for the night. However, there is much relief to be gained from comfrey root, syrup of coltsfoot, mullein and hyssop.

Comfrey root is both soothing and healing to the lungs. It can be drunk as tea or a decoction. Like mullein and slippery elm, comfrey is a mucilaginous herb, providing a calming effect on irritated lungs . . .

The pages blurred. It would it be too painful to continue growing my herbs. Nor must I remain on the infirmary committee. Deep inside that shattered, war-scarred shell was the youth I had loved so deeply.

A tear splashed the page and I reached for my blotter.

31

Town House, Truro
Saturday 10th February 1798, 2 p.m.

We heard them before we saw them, William and Henry skipping by the side of a rather distinguished-looking gentleman, their happy laughter echoing down the street. The man with them was of medium height, elegantly dressed in a dark jacket and breeches, his white cravat folded neatly and secured by a silver pin. He wore no coat, his tall hat resting on his slightly receding hair. His boots were polished, his hands gloved in fine leather. He was closely shaven, and though he was ten years older, and a little stouter, I recognized him at once.

'Well, well, *Miss* Carew,' he said, smiling broadly. 'This is such a pleasure. It's been a rather long time.'

'Emerson, it's lovely to have you back — the boys have been counting down the days. We all have. May I introduce Miss Constance Melville? Connie . . . this is Dr Polgas.'

He bowed, smiling broadly. 'A pleasure to meet you, Miss Melville. I must say, I've forgotten how cold England can be.'

She smiled shyly. 'Welcome home, Dr Polgas. You survived the Italian biscuits?'

His laugh was throaty, joyous. 'They were delicious, thank you.' He glanced at his nephews, lowering his voice. 'Fortunately, I'm used to ship's biscuits!'

William beamed with pride. 'Grandmama will be so pleased to see you.'

His hair was greying at the temples. He had his mother's long nose and Cordelia's slightly hooded eyes. His skin was sunburned but not weather-beaten. He looked well, refined and elegant, a man in his prime. 'Miss Melville, I hate to say this, but you were *very* young when I saw you last. And I'm thrilled to hear of your brother's safe return.' He glanced at me. 'I believe Sir Edmund was commended for valour. You must be very proud of him.'

There was compassion in his glance, a look of understanding, and I smiled back, comforted by the warmth in his eyes. 'Yes, we are both . . . very proud of him.'

'Mother tells me she's on the infirmary committee with Lady Clarissa,' he said in such a way I had to smile.

'Yes. And it makes for some very lively discussions.'

He rubbed his gloved hands together. 'Indeed it must. No wonder Dr Nankivell is ready to step down! I must say, this meeting is very fortuitous as we're on our way to visit you.'

We reached our house, the white pillars of the portico shining in the sunlight. It was another beautiful day, the sky a brilliant blue. The boys had run ahead and were tearing from room to room, searching for Mother. Papa stood at his study door, greeting Dr Polgas with an affectionate smile. 'Emerson, dear boy, welcome home.

267

Splendid . . . splendid.' He put his hand on his shoulder, patting him warmly. 'When you've finished with the ladies, come and have some brandy. Survived the biscuits, did you?'

Footsteps stopped halfway down the stairs and I looked up. Luke was staring down at us, his dear face frozen in sudden sadness. I had been smiling, laughing at Papa's invitation. I was carrying hat boxes filled with Connie's new bonnets. I looked carefree and unconcerned — everything but what I felt. I could see the pain deep in his eyes; we were closing ranks, laughing and joking with Dr Polgas and Edmund's sister, welcoming them into our family as once we had welcomed him. A well-connected family looking after its own.

A blush burned my cheeks. I had not known he was coming — this must be his last visit to Mother, his last visit to our house. He looked thinner, his cheeks gaunt and I forced back my tears. There was such anguish in his eyes.

Papa looked up. 'Ah, Luke! May I introduce Dr Polgas, Cordelia's brother . . . my eldest son's wife — *Old* Emerson, as opposed to *Young* Emerson?' He laughed heartily. 'Have you freed Lady Clarissa from her shackle, Dr Bohenna?'

Luke walked slowly down the stairs and my heart burned like fire. He would never hold me again, never bend to kiss me, never look up from his books and smile his loving smile. We would never sift through hospital statistics again, never discuss the efficacy of different remedies. Never draw maps of where illness was rife — his absolute certainty that particular areas of Truro

268

held sources of contagion.

'I have freed her, Lord Carew, with strict instructions to bear weight on that ankle for only *two* hours a day. She must take things easily. Use it, but not over-use it. Am I right, Dr Polgas?'

Emerson Polgas nodded vigorously, holding out his hand to clasp Luke's. 'Dr Bohenna, this is an honour.'

Luke smiled warmly. 'No, believe me, the honour is all mine.' He turned to Constance. 'Miss Melville, I'm very sorry to hear the news of your mother's death. I'm so sorry I couldn't help her.'

'Oh, but you *did* help, Dr Bohenna. Your visit brought her great comfort and relief.'

He did not look at me. He was looking everywhere but at me. 'You're a surgeon, I believe, as well as a physician, Dr Polgas? Physician-in-charge of Port Royal Hospital in Jamaica. I've read your Treatise on Marsh Miasma. Your expertise will be highly valued by those of us treating patients returning with such diseases.'

Emerson Polgas looked surprised. 'Thank you, I'm honoured — you didn't find my treatise too controversial?'

Luke smiled. 'No, I found it very interesting. You tell us Marsh Miasma is most contagious at night yet those who anchor away from the shore rarely fall foul of the fever. That the source of these fevers remains the same, but the seasons affect the onset of the illness.'

'Indeed.'

'And the disease can be on one side of a river, and not the other?'

269

'Indeed. Whole regiments have suffered on one side of the river, yet those camped on the other side remain unaffected. With the same prevailing winds.'

'With no contagion from person to person?'

'Indeed. Healthy men who enter the marsh can become ill *without* being in contact with an infected man.'

'So it's not contagious but maybe something in the marsh itself? And sailors continue to suffer these remitting fevers even after they return to British waters.' Luke looked up. Mother was standing at the top of the stairs.

'Emerson, how lovely to have you back.' She began her descent, holding the banister carefully.

Emerson Polgas bowed. 'Lady Clarissa, you've not changed one little bit. Can it really be ten years?'

Mother smiled, stopping halfway down the marble stairs. 'Thank you, how very kind. So Marsh Miasma is *not* contagious?'

He nodded, glancing back at Luke. 'My findings never differed. Those with the disease — and by that I include both remitting and unremitting fever — who left the area where they contracted the disease, never communicated it to others. The foul air of the miasma can be cleared by strong winds and harsh weather conditions, yet the miasma stays *within* the marsh area. The illness does not spread across the sea, nor does it spread from person to person.'

Mother was watching me and I forced a smile. Luke kept his eyes firmly on Emerson Polgas. I could hardly breathe watching him standing there so formally, *all that honour and stiff resolution*. I wanted to cry, I wanted to run to his side. I wanted him to sweep me into Papa's study and hold me tightly.

He looked desperate to be elsewhere. 'My work here centres around the disease caused by putrid and stagnant gutters — the pools of stinking detritus left to rot in our alleys. Illness spreads rapidly — whole households coming down with typhoid and the flux, yet other areas remain unaffected. Unlike the disease of smallpox or influenza — which are definitely contagious — it seems to be the miasma causes the illness. It sounds rather similar to your marshes . . .'

Emerson Polgas's hooded eyes sharpened. 'I understand your advice was to deepen and flush the sewers away from town? You've instigated broader streets and the removal of filth — and you want a system of water pumps separate from the drains. I've seen your proposals for the new infirmary, Dr Bohenna, and I must say I'm impressed.'

'Thank you.' Luke nodded at the footman who held out his coat and hat. 'Most importantly, I believe we should start to inoculate against smallpox. The evidence is now quite compelling.'

Emerson Polgas raised his eyebrows. 'A controversial view, I believe, Dr Bohenna?'

Luke put on his hat and fastened his coat, a slight tightening of his lips. No smile, no glance back at me, just a rigid set to his shoulders and a formal bow. 'I'm afraid I must leave you . . . I have patients waiting. If you'll excuse me.'

Mother finished her descent of the stairs and

tapped Emerson's arm with her fan. 'Be warned, my dear, Dr Bohenna is a serious contender for the job you assume is yours.' She tapped his arm again. 'Believe me, it is not a foregone conclusion. Dine with us tonight — if your dear mother can spare you. Sir Edmund Melville is expected, and I'd like you to meet him.'

'Lady Clarissa . . . I would dearly love to, but I'm engaged to have dinner with Lieutenant Halliday in the White Hart tonight.'

Mother's smile broadened, a conspiratorial glance at Constance. 'George Halliday? Sir Hugh and Lady Imogine's son? Well now, how splendid. I haven't seen George Halliday since he was commissioned. What a lucky coincidence. I shall expect you both at six.'

Papa pointed Emerson swiftly into his study and Mother drew a contented breath. 'Not just one, but *two* highly suitable matches,' she whispered, lifting the hem of her skirt to admire her bandage-free ankle. 'Don't look so stricken, Connie my love, it's only to please your brother. At least, he must *think* I have your marriage in mind.'

32

My apricot gown glowed in the firelight, the Mechlin lace at my sleeves catching the light. Bethany stood back. 'No, a little higher. Let me pin it again.' She was more flustered than usual, running from one of us to the other, tweaking our hair into curls, smoothing our gowns, but I could see her heart was not in it. Nor was mine, though I tried to smile for Connie's sake.

Bethany glanced at the gowns abandoned on the bed, the discarded shawls hanging over the chair. We had even changed our minds on how to wear our hair, but now we were finally ready: two elegant ladies in our finest silk, even though we did look pale and less excited than we should.

We stood in front of the looking glass. 'Would you like a faint blush of rouge, Miss Melville? Only black drains a lady of all her colour . . . '

Connie shook her head. 'No, thank you, Bethany. When I get embarrassed I blush terribly. If either of them — ' She stopped.

I looked just as pale, just as fearful. 'Mother's promised, Connie, and when Mother promises something she *never* goes back on her word. She's *not* matchmaking.'

Her lips quivered. 'I think she is . . . Amelia, I made a terrible mistake.' She glanced at Bethany, now busy at the dressing table, and her voice dropped. 'I was telling her about the funeral . . . about Reverend Kemp and somehow

273

. . . somehow, I told her how much I loved Adam Kemp. I couldn't help it. I just came out with it.'

I held her gaze in the mirror. 'Don't give them any undue encouragement . . . just be polite and smile. They're both charming — George is very like Frederick and you've nothing to fear from Emerson. Mother will never force you into a marriage you don't want.'

Bethany lit another candle, the wax dripping from the one she held in her hand. As the flame flared, I saw her eyes fill with tears. She picked up my jewellery case and came quickly to my side. Her fingers trembled as she opened it. 'Do you think you might like to wear these earrings, Miss Carew? As befitting . . .'

The diamonds glittered on their velvet lining and I nodded, fastening them to my ears. Her voice had rung with hurt, her unsaid words hanging between us. *As befitting the next Lady Melville.* The clock struck the quarter hour and I knew we must go down.

'You look beautiful, Connie. Come, we better go. Mother asked Edmund to arrive a little earlier.'

Halfway down the stairs, we stopped. The drawing room door was ajar and we saw Edmund leaning over a newspaper that was lying open on the table. 'Oh no! Connie, look! He's reading the paper. Mother must have left it open.'

Her face fell. 'He won't be able to read it — he's not holding a magnifying glass.' She sounded as shaken as I felt.

He turned sharply at our entrance and my fear spiralled. He looked horror-struck, worst of all, a pair of iron-rimmed spectacles sat heavily on his nose.

'Edmund . . . how lovely you've come to Truro.'

His fine silk jacket stretched impeccably over his broad shoulders. He looked elegant, expensively dressed, his waistcoat delicately embroidered, a pair of silver buckles at his knees. His boots were highly polished, his cravat fashionably tied. His short hair was newly washed. A perfect gentleman, expect for the panic behind his new, rather ugly glasses.

'Amelia . . . Connie . . . have you read this? *Fox and Fox Insurance are seeking Mr Philip Daniel last seen yesterday on the quayside in Truro.*' He ran a shaking hand across his forehead. 'Philip Daniel is the man who signed my letter — he's the agent from Sumatra . . . the one who's bringing back my shipment.'

A fine layer of sweat covered his upper lip. His cheeks were flushed, his hands clenching into fists by his side. 'Why are Fox and Fox seeking Philip Daniel *here* in Truro? The *Swift* was bound for Bristol — she can't have docked here because her hull would be too deep.' He swung away from us, his shoulders stooping. 'Something's happened. I'm sorry . . . please, give me a moment.'

The fire was blazing, the candelabra glittering above us, and we stood in silence, waiting for his shoulders to straighten and his fists to unfurl. 'I'm sorry.' He was fighting his emotion, almost choking on his words. 'Why are Fox and Fox shipping insurance seeking Philip Daniel?'

The keepers of secrets, both of us instinctively

staying silent. To tell him of our fears just before he faced company would be too unkind: now was not the time to dash his hopes.

'Maybe he's looking for you . . . perhaps he called into Pendowrick and was told you'd left for town?'

Connie shook her head. 'But his letter was sent to Father in London — it was forwarded to Pendowrick. Does Mr Daniel know our Cornish address?'

Edmund's face cleared, a new hope to his nod. 'Yes . . . I believe so. It was a very long time ago, but I believe I told him our estate was in Cornwall and questioned the chance of shipping it to Truro.' He brought out his handkerchief, blowing his nose. 'Or maybe he's been to London. We need this shipment — everything rests on it. I should imagine he's stored the spices safely in Bristol and wants to hand over the papers. Yes, that must be it.'

He smiled, adjusting the heavy frames. 'Amelia, let me look at you. My dearest love, you're even more beautiful now I can see you properly . . . ' He lifted the frames, dabbing his tears, 'At least I *could* . . . there, that's better. Are these so very terrible? I need to get used to wearing them . . . '

He was so eager and my heart lurched. His pitted face, the scar above his lip, even the coarseness of his skin was beginning to look familiar. I breathed deeply. I would find a way back to loving him. I could. I would. I had to.

'Not at all. I'm glad they work so well. That newsprint is really quite small — it's a wonder you can read it.' I smiled, but he did not smile back. There was a sudden tension in his shoulders, a stiffening of his back.

In the doorway Mother stood resplendent in her finest blue silk. Matching feathers clustered to one side of her elegantly swept-back hair, a pair of sapphires dangling from her earlobes. Papa stood behind her, bewigged and uncomfortable in his most formal jacket. A gold watch hung from his waistcoat pocket, which he flicked open with one hand.

'Splendid. Excellent timing. Four years too late, but you're very welcome.' He strode forward, clasping Edmund by the hand. 'Very welcome indeed. Excellent. Those glasses actually help, do they?'

I could see them hiding their shock, both of them glancing away, not wanting to appear discourteous. Edmund's face was a livid red, his hands twisting against his embroidered waistcoat. 'Six years since I was last here . . . six very long years . . . interminable years . . . but I'm back now and never has Truro looked more beautiful . . . or Miss Carew.'

Mother drew herself to her full height, her smile gracious, though it did not reach her eyes. 'There are going to be seven of us dining tonight,' she said, folding the newspaper and handing it to the footman.

A pulse beat in Edmund's neck. He loosened his collar. 'Lady Clarissa . . . if you don't mind . . . I don't think I can face society just yet. I look well but I find society very difficult. Please, if you don't mind, I'll return tomorrow.' His eyes sought mine in panic.

Mother's voice was soothing, full of reassurance. 'Sir Edmund, I understand. Believe me, I understand. But my advice is to take one small step at a time. What is difficult now will only get more difficult the longer you leave it. Admiral Sir Alexander Pendarvis has told us what you have been through and how it has affected you — indeed how it would affect anyone. I don't believe in mincing my words. I believe gallant heroes who put their lives at risk for their king and country need to be nurtured back into society. Your terrors will leave you — but only if you allow us to help.'

He looked shaken, bowing courteously, but I saw panic in his eyes, a sudden hardening of his mouth. 'Lady Clarissa . . . your kindness means everything. I do not deserve such generosity of spirit.'

'Your extraordinary bravery under fire is what we must dwell on. The enthusiasm of a youth, too impatient to go to war to bid goodbye to his fiancée, will, in time, be forgiven.'

She had said it. Dear God, she had said it. Reprimanding him as if he was still in the nursery. I could hardly contain the thumping of my heart. I knew I must go to him, stand by his side, let him know I held no such poor opinion of his sudden departure.

Edmund lifted his chin, as if awaiting the next blow. 'Thank you for speaking so candidly, Lady Clarissa.'

Papa nodded, smiling with the same slight reserve. 'Stay, Sir Edmund, though by all means feel free to leave us if you must — rest assured you will be among friends. Dr Polgas has worked in the navy his whole career. He's recently returned from Jamaica and if anyone understands the *inflictions* of the Tropics, he does. And we're to be joined by Lieutenant George Halliday. I believe you know the latter, if not the former.'

Mother put out her arm, leading Edmund to the window. 'Lieutenant Halliday has extremely good credentials,' she said softly, glancing back at Connie. 'He's well connected and in need of a wife to help him spend the rather large amount of prize money he's accrued.' Her voice dropped even lower. 'Dr Polgas is already family, and also in want of a wife. Stay for your sister's sake. Approve one of them and leave the rest to me.'

The clock struck six and through the open door we heard two men leaving their coats with the footman in the hall.

Just one glance at Emerson Polgas and we knew Lady Polgas had instructed him what to wear. His dark blue silk jacket had a cut-away collar, deep lapels and brass buttons that looked almost, but not quite, like a naval uniform. A gold pin held his immaculately folded silk necktie in place; his damask waistcoat was finely embroidered, his breeches elegant, his shoes polished and new. He looked poised and elegant, his hair worn short, greying at the temples, his slightly hooded eyes glancing straight at Edmund.

Younger by ten years, Lieutenant George Halliday stood resplendent in full navy uniform.

A friend from childhood, I caught the same charming smile, the polite but shy glance he risked at Connie. He had the same mass of blond hair he had had as a youth, the same ruddy complexion, the familiar round cheeks and boyish dimples.

'Lady Clarissa, thank you for inviting me. It's such a pleasure to see you all again.' The same charming voice, another shy glance at Connie. 'Miss Melville, this is indeed an honour.' He bowed to Edmund. 'Sir Edmund, I've heard about your exploits . . . we've all heard . . . Suffice it to say it's men like you who make our navy great.'

'I hardly think — '

'Your valour can only be admired . . . your escape, well, little did we know all those years ago how things would turn out.' He tapped his jacket. 'Gieves did a splendid job, didn't he?' He turned to address us all. 'The last time we met, we were being measured for our uniforms.'

He risked another glance at Constance and Mother smiled. 'Miss Melville is staying with us for a while — after the recent sad death of her mother.'

His bow was respectful, immediate kindness in his voice.

'Please accept my sincere condolences, Miss Melville.'

Constance forced a smile. 'Thank you. Are you in Truro for long?'

'My ship's undergoing repairs in Plymouth so I've a week, maybe ten days. This is my first long shore leave for four years.'

'Splendid, let's make the most of it.' Papa stood by the table, a silver cup poised above the glass punch bowl. 'Rum for you navy men . . . just a drop or two of brandy . . . lemons . . . and sugar. I have this recipe from Lady Pendarvis and I must say it's rather good.'

My heart was thumping so hard I thought it might burst. Edmund was smiling but in the mirror I could see his hands clenched into fists behind his back. His knuckles looked white, his breathing laboured. Mother was wrong to put him through this, and I was wrong not to intervene. I should have stopped her; he was not ready, he would freeze, forget his words. He needed more time.

Pana handed a glass of Dunch to George Halliday. 'You shared a tailor? Splendid cut — very fine.'

'I've since had the cuffs and lapel changed to blue, but you were right, Edmund. You warned me not to have it lined with silk and I took no notice.' He smiled at Mother. 'The Tars don't like any undue signs of wealth — it's inappropriate and Sir Edmund knew that. You've to earn their respect, not parade around in velvet collars and silk-lined pockets.'

Edmund shrugged. 'I was not immune to censure, even though I chose the basic cloth. Which is your command?'

'I'm with the Channel Fleet under Admiral Lord Bidport — my ship's *HMS London*. She's a fine ship, though she's getting on a bit and in need of repairs.' He smiled at Constance, his boyish dimples creasing. 'She's a second-rate

281

ship of the line — ninety-eight guns . . . and she's seen us through a few tight spots, I can tell you.'

Connie's blush deepened. Her black hair was entwined in pearls, a silver pendant hanging round her neck. She smiled stiffly, her large brown eyes beneath her heavy dark brows plummeting to her hands on her lap. She remained by Mother's side, hardly sipping her drink.

Papa swilled the punch in his glass. 'The Channel Fleet? Caught up in the mutiny, were you?'

'I was. It was disgraceful, if a little frightening. It came from nowhere and took us all by surprise.'

Edmund straightened, squaring his shoulders. 'I read about it while I was in the hospital. They wanted better living conditions, more pay . . . better victualling . . . increased shore leave and compensation for sickness. Well, perhaps they should try prison hulks!' He smiled and a rush of pride surged through me. 'I understand they wanted certain officers removed — and I have to admit, I'd be with them in that!' His laughter cut the ice, and I started to breathe. Perhaps seeing an old acquaintance was just what he needed.

Emerson Polgas raised his glass. 'To your safe return, Sir Edmund, and to your ten days of shore leave, George.' He took a sip of his drink. 'As far as I've read, the mutineers weren't complaining about flogging or impressment — just their conditions.'

George Halliday nodded. 'It was all about

conditions and pay. They're calling it the *Breeze* at Spithead, but it could have been far worse — it could have been a *gale* or a *hurricane*.' He smiled at his joke, raising his glass. 'Lord Howe smoothed the waters, and just as well.'

Edmund was talking amicably but I could see the knuckles in his fists were still white. 'But it sparked another mutiny — at Nore, I believe.' He glanced at me through his heavy iron frames. 'The one good thing about Stonehouse Hospital and the interminable waiting for doctors — present company excluded — is that you catch up very quickly with what's been happening.'

He seemed to be managing well; it was me who seemed more nervous.

Papa shook his head. 'Ah, but Nore was different. The mutineers were blockading the port of London and interrupting trade. Merchant vessels had every right to bring their cargo upriver to unload.'

'Indeed, Lord Carew, and they were dealt with very swiftly. The Admiralty was right to make no further concessions. Many believe the mutineers were puppets of France — spies placed in the ships.'

'Goodness, can that be true?'

A blush deepened George Halliday's cheeks. 'It could well be true. Did you know we no longer ring five bells for the last dog watch? That was the signal to start the mutiny.'

Constance's eyes plummeted again. 'No, I didn't. How interesting.'

I should have prevented this, both of them forced into polite conversation. Edmund and

Constance were grieving their mother, both looking so fragile; Constance with her downcast eyes, Edmund trying to hide his panic. Mother glanced at the clock and put down her glass.

'Shall we eat? Emerson, you must tell us all about this hospital of yours. The West Indies must seem a very long way away now'.

I glanced at Edmund and my heart froze. Behind the glint of his glasses was a look I had never seen before. A hard, piercing look that made my blood run cold.

33

I could not eat. Candlelight flickered across the mahogany table, dancing on the silver tureens and gold rims on the plates. The huge centrepiece swelled with fruit and nuts, our crystal glasses matching the cut-glass bowls placed beside us to wash our fingers, Mother's sapphires glinting at her ears. Papa sat back on his chair. I knew he wanted everything cleared away. He would rather be in his corduroy jacket and felt hat, drinking potato soup and eating hearty rabbit pie, but at least the claret was one of his favourites.

He held up his glass. 'Emerson, I salute you. Physician-in-charge of Port Royal Hospital in Jamaica. To be responsible for the care of so many. Indeed, I salute you.'

'Thank you, Lord Carew, but sickness is sickness, wherever you are. One hospital is very much like another, though I have to say I'm grateful to see the back of tropical disease — for a while, at least. We've lost more men to disease than we have to war. Whole regiments, one after another. It's not easy to witness, let alone treat.'

'But quinine has made a difference?'

'Yes, Amelia — quinine, bark, wine and laudanum all play their part. But there's a dearth of provisions out there. Ships' doctors need more than they can carry. They pack their chests at the onset of each voyage yet by the time they reach

285

us, they need more. Supplies were hard to come by and I had doctor after doctor hoping to restock their chests.'

I had hardly dared look at Edmund. Perhaps I was mistaken and the look I had seen earlier was just some distortion of his thick lenses. He was talking freely now, answering their questions, telling us about his capture, his harsh detention in the prison hulk and his subsequent escape. His voice faltered with the telling, his tone hesitant, growing stronger as he recognized the sympathy with which he was being heard, but I saw his hands clench beneath the table, the tapping of his heel as he spoke of the merchant ship, the interminable voyage down the coast of Brazil, the yellow fever he had suffered, and the clamping of chains as they forced him below deck in every harbour.

Mother was more subdued than normal, her usual affability held in check. She became increasingly quiet, nodding in encouragement, smiling back at Edmund when he stumbled on his words. Maybe she was right to make him endure this; perhaps talking to like-minded people was all he needed. I tried to calm the beating of my heart; perhaps that look had been fear, not hatred.

He cleared his throat. 'Dr Polgas, please assure me this brain fever I suffer from will pass. I get blinding headaches and at times I'm very forgetful. It's rather disorientating.'

Emerson's hooded eyes sharpened. 'All symptoms I've seen before. Come and see me tomorrow, or at your convenience. I'd be delighted to examine you and tell you all I know.'

'Thank you. I will.' Edmund's smile ripped through me, giving me sudden hope. The more he talked, the more he seemed to relax.

Constance must have felt it too. She smiled at Emerson Polgas. 'I'm afraid you're not quite finished with tropical illnesses, Dr Polgas. Dr Bohenna was right when he said your expertise will be needed.'

He returned her smile. 'These diseases can return with no warning. A person may be well and happily employed one minute, then shaking with fever the next. Returning soldiers and sailors can be affected for many years.'

Edmund cleared his throat. 'You've all been very kind. I believe you haven't pressed me because you believe I don't want to talk about my ordeal . . . but I only did my duty. We were all just doing our duty. I must have been thrown well clear. I managed to drag myself away but was captured. They held me in a prison hulk right below the fort — you can imagine the conditions were far from ideal . . . '

He looked round at the sudden silence and I forced back my tears. Those were the exact same words he had used only an hour ago. He was about to tell us again how he managed to escape.

Mother put down her napkin, indicating to the footmen to pull back our chairs.

'Perhaps another time, Edmund, it's getting rather late? We'll leave you men to your brandy . . . join us when you're ready.'

Pana stood up, clearly thrown by Edmund's lapse of memory. 'I think we'll join you now. No harm in drinking brandy in the drawing room. Come . . . let's have no more talk of war.'

I gripped Constance's hand but as Edmund followed, I turned to slip my arm through his. His voice was a whisper. 'I think that went very well, don't you? Your parents are very kind . . . considering how they feel about my behaviour.'

He had no idea at all. I wanted to run from the room, bend double and howl. Somehow, I had to smile back at him, stop myself from crying. 'That was a kind offer from Dr Polgas.'

'He seems very understanding. Do you think I might ask to go and see him? He wouldn't think it too much of an imposition?'

'No . . . I mean, yes . . . Please do. Go tomorrow.'

Mother and George Halliday were standing by the fire, George admiring the three paintings of roses I had painted for Mother's birthday. He leaned in closer.

'Did you really paint these, Amelia? I have to say, they're very good. You have such talent. I remember you painted me once — do you remember? My mother still has it — you showed such promise even at eleven!'

He was trying to lighten the solemnity in the room, the terrible compassion we all felt for Edmund. 'Of course I remember — actually, I was quite pleased with the result, considering you couldn't sit still!'

George smiled, turning to Edmund. 'Was your miniature as good as mine? I have to say I was pleasantly surprised with the end result. He had very little time to capture our likeness, but he managed very well. Of course, all he had to do was get the face right — the uniform was already copied from the catalogue.' He smiled at Constance. 'Did Edmund tell you we had to choose our jackets from a very elaborate catalogue? The choice was far greater than I imagined. I think we were both a little overwhelmed.'

I hardly heard him. Edmund had his back to me, carefully choosing a bonbon from a silver dish. 'Unfortunately my miniature didn't arrive in time.'

'Oh, what a shame. Mine was in my trunk and very nicely framed. It was *you* who chose the frame, Edmund. You, who held back on fancy frills and velvet trims but insisted on an encrusted frame!'

I could not look at Mother, nor Papa, nor Constance. I felt winded, unable to breathe. Not a glimmer from Edmund, no sign he had been insensitive, that he understood how much it would have meant for me to have his portrait. Just the careful deliberation of which bonbon to choose. It felt like treachery, the sharp, sudden pain of being stabbed in the back. All these years of having no record of what he looked like — nothing to hold to my heart during the long tear-soaked nights of his absence. I had to fight to breathe.

George Halliday was smiling. 'I suppose they must rush them a bit, though I have to say mine was excellent.'

Mother and Connie came instinctively to my side, sitting next to me on the chaise longue and

I straightened my back, trying to look unconcerned. I had to understand. I had to let this
pass. Above all, I had to stop myself from crying.

He caught the sudden silence in the room,
everyone's averted gaze, and must have realized
his mistake. He came swiftly to my side, kneeling
on one knee as he reached for my hand. 'Amelia,
forgive me. It was a thoughtless oversight. I was
in such a terrible rush — the ship was only
docked for one night and I thought I was going
to miss it. I waited so long for Francis, I hardly
had time to change, let alone check the contents
of my chest. The portrait slipped my mind
— *completely* slipped my mind until I was on
board ship. When I found it wasn't in the trunk,
I assumed he hadn't finished it in time . . . then
I thought perhaps I hadn't ordered it correctly.'

Papa refilled his brandy, casting an anxious
glance at Mother. 'Thoughtless, certainly, but
not a crime. I'm afraid young men don't
understand the ways of women . . . It takes a
lifetime, old boy. You'll learn.'

Mother was less forgiving. 'Thoughtless, yes,
but not a crime. Just a serious case of misjudge-
ment.'

This time I was waiting for it and there it was,
the flash of hatred in his eyes, a fleeting look of
loathing before he looked down in penance. I
thought the ground would swallow me, a terrible
giddiness taking hold. He hated Mother, plain
and simple; he could not stand the sight of her.

Emerson Polgas sought distance by the
window. Picking up one of my bone animals, he
held it to the candle. 'This is exquisite . . . an ark

290

filled with animals. What a beautiful piece of work. Are these carved from bone? They are quite extraordinary.'

Glad for the change of subject, Papa boomed across the room. 'Yes, incredible, aren't they? Captain Pierre de la Croix made it for Amelia's birthday. It's not quite complete . . . he says there's a couple of giraffes missing, or some such creatures.'

George Halliday joined Emerson by the ark, likewise picking up an animal. 'I believe these French fancies are highly sought after, but this is particularly magnificent. Who is Captain de la Croix? I presume he's a prisoner on parole — with enough time on his hands and mutton in his belly to whittle the day away making these exquisite animals?'

'Yes . . . in Bodmin along with two hundred others, I'm told.'

'Do you think he could make me a model of *HMS London*? That would be rather splendid. Could you ask him for me?'

Papa did not see Mother's warning shake of her head, nor my frantic stare. 'Certainly . . . he's a good chap is Pierre. We've all grown very fond of him. Frederick's ship — you know, *HMS Circe* — captured his ship off Guadeloupe. The crew were ill and Admiral Penrose set them all ashore — but brought Pierre de la Croix back along with his ship.'

'Good prize money then for them. Though unfortunate for Captain de la Croix.'

'Indeed, George. But Pierre has a certain charm about him. A certain *resignation*. He stayed with us in Trenwyn House for a short while and we got to know him. Now he's in Bodmin making these rather lovely fancies. I believe he teaches French . . . and epee fencing. You'd like him. But for the war — ' He stopped as Edmund's strangled sob filled the room.

His fists were clenched, his face white. 'You've . . . befriended . . . a French captain from *Guadeloupe*?'

'Merely doing our duty to Frederick's prisoner, old chap. Frederick took his parole.'

In the silence I could hear my heart thumping. Edmund remained thunderstruck. 'A man who patrolled the very harbour where you knew I'd fallen? A man *responsible* for attacking the troops I was sent to protect?' His shoulders began shaking, the tremor back in his hands.

Mother's eyes filled with compassion. 'He's a prisoner, Edmund. He's given his parole — he can no longer hurt you.'

Edmund tried to steady his voice. 'I understand . . . of course, I understand. Only in my prison I didn't have the luxury of eating meat and whittling away the day carving bones. They didn't afford me the privilege of choosing to teach English or cricket. Perhaps I should have offered lessons . . . maybe that's where I went wrong? Forgive me, but I must leave.'

Clutching his head between his hands, he rushed to the door and I ran after him, fighting back my tears. He thought we had betrayed him, and in a way we had. He was not ready for this, I should have warned him about Pierre de la Croix. The very mention of our friendship with someone he regarded as his enemy was clearly more than he could take.

The front door was open, Edmund striding away, and I ran after him into the moonlit square.

'Edmund, stop. Don't leave like this.'

His face was livid, the look of cold hatred back in his eyes. 'I can't do this. I can't pretend everything's all right. Leave me . . . please. None of you understand.'

'I'm so sorry that happened . . . it must be a terrible shock — I do understand . . . honestly, I do. Tonight's socializing was too soon for you — we should have waited. Edmund, with Dr Polgas's help you will get better. Let me help you.'

'By accepting presents from a man who might have killed me?' He swung away from me, hugging his shoulders in the freezing night air. A few people had stopped and turned, but mostly the square was deserted, the footmen watching us from inside the hall.

We stood in silence, his shoulders heaving. There was such anger in him, such rage. 'No, it's me that should apologize,' he said through clenched teeth. 'I've behaved despicably. I'll write to your parents in the morning and apologize for my outburst.'

'They understand. Believe me, they understand.'

His voice softened. 'It's just so hard to contain the fear . . . it's like a wave that comes from nowhere and it leaves me so scared. My head's clearing now. I'll be all right. Goodnight, my

293

dearest love.' He sounded calmer but his hands were still shaking. 'Go inside. The last thing I need is for you to be ill. I love you, Amelia. I just wish your parents didn't hold such a low opinion of me — but they're right to be like that. I would be just as protective of any daughter of mine.'

'They'll come round. They understand, honestly they do.'

He shook his head, his look of resignation flooding me with sadness. 'How can they understand when they didn't even let me tell them what happened? Your mother stopped me from speaking — they just *don't want to know.*'

I froze, but not from the cold. If this was my future, then I must make a choice. A vulnerable youth, now a vulnerable, confused man. I would not abandon him; already I had hidden my knowledge about his shipment, but if our future was to have any meaning, it had to be based on honesty. I had to speak plainly, summon every ounce of courage, start the way I meant to continue.

'You *did* tell them, Edmund. You told them everything . . . but you forgot that you had.'

His cry tore my heart, his hands gripping his head as he staggered blindly across the square and I ran to the footmen, calling out through a wave of despair. 'Go with him . . . see he gets safely back to the Red Lion. Help him . . . please. Make sure he comes to no harm.'

34

Town House, Truro
Sunday 11th February 1798, 9 a.m.

The clock on the mantelpiece struck nine, the chimes cutting through the awkward silence. Finally, I could bear it no longer.

'Mother, may Constance and I visit Edmund at the Red Lion to check if he's all right? Only I'd like to bring him back here to clear the air between us. It must come from us. He was embarrassed by his behaviour last night, and I'd hate there to be any bad feeling.'

Mother was writing at her desk; she looked up at me and smiled. 'By all means. He is welcome here at any time, you know that, my dear. Both of you are extremely welcome.' She smiled at Constance. 'This is a very difficult time for all of you.' Bethany joined us as we set off to cross the square, our cloaks wrapped firmly round us, our hoods pulled low against the bitter wind. 'Thank you,' Constance said, 'for being so understanding. I don't know what I'd do without your family.' A flock of gulls were flying in a wide circle above us, their plaintive cries fuelling my sense of unease. I had to convince Edmund that Mother had his best interests at heart, that he was safe and welcome in our house, that it would take time for him to recover and I would be at his side at all times. The Red Lion came into view and I breathed deeply. I had to make Edmund understand that I was not going to forsake him.

The door of the inn opened and a man bowed as he held it open. An elderly lady with several pelisses watched us from the bottom of the huge wooden staircase, her maid fussing over the last of her boxes. The landlord saw us from behind the bar and came rushing forward, wiping his hands on the vast white apron tied round his waist.

'Forgive me . . . I didn't see you there, m' lady. It's Miss Carew, I believe? How can I be of service?' His bald head shone with sweat, his face flushed, his smile warm and genuine. If he was surprised to see me, he showed no sign, but stood, half-bowing, as I leaned nearer.

'Could you tell Sir Edmund Melville that we are here? His sister and I would like a word with him.' I spoke softly, not wanting Edmund's name to be heard by the men at the nearby table.

The landlord shook his head, answering loudly. 'I'm sorry, you've just missed him. He's kept his room, but he's gone fer a day or two. Took a bag but said he'd be back. He must've left shortly before nine.'

I felt my legs weaken. 'Did he say where he was going?'

'Said he was goin' back home — up the moor. I know that, 'cos he told me if a man called Philip Daniel were to come here lookin' fer him, I'm to tell him to stay in Truro . . . that Sir Edmund will be back. He doesn't want them to keep missin' each other.'

'Thank you. You're very kind.'

We stood on the pavement, both thinking the same thought. Constance voiced it first. 'He's returned home in case Philip Daniel's gone there. We should have told him . . . we should have taken him to Mrs Fox . . . Amelia, we need to be with him when he finds out.'

We linked arms, walking slowly back home along the street. Bethany had remained by the corner shop and we returned to find her deep in conversation with Seth. Their words sounded urgent, her blonde hair swinging as she shook her head. Seth was not dressed in his livery but in a felt hat, a corduroy jacket and a large leather apron tied around his waist. His boots were soiled, a leather satchel slung over one shoulder. He saw us coming and stopped mid-sentence. Bethany swung round, anxiety in her eyes.

'What is it?' I asked. They did not answer but stood looking down at their feet. 'Tell me, please.'

Bethany's cheeks flushed. 'Tell her, Seth. Tell her just as you told me.'

His blue eyes looked straight into mine. 'I'm not one to meddle, Miss Carew. You know I don't gossip or spread alarm.'

Something in his voice made my heart race. Something in his eyes. My trusted coachman had never looked at me like that before. 'You've heard something? Seth, please tell me.'

He swallowed; when he spoke his voice was gruff. 'Not heard but *seen* somethin'. I'd like to say I might be mistaken, only I know I'm not. I've been worried about one of the mare's fetlocks . . . a farrier works at the Queen's Head and I was talkin' to him when the stagecoach left. A man was waitin' in the overhang an' I get a feelin' with some men. It's like ye know they don't want to be seen. They act different, not pushin' forward so they get the best seat, but waitin' behind, gettin' on the coach at the last minute.'

My heart began pounding. 'Who was he?'

'It was Sir Edmund, Miss Carew. Dressed plain — black overcoat, black breeches, boots, black leather gloves. He wore a large hat, bigger than mine, pulled low. His collar was pulled up an' I'd not have noticed him, except fer the fact that he was actin' like he didn't want to be seen.'

I could hardly speak, my panic turning to fear. 'Where was the stagecoach going?'

'Bodmin.'

'Sir Edmund's gone to Pendowrick . . . he's meeting someone there. That's why he's gone.' My words sounded stilted, my head trying to make sense of it, my heart warning me otherwise. 'He must have decided to take the stagecoach.'

Seth and Bethany looked at their feet; they would not contradict me, but Constance shook her head. 'Even if the coach stopped for him to get off, he'd have to walk down the lane to Pendowrick. That's two miles off the turnpike. He hasn't had time to send word for someone to meet him — and why would he take the stage-coach when he has his own horse?' Her voice strengthened, a note of steel entering her tone. 'You're absolutely sure it was Sir Edmund?'

'I am, Miss Melville. As ye recall, I spent several days up at your house.'

'Where is Sir Melville's horse stabled?'

Seth held her gaze. 'That's where it don't make sense. I was in the stable when he brought in his mare. He left the horse an' then waited in the overhang.' He paused, glancing back at me. 'Sir Edmund had a bag with him, Miss Carew. I can swear he was on that coach, an' it's my belief he was expecting to stay a night or two.'

Bethany shook her head. 'We're not gossiping . . . honest we're not. It's just that . . . '

I felt winded, my senses reeling. 'I know, you all heard what happened last night — it was very disturbing. It's not something to spread around and I know you won't . . . I'm very grateful you've told me. Seth, would you go to the Red Lion and see what instructions Sir Edmund left . . . and then go back to the Queen's Head and enquire about the horse you saw him bring in.'

'Straight away, Miss Carew.'

Bethany walked ahead, knowing we needed privacy. Constance gripped my arm, drawing me back. 'You saw the rage in him last night, didn't you, Amelia? I watched your face . . . I saw it in your eyes. You recoiled in horror, just like I did when I first saw it. It's rage he can't hide. It's frightening . . . it's why I've been holding back, but now you've seen it we can talk about it.'

Her words churned my stomach. Yes, I had seen rage, and I had seen hatred; I had seen the power behind those clenched fists. 'Connie, do you think Captain de la Croix could be in danger?'

Her reply was instant. 'You know he is.'

'Then I have to go to Bodmin. I have to warn Pierre.'

Mother was still at her writing desk, the lace at her sleeves protected by bands of cotton. She had seen us hurrying across the square and put down her quill, carefully dusting her letter. 'What is it, my dears?'

I shut the door behind us. 'Mother, we must go to Bodmin. Straight away. We have to leave as soon as possible.'

Her eyebrows rose, her eyes immediately alert. 'We? Why might that be?'

I had been trying to remain calm but voicing my fears brought tears to my eyes. 'Edmund's gone there, and I think he means harm to Captain de la Croix. I think he might challenge him to a duel or . . . or do something dreadful.'

'You really believe so?'

'Seth saw him get on the Bodmin coach. He had a bag with him . . . Seth only noticed him because he looked furtive, as if he didn't want to be seen.'

'Seth is a very good judge of character. I trust him implicitly.'

'So do I.' I took a deep breath. 'Mother, Connie and I have both seen an anger in Edmund that frightens us.'

She nodded. 'Yes, great anger. I saw it too. Anger, disappointment, even jealousy. All very natural emotions if you've spent the last three and a half years in dreadful circumstances and you witness your fellow men reaping huge rewards for what you consider an easier war.' She drew out a clean sheet of paper, dipping her pen into the ink. 'You believe Edmund sees Captain de la Croix as one of his captors and seeks revenge?'

300

'I think that might well be the case.'

'Then we have a duty to prevent it. We must warn Captain de la Croix that Edmund may seek him out and do something very foolish.'

She looked so calm. She had no idea of the urgency of the situation. 'Mother, we need to leave *now* — that way, we'll be right behind him. We can't trust it to a letter. Can't we just go? I need to explain everything to Captain de la Croix . . . the reasons behind what we fear.'

Her eyebrows rose. 'Goodness me! I can't suddenly pick up sticks and go with you to Bodmin. My ankle still keeps me at home . . . and your father's been *very* unwell this morning. Besides, it would be foolish to take our coach as Edmund would recognize our crest and know you've hurtled after him.'

'Papa is ill? You didn't tell me. Is he very ill?'

'Nothing that a few days' rest won't put right.' She was busy writing, her pen scratching noisily over another sheet of paper.

'May I go with Bethany? Please, Mother, I have to go.'

She sighed deeply, glancing up at me. 'I've just written to Mary on the *off chance* that she might be able to take you in her coach. Edmund will not recognize it, nor has he ever met her. Bethany is needed here — and anyway, Edmund knows her, and Constance *certainly* can't go.' She returned to her writing. 'Your only chance is if Mary is free. *If* she agrees, then you may go. Mrs Hambley in Bodmin will accommodate you — I'm sure Mary will find Mrs Hambley's rooms very comfortable.'

I ran to kiss her. 'Thank you, Mother . . . thank you so much. I'll take the letter straight to Mary.'

Mother pulled off her cotton protectors, spreading the lace at her wrist. She pulled the bell rope with an elegant sweep of her hand. 'No dear, go upstairs and prepare for your journey. Bethany will pack a small bag for you. Ah, thank you. See these letters are delivered — *urgently*, please.' She handed her letters to the footman.

Through the open door, I saw Seth standing in the hall, the footman glaring at his mucky boots. One glance at his face and I knew the answer.

'Sir Edmund ordered his horse to be saddled first thing an' he left the inn just after eight thirty.' He swallowed, lowering his voice. 'But the horse was left at the Queen's Head shortly after — that's when I saw him. He left instructions to stable the horse until he returned.'

'Thank you, Seth.'

His huge hands gripped the strap of his shoulder bag, his cheeks florid. 'There's something else I need to tell you, Miss Carew. Sir Edmund gave his name as Mr Owen — the horse is booked in under a Mr Owen from Falmouth.'

★ ★ ★

Mary Lilly sent word the coach would be at my disposal and I hurried to her house, carrying the small bag Bethany had packed for me. I felt winded, my unease growing. Not only had Edmund lied but he had gone to extraordinary lengths to hide his whereabouts.

I was wearing my blue velvet travelling gown

which Edmund had not seen; my cloak was borrowed, my hood pulled low. I would warn Captain de la Croix and beg him not to rise to Edmund's anger. I would explain everything. Behind me, the church clock struck ten; I was an hour behind the stagecoach.

The door opened and a flood of disappointment made me catch my breath. Mary Lilly was not waiting for me; there was no sign of her bag, her hat, nothing to show she was ready to travel, and I hurried across the panelled hall into her darkened drawing room. The drapes were closed, the fire roaring. Mary Lilly lay on the couch, a damp towel pressed to her forehead.

'Mary, you're not well?'

'Amelia, my love . . . come in. No, I feel very unwell. A terrible pounding in my head, and flushes like I've never had before. My joints ache something terrible, but the coach is yours, my dear. I've told the coachman to get everything ready. Take a look through the window and see — only, don't let in too much light, my dear.'

I peeped from behind the curtain. The coach was almost ready. 'Mary, what have you taken? Some willow bark? What can I get you?'

'Nothing, my love. I've called for Luke, and he'll be here soon. I'll await his instructions.'

My hopes were fading. Mother would never let me go alone. The front door banged, and footsteps came hurrying across the hall. Luke rushed to his mother's side, lifting her wrist to feel her pulse. He had not seen me in the darkness and my heart leapt, scorching my chest.

'Mother, this is all very sudden. Where's the

pain? Are you nauseous? Your pulse is normal — it's regular and strong. It's not racing and you're not hot, so it's not a fever.' He turned round, his eyes flooding with love. 'Amelia, I'm so sorry . . . I didn't see you there. Have you given her something? She's not feverish and her pulse is normal, only a little fast.'

My pulse was anything but normal; it was racing, my whole body aching.

'Well, that's a relief.' Mary lifted her blanket, sitting up slowly. 'Though the headache is quite terrible. I'm quite well in myself, but not well enough to travel.'

'No travelling at all.' Luke reached for his bag, fumbling with the catch.

She rested her fingers on her forehead, her white hair elegantly tied in a loose bun. 'Can you stay, or are you busy with patients?'

Luke smiled. 'It's Sunday. I've some notes to write — but I can stay and work here.'

'Well then, that's very fortunate.' She stood up, walking across the room, opening the curtains. In the courtyard behind, the coach stood ready to leave, the four grey mares throwing back their heads in anticipation. 'That means you can take my place. Just to Bodmin, my love. Only Amelia needs to go . . . and quickly, too. So if you hurry and change you should be off within, what shall we say, ten minutes?'

His eyes caught mine — dependable, loving eyes; ones I knew I could trust. His voice was firm, no hint of hesitation. 'Ten minutes it is, then.'

35

Mary's coachman was ready, but there were four other men waiting by the coach. Seth nodded, taking my bag, holding open the door so I could climb the steps. Mother's three footmen wore no livery, each dressed in thick leather coats, warm hats and scarfs, each, no doubt, with a pistol concealed beneath the heavy folds of his coat.

Mary stood by the kitchen door, handing Luke a small bag as he passed. He nodded to the coachmen, smiling at the footman to pull up the steps. Taking the seat beside me, he knocked the roof with his knuckles. We heard the crack of the whip, felt the sudden lurch, and I reached up, closing the curtain against prying eyes. Luke did likewise and we jolted forward, in what could only be considered unseemly intimacy.

His smile was rueful, apologetic. 'Most parents do their utmost to prevent this sort of thing. Our mothers, it seems, have gone to extraordinary lengths to throw us together.'

I had to turn away. He had dropped everything to come with me. 'It's only your mother.' I whispered. 'Mother hoped Mary would come with me.'

He unfolded a letter. 'I'm afraid it's both of them. This *urgent* letter from your mother informed me Mary was unwell and needed me *immediately*.'

The writing was definitely Mother's. I could

see the word 'immediately' underlined and panic seized me. 'Oh, goodness. Luke . . . you know what this means?'

He shook his head, his smile ripping through me. 'No, what does it mean?'

'It means Mother must think there's going to be bloodshed.' He put the letter back in his jacket pocket. 'Why are we going to Bodmin, Amelia?'

Seeing him, being so close to him, the love in his eyes, knowing that he was willing to drop everything and come with me. He looked paler, thinner, the sadness in his smile tearing my heart. I stared ahead, the wheels ringing across the cobbles.

'We need to warn Pierre de la Croix that Edmund knows he patrolled the waters around Guadeloupe. Last night, Papa told our guests about our friendship with Pierre and Edmund showed such anger. It was horrible . . . it made my blood turn cold.' I needed to take a deep breath, stop my lips from quivering. 'Luke, he's changed so much. One moment he's polite and loving, the next a coldness seems to sweep through him . . . and an anger that makes him turn away and clench his fists.'

His voice was gentle. 'Anger, jealousy, the desire for revenge — they're all natural emotions if you've been cruelly imprisoned or spent years in harrowing circumstances.'

'You've been talking to Mother?'

He nodded, leaning back against the soft leather upholstery of his stepfather's carriage. 'Lady Clarissa asked me what they could expect

306

and how they could help Edmund. And I told her there's growing evidence that some prisoners who witness great atrocities — or who've been subjected to such things themselves — can't simply return to the lives they once lived. They see others living in prosperity or reaping huge rewards for what they consider an easier war and their resentment builds. Many may never speak of what they went through. They want to free themselves from the memories, or they keep it to themselves, knowing they should feel grateful they've returned home and are no longer living in torment. But hidden emotions can often surface.'

He looked pale, he was thinner; he had not been eating.

'I saw that last night.' I was fighting back my tears. 'We put Edmund through a terrible ordeal — George Halliday was with him when they were measured for their uniform. They were equal then — idealistic young midshipmen — but now George is a lieutenant and has amassed huge prize money and Edmund faces a bankrupt estate. Also . . . ' It was too hard to continue.

'Also?'

'Emerson Polgas was there.'

'Ah, yes. The affable Dr Polgas.'

'Luke . . . Emerson Polgas is Cordelia's brother . . . he's family. It doesn't mean — '

'The job's his, Amelia. I'm not going to apply for it . . . I'm going back to Falmouth. There's much sickness there — a great need for medical provision.'

The horses began to slow, beginning the steady incline up onto the moor and he reached for the curtain. 'I think we can risk opening these now, no one will see us.'

'No . . . keep it shut. Please — just a little longer.' He must not see the tear rolling down my cheek. He was to leave Truro. Of course he was. He would leave and I must never see him again.

I composed myself and pulled back the curtain, watching the wind blowing the gorse, rippling across the grass. Bands of heavy-bellied clouds blanketed the sky, the vast moor opening before us in muted colours. Luke had sat next to me on purpose, side by side, so we could avoid each other's eyes.

He, too, was staring out of the window. 'Edmund's not alone in finding his return more difficult than he thought. I've seen several men retreat into corners and shake with fear — some show great aggression, as if it's *kill or be killed*. Others turn to drink to dull their memories. I believe we can help him.'

He turned and our eyes locked. The kindness in his voice, his understanding, the compassion in his eyes; I fought the terrible yearning to slide my hand nearer his.

'We?' I whispered.

'Yes, *we*. I'll do everything in my power to bring Edmund back to full health. There are others we can call upon — men who've gone through the same living hell and who understand this period of adjustment.'

The coach was swaying, a gentle rhythm on

the best of springs. Far superior to Papa's carriage, the plush leather seats were ruby red, the matching silk curtains held back with plaited gold braid. The rails were brass, so, too, the door knobs. The dark wooden interior was polished and gleaming, beeswax candles standing ready to be lit in shining brass candlesticks. Even the carriage lanterns on either side were so clear, there looked to be no glass.

I stared at the barren landscape, at the desolate bleakness that stretched as far as I could see. *And where thou art not, desolation.* A tight band constricted my throat; I could neither breathe nor swallow. I did love Edmund. I did. Or at least, I could care for him.

I would honour him, be there for him, in sickness and in health; I would oversee his recovery and he would get well again. The youth who had raced across the moors and jumped the ditches was still there: the man I had vowed to love, who had stood tall, laughing back at me, his shirt billowing in the wind, was still there.

Luke turned and I forced myself to look at him. 'You may be mistaken; Edmund might be angry but would he go so far as to seek out Captain de la Croix?'

I stared in surprise, I had not told him. 'Luke, he's *already* gone. He left this morning . . . we're an hour and a half behind him. He has every chance of finding Pierre before we get there.'

His interlocked fingers tapped his against his mouth. 'So that explains the rush. Where is Captain de la Croix lodging?'

'With Mrs Hambley at 25 Bore Street. She

runs a guesthouse, or rather she used to run a guesthouse but now she has two parole prisoners. It's opposite the White Hart. We visited them before Christmas — Mother and I took Captain de la Croix a hamper.'

'Did Edmund leave by coach or horse?'

I could not tell Luke about his horse — he would think so ill of him. 'He took the nine o'clock coach from Truro this morning. It stops in India Queen to change horses — it's very fast. It's due in Bodmin just after two.'

His voice was strong, immediately reassuring. 'There's a lot we can do to calm Edmund's state of mind. Our priority is to warn Captain Pierre — but after that, I'll do everything in my power to help Edmund. From what you've told me, his instincts are gentle. He's perplexed and he's hurt, but he's not ruthless. By the time he arrives in Bodmin, I feel certain his rage will have lessened and he'll be himself again. I don't believe there'll be a duel, or one drop of spilt blood. You must trust the man you love.'

He glanced at his fob watch, his voice matter-of-fact, almost distant. 'With luck, we'll be no more than two hours to India Queen, then another two to Bodmin. I suggest we change horses.'

I matched his tone, forcing my words through my constricted throat. 'I think that's best.' He did not look at me and I was grateful for that mercy. I, too, was staring out of my window. 'Thank you for coming with me, Luke.'

His eyes remained fixed on the horizon, his tone formal. 'I'm glad to be of assistance. It's my pleasure to help you — while I remember, I've been to see young Joe Oakley. I think the wheeze will settle with tincture of opium. It'll calm his spasms. I've prescribed it just at night — for the day I've suggested comfrey root and syrup of coltsfoot, and some hyssop to soothe his lungs.'

The road was flatter now and wider, the horses racing at full speed, hurtling across the windswept moor with every ounce of their strength. The vast moorland lay shrouded in mist: there were no trees, only hawthorns bent sideways by the prevailing wind. On a clear day we would have glimpsed a band of blue sea to the north, but not now. The land was indistinguishable from the sky, just brooding dampness, the grey mist pooling in the vales and obscuring the lakes.

★ ★ ★

Luke pulled down the window. 'This is India Queen.'

The horses slowed to a walk and we turned into the courtyard of the inn. A dog barked, chickens scattering as our wheels rattled over the cobbles. Grooms put down their brushes and came rushing over to await their instructions. Seth opened the carriage door and pulled down the steps.

'We'll change horses,' Luke told him as he helped me alight. 'Insist on their four best — regardless of cost. I'll see to the paperwork.'

'Right away, Dr Bohenna.'

It was not his coach and Seth knew to leave

the choice of fresh horses to Mary's coachman. He looked round, smiling as the older coachman invited him to join him in his choice. Behind us, a booming voice greeted us from the inn.

'Sir . . . ye're very welcome. Come this way . . . some refreshment? I'm sure yer wife will want to freshen up and sit by the fire. This way, please.' His florid face wore a genuine smile, his eyes jovial, his stained white apron covering his ample belly. 'We'll see you get the best horses we have. Oh, mind the hens — go away . . . shoo. This way, if ye please.'

'The stagecoach to Bodmin left on time? When would that have been?'

'The stroke of eleven thirty, sir, right on the chime.' He looked at the large clock above the arch. 'Should make good time, too. The road's good. There's nothin' untoward as I've been told — an' this mist's liftin'. A jug of ale, sir? What can I get fer yer wife?'

'A small glass of ale, thank you. And I'd like to freshen up.' I replied.

An equally jovial woman, wearing the same welcoming smile and an equally stained apron, led me down a dark corridor to a wash room and I caught my reflection in the mirror. She reached for the enamel jug. 'I'll bring ye some hot water. Ye feel poorly, m'lady? 'Tis all that rattlin' about. Some are very sick when they get off the coaches. I'm forever settling stomachs an' easin' achin' bones. There, I'll be back. Ye'll soon feel better.'

We had made excellent time. Even with the stop, we could only be an hour behind the stagecoach. Through the open window, I heard Seth questioning one of the grooms.

'Yes, sir, I recognize that description. Big hat, an' black overcoat? Yes. No, he didn't get off. Not fer nothin'. Stayed on the coach while we changed the horses.'

36

The mist had lifted, a watery sun casting shadows across the moor. 'That's the last of the mines.' I was counting down the chimneys on the engine houses and knew we were getting close. 'This is Five Ways crossroads.'

We started descending the vale, the gorse and bracken giving way to well-tended orchards and neatly ploughed fields — the verdant and abundant pastures that brought prosperity to Bodmin. The road began to widen, a few small cottages marking the outskirts of the town. An ox wagon lumbered in front of us and we slowed to a walk, the air taking on the smell of malt and woodsmoke.

'I've asked them to stop just short of the inn, so we can alight without being seen.' Luke sounded confident, but my heart was hammering.

A plume of smoke rose from a blacksmith's chimney, the rhythmical banging of a hammer hitting an anvil. Shouts rang from a cooperage, men rolling barrels onto a waiting wagon, and I tried to stop the fear rising within me. Edmund could have got off the coach at India Queen. If his anger had abated, he would have turned back to Truro.

Luke flicked open his fob watch. 'He's had just over an hour to find Captain de la Croix, but duels require seconds and weapons — and they're usually conducted at first light. If he's after a fight, he'll no doubt wait until nightfall.'

A ditch of clear water ran along the pavement, the first of the fine double-fronted houses with their elegant front doors and iron railings, and I wrapped my cloak tightly around me, pulling the hood over my bonnet. We were entering the west of the town, the church and law courts were to the east, so we would avoid the congestion in the centre. The coach stopped and Seth drew down the steps. A short distance up the road, the sign of the White Hart swung from its chains.

'He might be watching the house from the inn. We need to go round the back so he can't see us — there's a lane to the side of her house.'

Luke nodded, taking the bags, and we walked quickly, our steps in time. Not too fast, or we would draw attention to ourselves, but purposefully as if we were in a hurry to get to our lodgings. The shrubs in the front garden came into view, followed by the old stone house with its slate roof and path leading to a gleaming black door. A wrought-iron gate led to the garden behind, but we used neither. I slipped my hand through Lukes arm, leading him down the narrow lane and in through the wooden back gate to her immaculate garden. Well-tended vegetable beds stood in regimental rows, a brick path leading us through fruit trees and past the most elaborate chicken coop I had ever seen.

A huge ginger tomcat watched our approach, scowling at us as we knocked on the back door. 'That's Gustave.' I whispered. 'He's actually very sweet.'

315

Luke's smile was instant, a lift to his eyebrow. 'If you say so!'

I smiled back. 'No, he is. Honestly. Mrs Hambley won't tell us why she calls him Gustave, or how she even knows the name. She gets very giggly and blushes . . . Mother thinks — '

The door opened to a short, round-faced lady, almost as broad as she was tall. Under her white mobcap, her hair was streaked with grey, her cheeks aglow with good health. One look at us and her hands flew to her bosom. 'Dear Lord, Miss Carew! What a surprise. No . . . no. Don't tell me. I can see it in yer faces. So much in love ye've run away together. Dear Lord, what am I to do? Keep ye hidden? Ye want me to hide ye fer a while, is that it?'

She threw out her arms, gathering us into her kitchen. 'Ye were right to come here. I won't say a word . . . but ye'll have to tell yer mother. She'll come round to the idea, honest she will . . . If there's one lady with love an' compassion oozing out of her soul, it's Lady Clarissa.'

No amount of protestations could stem her delight. Forcing us through the door, she glanced quickly over her shoulder. 'Well, ye're not the first, an' ye won't be the last. God knows, everyone is welcome. Ye seem a very nice man, sir . . . a gentleman. Very genteel. Very kind eyes. Lady Clarissa will give in, honest she will — but ye *must* tell her ye're safe.'

'No . . . Mrs Hambley, it's nothing like that. This is Dr Bohenna . . . Mother would be with us if she could, but she can't . . . and nor could

316

Dr Bohenna's mother. We're here on urgent business. Is Captain de la Croix at home? Has he had a visitor?'

Her puzzled eyes looked at each of us in turn. 'Well, that's a shame.'

'Shame we've just missed him? Shame about what . . . ? He's had a visitor, hasn't he? Is he all right?'

She shook her head, reaching to fill the heavy kettle. Luke held it for her, and her smile broadened. 'No, Miss Carew. It's just a shame ye're not eloping.' Her eyes filled with mischief. 'Doctor, ye say?Well, are ye hungry, Dr Bohenna? No . . . don't tell me, let me guess. Buttered buns? Or lardy cake? I've got both . . . Perhaps I should just give ye everything I've got. Ye both look half-starved. Both of ye so gaunt an' in need of a good meal. Miss Carew, I hardly recognized ye, ye've grown so thin.'

Luke shrugged his shoulders. '*Everything you've got* sounds rather perfect.'

Mrs Hambley blushed, her happy giggle filling the room. 'There now, that's what I thought.Ye need feeding up.'

I tried again. 'Is Captain de la Croix here? Only it's *very* urgent.'

She looked reluctantly away from Luke. 'Yes, Miss Carew, go on through to the parlour, he'll be that glad to see ye. He's upstairs with those old bones of his. Perhaps ye'd like to freshen up first, an' I'll make ye some tea?'

The parlour was warm, the fire casting a red glow across the lime-washed walls. The rug was a mix of assorted colours, plump cushions neatly placed on the high-back chairs, but I did not sit. I went straight to the small leaded window, watching the inn from behind the floral curtains. There was no sign of our coach, just two horses drinking from the trough. Luke stood by the fire and our eyes caught.

'Mrs Hambley was once very good to Charity's sister, Celia, and we've got to know her very well. She doesn't mean to be so familiar . . . it's just her way. Please don't mind — '

I turned at the sound of footsteps. Pierre de la Croix ducked under the lintel and stood bowing in the doorway, his black hair falling across his forehead. His dark brows lifted, the lines on his face creasing into a welcoming smile. 'Miss Carew, Dr Bohenna, what a lovely surprise.'

In Mrs Hambley's care, his cheeks were fuller, the blue jacket of his French uniform buttoned neatly across his slightly broader stomach. Hints of grey framed his face, his black hair tied in a bow behind his neck. Only his stiffness remained, and his charming manners. 'I am overjoyed to see you.' His eyes sparkled, looking from one of us to the other, as if expecting some news, and I walked quickly towards him, holding out my hand for him to kiss.

'I'm afraid we're here under rather difficult circumstances — no . . . no one's ill. But there's something we need to discuss.'

'Of course, shall we sit? Dr Bohenna, they have let you leave your patients?' His English, with its heavy French accent, was improving by the day. 'Mrs Hambley says she will bring us some tea. If you make yourselves comfortable, I

318

shall help her with the tray.'

'No . . . no, I can manage. Captain de la Croix, ye spoil me!' Mrs Hambley squeezed sideways through the door. 'Carrying an' fetching fer me all the time — an' making me such a lovely chicken coop. Honest to God, I'm the envy of the town.' She smiled broadly, placing the laden tray on the table between the windows. 'But perhaps a few more logs on the fire? There now.' She surveyed the four plates piled high with food. 'I'll go an' get the rest. Then I'll make up yer rooms. Ye are staying, I hope, only the inn's a rowdy place an' ye'll get no sleep?'

I glanced at the carriage clock above the fireplace. Half past three. 'Thank you, Mrs Hambley, that would be very kind — we'd like that, if it's not too much bother?'

Luke raised his eyebrows, rubbing his hands together. 'This is an absolute feast.'

'Well, now . . . see what I'll make ye for supper. We'll have rabbit pie. There now . . . that's settled. I'll get Susan to make up yer rooms an' I'll get going with that pie.'

I poured the tea into her best china cups and handed them round. With the warmth of the fire and the glow of Mrs Hambley's welcome, I suddenly realized how hungry I was, and I helped Luke and Captain de la Croix sample something from each of the piled plates. Now we were here, my fears were beginning to subside.

'You've had no visitor this afternoon — a tall young man with short dark hair . . . wearing a thick overcoat and a large hat?'

'Non, Miss Carew. I finished the hen house

319

and went straight upstairs. I've been in my room . . . I've finished nearly the last of the animals for your ark. Thank you for your kind letter, but it is my pleasure. Your family have been so good to me — I would not be here with Mrs Hambley, if you had not arranged it.'

He put another log on the fire, wincing slightly as he bent down, smiling at Luke's obvious concern. 'Nothing to worry about, Dr Bohenna — just an old sailor's *rhumatisme*. We get wet, and we stay wet. Damp clothes, damp bed — *et voilà*, stiff joints!' He sat back on his chair. 'Who am I to expect, this visitor?'

I put down my teacup. 'This is very difficult . . . for me, at least. On my birthday, I had the very good fortune of hearing that my fiancé . . . who we all believed was dead . . . had escaped his captivity and has since returned.'

His dark eyes shot straight at Luke. 'I am so pleased. What wonderful news.'

'Yes, it is.' My heart was thumping, the fire too hot. 'But his return sees him a troubled man. His imprisonment was exceptionally harsh and his subsequent escape led him to further brutality. He is struggling . . . '

'I believe many are troubled. It is troubling times.' His voice was warm, filled with compassion. 'You are fearful, Miss Carew. I see a change in you, a sadness in your eyes. Tell me what you want of me. Am I to understand I am never to contact your family again?'

'It is not our wish . . . but it might be a necessity. But if it were only that I'd have written to you before I came. The problem we face is

320

that my fiancé, Sir Edmund Melville, was imprisoned in Guadeloupe for a year before he escaped, and I believe that your ship patrolled the seas around the island.' The tight band round my throat was back, choking my words. 'My fiancé, Edmund, has taken the news rather badly. I think he believes you might have been part of the capture — and subsequent deaths — of the men he was meant to protect.'

A sad shrug to his shoulders. 'I see. He considers me his direct enemy. I was not part of the attack but, yes, I was part of the fleet. Certainly I was there. I sailed frequent into the port and I knew all the frigate captains.' His heavy brows creased. 'Tell me, when was your fiancé imprisoned?'

'In April 'ninety-four. Just under four years ago.'

Lines etched his face, a furrow crossed his forehead. 'Then I'm afraid he is right to consider me responsible. I was certainly there. Until my capture in May 'ninety-six, that was my patrol area. We were instructed to take back the island — attack any British ship sailing in those waters. My orders were to see off all enemy ships, because, of course, we were determined not to let Guadeloupe *back* into British hands.' He returned his cup to his saucer, his abundant black hair falling forward. 'And I am very sorry to confirm that there was indeed great brutality on the island. The new governor used his power with *no* mercy — everyone feared his guillotine. I say this not to upset you but because I understand why your fiancé would bear me no goodwill.'

321

'Thank you . . . I'm so sorry this has happened.'

'*Non, non,* this is the sad consequence of war. I am very aware of the conditions on the island . . . I know they are far from what they should be. I never saw them for myself because I never delivered any prisoners to the fort, but I know the dungeons are squalid and rife with disease, and I would not wish that on anyone. I understand what you are saying — that I must not meet Sir Edmund. I see it in your face. When war becomes personal, it is not good.'

Tears pooled in my eyes. 'No, it is not good, Captain de la Croix. Last night Edmund showed great anger when he found out about you and — '

'You fear he will come here and seek me out? To revenge his fallen shipmates? Why else would you rush to my side with a doctor in attendance? You fear bloodshed, Miss Carew. I see it in your eyes.'

'Yes. I'm afraid I do. I believe he may do something very rash. He left first thing this morning, which is why I'm so fearful. He's here in Bodmin, and I think it only a matter of time before we hear his knock on the door. And it scares me, Captain de la Croix.'

Luke rose from his chair, peering from behind the curtain at the commotion going on outside. 'There's a coach leaving — it's crowded . . . but no sign of Edmund.'

'Your fiancé must be a brave man, Miss Carew, if a little — how do you say — disturbed? To survive imprisonment means he is strong and courageous, and to escape is *heroique*. Indeed, I salute him. But I cannot hide from him. Nor can I deny where I was and what I did. Your brother captured my ship — both he and Admiral Penrose are very fine sailors. And I salute them, too.' He drew a deep breath. 'My men were very ill, we had suffered *la typhoïde* and we were weakened, but it could have gone both ways. I could have taken your brother's ship . . . *HMS Circe* could this very moment be sailing under a French flag. It is war . . . it is what we are sent to do. Our orders are to capture or be captured.'

He clasped his broad hands as if in prayer. 'I never expected such clemency from your family. It is the truest example of humanity. These are harrowing times we sit drinking tea and I forever thank my God that I have been delivered into such kind hands, but we both know your brothers remain in peril. We cannot deny that.'

No, we could not deny that. Tears pooled in my eyes. 'And I would hope that if they are captured . . . that they might receive the same humanity.'

'I hope so, too. But I cannot defend the conditions in Guadeloupe. If Sir Edmund has been treated so harshly, and he sees me amongst such kindness and *générosité* of the soul, then I believe he would find it quite intolerable.'

'Could you say you weren't there . . . ?' Even as I said the words, I knew it to be impossible.

He shook his head, another shrug of his broad shoulders. '*Non*, Miss Carew. He only needs to speak to any one of the other parole prisoners. He will ask who knows me, and they will tell him what they know. My record can be read . . . I cannot live a lie. I cannot deny where I was — nor can I hide from Sir Edmund. If he wishes me harm, then I must wait for him to find me. I can promise you I will not — how do you say? — *retaliate* with undue force, but if he wishes me harm, I must be able to defend myself.'

'Of course you must, Captain de la Croix. But I believe Sir Edmund does wish you harm, and it's too frightening to contemplate.'

Luke came to my side. 'Captain de la Croix, we *can't* risk Edmund doing anything foolish — for his sake as much as for yours. He needs time for his anger to abate — I believe any sight he has of you will fuel that anger. He must not find you.'

'I cannot hide. That is asking too much.'

'But we can't ensure your safety while you're here.' Luke paused, a tone of hope entering his voice. 'For Amelia's peace of mind, may I suggest we take you to Sir Alexander Pendarvis? He holds overall responsibility for all the French prisoners in Cornwall. I believe we should ask his advice.'

'Go to Sir Alexander — to his house?'

'Yes. He's Amelia's godfather and I believe he would want us to take you to him. Otherwise, the consequences could be very grave — for you and for Sir Edmund. We need to protect both of you — but we can only do it if you never meet. Would you agree to come?'

Captain de la Croix nodded, his mouth set firm. 'I consider that . . . very sensible. Thank you, Dr Bohenna.'

Mrs Hambley stood in the doorway, her large white apron dusted with flour. 'Some more tea for you all?' Her face fell. 'What is it, my dears? Did ye not like the lardy cake?'

Luke picked up the tray, handing it to her. 'No, Mrs Hambley, we loved it, thank you. The tea was very welcome . . . and your lardy cake was particularly delicious, but I'm afraid we can't stay.'

'Why, bless ye, are ye up an' off again?'

'I'm afraid we are. We must leave right away. Captain de la Croix must pack a bag and come with us.'

Her plump cheeks dimpled. 'Oh, no, Doctor. Captain de la Croix can't leave. He's only allowed one mile out of town. Up to the milepost an' back. He can't go with you or he'll be shot for trying to escape. An' we can't have that!'

'Captain de la Croix will be safe with us, Mrs Hambley, I promise. We have a carriage and we must leave straight away — if we get stopped, we'll say we're acting under Sir Alexander Pendarvis' instructions. The captain can't stay here, he's in too much danger. And if we go anywhere else, he will be shot and we'll be accused of helping a French prisoner to escape. This way, he'll be safe.' Luke turned to me. 'How long will it take us to get to Fosse?'

My heart burned, my whole chest on fire. There was such love in his eyes, and I had to turn away. 'No more than two and a half hours — it's about fourteen miles.'

He cleared his throat. 'That's what I thought.'

37

The clock on the wall chimed four, the daylight already fading. Mrs Hambley stood at the door listening to Luke's instructions.

'If you could send your maid to the White Hart — ask her to find Mr Tomkins and a man called Seth. They're our coach drivers. Ask her to tell them to harness new horses and bring the coach back to where they dropped us off as soon as they can. Tell her to be quick, but not to look as if she's hurrying . . . just as if she's passing the time of day. Have you got that?'

'Yes . . . Mr Tomkins . . . Seth . . . the coach as soon as they can, where they dropped you. I'll tell her this instant. Only to look like she's passing the time of day.' She stopped, shaking her head. 'That won't do at all. No. I'll tell her we'll do the usual. If it's to Fosse ye're going, then that's to the east. A carriage that sets off to the west, then turns of a sudden an' heads east draws too much attention. No, we'll do the usual.'

Luke smiled. 'And that is?'

'We'll put a hat against the chair so when anyone looks through the window they'll think Captain de la Croix is still here. Ye needs go back out the garden, turn right an' follow the lane past the old debtors' gaol . . . then past the court. Then wait under the tree by the church. That way, ye can't be seen. The carriage leaves with its curtains closed, ye get in, and no one sees ye.'

'You've done this before?'

She reached forward, adjusting Luke's cravat. 'More times than ye can imagine, Dr Bohenna. I'll get the hat. An' if anyone does come knockin' at the door, I'll tell him Captain de la Croix has gone up to Five Ways fer a walk.'

'Will she be safe?' I whispered as her sturdy footsteps rang down the hall.

'Edmund might force his way in and search the house, but he won't risk hurting her.'

Pierre de la Croix stood in the doorway, a bag in his hand. 'I am ready to leave.'

Luke nodded. 'Good. We're going to meet the coach by the church.'

Mrs Hambley plumped up the cushions on the chairs. 'Come then.' With open arms, she ushered us down the corridor. 'I'll light the lantern after ye're gone an' I'll bring in another tea tray. They can watch as long as they like, but they'll never guess he's not in. Ye'll be halfway to Fosse before they even think to knock.'

The warm kitchen smelled of fresh bread; the signs of baking, a huge rolling pin laying next to a ball of newly made pastry. On the window sill outside, Gustave flicked his tail. Mrs Hambley dusted the flour from her apron and reached for a woollen cloak. 'Cover ye uniform, Pierre. Don't give them even the smallest glimpse. Here. Wear this. I know ye'll be back. I won't worry at all.' She swallowed hard. 'There, that's Susan now. Did ye find them all right?'

A young girl with flushed cheeks and a

327

freckled complexion nodded from the doorway. 'Mr Tomkins says twenty minutes an' he'll pick ye up at the church.'

Mrs Hambley smoothed the thick black cloak over Pierre's broad shoulders, her fingers fumbling with the clasp. 'I've put a little somethin' in fer yer journey and the medicine for that stiff old back of yers. Go now. Walk slow, mind. Ye're out for a little air, that's all.' She took a deep breath. 'I'll not worry at all.'

* * *

We walked slowly down the back lane, trying to look unconcerned, Luke smiling, pointing out where the path was damp. We passed the almshouses with their tiny leaded windows, untidy gardens and empty pigsties, crossing the road to avoid the stench of the sewer running from the debtors' gaol. The light was fading, glimpses of the main street showing it was still busy; carts were passing, people wrapped up against the cold evening air.

'Down here.' Pierre de la Croix knew exactly where to take us.

The church bell struck the half-hour. The law courts were ahead of us, the lamps of the guildhall being lit, a woman throwing slops into the gutter. Under the overhang of a row of columns, men stood in groups, wearing the blue uniform we were so desperate to keep hidden.

'We'll go down Back Street, so they won't see me,' Pierre said, pointing us down a dark alley in front of the London Inn.

The church with its ruined steeple lay just in front of us, the large cedar tree perfect for concealment. Beneath it, the earth was wet, and we stood watching the road, the lowest branches hiding us from sight. We heard the rumble of wheels and waited for them to stop, stepping straight from the woody dampness into the smell of beeswax. Settling ourselves in the darkened carriage, Seth pulled up the steps.

'We reckon just over two an' a half hours, Dr Bohenna. The horses are fresh and the men rested and fed. By the look of it, there'll be a moon to guide us — we should be in Fosse by seven. When we're clear of the town, we'll light the lamps.'

He closed the door and Pierre de la Croix's voice came softly through the darkness. 'I am very grateful, Miss Carew. I appreciate your kindness — your concern for me. I have no desire to confront your fiancé.'

I smiled, but I felt sick in the pit of my stomach. Edmund had planned every detail — lying to the innkeeper, leaving his horse in another stable under a false name. 'You gave my brother your parole, Captain de la Croix — and you've become our friend. I'll not see one hair on your head harmed. My fiancé is not himself . . . he's troubled . . . he forgets things. His anger *will* abate, but he needs time. Your welfare is our prime concern.'

The coach picked up speed and Luke lifted the edge of the curtain, peering through a small gap. 'We're clear of the town but I think we'll leave the curtains drawn.' He settled back against the plush seat. 'Are you quite comfortable, Captain de la Croix? Are you warm enough? There are blankets I can reach. My mother believes in blankets but my stepfather believes brandy warms him better. In fact . . . ' He leaned forward, reaching under the seat. I heard a key turn, a bottle being drawn out. 'This rather fine French cognac has very warming properties.'

Captain de la Croix sighed deeply. 'Your stepfather is not only a wise man, but he has perfect taste. Maybe I am a bit cold?'

I knew Luke would be smiling. 'I think we're all a little cold.'

I lifted the edge of my curtain. Dusk was settling, black clouds streaking across a pink sky. Luke handed me a glass and the fiery liquid burned my tongue. Mr Tomkins urged the horses forward, giving them full rein and the pace quickened. It was as if they had been waiting for his signal to give him every ounce of their strength.

The moor lay before us in all its vastness, the air fresh, carrying the scent of bracken and damp vegetation. I had never been across the moor by night and as it stretched out like some ethereal wilderness, I breathed deeply, my courage returning. Bethany would have us believe it was the home of ghosts and goblins, every moon shadow hiding a restless soul, and perhaps she was right. It looked like a different world, the moon bright, the turnpike winding into the distance like a silver snake. Clumps of trees and rocky black outcrops stood silhouetted against the grey sky, moonlight dancing on the lakes, shimmering across the vast swathes of grass.

Pierre's head rested against the window; his eyes were closed, his body swaying to the rhythm of the coach.

'Edmund frightened me last night,' I whispered.

'I can understand that. I was there, I saw what happened.'

My heart jolted. 'You were in the square?'

His laugh was rueful. 'Sometimes I find myself passing your house at night.'

A tight band constricted my throat. 'Your house is in Pydar Street . . . it's the other direction. No one crosses the square unless they're going to church.'

'Maybe I wasn't *passing* your house. Maybe I was standing in the freezing cold, hoping to catch a glimpse of you.'

I was glad of the darkness, grateful he could not see the tears pooling in my eyes. 'That's rather foolish, Luke. You'll catch cold. Patients don't want their doctors to get ill.'

His sigh was gentle. 'Then I'll stop doing it. I'll go straight home to Mother's roaring fire instead.' He slid his hand across the bench, our fingers touching as he offered me his handkerchief.

And where thou art not, desolation.

His voice was stronger now. 'I think we should start Edmund on dandelion root tincture. Melancholy encompasses grief, sorrow, and fear, but it's just as likely to trigger anger and the desire for revenge. It's a vicious circle — nervousness and a sense of being overwhelmed leads

331

to lack of sleep, which in turn causes great agitation — leading to anxiety and nervous exhaustion. Thoughts get distorted, nightmares become a pattern, and that, in turn, gives rise to increased fear and a further rise in tension.'

He had read my mind; well, almost. 'What about skullcap? Your father swore by skullcap.'

'Skullcap tea at night. Or maybe we should start him straight on tincture of St John's wort? Two to three drops daily for three weeks and we should see a difference.'

'Thank you for coming with me, Luke.'

His hand rested on the seat between us, waiting for me to return his handkerchief. I dabbed my eyes, battling my tears. St John's wort needed to be freshly harvested, the tincture made only from flowers and buds picked in June. There was passion flower, too. And we could try lavender.

Captain de la Croix was breathing steadily, the carriage dark, and I slipped off my glove, sliding my hand slowly towards Luke's waiting fingers. I could not help myself, the yearning to touch him was overwhelming, too powerful to resist. Luke's hand closed over mine and a familiar warmth flooded my heart.

'Are you all right?' I whispered, the pain so intense I could hardly breathe. I waited, the pain growing worse, ripping my heart as Luke drew his hand away.

'I will be,' he whispered. 'And I believe Edmund will be too.'

★ ★ ★

Tincture of St John's wort: for melancholy, and for the nervous exhaustion of heart-break. For desolation and sorrow. For a sense of overriding fear, envy and anger.

Flowers of St John's wort must be harvested in full bloom, either in late June or early July. Once harvested, chop, crush and bruise the flowers until the juices run red. Pack the crushed flowers into a jar, then add brandy to cover the entirety. Seal well and turn daily for six weeks until the mixture becomes blood red in colour. Strain through a muslin cloth and keep the tincture in a sealed bottle.

THE LADY HERBALIST

38

We entered Fosse with its narrow main street, the shutters in the long row of houses closed against the cold night air and came to a stop, the lamps casting pools of light against the cottages on either side. Luke pulled down the window and peered out.

'It's going to be tight. These lanes can hardly take a carriage.'

Pierre eased his shoulders. 'This has been a most comfortable journey. And very quick.'

Men were hurrying along the quayside, a strong smell of grilled fish filling the carriage. Moonlight glinted on the black river, the masts of the ships rising above us. We pulled slowly up the hill, heading for the lamps burning against the vast redbrick house with its eight sash windows and large portico — Admiral House, my godfather's new house in Fosse. An arch led round to the stables but we remained on the road. The doorman stepped forward and I pulled down the window.

'Will you tell Lady Pendarvis that Miss Carew is here?' I asked.

He shook his head. 'Lady Pendarvis and Sir Alexander Pendarvis have just this minute left to spend the evening with Sir James and Lady Polcarrow . . . at Polcarrow.'

'Thank you. We'll go straight there.'

Light from the lamps filled the carriage and Pierre de la Croix shifted stiffly. 'But we will disturb their evening. This is very awkward.'

'Not at all,' I reassured him. 'Sir James Polcarrow may look very stern but we know him well and he'll welcome us — as will Lady Polcarrow. They'll understand.'

He shifted his position, reaching for the leather satchel. 'I am in your most kind hands, Miss Carew. But now we have stopped, I can take this opportunity to ease my *rhumatisme*.' He rummaged inside his bag and drew out a small brown bottle. 'Mrs Hambley kindly bought this for me. The doctor came to our door and she tells me she got the last bottle. Imagine . . . a London doctor in Bodmin. We are lucky, are we not?'

I reached forward, my hand knocking Luke's as we rushed to stop him.

'Pierre, stop! May I see that?' Luke took the bottle and held it to the light of the lamp. '*J. Reynold, chemist and druggist from Richmond, London, wishes to inform the nobility, gentry and public that all medicines, elixirs and lozenges are prepared . . .*'

'Luke — that's the same label . . . it's the same bottle.'

'Have you had any of this yet, Pierre?' I caught the fear in his voice.

'*Non* — not yet. I've just got it. It is for the aches and pains of *rhumatisme*. The doctor told Mrs Hambley it would be particularly effective for the stiffness I have.'

'He would . . . but it means nothing. This

335

concoction is particularly effective for *everything* and *everyone* — including horses. You mustn't take it. The man's a quack . . . a charlatan. May I take it with me to test? We need evidence of the harm these concoctions do. I'll write you a proper prescription — one that will help you, not *poison* you.'

'Of course, but Mrs Hambley was adamant he was a proper physician . . . '

'Did she say what he looked like?'

'An old man, with long white hairs. A beard, she said, and gloves with the tips of his fingers missing. He was very knowledgeable about sailors and the illnesses they face.'

Luke slipped the bottle into his pocket. 'Very knowledgeable. That's how he's so successful in selling his concoctions.'

A large gatehouse with heavy locked gates loomed in front of us. Luke pulled down the window and a gatekeeper in red livery stepped forward. 'I am Dr Bohenna and Miss Carew is a good friend of Sir James and Lady Polcarrow. We wish to speak with Miss Carew's godfather, Sir Alexander, who we believe is dining here.'

The gatekeeper opened the heavy gates to a line of lanterns leading up the long drive. Dark and forbidding in the winter evening, the lamps cast eerie shadows on the closely clipped privet, but last summer the drive had been filled with bleating sheep and we had been greeted with the laughter of two young girls chasing puppies down the grass, Lady Polcarrow hurtling after them, her skirts gripped above her knees as she called them back.

More of a castle than a house, the crenellations, tall turrets and pointed arched windows rose in front of us. Stone steps led up to the ancient oak door, two lamps burning on either side. A groom ran to attend us and I stood on the steps, breathing in the scent of jasmine and woodsmoke, but, most especially, the smell of the sea.

Below us, rooftops glinted silver, the new street lamps casting a soft yellow glow. Moonlight shimmered on the black water, lights shining in Porthruan on the other side of the river. Lanterns swung on anchored ships and I breathed deeply, relishing the fresh breeze that caressed my cheeks. I could hear the jangle of rigging, the sound of a fiddle. Pierre stood by my side, also breathing deeply, smelling the salt, no doubt feeling the lure of the ocean.

We followed the footman across the polished flagstones, past the heavily engraved staircase with its elaborate swirls of animals and birds. An ancient stone house, not dissimilar to Pendowrick, yet here there was such warmth — a fire roaring in the huge fireplace, a portrait of a smiling woman with a basket of flowers and a spaniel at her feet.

Heavy beams criss-crossed the ceiling above us, portraits of ennobled ancestors watching us as we walked down the corridor — a longcase clock with a painted face and shining brass hands, a Chinese vase, a bowl of rose petals, and a child's abacus. The footman announced us and we heard cries of pleasure.

Lady Polcarrow rose from her chair. 'Miss

Carew, this is a lovely surprise.' Her ivory silk gown shimmered in the firelight, the lace at her elbows falling in an elegant fan. She looked more beautiful than ever, her chestnut hair glowing red in the candlelight, loosely coiled and held in place beneath a wreath of silk roses. 'Dr Bohenna — this is an honour . . . I thought you never left your patients?' She smiled her devastating smile, her fiercely intelligent eyes now resting on Pierre.

'Lady Polcarrow, please forgive us . . . I hate intruding on you like this. May I introduce Captain de la Croix?'

Pierre bowed deeply. 'It is my honour, Lady Polcarrow.'

Across the room, I caught my godfather's eye. Sir Alexander Pendarvis stood stiffly, waiting for Sir James to greet us. James Polcarrow stepped forward, bowing to Captain de la Croix. 'You are very welcome, Captain de la Croix.' He turned, his stern face breaking into a radiant smile. 'And you are always welcome, Miss Carew . . . Dr Bohenna, I'm delighted to see you. Please, come to the fire. This is an unexpected pleasure.'

We had charged uninvited into their house but I knew their welcome was genuine. Sir James wore his dark hair short, his straight nose and square jaw as chiselled as the Roman bust we had just passed in his hall. A man in his prime, tall, assured, a wealthy landowner and Member of Parliament, a passionate advocate for the abolition of slavery and the adoring father of three daughters.

'*If* Mother knew we were here, she would send

her regards,' I said, smiling back into his extraordinary blue eyes.

'And are we not to tell her?' He looked amused, glancing at his wife with a rise of both eyebrows.

I shrugged. 'She thinks we're in Bodmin . . . but she was very particular Dr Bohenna came with me.' Another raise of his dark brows, another smile at his wife.

Uncle Alex stepped forward, grasping the handle of his ebony cane. He kissed my cheek, bowing to Luke and Captain Pierre. 'Captain de la Croix, I presume Miss Carew has brought you here for my protection?'

'Uncle Alex — '

He held up his hand. 'Amelia, my dear, no explanation is necessary. I've long been anxious that Sir Edmund might react badly to the knowledge Captain de la Croix is a friend of your family. I can guess why you're here. You wish to afford Captain de la Croix my protection because you believe Edmund might seek him out?'

I nodded, and Lady Pendarvis rose from her chair, tall, elegant, a sapphire brooch glinting in her turban. Her blue silk rustled as she held out her hands. 'Dearest Amelia, it is lovely to see you, and *Capitaine de la Croix* is indeed welcome to stay with us for as long as need be.'

She stood impassive as her compatriot bowed, her extraordinary hooded eyes under their perfect half-circle eyebrows pinning Captain de la Croix as I knew they would. In her late fifties, her coiled hair was still luxurious, no hint of grey, her movements retaining the grace of a woman half her age. 'Perhaps, you will be able to persuade me that my brothers' exile from their homeland and the ruin of their estates has made for a better society? That your Corsican *upstart* has the interest of his country at heart — not just *greed* and *self-aggrandisement*?' Her French accent had lessened after more than thirty years of marriage but was still discernible, especially when she was angry.

Pierre's dark hair fell forward as he bowed again. 'I am a simple sailor, Lady Pendarvis. I do my best for my country, but whether I can persuade you the blood that has been spilled is worth it will remain to be seen.'

Uncle Alex was watching me. 'Captain de la Croix, you are welcome to my protection, as would be any parole prisoner who faced the same circumstances. The Admiralty has strict laws governing *prisonniers en liberte condition-nelle* and they must be heeded. But as it happens I have something in mind that will adhere to these strict regulations yet go some way to alleviate the situation we find ourselves in.'

He was wearing his grey wig, his fine-boned chin closely shaven, his cravat pinned with a silver pin. He was always elegant, always immaculately dressed, his jacket well tailored, his waistcoat beautifully embroidered; his polished left black boot matching the ebony peg beneath the buckles of his right knee. Only his eyes looked shrewder, a hardness in them I rarely saw.

'I need to engage an agent to report to the French prisoners' board — someone who writes

340

his findings in French but who speaks good English. I need to document the monthly numbers — the general health of the prisoners and the conditions within which they're kept. We're to document everything — the food they're given, the state of their clothes, their hammocks, their access to exercise and so forth, and I've had you in mind for this position for quite a while.'

'Sir Alexander, I am honoured, but — '

'This is a genuine post, Captain de la Croix, and you are amply qualified to take it. We are all aware of the reason you're here, but it's not the reason I offer you this post.' He turned to me. 'My fears are grounded, are they, Amelia?'

I nodded. 'Edmund found out about Pierre last night . . . he was really angry. It frightened me . . . and this morning I found out he'd taken the stagecoach to Bodmin . . . and I was scared he might do something foolish. Please don't think ill of Edmund — he needs time and help . . . he's come back to find a man he considers a direct enemy is our friend and he's hurt. It must have been a terrible shock . . . '

Normally when Uncle Alex looked at me his grey eyes softened, but they held firm, the steel in them remaining. 'I've been rereading his Admiralty report.'

'And does it mention anger?'

His mouth tightened. 'Among other things.'

I felt cold to the bone. Lady Polcarrow must have seen me shiver. 'Amelia, please, take off your cloak and come nearer the fire.' She pulled the bell-pull, standing by her husband, tall, willowy, the circlet of silk flowers in her hair making her look like a Greek goddess. 'Henderson will show you where you can freshen up. Take your time, we're in no hurry, but I hope you're hungry. We've got roast pork tonight with apple dumplings and Sir James' favourite pudding — Mrs Munroe's sent us up a whortleberry pie and that's never to be missed. Make yourselves comfortable, all of you, please, and join us when you're ready.'

39

Achandelier hung from the heavily beamed ceiling, further candles grouped around the room. The room was bright, the yellow drapes at the windows bringing cheer to the surroundings; the fire was roaring, a set of colourful tapestries hanging on the wall, and an elegant china vase standing waist-height on the floor. Behind me, fine china ornaments crafted out of Sir James' clay stood proudly displayed in a glass-fronted cabinet.

A portrait hung above the fireplace filling the room with beauty — Rose Pengelly, holding a red rose in her hand: the fiery shipbuilder's daughter who had captured Sir James' heart so completely. She held it still, only more so; I could see it in his smile, in the hand he rested on her arm, the adoration in his eyes every time he looked at her.

He had carved the huge leg of pork with seamless ease, the piled-high tureen of roast potatoes was now empty, every last carrot and parsnip enjoyed. The Staffordshire plates were cleared away and a huge whortleberry pie now demanded our attention. Silver candlesticks glinted on the table, the soft light flickering across our faces. Steering the conversation away from war, Lady Polcarrow asked for news of my nephews and we talked of Lady Pendarvis's new grandson, of Lady Polcarrow's three daughters.

I smiled back at them, hoping they would not see my heart was breaking. Both kept glancing at me: Lady Polcarrow with her intelligent eyes in their thick black lashes; Aunt Marie, with her hooded lids and her uncanny ability to know just what I was thinking. They loved Luke: I could see concern deep in their eyes, their gentle hints that he was not looking well. They had pressed him to eat, their glances aching with unspoken questions.

Uncle Alex turned to Pierre. 'You're looking well, Captain de la Croix. Mrs Hambley is obviously looking after you.'

'Thank you, Sir Alex, she is too good a cook.' He smiled from under his black curls, 'My waist, it has increased.'

'As agent, you'll accompany me on my visits and your reports will be sent directly to the French authorities. I won't censor them. Our prison in Norman Cross is, I believe, quite exemplary — a first-class example of how to maintain a man's dignity whilst denying him his freedom, but you will also see conditions that fall short of *satisfactory*. There are nearly twenty-two thousand of you now — entire families from merchant ships, many from Africa, even India. Most speak no English and you must be their voice. My job is to see each prisoner treated fairly, yet even as we speak the numbers rise.'

James Polcarrow sat elegantly in his high-back chair, swilling his claret, his dark brows creasing. 'Still no successful exchanges?'

Sir Alex shook his head. 'All my attempts to exchange have fallen on deaf ears — *all* of them.

344

It's long been my opinion France doesn't want her prisoners back. Every day the cost to our government rises — money we can ill afford. The longer they keep them here, and the more we capture, the emptier our coffers become. I'm told it's running to nearly £300,000 a year — money we could otherwise spend on ships and provisions.'

Pierre de la Croix gave a sad nod of agreement, consternation in his dark eyes. 'A truth I would like to deny, Sir Alexander, but we, too, believe we are not wanted back in France. It will be my pleasure to act as your agent. You look after us very well — better, I have to say, than the treatment Sir Edmund Melville received. He has every right to detest the sight of me. The conditions in his dungeon were . . . far from satisfactory.'

I had to speak for Edmund, I needed them to know how much he had suffered. 'He wasn't in the dungeons, Captain de la Croix — he was in the prison hulk beneath the fort. But you're right, his conditions were brutal. He was frequently beaten . . . he was half-starved, forced to repair the battery and the defences. They worked him like a slave. But that's what saved him. He was able to watch the ships — he must have seen your ship, Captain de la Croix. He watched every ship enter and leave the harbour and he took his chance when he could. And thank goodness he did.'

I looked up at the sudden clash of Pierre's fork on his plate. He was staring at me, his eyes puzzled. 'Prison hulk . . . in the harbour?'

'Yes, directly below the fort. It's a despicable practice. It's to stop our ships from attacking.'

Uncle Alex leaned forward, taking a nut from the centre-piece. 'It's more and more apparent that the names of prisoners in hulks are not getting recorded. The poor men die nameless. Hulks are rancid and foul and the men not expected to live, so why bother with lists? We have many examples of men imprisoned where we have no records.'

'Forgive me, Sir Alex . . . Miss Carew, but there was no prison hulk under the walls of the fort. There are sharp rocks there — but besides that, Guadeloupe did not have a prison hulk. Never. Not while I was there.'

'They did, Captain de la Croix. Edmund was imprisoned there for a whole year.'

His voice was soft, yet insistent. 'No, Miss Carew, not in Guadeloupe. I swear to you. There was no prison hulk in 'ninety-three, 'ninety-four, 'ninety-five . . . or the first half of 'ninety-six. I know that for absolute certain.'

His eyes held mine, like shards piercing my heart, and I stared back, trying to breathe. 'There was . . . perhaps you just didn't see it?'

The fire crackled, the room suddenly silent, but for the terrible thumping of my heart.

Captain de la Croix looked Uncle Alex straight in the eye. 'Non. I swear, I do not lie. There was no prison hulk in the harbour — just the dungeons in the fort.'

'Are you quite certain? We have names of the prisoners inside the fort, but we have none for the hulk.'

The captain's reply was instant, spoken with absolute conviction. 'Because there was none.'

I could hardly hear Luke for the pounding in my ears. 'Perhaps Sir Edmund was confused? Perhaps without realizing it, he was taken to another island?'

I fought to breathe. 'No, Luke, he definitely said it was Guadeloupe. It's in all his records.'

Pierre de la Croix shook his head. 'Forgive me for speaking so bluntly, but one of us is not speaking the truth, and I know it is not me.'

I thought I might be sick, the room was too hot, no air to breathe. 'There'll be a reason . . . ' I was gripped by panic. He had lied to the innkeeper, he had stabled his horse under a false name, he had gone to significant lengths to hide his whereabouts. I tried to sound strong, but I could only whisper. 'There must have been a prison hulk . . . Edmund would not lie.'

Uncle Alex's voice sounded distant. 'Amelia, I'm not happy with this. Far from it. Captain de la Croix has no reason to lie. There are no records of a prison hulk, though one was suspected in Martinique. You said Edmund showed great anger? Setting off as fast as he could after he heard about a frigate captain who'd served in Guadeloupe? He saddled his horse and rushed to Bodmin?'

'He took the early stagecoach.' I could not say *and he lied to cover his tracks.*

'Amelia, I understand this is very hard for you, but it's vital I make this point. You saw great anger in Edmund . . . but what if the rage you saw wasn't the desire for revenge — but instead

347

was fear? The fear of a man who knows he must keep his story safe? If an escape *was to be believed*, how much better to be from a hulk floating on the water than a dungeon deep beneath a fort. A hulk where no names are recorded?'

'Uncle Alex! How can you even think that? It's just the wrong harbour — the wrong part of the island.'

'All his records state he was kept in a prison hulk under Fort Fleur d'Epée. If there was no prison hulk under the fort, then we have to face the distinct possibility that Edmund is lying.'

'You judge him too harshly. He's forgetful — that's all. His head injury makes it hard for him to remember. His vision's damaged and his hearing is poor. Sometimes he blanks out completely . . . sometimes his headaches render him incapable of even lifting his head. He's a sick man and he's made a mistake. That's all. He's come back and his mind's gone blank and he remembers it wrongly.'

I needed to breathe. I needed to hide the terrible twisting in my stomach, yet he would not stop. 'Amelia, my love, no British ship can verify or disprove his story, but a French frigate captain who sailed in and out of the harbour while Edmund claims he was in the hulk would be able to. What if he knew just *one word* from Captain de la Croix and his story would no longer hold? What if his sole intention is not to avenge his shipmates, but to silence Captain de la Croix?'

My chest was too tight. I had to gulp for air, control my sudden giddiness. They were all thinking the same; I could see it in their faces, the sudden horror in their eyes. 'It's not a *story*,' I whispered. 'He was praised for his valour.'

Luke rose from his chair and stood behind me. 'Maybe the blow to his head rendered Sir Edmund unconscious and . . . instead of capture, he found himself crawling to freedom? What if he was trying to reach a naval base when he was taken by the Portuguese ship?'

His words brought me sudden hope, but Uncle Alex merely frowned. 'And what if, as time passed, he couldn't bring himself to return to the navy?'

I hardly recognized my godfather; it was Admiral Sir Alexander Pendarvis speaking, one time Commander-in-Chief of His Majesty's Channel Fleet.

Aunt Marie had been silently watching. When she spoke her voice was soft, making it harder to hold back my tears. 'Amelia, dearest love, your godfather is not without influence . . . He *does* understand, and he will do everything in his power to see this confusion cleared. You think you have led Edmund into a trap — that you have exposed him to great harm, that your desire to see Captain de la Croix safe has led you to betray a man you once loved so very dearly. To help Edmund now, you must tell us everything because it will serve Edmund much better if we get to the truth.'

Luke was still behind me, his hand resting on the back of the chair. I drew a deep breath. 'Edmund hated the navy,' I whispered. 'He should never have taken the commission . . . he was very unhappy. He wanted to fit in . . . his letters were full of how hard he tried. He wanted me to be proud of him — like I am of my brothers — but in reality, he was desperately unhappy. The men in his mess hated him . . . he was the target of some very cruel behaviour.'

'He was the target of malice?'

'Yes, Lady Polcarrow. Edmund was, and still is, very impressionable. He didn't stand a chance. They stole from his chest — they took his money, his gold watch, his compass and his silver nutmeg grater . . . and some of his clothes went missing. He tried not to let it affect him — he sought advice from one of the other officers, but he was told it would make things worse if he went to Captain Owen. So he did nothing . . . and they never returned his belongings. There was very little left — they stole everything.'

James Polcarrow's dark brows creased. He had been following the conversation with deepening concern. 'Forgive me, Miss Carew. They were at sea and no one left the ship?'

'Yes. They kept off shore because of the fevers.'

'And they didn't return his property once he was declared dead?' His blue eyes pierced mine. 'That rather goes against the honour of sailors for their fallen shipmates. I'm sure your brothers would know this to be the case — fellow shipmates often pay more at auction for the clothes of their fallen friends than they're worth, and if personal property is *borrowed*, or taken out of malice, they would see it returned. Especially if no one had left the ship. Clothes and possessions are listed in their sea chests. Am I right to believe this, Alex?'

'Stealing from fellow shipmates incurs the severest punishment — running the gauntlet. It's harsh and strictly imposed. Very few risk it.' Uncle Alex's voice had taken a chilling tone. 'What was returned, Amelia?'

'His Bible, a shell for me . . . and my miniature portrait. Very little else — nothing of what they stole.'

His eyes narrowed. 'This makes it worse. We now need to consider a very *uncomfortable* thought.' I caught the glance he gave his wife, the returning rise of her perfectly arched eyebrow. A pulse twitched by his mouth. 'And that is this: we must consider whether they *may* or *may not* have actually been stolen?'

A bolt shot through me. I felt winded, reeling as if punched. 'But they were! He wrote it in his letters. I'm sorry to sound so angry but you're being really rather beastly.'

In the silence, the fire crackled. I thought they would hear the thumping of my heart. Uncle Alex had never spoken to me like this; he was kind, he was indulgent, he never questioned or probed. He bought me books, helped me study. He had pored over the designs of my herb garden, always encouraging, sending numerous pamphlets about physic gardens and the names of gardeners I could contact. I hardly recognized the fury in his face.

'I know I sound harsh, Amelia. I would protect you from this if I could, but this is something I've come across before. It's important to take money with you — a gold watch to sell, a compass for when you steal a boat.'

The room whirled round me. 'They were stolen from him . . . how can you think otherwise?'

The man questioning me was Admiral Sir Alexander Pendarvis, knighted for exceptional valour. He was not *without* influence, he was *the influence*, the adored hero of all my brothers and every last man who served under him. The Admiral whose word was law, who court-martialled and imposed the severest penalties.

Luke pulled out my chair, his hand resting on my back as he helped me put my head between my knees. Someone was fanning me, Aunt Marie, I think. Lady Polcarrow handed me a glass of water.

Uncle Alex addressed Sir James, his words slicing the air. 'This doesn't sound anything like a scared man running on the off chance. This was carefully planned — a cynical, well-executed desertion. He even had time to lie to Amelia in his letters.'

'I believe he volunteered to lead the landing party . . . ?'

'Apparently he was quite insistent. They carried powder bags over their shoulders — and no one checks the bags. It would be the perfect way to carry money to bribe a crew, even to buy a boat. Certainly a change of clothing. It sounds like the man had planned it down to the last detail; he gave orders for his men to return to the ship, waited until they were in the rowing boats — the heroic officer who wanted all his men safe

352

— then he lit a small fuse, fabricated his fall and lay there as if dead.'

'But I understood one of his men went back to save him?'

'Yes . . . and died later of *extensive* wounds in the fort. That's why I've been re-reading Edmund's papers.'

'Because the man was taken to the fort and Sir Edmund was imprisoned in the hulk?'

'Yes, but now I see it differently. According to the prison records, the man was found burning in a fire.'

40

The hateful conversation continued. 'Desertion is often a spur-of-the-moment decision — a sudden opportunistic chance — or it can be accidental, often unintended. Stragglers miss their ships for a number of reasons — poor transport, bad weather, ships needing to sail in an emergency. Some ramble too far ashore and through inattention or drunkenness miss their ships, some are always watching, waiting to seize the first opportunity.'

'It's not a hangable offence, is it, Sir Alex?' Luke returned to his seat, leaving Lady Polcarrow and Aunt Marie beside me.

'Not for the ranks, Dr Bohenna. If a sailor's marked absent for three successive weekly musters and is returned to his ship, the captain can enforce whatever punishment he sees fit. The runaway could face twelve lashes, sometimes more. Some captains show leniency, others charge them with more than one crime and demand twelve lashes for each crime. It depends on the circumstances — but we're talking about an officer, Dr Bohenna. Again, it depends on the severity of the situation — desertion is tried through court martial. And yes, it could be a hangable offence. It could involve several hundred lashes, flogging round the fleet — imprisonment in Marshalsea, or the severest fine. It depends on the evidence submitted at court martial.'

'Miss Carew has often spoken of Sir Edmund's gentle nature. What if his ability to reason was affected? What if his possessions *had* been stolen and he didn't plan to desert but was knocked unconscious and he managed to crawl away — only to watch his ship sailing away on the horizon? What would he do?'

Alexander Pendarvis regarded Luke through shrewd eyes. 'You are determined to defend him, Dr Bohenna? If he wasn't captured he should have gone straight to a naval base . . . find his way to an island under British control. There are many within close distance — Dominica, Grenada, Barbados. But instead, he tells us he was taken as a slave and they sailed the Caribbean Sea to the coast of Venezuela. To Brazil where he writes to Amelia.'

His voice was harsh, spoken through thin lips, yet Edmund had described it so clearly. I had exact images in my mind — the rancid bilges, the locked grilles, the way he had stared up at the moon; the men who had died in their chains around him, the relentless heat, the fortifications they had been made to rebuild. The ships he had watched, the chance he had taken at just the right time.

'He *was* imprisoned . . . ' I cried. 'He has manacle scars on his wrists to prove it. I've seen them — deep purple bands that cut into his flesh. It's in his medical records. He *was* imprisoned.'

In the sudden silence I saw pity in their eyes. Uncle Alex shook his head. 'It's the first thing they think to do. They get tight bands fitted to constantly chafe their skin; it might hurt, but it's effective.'

I stared back in horror, fighting my tears. Lady Polcarrow's frown deepened. She stood up, tall, elegant, the kindness in her voice making my mouth quiver. 'Come, Miss Carew. We will withdraw and leave the men to their brandy.'

Deep sorrow etched Captain de la Croix's fallen face. He remained silent, staring down at his plate, his fist held against his chin. He was a good man, kind and polite; there was no reason for him to lie, yet Edmund had lied this very morning. Lady Polcarrow slipped her hand through my arm, Aunt Marie's hand was on my shoulder, strong, supportive, leading me to the door.

I needed time to breathe, to compose myself. I felt winded, my senses reeling. Edmund should have told me the truth — that he had crawled to safety and tried to find a ship home. I would not have thought less of him — no one would have thought less of him. Only Luke understood. Only Luke. My legs were buckling, Rose Polcarrow and Aunt Marie leading me as surely as I was leading Edmund to the gallows, as if I had hold of his hand and was taking him straight to the hangman. Stabbing him in the back. The worst kind of treachery.

Uncle Alex's voice cut through my pain. 'James, do you have pen and paper — enough for four of us? If you don't mind, I'd like us to follow the ladies through to the drawing room. There's something I'd like to do.'

'Paper? Yes, I can certainly get some.'

'Thank you. Something's been niggling me,

and I'd like to try something while we have Dr Bohenna with us.'

They followed right behind us. I sat upright and tense, Aunt Marie smoothing her gown as she sat beside me. A footman brought a filigree silver tray with a glass decanter and crystal glasses, and I watched Uncle Alex swirl his brandy in his hand. He had never wanted me to marry Edmund; he thought Edmund weak, mistaking his vulnerability for foolishness, his sensitivity for lack of manhood.

I fought for courage. Uncle Alex would have to defend Edmund's character if it came to a court martial — I would plead with him, beg him to tell everyone Edmund was a good, kind, gentle man, that he was vulnerable, cruelly treated, and must have acted under the severest provocation.

Sir James was handing everyone a sheet of paper and Uncle Alex shook his head. 'No paper for me, James — just one for Lady Polcarrow, my wife, yourself and Captain de la Croix. Perhaps you should all sit round the table and use this inkwell?'

He pointed to a round table between the two French windows and waited while they settled themselves with a sheet of paper, their pens poised. 'Now, I want you to imagine that Midshipman Melville has suffered the rigours of a harsh imprisonment. He has been bartered for alcohol and finds himself heading for Sao Luis, in Brazil, on a ship that carries yellow fever. The crew are sick and dying, and Midshipman Melville is, himself, struck with the illness. The captain orders the sick men off the ship, and sends them in the direction of a sandy beach where he knows the good nuns of the Sacred Heart will take them in.'

He turned to Luke. 'Dr Bohenna, describe if you please, how Sir Edmund would feel as he rises at the first opportunity from his near deathbed, to write a letter.'

Luke cleared his throat, glancing at me. 'He'd be very weak — his legs especially. He'd be helped to the chair. He'd feel dizzy — light-headed. He may even have a pounding headache. Yellow fever causes aches in both the joints and the muscles so he'd be in pain and he might still have some residual fever.'

'Thank you, Dr Bohenna.' The lines round his mouth hardened. 'So, Edmund Melville takes up the pen and with shaking hand starts to write . . . now, write, please. Each of you — Captain de la Croix, write in French. You are Edmund Melville, and this is the first opportunity you have to let your beloved fiancée know you've survived and you're safe and will do your utmost to return to her as soon as possible. You're feeling just as Dr Bohenna described but you're filled with such elation. Now write, please . . . write from the heart.'

None of them had seen Edmund's letter from the convent but Luke had, and I searched his face, the fire reflecting his auburn hints, the dusting of freckles on his cheeks. There was sadness in his eyes, a glance of fear, and my heart thumped. He looked as if he were trying to warn me. He had guessed what this was about and knew it would do me harm.

Their pens scratched the paper, their words flowing as Uncle Alex hovered behind them, watching the lines grow into a paragraph. 'And stop,' he said abruptly. 'Stop now. Put down your pens. I don't need to read what you've written, but if you could lay your letters out so we can see them.'

Luke came to my side and we walked slowly to the table. Captain de la Croix rose for me to take his seat and I hardly thanked him, staring instead at the different writing: Lady Polcarrow's beautiful copperplate, Aunt Marie's flowing loops and fancy flourishes, Sir James' precise hand, the urgency in Captain de la Croix's hurried scrawl.

All the letters ended abruptly, all mid-sentence, just like Edmund's. They had written the name of the convent, the date, and had all started with *My darling Amelia*. But I was no longer his darling Amelia; I was his betrayer, the tightener of the noose that would hang him.

Uncle Alex pointed to each of the letters. 'You've all written the *Convent of the Sacred Heart* and the date, but not one of you has written for *whom* the letter is intended. How is it to reach its destination?'

Lady Polcarrow raised her hands in protest. 'But you stopped us before we could address it, Sir Alex! You gave us very little time.'

'You were going to finish the letter, then sign it, fold it, and write the address clearly, Lady Polcarrow?'

'Yes, of course I was. I'm in São Luis, Brazil, and the letter must get to Truro. I would have addressed it very clearly.'

She had said the words he wanted to hear. He nodded, staring down at each of the letters. 'Yes — you would leave an appropriate gap so that when you folded the letter, the address could be written on the front — and you would seal the letter on the back. But what if you knew you weren't going to finish it? What if you were going to stop mid-sentence and someone else was going to *find* the letter and send it for you? You would need to make sure they knew where to send it.'

Rose Polcarrow's bright eyes sharpened. 'I'm not sure I quite understand, Sir Alex.'

I understood, and so did Luke. I held his gaze. This was how the trial would go, each man made to write the same letter. Uncle Alex was addressing me, but I could not look at him. I remained staring at Luke, desperate to hold back my tears.

'Your parents told me Edmund had written the address on his letter — and it took eighteen months to reach you. But we're a hard-bitten, cautious lot in the Admiralty. We pick over every word — *every detail*. Prize money is at stake, a man's reputation. When officers return from unexplained absences we use a very fine toothcomb. Everything is questioned and indeed, everything Edmund told us *was* verifiable — the ship he escaped from *was* carrying what he said, and it *had* visited the ports he told us it had. The tides correlated to the seasons, the passage from Guadeloupe totally feasible, though he seemed to have had more wind in the doldrums than I would expect there to be, but his story added up. Everything he told us matched the seasons and the tides.'

'But something kept niggling me, and I've been over and over his records, trying to discover what was keeping me awake. And then it struck me. Would a man in his position start a letter with your full address? Who writes the address of the recipient first? Surely not a sick man who can hardly walk, whose head is throbbing, who wants only to tell his beloved fiancée how much he loves her and how he's coming back? And I think I've just proved my concern is a valid one.'

Sir James studied the letters. 'Miss Carew received a letter that finished abruptly — just like this?'

'Yes. And I believe it to be fabricated — an elaborate hoax. I believe we should mistrust the date, even the place. The fact it took eighteen months to arrive is not out of the question, but it does warrant caution. Edmund Melville would know to leave the West Indies before the hurricane months of August and September. Preferably he would leave in July — I wonder if he . . .'

Aunt Marie slipped to my side, tall, elegant, her exotic perfume too heavy for my reeling senses. Lady Polcarrow likewise stood by my side, her eyes seeking her husband's. 'Perhaps you could show the others your new urn on the terrace, James?'

Sir James smiled but remained looking at Uncle Alex. 'It's rather cold out there . . . and it's not very well lit. Perhaps in the daylight, my love?'

Her hand gripped my shoulder. She swallowed, trying again. 'Sir Alex hasn't seen your new book on minerals yet. Perhaps you may like to take everyone *to the library?*'

Sir James smiled, indicating the fire. 'I think they'd rather stay here. The fire's out in the library and this one's blazing.'

Lady Polcarrow's voice took on a definite edge. 'Captain de la Croix and Sir Alex will be very interested in your latest figurines, James. And so would Dr Bohenna. They will all be interested *when you take them back into the dining room* and show them.'

He smiled benignly, reaching for his brandy. 'To be honest, they all look rather the same to me.'

'*James?*'

He glanced up, suddenly aware of his wife's blazing eyes. He looked surprised, as if he might have missed something. 'Yes, my love?'

'The dining room. Your china. Your books in the library.'

He stood straight, a sharp swallow, his hand immediately on Captain de la Croix's shoulder. 'Allow me to show you some ornaments crafted from my own china clay. Come, sir. Come, Alex . . . Luke . . . this way. I have a very interesting new book on minerals . . . '

Pierre de la Croix had been following the exchange between Sir James and Lady Polcarrow with growing concern. He stood stiffly, bowing abruptly, his petrified expression hard to hide. Sir James kept his hand on his shoulder, leading the men from the room. 'You're a frigate captain, sir?' I heard him say. 'You ran a tight ship, had men jumping to your command?'

'Indeed, Sir James.'

I was holding back my tears, somehow managing to keep them from flowing. Sir James took hold of the door handle. 'You're not married, I believe, Captain de la Croix?' he said as he shut the door.

Rose Polcarrow sighed. '*Finally!*' she said, her arm slipping round my shoulders.

Aunt Marie waved her fan furiously. 'What was he thinking — behaving as if he were addressing a court? My dearest love, I am so sorry. Your uncle adores you . . . he loves you like a daughter, but I think that clouds his judgement. For such a slight man, he can have the tread of an elephant. How could he spring that on you? It was ill thought out and very unkind. Rose — you should have insisted on the terrace. A stay *outside* in the freezing cold would have done him no harm at all!'

Tears began flowing down my cheeks. I had stared at that letter, never thinking it was false. Was it a lie? If so, what else had he fabricated to hide the truth?

Aunt Marie held me to her. 'My poor darling. My poor, poor, darling girl. Weep. Let it all out. Don't try to be brave.' She turned to Rose. 'My love . . . I need some brandy.'

I could hear myself howling, sobbing, as if a cork had been removed from a shaken bottle; like a pipe bursting, a torrent flowing from a blocked gutter. I could not help myself, the tears streaming down my face as I gulped for air. At last I stopped, my shoulders heaving.

'Now, tell us, my love — tell us what you

cannot tell the men — what you cannot even bear to think. We are women and we understand. What is it that you are hiding behind those sad eyes of yours? Because you are hiding something, my love, and it is tearing you apart.'

'It's just the shock.'

'No it isn't, my love. Tell us what is really in your heart.'

41

They each held a hand; Aunt Marie, with her long aristocratic fingers, Rose Polcarrow holding the other tightly in her lap. Neither would let go, both waiting until I found my voice.

It was more of a whisper. 'Edmund lied to the innkeeper this morning. He told him he was going back to Pendowrick to meet a man who was looking for him. But for my coachman, I would believe Edmund to have gone home. But . . . instead, he left his horse in the stables of the Queen's Head and took the stagecoach to Bodmin — I only know this because my coachman asked in the stables and they told him Edmund gave instructions to stable his horse *under the name of Mr Owen*. And that makes it so much worse.'

Aunt Marie drew a deep breath. 'He did not lie to your face, but he went to considerable effort to conceal his true destination?'

'Yes.'

'And you believe you must protect him now because of the love you once bore him?'

'Yes . . . I do.'

'It was a very long time ago. You were so young. He swept you off your feet and you loved him with a passion. The first stirrings of a young woman's heart can be very powerful — and the flowering of passion can be *mistaken* for true love.'

'No, Aunt Marie, I really loved him ... I vowed to love him. No one understood him like I did. It wasn't just the stirrings of passion — it was so much more than that. It was as if I was sent to protect him. I had such strength — it was as if he needed my strength and together we were whole.'

Her voice softened, a sigh of resignation. 'And after such a long time, the passion returned — you felt the same great stirring as before? He took you in his arms and when he kissed you again, the years disappeared? You melted with the same urgency and now you seek to defend him, just like before? Is that how it is, my love?' She leaned forward, pressing my hand to her lips.

I needed to say it. I needed to speak my thoughts, like a boil to be lanced. 'No ... not at all. That's how I wanted it to be ... how I thought it would be. But it wasn't like that. I'm trying so hard to love him, but there's no draw, no sense of belonging or wanting. It isn't his scars, I'm used to that and I don't find them frightening. It's just ... I couldn't let him kiss me — my whole body went cold. I felt so fearful.'

'Of course you did, my love. After all these years — how can you just step back into loving him when you love Luke so much? You cannot kiss one man when you are so passionate about another.'

Rose Polcarrow's eyes held mine — beautiful mesmerizing eyes, fringed with dark lashes. 'Do you feel drawn to protect Edmund because you can't desert him — that *morally* you can't give up on him? Or do you fear he'll turn on you? Is it physical fear you feel?'

'I don't think he'd ever hurt me, but he's come back so angry . . . his rage flashes like a sheet of white fury across his face. His sister Constance has seen it — that's why she asked to stay with us — but I can understand his anger. I understand how men need help when they return from war. His estate's in ruin, he's spent years away from his responsibilities and his mother has just died. I can understand his anger.'

Those bright eyes held mine. 'Do you fear you can't break your promise to him? That you're *bound* to him?'

'Yes. Well . . . probably. But I've lost my trust in him . . . and my fear is that all those lonely years of heartbreak spent grieving for him might have been *better* spent.'

I had said it; dear God, I had said it. 'I've always defended Edmund against Mother's censure — I've always hidden my hurt at his abrupt departure, but last night . . . well, it's as though I'm finally seeing things clearly — as though I've been wearing blinkers all these years, that everything I believed of him was a lie . . . that he never really loved me. That all the love was on my side.'

Aunt Marie reached for her brandy. 'He told you, to your face, that he didn't love you?'

'No . . . he's very clear about his love — and how we're to be together. And there's definitely passion in him. In Pendowrick he wanted to kiss me — he was about to get very passionate but I

367

couldn't let him touch me. But it's not about *now* . . . it's really about what happened before he left.'

'You have reason to doubt him *before* he left?'

'I've always defended him rushing off like that . . . always found reasons to explain it, but I'm beginning to think Mother might be right. I think I've been burying my hurt all these years. I thought I was making too much of it, that I was being selfish. I told myself love was unconditional, that I must excuse him — but last night, he showed such insensitivity.'

'What did he say?'

'When he left for London I sent him a miniature portrait and he promised to return the favour. I reminded him the last time I saw him and he promised to sit for one. I know it sounds trivial but most sailors send their loved ones a token . . . a keepsake for them to hold.'

'Of course they do! I still have Alex's. A midshipman, just like Edmund.'

'Well, he never sent it, and never mentioned it. But last night, I found out he *had* commissioned one — that he'd sat for one and even chosen its frame, but he never sent it to me.'

I could have said the house was on fire for their sudden reaction, both of them gasping in horror. Aunt Marie dropped my hand. 'You are not serious? He sat for a miniature portrait and never sent it to you?'

'I wouldn't have known if George Halliday hadn't mentioned it. And Edmund just shrugged it off . . . he said he didn't think to look in his trunk when he collected his uniform, and that when he found it wasn't there, he thought he hadn't ordered it correctly.'

'Nonsense! The man left for war without either sending his picture to his fiancée or leaving a forwarding address so it could reach you? That cannot be. Who is George Halliday?'

'He's a friend from childhood. I knew him better than Edmund but by chance they were both having their uniforms measured in London at the same time. George said Edmund had insisted on an encrusted frame . . . but he never sent it to me.'

Rose Polcarrow let go of my hand, walking swiftly to the silver tray to pour herself a brandy. She looked back, her eyes flashing — the eyes of Rose Pengelly, the shipbuilder's daughter who kept every member of the Corporation under tight control; fiery Rose Pengelly with her chestnut hair and her unparalleled intelligence.

'I understand how you feel, Amelia, and I'd feel the same. What you're really saying is that either it was a genuine mistake and he really did forget it in the hurry of collecting his uniform — in which case he was hardly thinking of you and showing no regret at leaving you — or he sent it to *someone else*.'

To voice it like that. To bring it out into the open, it was as if I could breathe again, as if all the anger I was hiding had finally found its voice. 'It's not the only thing that makes me doubt him. He had my miniature with him on board ship . . . and if he really loved me . . . if he *was* planning to desert, then why didn't he take it with him? Frederick wears Charity's next to his

369

heart at all times, so why didn't Edmund? He left it behind and it was found with his possessions.'

Aunt Marie gulped the last dregs of her brandy. '*Mon dieu, l'homme est un bâtard insensible.* I know what my husband would think — that he left it behind to *prove* he wasn't deserting — why else would he not have it on him?'

Rose was still frowning. 'But if there *was* someone else? A maid? A married woman? Someone *unsuitable.* What if he joined the navy, planning to desert so he could be with her?'

'Yes . . . what if he has been with another woman? I'm beginning to doubt everything he's told me. Otherwise, why not tell me the portrait was with the artist?'

'Which often happens.'

Their furious support was everything I needed. 'If he had loved another woman, then I would have let him go. I'd have been heartbroken, of course, but I would have survived . . . it's just the terrible thought that all those years of grieving might have been for *nothing.*'

Rose Polcarrow's lips pursed. 'I'd feel just the same, only a *lot* angrier. Would it help if we could prove there was no other woman — that he was just insensitive and rushed off with too much on his mind? Or, even better, that he's a lying bastard and knows exactly where the miniature is?'

I smiled at her fury; her words *and mine.*

'I feel bruised by him. I can't explain it very well. I feel cold towards him . . . angry that he might have lied to me before he left.'

'He had his uniform fitted in London and they sent his trunk to be collected?' There was something in the lift of Rose's voice, a sudden a glint in her eye. 'I don't expect you know which tailor he used, and where it was sent?'

'It was Gieves in London. Frederick uses them. They sent it to Plymouth Dock.'

'Excellent.' Rose's smile broadened. 'You might not be aware of how tailors work, Amelia, because I can't imagine it's ever been an issue, but newly commissioned officers often can't afford their uniforms — they pay by instalments. Either when they get paid, or when prize money begins to trickle through. You know this, don't you, Marie?'

Aunt Marie nodded, her voice also lifting. 'I know what you're going to suggest, Rose, my dear, and it is definitely worth a chance.'

I must have looked blank, staring back at them with their conspiratorial glances.

Aunt Marie patted my hand. 'It is always better to *know* than to *suspect*. Suspicion is one thing, proof is quite another. What Rose means, my dear, is that naval outfitters often keep back items — watches, clothes, anything of value — until the last bill is paid. They hold the articles as *surety* and keep them in safe boxes . . . often in vaults. They also keep *meticulous* records.'

'They might have the miniature?'

Aunt Marie nodded. 'Sir Richard Melville was a gambler — a profligate man with no morals. A midshipman's sea trunk is very costly, and yes, I

371

think they might very well be holding back the miniature as surety, and Edmund may be too embarrassed by his lack of funds to tell you. Either that or they might have the forwarding address to where it was sent. One very quick visit to Plymouth Dock, and your mind will be put at rest.'

'But it won't be a quick visit, Aunt Marie. I can't go to Plymouth Dock just like that. I'll have to go all the way back to Bodmin and then take the turnpike, and it's not our carriage, it's Mrs Lilly's . . . I have to return it. And I'd never be allowed to go all the way from Truro when I get back. Mother gives me a lot of freedom but she'd never sanction that — especially in winter. What if we write to the tailor?'

Rose Polcarrow stood by the French window, pulling back the heavy drapes. Opening the latch, she stepped on to the terrace and a blast of salty air filled the room. Framed in the moonlight, her chin held high, she sniffed the air like Captain de la Croix had done. 'Perfect,' she called back. 'We shall sail there. The wind's south-easterly. It's a steady breeze and absolutely perfect. It will be cold, but it'll be quick. I'll have you back in no time.'

She left the curtains undrawn, moonlight drenching the terrace, flooding the balustrade in silver light. Her smile was radiant, and I found myself smiling back.

'You're not going to ask Sir James to sail me to Plymouth?'

Her smile broadened, a slight shrug of her shoulders. 'No, Amelia. *I'm* going to sail you to

Plymouth. *L'Aigrette* is my boat; my father built her for me. Well, not exactly for me, he built her for the revenue but she was stolen and James found her and gave her to me as a wedding present. She's the fastest cutter there is, and she's mine — but I believe James may be persuaded to come with us.'

I caught her mischief, her energy; it was as if I had come alive again. I could feel the blood pumping in my veins, the air in my lungs. In order to believe in Edmund, I needed the truth.

'But Mother will be worried. I can't go without telling her.'

Rose's eyes were alight. 'Then send your carriage back with a letter — after Plymouth Dock, we can sail to Falmouth, and upriver to Truro. You'll be just behind the coach, but at least she'll know who you're with. James always has business in Truro. My mother can stay with the girls. They love how she spoils them — they'll hardly miss us.'

She reached for the bell-pull, smiling at the footman. 'Tell Sir James he can return now,' she said. 'It'll mean an early start. We've missed this tide, but it turns again at five. If the wind holds — and I think it will — I can get you to dock in four hours. That gives you two hours to find the outfitter before we head to Falmouth. How does that sound?'

'It sounds perfect. Thank you.'

We were still smiling when the men entered. Just one glance at his wife and James Polcarrow's handsome face relaxed.

'James, Miss Carew would like to go to

Plymouth. There's something she needs to do . . . and as we're so close, it seems a shame not to take her.'

His smile broadened. 'I take it we're to catch the early tide?'

42

Polcarrow, Fosse
Monday 12th February 1798, 4:30 a.m.

I woke to Rose's soft whisper. 'Here's some hot water. There's food on the boat so we'll go straight to the harbour. Everything's ready.' Candlelight flickered across her face and I had to look twice. Her hair was swept back, concealed beneath a large cap; she was wearing a jacket and breeches, a pair of men's boots. 'Luke is with James. This is Tilly — she'll help you get ready.'

The young maid poured water into a basin and went to stoke the fire. I had not heard her light it. I'd thought I would never sleep but the mattress had been so comfortable and I felt refreshed. I slipped from the bed, splashing my face, my excitement mounting. Tilly helped me into my travelling skirt and I fastened the long row of buttons on my jacket. My hair would just have to do. Following Tilly's silent footsteps down the elaborate wooden staircase, I joined the others in the hall.

James Polcarrow was almost unrecognizable. Gone was his immaculate jacket and perfectly pinned cravat, in their place a heavily oiled jacket and leather breeches, a large hat and sturdy boots. Round his neck was a thick woollen scarf. 'Excellent. I hope you slept well, Miss Carew?'

'Yes, thank you, I did.'

Luke's thick overcoat was buttoned to the neck, his familiar hat in his hand. He took my bag from Tilly, glancing at me more in hope than encouragement. James Polcarrow nodded. 'All set? Come . . . '

A cart and horse were waiting on the moonlit drive, the air cold, a slight breeze against my cheeks. Rose slipped beside me on the wooden bench. 'The wind's still south-easterly,' she said, lifting a basket onto her knees. 'We'll make good progress.'

Luke and James Polcarrow squeezed next to each other on the bench opposite and a burly red-haired man shut the door of the cart. Seth let go of the horse's bridle and we started down the long drive. The gatehouse was open, the iron wheels ringing across the cobbles, jolting us from side to side as we approached the quay. *L'Aigrette* was moored along the harbour wall, her sleek black hull almost indistinguishable against the inky water.

Moonlight danced across the river mouth, flooding the ships' masts. The air was biting, the wind gathering, and I gripped James Polcarrow's hand as he helped me along the gangplank. It rose and fell beneath my feet and I lifted my skirt, Luke one step behind me. A burly man with thick-set shoulders and white hair helped me over the gunwale and on to the scrubbed deck. Already Luke looked pale.

He must have seen my concern. 'No, honestly, I'll be fine. They've given me ginger — I've a whole bag — and Lady Polcarrow's brought peppermint leaves. I'll be *fine*.' He was wrapped up against the cold, the collar of his travelling coat pulled up, his hat pulled low. He looked up at the mast. 'She's a beautiful boat. Have you been on her before?'

'Once, when they came to Mother's concert. They anchored below Trenwyn House. They had another captain then — Captain Lefevre — but we didn't sail.'

The white-haired man spoke. 'Do you require me to stay, Sir James?'

'Yes, thank you, Jago. Just as well if we're going on to Falmouth. Are we set?'

He nodded. He, too, was wearing a heavily oiled leather jacket, the same heavy boots, a thatch of white hair under his master's hat. 'Aye, set and ready to slip.'

To the east, a thin band of grey streaked the black sky. The town lay quiet, a group of men watching from the shadows on the quayside. Woodsmoke drifted on the air, the rumble of another cart. Lamps were swinging on the anchored ships, shouts rising from their decks. The turn of the tide; each ship getting ready to slip her moorings or heave up her anchor. James Polcarrow stood at the bow, peering across the water to the small gap between the cliffs. 'It looks clear — we'll get going straight away.'

'Yes, Sir James. Will you take the helm?'

'No, Lady Polcarrow will. We'll make it out in this wind, but others can't point so close — we can't risk getting caught behind them.' He ran down the deck. 'Take her as close as you can, Rose.' He turned to me. 'There's a stove below — you'll be very warm.'

I drew my cloak around me. 'I'm fine. I'd like to watch.'

Luke looked uneasy. 'Can I help at all?'

James pointed to the rope securing us to the harbour wall. 'On Rose's command, release this end . . . and pull it in from here. Then coil it neatly.' He smiled. 'It's always better to work a ship. It's being a passenger that makes you ill.'

Rose held the helm, grasping the tiller in both hands. Looking across the river, she shouted her command. 'Release the bow . . . we're with the current. Hoist the jib to port.'

The ship turned slowly from the harbour wall, pulled by the steady flow beneath us. James and Jago uncoiled the rope and the small sail filled. 'Now the foresail.' Working in unison they pulled the ropes and the sail unfurled, flapping as if out of control. It filled and we pointed across the river to Porthruan.

'Release the stern,' shouted Rose. 'That's you, Luke. Let the rope go, then bring it in on the other side. That's it.' Her laughter echoed down the ship. 'Well done — we're away. We'll make a sailor of you yet!'

We were pointing close to the wind, the swell increasing, the bow rising and falling. Pushed by the immense force beneath us, pulled by the sails, we were gathering speed, slipping silently out into the black sea, the first ship to get away. The wind was freshening, the waves building. The clock struck five and Rose waited until the last chime was carried by the wind.

'Ready about,' she called. 'Take the sail to starboard and hoist the mainsail.'

The sails filled, a sudden surge pulling us forward. James and Jago heaved against the ropes and the mainsail lifted, unfurling into a graceful arch. The ship leaned sideways, slicing the waves, and Rose wedged her foot against the seat beside her. The wind blew against her cheeks as her eyes searched the darkness.

'It's a lee shore so we'll have to keep well clear of the rocks before we tack. Then it's straight to Plymouth.'

Above us, braziers were burning on cliffs, the outlines of soldiers staring down from the battlements — the improved fortifications that Major Trelawney had worked so hard to rebuild. They were watching us, recording every ship that came and left. French spies had used these harbours before, and Major Trelawney was not the only one who thought they would return. James dipped a lantern as a signal, swinging it three times to the left, and I pulled my hood tighter.

The wind was fiercer now we were out of the harbour, cutting like ice, making me catch my breath. The swell was growing, the bow dipping deeper beneath the waves. Luke slipped to my side and we stared down at the white froth swirling around us. He was so close, his jacket against my cloak. 'Do you feel all right?' I said.

'Surprisingly so.' He drew a deep breath. 'Are you cold? Shall we go below?'

'No, let's stay on deck . . . ' I wanted to be with him. I was aching to be with him. 'Luke, you know you told me *to trust the man I loved?*'

He nodded, his cheeks now full of colour, the

wind whipping his hair beneath his hat. His voice sounded forced. 'Yes, but it's important to understand that you might question that trust . . . there's a lot we can do for Edmund. We haven't heard his side of the story yet . . .'

'Luke, I can't desert him . . . I must see he gets the best representation.'

He drew me away from the drenching spray. 'I know. He must have acted under the severest provocation. Here, don't get wet . . . or we'll freeze to death.'

I wanted the spray on my face; I wanted to breathe the air. 'Luke?' He was staring out to sea, gripping the polished rail, and I slipped my hand closer. 'I haven't lost trust in the man I love — I trust and love him more than ever. It's *Edmund* I've lost trust in.'

He turned and my heart burned with such ferocity. I saw the love in his eyes, his desperate attempt to keep his mouth steady. His hand grasped mine and we stood staring at the white foam breaking from the crests, the fine spray wetting our cheeks. I could see him fighting his emotion. I wanted to turn to him, to rest my head against his chest. I wanted him to hold me.

His voice was strained, a sudden sharpness. 'We don't know anything for certain. There may be a perfectly reasonable explanation. Don't judge him . . . we cannot know the stress . . . the situation he might have found himself in.' He took his hand from mine. 'Why are we rushing to Plymouth, Amelia?'

'Edmund sat for a miniature and never sent it to me. Rose thinks it might have been kept as surety, but there's just a small chance he might have sent it to someone else. He dismissed it so lightly and I need to know why.'

His mouth tightened. 'I'm sure it's the former. He could never love another woman — not when he had you.'

The love in his eyes made my heart burn. I had loved him from first sight — from our first tentative conversations, from his visits to my herb garden. His insistence I knew more about herbs than I was telling people, his determination to have my opinion heard. He had drawn me out, inch by inch, day by day, week by week, until I had laughed and danced again and wrote long essays on how hospitals should grow ascorbic fruit and plant their own physic gardens. He had called me *Lady Herbalist*, insisted I compiled my paintings into a book.

I had to fight the deep ache in my heart. 'Our mothers knew what they were doing — throwing us together like this — but it's so cruel. I was better when I couldn't see you . . . or touch you. To put you through this — to just abandon you like . . .'

His hand reached out, warm, comforting, filling me with such pain. 'You haven't abandoned me. And I wouldn't have it any other way. Love is love, Amelia. It's too powerful a force to resist . . . and if two men love one woman, then someone will get hurt. You need time . . . to know in your heart which one of us you will choose. I don't feel abandoned — I know it's tearing you apart.'

'It's like a knife, constantly stabbing me. I

expected to love him again. I thought I would . . . I keep telling myself I want to love him, and I'm trying to love him, but by loving him, I can't love you, and that's far worse. It's impossible.'

He clasped my hand. 'Edmund's been to hell and back . . . and his story must be heard.' He pressed my gloved hand to his lips. 'I love you, Amelia. I adore everything about you . . . and I will do so until my dying breath . . . but whatever you decide . . . I will honour your decision. Last night, I lay awake tormented by such hope. I've never wished ill on another man, especially one you hold so dear, but I lay there thinking such ill of him, wanting him to — ' He bit his lip.

The wind was whipping our clothes, the deck plunging beneath us, and I buried my face in my hands. He cleared his throat. 'I believe men don't change in essence — but when they suffer great hardship? Who knows how we ourselves would react under circumstances that push us to the limit? I believe you must trust in your love for him, because I don't believe you capable of misjudging a man's character. You need time . . . *we* need time.'

He handed me his handkerchief and I was glad of the spray on my face. Glad for the excuse to wipe my eyes. Behind us, a shout rang across the deck.

'Ready to go about. We're two miles off shore and that's enough to clear Lantivet Rock. I'm turning east. Full east — 90 degrees on the compass. Luke and Amelia, come back here, or you'll go overboard. I want you here, in the cockpit, or down — ' The wind was whistling, the waves splashing, Rose's last words lost to the wind.

'Ready,' James and Jago shouted back. They held their ropes, listening for her command. She waited for us to be wedged safely beside her and shouted.

'Going full east.'

James and Jago hauled the sails to the other side where the wind caught them, filling them like wings. We were flying now, ploughing the waves, the crests breaking over the bow, a steady stream of white froth washing over the lower deck. They pulled the sails taught and I gripped the rail, Rose holding her course, her leather gloves gripping the tiller, her thick oiled breeches taking the spray.

'Three hours, at this speed,' she said as James came to sit beside us.

His cheeks were flushed, his large hat with its turned-up brow framing his face. 'How about some breakfast?' He turned to Jago. 'Is it my turn or yours to make the coffee?'

Jago's response was instant. 'It's yer turn, Sir James, but stay where ye are. I've got it ready. There's coffee an' ham buns. And plenty of it, so I hope ye're hungry.'

We were pointing east, the grey streaks of dawn turning pink, lighting the sky ahead. The stars were fading, the moonlight less intense. A faint shadow of land rose to our left and James pointed to some lights just visible through the swell. 'That's the entrance to Polperro harbour — we're making excellent progress. I'll get us some blankets. The moment you feel too cold, you're to go below. I'll not have anyone on my ship incapacitated from cold.'

★ ★ ★

For the effective cure of motion sickness, whether it be in a carriage or on the sea: add a full half-teaspoon of freshly grated ginger, or two teaspoons of dry powdered ginger, to a cup of newly boiled water. Add a pinch of sugar to taste and the top two leaves of a fresh sprig of peppermint. Leave to infuse, then strain through muslin and drink whilst warm.

The chewing of raw ginger, though efficacious to some, is found unpleasant by most, and therefore it is not recommended.

THE LADY HERBALIST

43

The distinctive chapel on Rame Head was to our left and I grasped the seat. The swell was strengthening, huge white crests blowing foam across the sea. The wind had freshened, the bowsprit plunging deeper beneath the waves. James gripped the tiller.

'That's the entrance to Plymouth Sound. We'll turn to port . . . take care, the wind will be behind us and the current's strong.'

We had watched dawn breaking, now a glimmer of wintry sun. Clouds scudded before us, the bitter cold biting my cheeks, but it was bright, the visibility good, the bay opening out like arms welcoming us to safety.

Rose held the telescope to her eye and pointed across the sound. 'There's the citadel . . . that's Drake's Island. Looks like twenty or more ships anchored.' She swung the telescope to her left. 'That's Cawsand and Kingsand . . . there's another ten ships in the bay — maybe more. The fleet must be gathering.'

She handed me the telescope and I focused on the huge ships of the line, the sailors scrubbing the decks, the ensigns flying in the wind.

James strained against the force. 'Ease out the sails. We'll stay clear of these rocks then cut through to the Hamoaze.' Jago released the ropes, tying them tightly as the wind whistled through the rigging. 'Rose, can you take the tiller?' She nodded, swapping places with him. 'Head as far into the bay as you can then point to wind. We'll stand by, ready to take down the mainsail.'

We were flying, skimming across the bay. Rose pointed to wind and James and Jago eased down the sail. With the mainsail furled, the pace slowed and we skirted Drake's Island, weaving our way through the towering hulls of the anchored ships, slipping close enough to see the cannons behind the gun ports, smell the tar and pitch on the newly caulked decks. Smoke billowed from the land, the sound of banging, a host of small crafts rowing close to the shore. The citadel rose above us, yet more smoke rising, yet more ships anchored as we steered towards the river.

James Polcarrow had one foot on the deck, the other balanced on the bulwark. He looked so at ease, pointing the way for Rose to steer. 'Dock's further up. We'll anchor in Millfield Creek — off Stonehouse Pool. A walkway will take you along the river to Plymouth Dock. Starboard a bit, Rose; these rapids always cause turbulence. Aim between that lugger and the brig. We'll go in under foresail.'

In the lee of the land, the wind dropped. Jago was on the bow, leaning close to the bowsprit, standing ready to drop the anchor. I heard a loud splash and he called out the depth. 'That'll do nicely.'

The anchor held firm and *L'Aigrette* swung round, pulling gently against her rope. Mud fringed the edge of the creek, several boats lying half-submerged along the shore. The tide was not yet at its height but the river was busy, a myriad of small boats rowing to and from the anchored ships.

Luke emerged from the hatchway carrying a tray of steaming mugs. He handed them round and we clasped them in our frozen hands. 'You didn't tell me there was a cat on board!' he said, looking back at the hatchway and the sleek black cat that had followed him up.

Jago's bushy white sideburns almost met beneath his chin. His weather-beaten face creased in a smile. 'That's Purdue. She's the real master of this ship.'

James reached into his pocket. 'I've got a letter of introduction here — Sir Alex wants me to go to the Stonehouse Hospital and make some discreet enquiries.' He looked up. I could not help my sudden gasp — I felt fearful, as if they had only brought me so they could find evidence against Edmund — as if I had given them an excuse to come looking for something that would convict him.

He must have seen my concern. 'Amelia, please be assured, I'm not condemning Sir Edmund in any way — I believe a man to be innocent until proven guilty.'

He had taken off his oiled-leather coat and was wearing a thick woollen jacket, working men's breeches, a white-cotton shirt and a red scarf round his neck. His boots were wet, his gloves soaked. He peeled them off.

'As it happens, I understand provocation very well . . . I myself have been the recipient of great

387

cruelty. I've been impressed, flogged and kept in irons, but very few know that about me.' He glanced at his wife. 'I, too, was kept below deck in port . . . for nearly two years. I know how it affects a man's soul. I may not be in the navy, but I have seen *good* men pushed to the limit of their endurance. And so has your godfather . . . but if we're to defend Edmund, if Sir Alex has to stand up in a court martial and *defend* his character, as well as any actions he may have taken, then we must *all of us* understand why a kind, gentle man who couldn't even kill a chicken — a first-born son with an estate to inherit — joined the navy and then deserted his ship.'

There was always compassion in James Polcarrow's eyes, but none more so than now. I had heard his story, of course I had. How he had been kept prisoner on a French ship, chained and kept below decks in harbours. Perhaps that was why I held on with such hope to my belief that Edmund would emerge from this ordeal like James Polcarrow. That he would prove honourable, restore his estate, be compassionate and love his family, and serve his community as well as Sir James did.

Most of all, I wanted Sir James to know what Edmund had gone through. That his father had treated him with disdain and favoured Francis. That Francis was his brother. But I had promised Constance — the keeper of her family's secrets — that no one would hear it from my lips.

He was waiting for me to speak but I could say nothing, and he returned the letter to his pocket.

'Rose and I will visit the hospital while you find the outfitters. Take the new walkway round the river and be careful. It's a rough place. Don't take a bag and keep checking behind you.' He consulted his fob watch. 'It's just gone nine. We've two hours before we have to leave. Jago — could you show them the map?'

Jago spread out the map, pointing to where we were. 'This wall here goes right round the dock — like a fortress. These are the dry docks . . . these here . . . five in all, so steer clear of them. Take this walkway as far as Mutton Cove. Here . . . see? Then go straight up the slipway. The streets form a grid so just keep goin' up from the slip. Where d'ye need to get?'

I tried to remember what Uncle Alex had said. 'George Street.'

'Then it's here, behind Mount Wise. Go up here. It's busy, mind — specially round the victuallers. Careful round the rigging house . . . these are the bakehouses . . . an' here's the coopers. Watch yer step at the blacksmiths — carts will come at ye with speed. Always keep a watch behind ye. Once past the rope house, ye'll see the mast house an' the ponds below. It's steep for a while. Don't go near The Lugger tavern — they're thieves, the lot of them. Ye're as like to get your throat cut. Here, take the map. George Street is a long street — got a number?'

'I'm told it's number sixty-three.'

The old man scratched his white whiskers. 'Well, let's just hope it's the better end.'

44

James lowered the rowing boat into the water and I climbed down the knotted rope ladder, the boat rocking as I sat beside Luke. James pulled on the oars, rowing us swiftly across the muddy creek. He steadied the boat, looping the rope round an encrusted hoop, and I followed Luke up the steps to the small wooden jetty.

The docks lay ahead of us, a forest of tall masts. Luke pointed the way and we hurried along the cobbled walkway with its huge wall on one side and the crowded river on the other. Frederick had described it to me, but I had no idea the dockyard was so vast. The walkway stopped at a small stone harbour with fishing boats moored against its side and we looked around. The top of a slipway was just visible behind huge piles of nets and crates of fish.

'This must be Mutton Cove. We're to go up there.'

Seaweed lay glistening across the stones at the top of the slipway and I was grateful for my stout shoes. The rise was steeper than I expected, the street widening to a steady stream of carts and mule packs, all hurrying past us. We stepped behind a cart laden with barrels and followed it uphill, but halfway to the top, I had to stop to catch my breath.

'Are you all right, Amelia?'

I shook my head. Smoke was choking me,

stinging my eyes. Shouts and clanging echoed from a building and I stood, rooted to the spot, staring at the burning inferno spewing out thick black smoke. It was the largest building I had ever seen — a mass of furnaces, their red flames leaping like the fires of hell. The noise was deafening, huge cranking chains lifting enormous bellows to keep the fires blazing. Cranes were dragging heavy bars that glowed so brightly it hurt my eyes to look. Sprays of yellow sparks cascaded like fountains, lighting up silhouettes of naked men.

Luke searched my face. 'Amelia . . . ?'

I could not breathe. 'I'll be fine,' I whispered.

'You look very pale. Let me get you away from here.' I felt his arms around me, his sudden lift as he carried me along the cobbles. A stack of crates lay by the road and he put me down, freeing my hood so I could breathe more easily.

'I'm sorry. I'll be all right now. It's just . . . Francis was murdered here . . . his killers worked in the forge. He wasn't set upon on his way back to London like we thought he was, but he was murdered — right here, in Plymouth Dock. And seeing the forges suddenly made it seem so real — it was so brutal.'

I felt cold to my bones. 'He was beaten — then thrown into a pigpen — his legs were dangling over the side with his boots on when they found him. Only, now I can understand why it haunts Edmund so much. I couldn't picture it before, but I can see it clearly now. Edmund feels he should have stopped it.'

'How could he have?'

'Francis took a fancy to a married woman — he was so different from Edmund. There's more to it than that . . . but I can't tell you. I'm all right . . . honestly I am.' I took a deep breath. 'Where do we go?'

He smoothed out the map, looking around. 'That large building must be the mast house — see the masts floating in the pond? So that means we need to go up there.'

Huge warehouses lined the road. I could smell bread baking and cabbage boiling. Wagons were queueing, the sound of whips and angry shouts. People were yelling to clear the way to allow their carts to pass; men rolling barrels, stacking carts, sawing or hammering, or making wheels or barrels, or baking for the king's navy. Like ants in a nest, or bees in a hive. The bustle and noise were incredible. Sewers ran either side, overflowing with fetid water, horse dung piled on the streets, children with pale faces and running noses handing staves to the coopers. Boys were holding mules, women dodging the carts with huge baskets on their heads.

We turned right and Luke pointed to the sign — *George Street* — hanging from an iron pole. To our left, the houses looked dirty and cramped, crowding together amid piles of filth, paint peeling from the doors. Men were sitting on benches, their limbs wrapped in filthy bandages, their crutches stacked against the damp walls behind them. Some had lost legs, some arms, all of them staring at us from beneath dark scowling brows. The door of the Lugger Tavern swung open and a man was thrown to the cobbles. He crawled to the ditch and vomited, and Luke's arm tightened.

'Let's hope this isn't the *better* end,' he said, leading me away. 'Come — we'll go right. Those houses look smarter.'

A fine row of red-brick terraces with large sash windows stretched ahead of us, their doors gleaming with fresh paint. Many had brass plaques on the doors and rails outside for horses. A water pump stood by a water trough, and several horses stood drinking while their riders held their reins. The men beside us were now smartly dressed in frock coats and tall hats and I caught a glimpse of a large white building at the end of the street.

A shop with a black sign caught our attention and we looked up at the huge white letters, *GIEVES*, and the slightly smaller writing, *Royal Naval Outfitters. Established 1785.*

'We're here,' said Luke.

I stared at the black door in sudden panic. Luke's hand was already on the handle.

'Luke, stop. This doesn't feel right. I can't explain it . . . but it feels wrong.'

His voice was soft. 'You think you're being disloyal to Edmund?'

'Yes, I do. It suddenly seems very underhand — it's not kind . . . and you're right . . . it feels disloyal.'

'It's *not* disloyal or underhand and nor are you being hurtful. If the miniature is here, I'll pay the amount he owes, and you can take it home. But, Amelia . . . we wouldn't be doing this if you didn't feel something was wrong. Your loyalty to Edmund goes without question. We're doing this because you don't want to think ill of him — because you need to believe in him.' His voice caught. '*And so do I.*'

The shop smelled of polish. Vast wooden cupboards lined the walls, three large windows filling the room with light. A wooden counter with a bank of small drawers stood at one end, each drawer with a brass handle and a carefully written label. A tall, thin man with a bald head was staring at us from over the rim of a pair of spectacles. He wore a striped blue apron, a sharpening file in one hand and a large pair of scissors in the other. Next to him stood a young man, equally pale and gaunt, but without the glasses and with a shock of brown hair.

The older man put down his scissors. 'May I help you, sir?'

Luke closed the door. 'I hope so. My name is Dr Bohenna, and this is Miss Carew. We'd like some clarification on an account you hold.'

'Indeed? I am Arthur Henderson, and this is my son, William Henderson.' He leaned forward on the polished wooden counter. 'I'm afraid I'm rarely at liberty to disclose details of accounts — without authorization.' An open letter lay on the counter in front of him, but everywhere else was clear of clutter, everything put away in its proper place. He did not even glance at me but stood regarding Luke through professional eyes.

'It's Sir Edmund Melville's account I'd like to discuss. I believe a miniature portrait might have been left here — perhaps as surety? I'm here to make sure the account is cleared.'

Arthur Henderson stiffened, gave a sharp

sniff. He gripped the edge of the counter, staring back at Luke. 'Am I bein' accused of theft? Is that what this is about?'

He sounded angry and Luke shook his head. 'No, of course not.'

The tailor reached for the letter, sliding it along the polished counter. 'Meaning no disrespect, sir, but it seems like an accusation to me.' He held up the letter. 'I've just received this *express* — asking for the same such miniature. For years we hear nothing, and then both you and this letter arrive on the same day — all of you comin' from nowhere, makin' out I've got something of yours. When I *don't*.'

I stared at the letter. I could not see the writing, but I knew I would recognize it. 'Is that from Sir Edmund Melville? I'm his fiancée, and Dr Bohenna is his physician. May I read his letter? Only the miniature is missing, and we believed it to be here . . . but . . . if it isn't . . . Please be assured we're not accusing you of anything — we're just trying to trace where it might be, that's all.'

He remained taut, unsmiling, handing me the letter with an angry thrust, and I tried to steady my hand. The words swam in front of me . . . *that I rushed off in such haste and forgot to leave a forwarding address. I felt certain I had asked for the portrait to be sent in my trunk, but I can only imagine that it arrived too late and you may be keeping it for me. If this is the case, please do me the very great honour of sending it to me as quickly as you can — the address is as follows . . .*

He had been telling the truth; dear God, I had so maligned him. It was just as he had said; all my doubts were groundless, founded on hurt and suspicion when I should have believed him. Luke handed the letter back to Mr Henderson. 'We were just passing and hoped it would be here, but it was obviously never sent to you — it must still be with the artist in London. I'm sorry to have bothered you.'

Arthur Henderson reached beneath the counter, bringing out a leather-bound ledger. 'I know I don't possess it because when that letter came, I looked up his account. Soon as I read it I went straight to my books. Sir Edmund puts the date when he collected his uniform so I went straight to the page. He wasn't *Sir Edmund* then, just Midshipman Melville, but it's here right enough.'

He turned the pages of his ledger, each entry written in the same immaculate hand. List after list of everything in every officer's sea chest and underneath each list were the alterations required and the special instructions given for collection. As he turned the pages, I glimpsed . . . *watch as security . . . diamond brooch . . . pledges held . . . money to be paid on first payment* and then he stopped and I read *Midshipman Edmund Melville Date of trunk received: August 2nd 1793. Date of trunk collected: August 4th 1793. Ship: HMS Faith* and the long list of everything sent from the outfitters in London: *1 frock coat, 2 jacket suits, 6 prs trousers, 14 plain shirts, 4 ruffled . . .* At the end of the list were the words *Paid in full.*

'There . . . I can assure you it was not in the trunk and it was *never* sent here. Something as valuable as that would need to be signed for — I'd have signed for it. Here . . . right here . . . *nothing*. That's where I put further instructions about what to do with things that are sent too late.' He pointed to the bottom of the page. 'It would be here under *instructions*.'

He drew a deep breath, looking over the rim of his glasses. 'We're a family firm and I run a good business. I've never had any complaints. I'm as honest as the day is long — my reputation's as clean as a whistle.'

'Please don't think we've any reason to doubt your honesty. May I?' Luke turned the ledger round. 'This . . . here . . . it looks like a number?'

Arthur Henderson adjusted his glasses. 'That's not *instructions*, that's number *24*. That's something different. That means he left something behind. They leave all manner of stuff. Rushin' here, rushin' there. They never leave enough time — I've a wardrobe full of what they leave behind. Coats and hats and canes. Most of them come back, sometimes years later because what they leave can be worth a lot of money. We store them all because I don't want to be *accused of theft*.' He nodded to his son. 'See what twenty-four is, William. It's 'ninety-three, so I reckon that'll be the second cupboard.'

His son sifted through the garments in the wardrobe, lifting out a jacket with *24* pinned to the front, and as he walked towards us my heart seemed to burst. A searing pain made me catch my breath and I reached forward, gathering the

397

familiar jacket from the counter. Tears flooded my eyes; I could not help but hold it to me, a terrible compulsion making me clasp it to my heart. It smelled musty, unworn, but still it held his shape. I wanted to hold it to me, to kiss it, the pain so intense I thought I might cry out.

Luke was watching me but I could not help it. I could not look at him. I could only clutch the jacket against my cheek, breathe in the smell of it. I was back in Pendowrick with Edmund, running across the moor, stopping to catch our breath. He had been wearing this jacket in the dream I had had when he was running from me. It was as if I had caught up with him and was holding him to me, as if he were still wearing it. I could do nothing but clutch it to my heart, the pain so intense, so visceral, like flames burning me inside.

Luke was thanking them, signing papers, bidding them goodbye, but I could not move. I just stood where I was, clutching the jacket to my heart. 'Yes, no problem. I'll sign for this . . . we'll take it straight back to Sir Edmund. Thank you, Mr Henderson . . . thank you, yes . . . Good day to you, sirs.'

He led me down the street and we started retracing our steps, but I hardly saw where I was going. I could not let go of the jacket but kept it clasped to my heart as if I could never let it go. I could see Edmund in it, feel him in it — his old jacket bringing back all the love I had for him, the hope for our future, everything flooding back and I clutched it firmer, knowing I must never give up on his love. I had to save him from the gallows, from prison, from their cruel lashes — from everything they were about to inflict on him.

Luke's arm was firm, leading me along the crowded street, pulling me back from passing carts, yet all I wanted to do was curl up in a ball and clutch the jacket to me. 'Come, Amelia . . . come. We're nearly there.' Men were loading wagons, people yelling, the smoke billowing from the forges. The repulsive smell of boiling offal adding to the stench of the gutter. 'Just down these steps. Here's Mutton Cove. It's high tide so we have to hurry. Along here . . . that's it, up these steps.'

Waves were lapping the top of the slipway, men unloading crates of fish, seagulls screeching above us. Luke's voice kept urging me forward and I fought the yearning to wail. I could not help it. It was beyond my control.

'Here's the walkway — there's Stonehouse Pool. Mind this puddle. Sir James will be waiting in the creek. It's not far now.' He helped me on to a rock, standing beside me. 'There he is. He's seen us.'

I sat clutching the jacket. 'I'm so sorry, Luke . . . I can't help it . . . I can't explain it. It's just holding his jacket is so painful. So raw . . . like the years haven't passed at all. It feels like how it was — how we both were. Like he's just taken it off and left it on a chair — and he's coming back for it.'

He swallowed hard, staring across the water as he fought to speak. 'Well, there you are. It's very important . . . very important that this has happened. Far better it's happened *now* rather than later . . . if we were married. Your love for Edmund is obviously so deep, and I must understand that. I *do* understand it.' His voice caught. 'You needed to feel this way again . . . and I needed to witness it. It's for the best.'

45

James Polcarrow said nothing but rowed us quickly back with powerful arms, steadying the bottom of the rope ladder as I climbed *L'Aigrette*'s hull to the safety of the deck. I still had the jacket gripped firmly in my arms. I could neither let it go nor hand it to anyone. An empty numbness had taken hold of me.

Just one look from Rose and she hurried me down the hatchway and I stood leaning against the polished steps. A stove was burning in the galley, a thick black pipe leading to the deck above; everywhere neat and tidy with plates and cups stashed behind wooden grilles, the cooking utensils swinging freely from brass hooks. A lantern drenched the wood with yellow light, everywhere polished and gleaming.

'Come,' whispered Rose.

A brass clock and barometer glinted above the desk, a chart laid out, an open compass. There were no portholes but a central hatch filtering daylight onto the end table. Two carved benches were upholstered in blue velvet, the black cat asleep on one of them. Rose slipped along the bench opposite, looking furious. 'So there *is* another woman. Did you get the address?'

'No — there's no one else. He was telling the truth. He was in a hurry — he changed into his uniform and rushed off just like he said he had. He wants to find the miniature as much as we do. He sent an express.'

'To the tailor?' Her hair was still pinned beneath her large hat, spray lingering on her thick leather jacket. She was so beautiful, those long dark lashes in her perfect oval face, her cheeks now full of colour.

'Yes, we read it. He must have sent it straight away — that very night. He asked if the miniature was there and if so, could they send it to him. Oh, Rose, I've wronged him and I feel terrible.'

She was staring at the jacket still clutched in my hands. I wanted to put it to my lips, but I kept it pressed to my heart. 'He left his jacket behind in his hurry . . . and just seeing it, just holding it . . . has brought him back to me. Over the years, I'd grown distant from him — I had no image of him — not in my hands, nor in my mind. I'd lost sight of him, and when he returned I was almost ready to let him go. There just wasn't the same sense of love . . . but holding his jacket — holding this worn, familiar, rather messy jacket — brings back all my love for him. It's so painful, so fierce. It's come from nowhere and it's making me remember how much I loved him . . . as if all my love has just come flooding back. He needs me, Rose. He loves me so much, and I love him. I won't let them hang him — I won't. Uncle Alex has to clear his name.'

She stared at the jacket. 'You've been very angry with him and suddenly that anger's lifted. It's as if it's freed you to love him again like opening a floodgate that's been holding back your love. I can understand it very well.' She reached out, squeezing my wrist. 'Amelia, I have to go above — they need my help. The tide's turning and we must catch it. Stay below. Getting out to sea is going to be rough but it'll be more comfortable once we point to Falmouth. We'll get you home as quickly as we can.'

She stood up. 'I've never met Edmund and I'm more than a little fond of Luke which makes this very hard. But love is love, Amelia, and once it has you in its grip there's nothing you can do about it.'

James Polcarrow's shout echoed down the hatch and a shadow crossed above me. The sails were rising, the boat beginning to tip, the sudden sideways lurch confirming we had slipped anchor. I needed to compose myself. The black cat with her huge green eyes was staring at me as I laid the jacket on the table. I remembered it so clearly; he was wearing it as he knelt beside me at the altar.

I smoothed it out. The back was scuffed, a small tear by the pocket. Suddenly, my heart jolted. A hard lump, definitely a hard lump. I turned it over, searching the pocket for what must be inside. It was empty. The lump was not in the pocket but lower down — somewhere between the fold of the back pleat and the pocket lining. There must be a hole in the pocket and I ran my fingers round it, turning it out as far as it would go. The top side of the pocket had become unstitched — there was a small gap, and I reached inside it, expecting the line of stitches to give way. They stayed secure, not opening under the pressure of my fingers. I examined it carefully — it had not become unstitched but had been deliberately unpicked and sewn again.

Squeezing my hand through the satin lining, I felt the smooth outline of a package and pulled it back through the gap, slightly tearing the lining. My name and address were on the front — Edmund's writing, but it looked scrawled and written in haste. Four seals held the package closed, the red wax brittle, and I pulled off the string, slipping my finger beneath each seal in turn.

A letter was wrapped round something hard and my fingers fumbled as I unrolled the pages. I could hardly breathe, but found myself staring into the frightened eyes of a black-haired midshipman. I barely recognized him. He looked so gaunt and a shiver ran down my spine. He looked ill, thinner, his vulnerable eyes haunted and sad.

His writing was wild, untidy, the pages covered with blotches.

24 Hanover Square
London
July 10th 1793
My darling Amelia, my wife, my only love,
I am coming to you. Expect me within weeks — I need to leave London. I can't stand this torment a moment longer. At first, I thought I was imagining it. I'm so used to Francis mocking me — he always has — but recently, there's a new

viciousness in him which scares me terribly. He watches me constantly. He copies me — all my mannerisms, even the way I wear my hair. He sits at the dining table and his eyes bore into mine, and I then I realize he's copying me exactly doing what I'm doing — tapping his fingertips, tossing his hair, smiling back at me, his grotesque leer stopping me from eating.

It's as if he's turning into me — his clothes, the way he wears his hat, the way he holds his cane. I turn round to find he's walking behind me, copying the way I walk. And all the time there's evil in his eyes, as if he knows he's scaring me. I can see he enjoys it and takes pleasure in my fear. He's making me doubt myself — I can tell that's his intention. And it's working. I can't eat. I barely sleep. I don't want to leave my room. Last week, it got worse. I went back to the office and all my accounts had lines drawn straight through them. Right through all my careful lists of which spices to buy,from where, from whom — everything had been defaced and it must have been him.

Who else would do it? I couldn't take them to Father because I knew Francis would deny it and one of the clerks would be dismissed with dishonour. They are good men and they need their jobs and Francis knew I'd say nothing.

He has Father's ear, he manipulates him, but Father thinks the world of him. He does everything Francis tells him. Francis plies him with drink — I even think he puts laudanum in his brandy. He takes him to brothels and I can say and do nothing. They taunt me so constantly.

But that's nothing to what I've found out. My dearest Amelia, Francis has been taking your letters before they get to me. I wait for them, I long for them, but he must have been paying the footman. I realize that now. I saw him hand a letter to Francis and I never thought it might be yours. More and more, I began to think you weren't writing to me. And then yesterday, with Father's head laying on the dining table, he quoted my letter back to me word for word — the exact words I'd written to you. My loving words but with such hatred in his voice.

He was mocking me, and I just stared at him in terror. He'd taken my letter from the tray before it could be posted and I believe he has done that many times. He was looking at me with such hatred — such a cold, white, furious hatred — and my bowels just turned to water.

That's how scared I was. He takes the letters I write to you. I don't know which ones you've received, if any. Then he said, 'I'm writing to her. She lives for my letters. Perhaps you should know it's me she loves, not you. She's always loved me. We used to kiss in the barn when you weren't looking — deep, throaty kisses and I knew she wanted more. She used to beg me for more, and I'll give her more, too. I've a lot more to give her than you have. Do you even like women, or is it men you prefer?'

I took to my room. Amelia. I know that was weak, but I didn't know what to do. I didn't believe him — not for one second — but his voice and his spiteful face so full of loathing stayed with me. He said it with such a smile — an evil smile — and I feared for my sanity. I hate him, Amelia. I've always hated him, but now he knows I do, and I don't feel safe. That's why I must come to you. I'll tell your parents everything, and I'll beg them to let us marry. We'll stay with them until I'm twenty-one, and then my allowance will start, and I'll not be beholden to my father. Expect me soon — within the week, if I'm lucky. I need your strength, my darling Amelia. You're my rock. I need you so very desperately.

I turned the page, my hands shaking. The next section was written in different ink, dated three days later.

July 13th

My dearest Amelia, I have carried this letter with me, and as yet I've had no chance to post it. He follows me everywhere. I can't leave the house without him by my side. If I go to post this, he'll grab my wrist and force it from me. I can't trust any of the servants, not now. I'm like a prisoner, his cruel smile always mocking me, his spiteful comments drawing laughter from Father. Yesterday he

407

locked me in my room, and I didn't even bang on the door, I just stayed there without food. And then he came. He just unlocked the door and strode in, locking it behind him. He was smiling that horrible taunting grin, opening every drawer, tipping the contents on to the floor, and I couldn't stop him. I just stood and watched. He had a huge whip in his hand, and he kept slicing the air with it — so close to my face, I could feel the draught on my cheek. He said, 'You're not writing Amelia another whinging letter, are you?'

He emptied my ink on to the carpet, and he laughed because I had soiled my trousers again. That's how terrified he's made me. And he loves that. He kept saying, 'You're not man enough for Amelia — she needs a real man. One who knows just how to please her. And I do.'

I gripped the table, fighting my nausea. The petrified eyes in the miniature were staring back at me. I turned the page. The ink was the same, but the writing almost impossible to read.

46

July 14th

Amelia. I have such reason to fear. Last night I went downstairs. It was late, and I thought no one was up but the door to Father's study was open and I stared through the smallest crack. Father was slumped on his desk with Francis beside him, holding open a large book. He pulled Father's head up, forcing Father to look at him, and as Father's head lolled back against the chair I saw such terror in his eyes.

Francis was mocking him, just like he mocked me — holding open the book and whispering so cruelly. 'I'm your eldest son, for God's sake. I need recompense. I need provision. I'm not prepared to stay quiet any longer. I'm nearly twenty-one and I need recognition. You need to pay for the terrible ill you did my mother. You used her. You used that poor woman and if you don't change this will, I'll expose you — I'll tell everyone that while Lady Melville was about to give birth to your son, her sister, only three months earlier, had given birth to his elder brother.

Yes, Amelia — my <u>brother</u>. I can hardly take it in, but I know it to be true. We've always looked like brothers. There's very

409

little difference between us except Francis is stronger, and Father didn't deny it. He just shook his head. He sounded so pitiful, crying as he answered. 'I've given you an allowance — more than I can afford. You're bankrupting me. I won't change my will. I can't do that to my wife, or my children.' I thought Francis was going to kill him. 'Your children?' he mocked. 'I'm your eldest child.' And he grabbed him by the collar, shaking him violently, and then Father just picked up the pen and wrote on the will. I didn't see what he wrote but I saw the gluttonous smile on Francis's face as he stood over him. His tongue ran over his lips, his eyes pinpoint cruel.

I watched Father hand it over for his approval and Francis just stood there reading it. Then he walked to the safe and turned the lock, but he didn't give the key back to Father. He put it in his own pocket. I could barely walk, but somehow I staggered back up the stairs. I wanted to lock my door, but the key was missing. I just lay there, thinking he'd come in. I must have fallen asleep because when I woke there was a shadow by my bed, a man standing beside me, but the shadow looked wrong and I saw Francis holding a pillow. It was poised above my head and I just stared at it, knowing that at any moment he could bring it down against my face and I would stand no chance against his strength.

Then I saw his face. There was murder in

it. He was smiling that grotesque smile and then he walked away — he just walked away — but at the door he turned and laughed. 'You didn't want this pillow, did you?' he said, and I just lay there. I couldn't breathe. Amelia, I was so petrified, I think I passed out.

This morning I knew I had to summon up my courage and talk to Father. I had seen his fear and knew I must go to him. I was terrified but I went early and locked the door behind me. Father was surprised to see me, but I just walked up to his bed and came straight out with it. 'You've acknowledged Francis as your son?' And he answered, 'Yes, but he's not my heir. You are.' And I just stood there. 'You've just signed our death warrants.' I said. 'Now Francis will kill both Connie and me. He's evil. He's always been evil. I saw what he did to you last night, and I woke to see him holding a pillow above my head. It won't be that, though — it'll be poison. He'll get me first, and then he'll go down to Cornwall and poison Connie.'

Father just gripped me to him. 'I'll write another will,' he whispered. 'I'll call for my attorney and I'll get him to keep it safe — it'll be dated after the one I wrote last night so it will be my last, valid, will. I'll say Francis is not my son . . . I'll leave him an allowance as my nephew . . . I'll get my attorney to sign it and keep it under lock and key. Only Francis must never know I've

411

changed it. Never tell him.' He was shaking, looking over his shoulder at the door.

Yet even in my terrible anxiety, I understood what my father clearly didn't. 'But he must know,' I cried. 'That's just the point. He must know he's not to inherit after our deaths . . . because if he doesn't know that he'll kill me, and he'll kill Connie. He has to know there's no benefit to killing us. He has to understand that he has no claim to your estate. What proof does he have that you're his father?'

He was crying, sobbing, his eyes pleading. — 'There's no proof,' he whispered, 'nothing at all. No one knows, not even your mother. There's no proof whatsoever. Edmund, I promise. Francis wheedled the truth out of me six years ago and I've given him a vast allowance ever since. He's ruining me.'

Then he put his hands on my shoulders and stared into my eyes. 'I want you safe, Edmund. I want you away from him. I want you where he can't get you. He needs to think you're far away. You must join the navy and you must hurry. We'll take up Captain Owen's offer, but it will be you that goes, not Francis. We'll get everything ready — but we have to hurry. The ship leaves on August 4th. You've got three weeks. Three weeks and you'll be away from him. After six months, resign your commission — do anything you want, but stay away from Francis. Go home and marry Amelia and

412

take her somewhere safe. *Promise me you'll stay away from Pendowrick? Send me word where you are but keep changing your name. Use the word <u>glorious</u> in each letter and I'll know it's you. I'll sort something. I can't have him keeping this hold over me.'*

The boat was rising, falling, plunging up and down, a slight roll as the bow sliced the water. Timbers were creaking, the cutlery jangling on the brass hooks in the galley. Glancing through the hatchway, I saw the sails hauled tight, the sky a brilliant blue. The cat was still staring at me, the table sloping at a definite angle. I turned the page.

The ink had changed, the writing neater and more compact.

Dearest Amelia, *I've just sat for a miniature portrait. The artist is employed by the tailors and he assures me it will be ready before i go. He had a number of portraits with the uniform already painted, so I chose the one most like my uniform and he only needs to paint my face. George Halliday was there, and it was wonderful to talk to him of home. He said he'd seen you about six months ago and said you were looking well. He helped me choose my uniform, but I wasn't at all interested because I'm not going to wear it for long. He was so excited to be joining his ship — he was so proud, and I tried to pretend I was, too.*

I left Francis in the office and hurried out

of the back door and every moment during the fitting, all I could think was that Francis might have followed me and was spying on me like he always does. I kept looking out of the window — I even thought I'd seen him — but that's how scared I've become. He was back in the office when I returned so it can't have been him. It's vital he doesn't know. He mustn't stop me going.

It was only afterwards I realized I should have given this letter to George — I had it with me but I'm not thinking the way I should think any more. I jump at the slightest shadow. I shall join the ship and after a short while, I'll resign my commission, just as Father has instructed — and I'll come straight to you. You can help me decide what to do, but I can't be with Francis a moment longer.

When we got back, Father said it had been a glorious day and I knew that was a sign that his attorney had been, and I started laughing — terrible nervous laughter like a madman in Bedlam — and Francis started laughing too. 'Yes, it's been a glorious day,' he mocked, and he just kept laughing long after I had stopped. And now, it's just struck me. What if he knows? What if it really was him I saw from the tailor? What if he overheard my conversation with Father?

I won't post this letter until I get the portrait. He'll have it ready when I go for my next fitting. I've ordered most of the shirts from the shelves but the uniform needs to be fitted. I leave for Plymouth in two weeks and they are adamant they'll have everything done in time. Once I'm safely on board, Father will tell Francis about the new will — and that it is with the attorney for safe keeping. He will know it post-dates the one in the safe and he'll have no access to it. Francis is not to be acknowledged as a son, but he can expect a generous allowance. I don't believe Father will change his mind, I believe he means it. I can sense a new coldness between them now and though he smiles and laughs at Francis's mockery, I no longer find it hurtful.

With no chance of him inheriting the title and estate, there's no reason for him to kill me or Connie, but I have to get away because just the sight of him makes my heart pound and I fear for my mental well-being.

I'll wait until the last moment to pack my belongings. The trunk is being sent from Gieves to their shop for collection in Plymouth Dock. I'll take as many silver ornaments with me and as much money as I can because I'll need money if I'm to resign my commission and find my way back. I love you, my darling. I'm a shadow of my former self but the moment I see you again I will blossom. You are my rock — I draw my strength from your laughter, from your smile, from all the love you have not just for me, but for everyone; for the whole of humanity, for every servant and estate worker who you stop and talk to — they all

*love you, but only a fraction of how much I
adore you.*

*We will be happy, my darling. We'll raise
a brood of children and I shall hold you in
my arms and never — never, ever — will I
let you go. I will honour our vows, because
I love you and I will always love you. I'm
coming home, my darling. Watch out for
me. I'm coming home.*

Tears blurred my eyes, my sobs beginning to
choke me. I must have cried out because Rose
hurried down the gangway. 'You've found his
portrait? Goodness! Where was it? And a letter,
too?' She swayed towards me, holding the table
as the deck plunged beneath her.

'It was in the lining of his pocket. I think this
letter will save him, Rose. It's harrowing to read
— but it shows Edmund wasn't in sound mind
when he joined the ship. They sent him instead
of Francis — Captain Owen offered Francis the
commission, but Edmund went instead. Captain
Owen can testify he offered the position to
Francis, but Edmund came instead.' I was
fighting the pain, the terrible sense of wrong.
'Edmund was terrified — he was provoked
beyond endurance. He wasn't in sound mind
when he joined the ship — Captain Owen
should never have accepted him in the state he
was in. Edmund should have come to me.'

She raced through his words, disgust mounting in her face, the same terrible anger. She put
down the letter, yet the look in her eyes made me
catch my breath.

416

'Do you think Luke can use this to testify that Edmund wasn't in sound mind when he joined the navy?' I whispered.

She breathed deeply, staring at the letter, her mouth drawn tight, no sign of hope. I had a letter that could save Edmund from the gallows and yet she was frowning? 'Amelia . . . Luke and James have just been talking about Francis's death — how he was found dangling in the pigpen. Are you *sure* you want everyone to see this letter?'

She handed it back. 'This last bit . . . '

I had not read the last *two* scribbled lines.

He accompanied me to Plymouth — he's here! He's taken rooms next door. Amelia — he says he wants to see me on to my ship. I hate him so much — I hate him. Hate him. I have to be rid of him.

I stared back at her, terrible dread churning my stomach. 'No . . . no, Rose . . . no. He's not a murderer. He was very weak — look at his face — he has no strength. He *couldn't* have killed Francis.'

Her voice was kind but firm. 'He had money, Amelia, and that's all it takes in some places — and believe me, Plymouth Dock is one of those places.'

'No. He wouldn't even think of it.'

'Amelia, I have to tell you . . . when he got home last night, Sir Alex sent Edmund's file to us and we read the cuttings from the newspaper about the trial. The woman's husband and

417

brother denied everything — they swore their innocence — and some people were never called to witness. Many believed they should have been called and that someone with authority stopped them from taking the stand. What if the motive behind the murder wasn't a wronged husband seeking revenge but a desperate man trying to rid himself of his tormentor?'

I stared back at her. 'Edmund wouldn't have known how to go about it.'

'But a man like Sir Richard would. Read these lines again . . . these ones about what Sir Richard said — *I'll sort something. I can't have him keeping this hold over me.*'

She gripped my hand. 'I may be wrong, but Francis was terrorizing both of them. He was blackmailing Sir Richard and ruining him. They *both* needed to be rid of him.'

47

My mouth tasted of salt, a terrible nausea sweeping through me. The motion of the boat was building, the angle of the table deepening; through the hatch the white sails were arching and I knew we were well out to sea.

'Come on deck,' Rose whispered. 'Put these away while you decide what to do.'

I steadied myself for a moment, grabbing the handrails as I swayed from side to side, and followed Rose up the gangway, wrapping my shawl tightly round me. It was bitterly cold, long thin clouds streaking across the blue sky, the sun reflecting on the sea, catching the white sails. Jago was on the tiller, Luke and James wedged against the bulwark on the high side. The bowsprit was plunging deep below the surface, spray covering the bow, white foam swirling along the lower deck, and I gripped the rail, trying to rid myself of my nausea.

To our right, the land was fast disappearing, nothing but a sea of vast, heaving waves breaking into crests. My cheeks stung with cold and I stood watching the sun glinting on the sea, like thousands of small mirrors. The ship's motion seemed steadier now the sails were broader, and I breathed deeply, filling lily lungs with the courage I so desperately needed. I felt bruised and shaken, yet I must stay strong. I was Edmund's rock and I must stay his rock. My love was still there, I just needed more time.

Rose took the helm and I envied her her strength. I had sailed these waters all my life with Frederick and Uncle Alex, but never in such pain. The Dodman was straight ahead of us, the bay that swept round Fosse and St Austell now lost to sight. We were flying, the wind lessening, though strong enough to heel the boat and push us home. Luke came to my side and we sat, side by side, staring over the rolling waves.

At last, he spoke. 'Clothing holds a person's shape — it holds their scent, their perfume . . . the oil they use in their hair. It's not surprising it brings such raw emotion back to the surface. Holding a loved one's garment often unlocks pain, giving rise to intense sorrow.'

'That's just how I feel, Luke. It's brought him so close again.'

His hand was almost touching mine and he pulled it away. He would never touch me again. I knew that now.

Rose handed the tiller back to Jago and called to us. 'We better have something to eat. I don't know about you, but I'm famished.'

We followed her down the hatchway, Luke's hand fleetingly on my back before he whisked it away. He could not look at me, and I could not look at him. Rose and James were opening drawers, laying out plates, the huge ham carved again, fresh bread sliced, pickle retrieved from behind the glass-fronted cabinet, and we sat at the table with the black cat watching us. No one, it seemed, dared to move her.

I had loved Edmund so dearly, his jacket had

brought back so much pain, yet why was I was struggling to love him? Why was it so hard? Was it because I could sense his lies? Luke ate sparingly, slowing drinking a cup of fresh mint tea. James Polcarrow had finished his meal and was leaning back, stretching out to stroke the cat.

Luke smiled as her loud purr filled the cabin. 'Was your visit to the hospital useful, Sir James? I've been there many times. It's a very impressive place. The wards are built to prevent spread of contagion — they're large, with good space between the beds — and they have very fine operating rooms . . . a lot of circulating air . . . and I believe the food is very good.' He was clearly trying to make conversation.

James laughed. 'And the hugest wall to keep the impressed men *in*. The sailors get there under all sorts of medical pretences, the poor men believe that once there, they're just going to *stroll* out, but it's like a fortress — there's no way out. The only way in is through the arch from the creek, and the only way out is through a heavily guarded gate. They row them directly from the ships and then the portcullis falls tightly shut.'

He lifted the cat on to his lap. 'Rose and I were waiting outside the chief surgeon's office — we must have looked like pressed sailors because along comes this janitor and offers us all sorts of potions and advice.' He smiled as Rose took off her hat, shaking her luxurious chestnut hair around her shoulders. 'Just as well they didn't see you do that!'

Luke handed a small piece of ham to Purdue,

who purred even louder. 'They thought you were pressed men waiting to be seen? What did he offer you?'

'He said he could give us lists of signs and symptoms for various illnesses — how to pretend you had a twitch — or a *nervous tick*, as he called it. For two shillings he could give us an emetic that would have us *retching our guts out*, and for a guinea, we could have a vial of belladonna — that's a guinea *each*, not a guinea for two! He said all we had to do was drop it in our eyes and pretend to be mad. We had to wave our limbs *loosely* — actually, he demonstrated it and he looked very convincing. We were to pretend not to remember things and stutter and stammer. But we weren't to use it straight away or they'd know it had come from him. We were to wait two weeks and then pretend to bang our heads and we'd be discharged as insane.'

Luke was laughing. 'Just as well you saved your money — it's the first thing a physician would think to look for. And you'd have to keep the drops going — you'd be searched, and the effect would wear off, then, suddenly, you'd be sane again.'

My stomach wrenched, a sudden petrifying jolt. Edmund had kept his eyes shaded with dark glasses, hidden behind thick lenses, kept the rooms dark. I thought I might be sick. What if Edmund had not had a head injury? What if he was not forgetting things?

'*Belladonna* — to make your pupils huge?' I said, gripping the table. Huge, black, vulnerable eyes. How could I have missed it?

They were all laughing, discussing the chances of the bottle being found — how long the drops would last, and how often you would have to apply them. I could hardly hear them. *Belladonna* — what if Edmund had used belladonna?

My head reeled. What if he had not forgotten the miniature was in his jacket — what if *he did not know it was there?* The empty plates swam in front of me. He had written to the tailor asking if the miniature was there but he had not mentioned the jacket. If he had not had a head injury, and was using belladonna, then he would have remembered placing it in the lining. Why had he not asked if the jacket was there?

I fought for breath. Belladonna was a poison. *He'll use poison.* Surely I had just read that in Edmund's letter? *He'll use poison.* I reached for the empty fruit bowl, trying not to vomit.

'Amelia? Quick . . . Let's get you on deck.'

'No, it's passing. I'm all right.'

Poison! My mind was whirling. Connie had sensed something was wrong the morning Lady Melville died and I had smelled the distinctive smell of almond oil on Lady Melville's lips — but what if it was not almond oil at all? I could see the page in Luke's father's herbal.

Cherry laurel water is a dangerous, ineffective treatment that has been used for coughs, colds, insomnia and stomach cramps but I advise against all such treatment. The distilled leaves of the cherry laurel, once infused with water, are poisonous in all but

423

the minutest quantities and will always lead to death. The smell of almonds on the breath is often the only sign that laurel water has been ingested. Do not keep laurel water in your cupboards and dispose of your bottles forthwith.

'*Poison*,' I whispered. 'What if it was *poison*?'

They stopped talking, Luke immediately puzzled. 'Belladonna is poisonous if used incorrectly but as eye drops it's relatively harmless — but you know that.' He stopped. 'Amelia, what is it?'

Rose's voice was firm. 'Show them the letter, Amelia. Show them the miniature.'

I fumbled beneath my cloak, pushing the letter across the table, sliding the portrait into the centre. Edmund's petrified eyes stared back at us as they read the contents.

Luke shook his head. 'I'm not sure what you mean, Amelia. There's definite provocation here — I'm not sufficiently knowledgeable about navy matters, but, medically, there's enough in this letter to plead Edmund was not of sound mind . . . that he was following direct orders from his father, and that this undue strain would make a man incapable of knowing what he was doing. The poor man's clearly scared out of his wits. But why do you think of poison? Are you saying Edmund *poisoned* Francis and left him in the pigpen?'

'No . . . Luke . . . It's Lady Melville . . . I smelled almonds on her breath just after she died . . . Laurel water lingers, doesn't it? I smelled almonds, but she'd been using my salve

424

and I thought it was the almond oil I'd used — we even put some on her lips. Oh, dear God!' I clasped my hands over my mouth.

'Lady Melville poisoned by laurel water? Who would possibly want to poison her?'

'I think Edmund's been using belladonna to make his pupils large. I didn't suspect it at all but once you mentioned it, it seems very likely. What if he never had a head injury and he's lying to us all?'

'I'm not following you. Are you saying you think Edmund is somehow responsible for his mother's death?'

I could hardly speak. I had felt such love for a jacket yet no love at all for the man who had worn it. Connie had sensed something was wrong that morning, with her blue flames and rushing water, her crows, her searching the shadows and looking for signs. She had sensed wrong — sensed the house had witnessed great evil.

'I don't know what I'm saying . . . it's just something's so wrong. Why can't I love the man, when I loved the youth so dearly? It's as if Edmund has come back another man.'

'That's hardly surprising, Amelia. He was gone a long time.'

I stared back at Rose, my heart thumping. Was it possible? Was it? 'He's been gone so long, I hardly recognize him . . . but what if he really has come back a different man? What if he didn't kill his mother who he adored, but his aunt who he hated and who had always hated him?'

James Polcarrow blew out his cheeks. 'Are you

saying that you think Edmund is really Francis Bainbridge?'

'Yes, I am . . . reading that letter makes me certain of it.' An ice-cold grip had clamped my heart. 'Edmund writes that Francis is turning into him . . . it's obvious he was studying him, learning everything he could. He'd no reason to accompany Edmund to Plymouth. I think he killed him to take his *rightful* place. I think the man who calls himself Edmund is lying about his head injury. His memory is perfect — and he doesn't know the miniature was in the lining of the jacket.'

'Absolutely right! He'd have written asking if they still had the jacket — not whether the miniature was there.' Luke turned the jacket over and examined the lining. 'We need to think this through . . . Edmund obviously hid his letter and miniature very carefully. He was petrified Francis would grab the jacket and find it in the pocket. He needed to post it, yet his half-brother had accompanied him to Plymouth and Edmund was petrified he'd find it. So he sewed it into the lining of his jacket. And Francis didn't find it.'

James Polcarrow took the jacket. 'Only Edmund knew the miniature was in there — Francis didn't, and *he still doesn't*. But you need stronger evidence than just suspicion, Amelia. What if his head injury is real? What if he's not using belladonna?'

'He's Francis . . . I know he is. I think he did follow Edmund to the outfitters. He was always listening at doors. I think Edmund's fear was correct — Francis *was* listening when his father

426

decided to write the new will. He overheard their plan and knew that he would never inherit the estate — even if Edmund and Constance both died childless. That's the whole point. Francis *was not* going to inherit the estate — *ever*. Sir Richard has a brother and there are cousins who'd inherit. Francis had no proof he was an illegitimate son — only an inscription in a book that would hold no sway. He considered himself the eldest son and was driven insane by jealousy. He considers the estate his birthright.'

'So Francis killed Edmund and took his place.'

'Look at the back of Edmund's jacket . . . Here, there are scuff marks — signs of a struggle and here's a tear.' I smoothed out the jacket. 'He must have forced Edmund to the ground but he didn't knife him because he needed to swap jackets and boots and there mustn't be any blood. He must have strangled him and then had to hide the body.'

'No . . . not hide the body.' Luke's voice was like steel. 'The body needed to be found but not recognized as Edmund. His father must think Francis was dead — they must all think Francis was dead. The face had to be unrecognizable so he balanced Edmund over the pigpen to be eaten. He must have watched until the face and neck were unrecognizable and then rushed to collect his uniform. Then he went straight to his ship — Midshipman Edmund Melville reporting for duty.'

James Polcarrow held the miniature in his hand. 'No one knew him on the ship, and he'd make sure he stayed away for years. It's very plausible — stolen identity is far more common than we think. He stepped into Edmund's shoes — or uniform — but he had to leave the navy as soon as possible because old friends would recognize him.'

He put the cat to the floor. 'If you're right, this was a callous, well-planned murder. The landlord of the inn states Francis didn't sleep in his room that night. He must have spent the night planning where to meet Edmund and how to dispose of him. In the morning, he must have sent him a note, asking to meet him — probably demanding money. And Edmund would have gone down that treacherous back alley hoping one last payment might suffice.'

Rose was searching the jacket, running her hands behind the lining. 'We need to find that note. It would have been in his pocket.'

I shook my head. 'No. Francis would have taken it. He killed Edmund, swapped jackets, and the first thing he'd do was check the pockets. But Edmund had made the hole at the top of the pocket — so a downward hand would not feel the gap and the letter and portrait remained safe.'

Luke's eyes caught mine. 'Francis rushed to the tailor, put on his uniform and ordered a trolley for his trunk. Fortunately for us, he was in a hurry and forgot the jacket in his haste.'

Rose slipped to my side. 'Amelia, did you sense anything from his letters? Does the writing change after he gets onboard ship?'

The pain was so intense, I thought I would cry. 'No . . . the writing doesn't change — that's

428

what's so awful. It looked like the same writing.'
A scream was rising within me, a terrible need to
howl. Francis had written those letters from the
ship. The exact same writing as on the letter Sir
James held. The exact same curls and flourishes,
the same elongated cross to his *T*.

I took the letter. 'Francis must have studied
his writing, as well as the way he walked and
tapped his fingers. Read this bit . . . *It's as if he's
turning into me*. Francis knew just what I'd look
for — what we'd all look for. He used to watch
us all the time, creeping up on us, staring at us
from doorways, but he had to kill Lady Melville
because a mother would know her son . . . and
his beloved nurse, Mrs Alston, would know every
mole and birthmark . . . so he had to kill her,
too.'

Both Constance and Bethany had felt the evil.
'Francis must have been waiting for Mrs Alston
in the shadows and tripped her up as she passed.
He must have stood over her, laughing like he
had laughed at Edmund, before reaching
forward and thrashing her forehead against the
stones to crack her skull.'

The stove was too warm. The ship's motion
had calmed, but it was not that making me ill, it
was the terrible realization I had held his letters
to my lips, to my heart. I had slept with them
under my pillow. I had kissed them, cried over
them, cradled them. I wanted to vomit.

James Polcarrow's voice was firm. 'There's no
evidence in this letter to substantiate a claim of
false identity — nor of murder. It's just the
rantings of a petrified youth. Show any court

429

martial this letter and they're very likely to acquit Edmund as being of unsound mind. I think Luke's right. I think this would act in his favour and, what's more, if we were to take him to court, you'd be under oath, Amelia — you'd have to say you thought the writing was the same.'

A gleam of hope made me look up. 'What about the letter to the tailor? He didn't even consider asking if he'd left the jacket. Surely that proves he didn't know the letter and miniature were in the jacket?'

'It's not strong enough evidence. He'll just say he forgot the letter was there . . . even the jacket. His records all show he's being very forgetful.'

'But surely a clever lawyer could trip him up?' Even as I said it, I knew he was too clever. When questioned, he would tell it just as it was — that he was being tormented beyond endurance, that he was not in sound mind when he joined his ship. 'What about the smell of almonds? What about poisoning Lady Melville?'

Luke shook his head. 'That's just your knowledge, Amelia. You smelled almonds, but there was almond oil in the salve. How can you be sure you smelled laurel water? Lady Melville's heart was weak and Annie was frail. She could easily have caught her foot in her hem and tripped down the stairs. The doctor signed the deaths as natural causes. He'd no reason to think other-wise. There's nothing we can pin on Francis.'

James Polcarrow drew a deep breath. 'If Sir Alex speaks in defence of Midshipman Edmund Melville, he would either be defending Edmund's

430

murderer, or he might be defending a totally innocent man who'd been terrorized by his step-brother and lost his reason.'

Rose shook her head. 'He's Francis, James. Amelia *knows* that now.' She picked up the miniature. 'She loved this poor frightened boy and who wouldn't? But the man who has returned repulses her. She feels no love for him — and he's manipulating her emotions. He knows exactly what he's doing . . . he's relying on her natural goodness, her pity, and capacity for compassion. It's all here, in Edmund's letter — Francis was insanely jealous of Edmund. They were so similar — they shared all four grandparents. All he needed was time to change from the youth he was into the man they'd both have become.'

The lines hardened round James Polcarrow's mouth. 'We've got Captain de la Croix safe, who else needs to be warned?'

The band tightened round my throat. 'George Halliday and Constance — George because he may refer to other conversations they had, and Connie because I have a terrible feeling he knows she suspects him. I think that's why he wanted her to come to Truro. He has to kill her, but he can't do it too soon or suspicions will be raised. He can't use poison again or have her fall down the stairs — but he'll think of something. She'll have an accident — a coach will run her over or he'll push her into the river and she'll be sucked under the sluice gates.'

James glanced at the clock. 'Three o'clock — it looks like the wind's dropping. We're losing speed. It's going to be tight.'

Rose reached for my hand. 'We need to be in Falmouth by five if we're to catch the flood tide. If we miss it, one of us will have to ride to Truro.'

Luke nodded. 'Put me ashore and I'll hire a horse. We need to warn to them.'

48

Falmouth 5 p.m.

Pendennis Castle loomed on the prow, the wide waters of Falmouth opening up. The tide was with us, the wind still behind us. We were nearly at Black Rock in the waters I knew so well. Ships crowded the harbour, some swinging to anchor, others moored against the wharfs. The sun was setting, twilight turning the sea a dark grey. Visibility was fading, soft pools of yellow lamplight just discernible on the land. We could navigate the Truro River with a good moon, a strong incoming tide, and enough wind to blow us round the bends.

They had left me to my grief — to the awful realization I had stood by Edmund's grave that day in Pendowrick, not knowing I was burying the man I loved. We had followed his coffin just like we had followed Lady Melville's, Sir Richard reading a lesson, Lady Melville tight-lipped and silent. I had stood and watched, thinking only of my hurt that Edmund had left so abruptly. Hurt and angry yet there he was, lying in the coffin in front of me.

Luke came to my side.

'Edmund is dead. I know he is. And it feels just as raw as it did the first time I heard of his loss. Only this time it's so brutal . . . I can't bear to think what happened. The first time I was

433

cross with him for leaving, hurt by his lack of letters, but now I feel such deep love for him. I feel I let him down. He needed me and I did nothing. He was struggling — desperately struggling — and all I could do was chide him for not writing.'

I wiped my tears. 'Yet he *had* been writing, and Francis had been taking his letters out of spite . . . to keep control over him, interfering with our correspondence — a vicious pleasure to him. Yet all the time Edmund was in the coffin and I never knew it. All these years of heartache, he's been in Pendowrick — lying in another man's grave.'

'He's in his beloved Pendowrick, Amelia. He's where he'd want to be — not buried in some unmarked grave, not heaped with other nameless soldiers beneath hot white sands. He's not in the sea, or burnt because of the contagion he carried. He's where he loved. He's with the birds he used to watch — his spirit's picking apples in the orchard, running on the moor. He's home, in Pendowrick — the home he adored and you must take comfort from that.'

'Just recently I saw him in a dream, Luke. For years I hadn't seen his face and then I saw him so clearly. He looked so well — he was happy, his hair bouncing like it always did, but he was running from me. He was wearing this jacket, but he kept running away, looking over his shoulder, laughing that I couldn't keep up with him. And I realize now he had come back to say goodbye. And that makes it even more unbearable. He'd been so tormented and I had no idea.'

'Hold that dream in your heart, Amelia. You say he was well and laughing . . . then you must remember him like that. That's what he'd want. Remember his laughter and his joy. Remember everything you planned and everything you loved about him. Remember the way it was, and never let it go.'

He stayed by my side, the tide drawing us closer to Trenwyn House. The sea was calmer, shouts echoing across the water. Dusk was falling, a misty haze hovering over the darkening water. Rose was on the helm, Jago and James adjusting the sails, drawing them in. They heaved them to the left and we inched slowly upriver, to the bend I knew so well.

'We'll go on,' shouted James. 'The moon's clear. The wind's strong enough — it's keeping south-easterly. We'll just get clear of this sandbank, then we'll keep to the middle of the river. If we lose the wind, we can row back to Trenwyn.'

Ships often lost the wind or ran aground by our house. As children we used to hear their shouts and rise early to row upriver to watch them float free on the incoming tide. Sometimes, they would attach ropes to rowing boats and try to row the boat forwards. Frederick and I used to climb trees and bet on who would get stuck on our sandbank. Once, I caught him moving the poles that marked the outer edge so he would win.

The façade of Trenwyn House stood silhouetted against the darkening sky. Lamps were lit against the coach house, lanterns burning outside the kitchen. Spring would see us return to the house we loved so much, Mother would build more treehouses for the boys, Papa would stride through his fields, picking up handfuls of earth to feel its quality. He would talk to his animals, scratch the head of his beloved black pig. We would play cricket and host concerts on the lawns. I would return to my beloved herb garden and sow new seeds.

L'Aigrette was being slowly pulled by the tide, her sails limp one moment, filling the next as they caught the wind. James stood on the deck, holding tight as he leaned over to watch the silent water. 'We're clear of the starboard pole. Ease out the sails.'

The wooded banks were lost to the darkness, owls hooting in the trees around us. Moonlight shimmered on the black river, the wind lessening, the same pattern as the sails flapped, then swelled again. The night sky was clear, a hazy ring around the moon, and I shivered but would not go below. We were all needed on deck, each of us poised to shout the moment we veered too close to the bank. Flotsam floated alongside us — a plank, an upturned wooden bucket, an empty crate. The river was silent, not a splash against the bow: *L'Aigrette* was gliding soundlessly, spreading her white sails wide, taking us home.

Jago stood at the prow. 'There's the lights of Malpas. The wind's droppin'. I reckon we should cut our losses and anchor there.'

James came to Rose's side. 'Jago can stay with the ship. We'll get someone to take us — two

436

miles by cart will be quicker than two miles with no wind. Let's gather our things.'

Woodsmoke was drifting on the air, lamps burning against the side of the Heron Inn. We had often rowed this far. The summer we got engaged, the four of us had piled into our boat and set off laughing, our baskets crammed with Cook's raised ham pie and freshly baked bread — Frederick, Edmund and I, and Francis. Always Francis. Always watching, always five feet behind. We had run from him, hidden from him. We had dived beneath hay carts, raced along the long drive, holding our breath as we searched for the widest oak we could find. We would hide behind it, sitting at first, then sliding down to lie on our backs, watching the birds above us and imitating their sounds.

It was too painful to remember.

James Polcarrow lowered the rowing boat with hardly a splash. 'We'll make two journeys. Rose can row me over, then she'll come back for you. In the meantime, I'll get us a cart. There's always someone ready with one.' He smiled, though his face remained stern. 'We'll have you home within the hour.'

★   ★   ★

Moonlight shimmered on the black water alongside the road. James Polcarrow sat next to the driver, the rest of us bumping uncomfortably on the hard bench. Luke clasped the seat as we lurched over a rock.

'We can't be that far behind him. He might

even be in Bodmin, still looking for Pierre.' He reached for my hand, firm, secure, gripping my fingers tightly.

'I know he's Francis, Luke. So many things make sense now. When I was with him, I was waiting for him ... hoping ... thinking, he would say something, but he never mentioned our vows. I wanted him ... to convince me they meant as much to him as they did to me, but not once did he refer to that day. Yet in his last letter, Edmund addressed me as *wife*. Edmund believed in those vows as much as I did ... '

'Yes, I saw that.'

'Francis thought he knew everything there was to know about us, but we kept that to ourselves. Only my maid and her fiancé knew, and they were sworn to secrecy.'

'A good lawyer may be able to use that ... '

'There's something else. I've been going over a word he used. It hurt me at the time, but now it takes a darker meaning. He said I *dabbled* in herbs — that's insulting, isn't it? It implies I don't know very much, doesn't it? It implies he thought he knew more than me. Now I'm convinced he's been studying poisons — and that's what Edmund meant when he said *he'll use poison*.'

The ruts were deep in places and difficult to avoid. Rose grabbed my arm to stop herself from slipping off the bench. 'I agree. It does imply he knew more — it's very useful to study poisons if you have murderous intent and plan to use belladonna and laurel water.'

The road was firmer now, widening out before

438

the bridge. Ships were crowding against the wharf, not a breeze blowing, the rigging silent, hardly a creek from the timbers. Smoke rose in tall plumes from the chimneys, the pungent smell of roasted herrings wafting across the river. Fishing nets were hanging up to dry, shouts filtering from a nearby inn. We crossed the bridge as the church clock struck ten. We were almost home.

I threw myself through the door, hurtling across the hall and into Mother's drawing room. Constance was sitting by the fire and I ran to her, reaching for her hands, tears stinging my eyes. Mother stood behind me.

'You've made very good time.' She turned to greet the others, her smile broadening as she saw Rose's breeches. 'Lady Polcarrow — how wonderful, you're wearing men's clothes! I must get some just like that. And Dr Bohenna — you've forgiven me, I hope?'

'You received my letter, Mother?'

'Seth came back with it this afternoon. How was Plymouth Dock?'

'Terrible. Mother could we call for Seth?' I turned to the footman. 'Could you ask Seth to come — if he wouldn't mind?'

Papa was already changed for bed. He stood in the doorway, his red silk dressing gown tied with gold braid, the jewels in his pointed Chinese slippers glinting, his beloved felt hat perched sideways on his head. 'A bit cold to sail, but successful, I hope? You're looking very well, Sir James. My dear Lady Polcarrow, is that what they wear in Fosse these days?'

Seth stood in the doorway. 'Seth, could you check Sir Edmund's horse? I'd like to know if he's back or not.'

'He's not back, Miss Carew. First thing I did — an' I'll keep checking. Nor has he returned to his room in the inn, and no-one answerin' to his description has taken the coach back from Bodmin. I've asked the stable lads to tell me the moment he arrives in Truro. Is there anything else I can help you with?'

'No, thank you. That's very kind. Thank you.' I had to sit down. Now I was home, I found I was shaking. All I wanted to do was lock the doors to keep my family safe.

Mother took my hand and drew me to her, reaching out her other hand for Constance. 'Did you find out anything about the miniature, my love? Had he sent it to someone else?'

I took Edmund's jacket from under my cloak and watched Constance's face crumble. Her hands flew to her mouth, her eyes filling with tears as she stared at the jacket. 'Yes . . . I did find it. And I found this letter . . . from Edmund.'

They stared at the miniature, passing the pages of the letter between them, waiting until each had finished before swapping to the next. Papa was last to finish. He put down the letter, his thick white eyebrows slicing in a frown. 'It's treacherous. It's outrageous. It's quite unpardonable, but it doesn't account for your fear. What's making you so fearful, my love?'

'We believe . . . Sit down, Papa. And you, Constance. This will come as a shock. We believe

440

. . . that night in Plymouth . . . it wasn't Francis they found, but Edmund.'

'Edmund?'

'Yes, Connie . . . We think Edmund is really Francis . . . we think Francis killed Edmund and took his place on the ship.'

'Are you quite sure? This is a grave accusation? Alex's letter tells us of his suspicion that Edmund deserted . . . in fact, his tone implies he thinks it's the most likely explanation . . . but is he Francis?' Papa handed the letter to Mother. 'Can you think it possible?'

She nodded. 'Yes, I believe it very possible. Francis was always a jealous, watchful child — there was something very unpleasant about him — and I saw a glimpse of that when he was here. I would not be surprised in the slightest if once he found out he was the *elder* brother, albeit illegitimate, his resentment knew no bounds.'

Constance's voice sent a chill through me. 'He *is* Francis, I know he is. I felt it right from the start. He didn't love me like Edmund would have loved me. He watched me just like Francis always did. I begged him to let me marry Adam Kemp and he was horrible — there was such hatred in his eyes — yet Edmund had always thought so highly of Adam. He even joked he was jealous because he thought I loved Adam more than him.'

'There's more . . . I smelled almonds by your mother's bed . . . on her lips the morning we found her. I thought it was the balm, but it's the only trace the poison laurel water leaves. I

441

believe Francis poisoned your mother . . . and pushed or tripped Mrs Alston down the stairs.'

Constance clutched her chest. 'Yes. Absolutely . . . Absolutely I believe that . . . The morning Mama died, I felt such torment. I felt evil in the room — I felt unsafe. Mrs Alston knew those stairs like the back of her hand . . . she always took great care. Her death was no accident.'

Mother drew a deep breath. 'Well, I must say that's a shock I didn't see coming. But what proof do you have that any of this might be true? Can you remember any birthmarks, Connie, my love?' Constance shook her head. 'No? And did you find the poison? No? Then is there sufficient evidence to bring about a prosecution, Sir James?'

James Polcarrow shook his head. 'No evidence whatsoever. There's no proof at all. The only thing on our side is that we suspect him and he, as yet, doesn't know we do. He may discover Amelia has whisked Pierre de la Croix away from his clutches, but until he sees that jacket he'll not suspect she, or any of us, are questioning his true identity. Our priority is to keep Constance and George Halliday safe. I believe we should take George into our confidence — but no one else. We'll have to get advice . . . maybe even set a trap.'

Papa had poured several large glasses of brandy. He handed one to Mother. 'Yes, indeed. Set an ambush. He can't keep up this pretence — not now we know. Brandy, Luke? James, Rose . . . You all look like you need one. Here, Connie, you've had a terrible shock.'

They took a glass in turn, James Polcarrow finishing his in one quick gulp. 'Rose and I will go straight to George. Then I intend to wake up my very good friend Matthew Reith and pick his brains about how to proceed.'

We walked James and Rose to the door. Mother took a candle and handed one to me, following me up the stairs as I knew she would. We closed the door, and I drew out the cream purse with its blue satin ribbon, laying out the letters on my desk. There was no discernible difference in the handwriting, no trace of the switch, and tears flooded my cheeks.

'How could anyone be so evil?'

She held me to her. 'He must have taken one of Edmund's letters with him. He would have had to copy it very carefully.'

'I think he'd been studying Edmund's writing for years. He thought he'd be safe, that none of us would suspect, but even with the belladonna, he can't hide the rage in his eyes.'

'Why use belladonna?'

'Because head injuries can cause large pupils . . . and belladonna distorts the function of the eyes — it's a clever ruse to appear blinded by the cannon's fire so he can wear shaded glasses. Perhaps he knows eyes are considered windows to the soul, and he can't hide what others will see in there.'

'Francis must have seen the church register before Lady Melville tore it out. He must have stood, side by side, with Edmund and seen too many similarities between them — so close in age, all four grandparents. They were a mirror to each other, too similar for it to be a coincidence. He decided long ago he would swap places with Edmund but he needed time to be away. He must have blackmailed Sir Richard in order to have funds to finance those years away.'

'He terrorized Edmund, Mother. Perhaps he thought he'd drive him insane. And then the perfect opportunity arose and he was ready to snatch it — right from the start he must have been planning to do Edmund harm.'

'The poor boy . . . the poor, poor boy. I think you're right. Do you remember Edmund was distraught at the thought his father was to send them to Sumatra? Yet I remember when Sir Richard told us, I saw such brilliance in Francis's eyes. They lit up, cold and calculating, yet burning as if it was the best news he could have been given. I think he planned it then — a long journey, a terrible accident, and he'd swap places with his step-brother. All he had to do was remain away long enough for no one to recognize him.'

'I think he received the letter from Lady Melville telling him about Sir Richard's death. He told me it never reached him — and her letter wasn't among his personal effects — but I think he threw it overboard. He *knew* his father had died. All he had to do was come home and murder Lady Melville and Mrs Alston. That's why he came back. When he was here in November he found out I was in love with Luke and assumed I'd call off our betrothal, only I didn't.'

'He'll make a mistake, Amelia. Sir James will

inform Matthew Reith. He's the foremost attorney in Cornwall. He'll find a way to trap him.'

49

Bethany pinned my last hairclip in place, her fingers fumbling as she tried to do up the clasp.

'No, perhaps a bit higher. There. That's better.' She had washed my hair and dried it by the fire, her eyes glancing at the portrait in my hands. She cleared her throat. 'I've been thinking . . . a lot . . . I don't want ye to worry. I'll go with ye to Pendowrick, Miss Amelia. I'll leave Truro and I'll come with ye.'

My heart jolted. 'Thank you . . . That's very kind of you, but there's no need for either of us to leave Truro. Neither of us will ever live in Pendowrick.'

Her cheeks flushed, a sudden hopeful smile. She returned the brush to my dressing table and picked up the damp towels, darting round the room as she tidied everything away. She glanced out of the window. 'Oh, it looks like ye have a visitor, Miss Amelia. Isn't that Mrs Oakley running across the square? Young Mrs Oakley — the Portuguese lady?'

I hurried down the stairs. Sofia Oakley was handing her cloak to the footman. She looked radiant, an enormous smile lighting her face. She was slightly breathless, curtseying quickly, smiling at me with such elation. 'Oh, Miss

Carew, I had to come straight here, you and Lady Clarissa have been so kind to me . . . I had to come to tell you.'

She was carrying a small basket and reached into it. 'I've just received this letter from Mrs Fox . . . it's such good news.' Tears pooled in her large brown eyes, her cheeks flushing.

'Come into the drawing room. Mother will want to know.'

Mother was at her writing desk, Connie reading by the blazing fire. Both looked surprised as I hurried Sofia through the door. I needed Connie with me. I knew what the letter must contain.

Sofia handed the letter to Mother. 'I've just received this letter, Lady Clarissa. My silks were insured — clever Mr Daniel had taken out further insurance. The ship might have been sailing without escort but he'd paid extra for that. He needed his spices to reach the Christmas market, so he doubled the insurance for the ship to sail. Which means that as soon as he can identify me, I can claim the insurance. Mrs Fox says she's bound to trace him through her contacts. Apparently, he's already put in a claim for his spices so that's . . . Well, it's the most wonderful news.'

The colour drained from Connie's face, but Mother was thrilled. 'My dearest, how wonderful. Of course Elizabeth will find Mr Daniel. He'll be able to swear to the insurers that you were on the ship, and that you are who you say you are. It really is wonderful news. I'm so pleased for you.'

She rang the bell for refreshments and I

447

watched the anguish in Connie's eyes. Edmund's shipment, ordered all those years ago, would arrive in time to save the family estate. We should be celebrating, but both of us knew Edmund would never have wanted his beloved Pendowrick saved by such callous disregard for life. Philip Daniel had sailed those men straight to their deaths.

My stomach tightened, remembering how Francis had sat reading the letter — claiming it was *his* shipment, *his* spices. Taking the credit as if he were Edmund.

'I'm so sorry, I can't stay for any refreshments, Lady Clarissa. I'm on my way to find Dr Bohenna. I searched all day for him yesterday, but his mother said he was away. Joe's wheezing is much better after Dr Bohenna's treatment, but he's developed a rash. It's not painful or itchy, but it's getting worse and I'm very worried.'

'A rash — on his body or his arms and legs?' I tried to hide my rising panic.

'It covers his throat and chest, Miss Carew.'

'Does he feel hot? Does he have signs of a fever?'

'Perhaps a little. He was shivering this morning — we're neither of us used to this cold weather.'

'May I come with you? I'd like a walk and I'd to see this rash. Can I go, Mother?'

Mother nodded and I reached for my hat and cloak, pulling on the fine kid gloves Elizabeth had given me for my birthday. Bethany was right behind us, smiling back at me as she tied the ribbons on her hat. The day was overcast, a blanket of grey clouds threatening rain. There was no sign of the wind that had blown us across the sea, just the cold and damp of a February day. I tried not to look concerned. A rash on the throat and chest . . . Luke would need to see that.

The pavements were busy, the usual bustle and noise increasing as we got nearer the quayside. 'Dr Bohenna will be in his rooms behind the library. I think we should try there first.'

A man was hurrying in front of us, his head bent, white shoulder-length hair flowing beneath his hat. He wore a long black coat, black boots and was limping, carrying a black leather bag in one hand, leaning on a heavy cane with the other. 'Oh, my goodness — look! That man fits the description Mrs Hambley gave Pierre . . . Quick. It may be the horse doctor. I have to follow him.'

We had to walk faster, dodging the crowds coming towards us. The old man was striding purposefully and people were moving quickly to get out of his way. He fitted the description perfectly. He looked to be in his seventies, but his movements were strong. 'Quick, we're losing him. He's among that crowd there. Where's he gone?' I looked up and down the quayside but there was no sign of him. 'Did you see where he went, Bethany?'

She shook her head and I turned to look again. I would have to warn Dr Nankivell. He must put up more posters; people must not be taken in by this quack. I searched the crowds

449

again, scanning the gangplanks and decks of the ships, but he had completely disappeared. A group of men were crowding round a man with a mechanical monkey, but he was not among them. He was nowhere to be seen. A stack of crates were just in front of me and I hitched up my skirt, climbing to the top of them. I could see over the heads of everyone and a sudden movement of black caught my eye, a glimpse of white hair.

'Sofia he's gone into your shop. He's just entered the door.'

We ran along the cobbles as fast as we could, but when we reached her shop, I drew her back, watching the man through the small leaded window. He was talking to Mrs Oakley, his back to us. She was shaking her head but he was taking no notice; instead, he was opening his bag and laying out his bottles.

'Go in,' I whispered, 'keep him talking. Make him think you're going to buy his medicines. Get him to explain everything but just keep him talking. Don't taste anything. Do you understand? Don't try *anything*. His medicines are harmful. They don't cure, they kill.'

I turned to Bethany. 'Go and get Luke. Tell him the horse doctor is with Mrs Oakley. Tell him to hurry. Sofia, is there a back way into the shop?'

'Yes, down the alley. It's the door with a new plank of wood. It's right in the middle of the row. It won't be locked so you can just go through. You really want me to buy his medicines?'

'Yes — no — yes. Buy as many as you can — whatever you do, just keep him with you until

450

Luke arrives. Bethany, after you've found Luke, go for Dr Nankivell and tell him to come at once. Then watch the front of the shop and follow him if he leaves. Can you do all that?'

'Course I can.'

She was off, and I leaned against the red bricks as Sofia opened the door. She stood frowning on the doorstep. 'And who are you?' I heard her ask.

'I'm Dr Lovelace,' replied a Scottish accent. 'I'm in Truro and I'm finding so much more illness then there should be. I've my medicines with me, and I can see this poor wee lad is not well at all.'

'I doubt we can afford your medicines, Doctor — though I'd try anything for my poor boy.'

'That, my dear lady, is where I differ from the greedy physicians that hold you all to ransom. My medicines are affordable. May I show you what I recommend?'

'Doctor, I believe you've been sent straight from heaven. Can we shut the shop for a little while, Margaret — just while this good doctor examines Joe?'

The door closed and I heard her turn the lock. The alley was only accessible from the end of the quay and I ran like I've never run before, dodging men rolling barrels, the nets left drying against the houses, the empty crates of fish. I found the entrance hidden behind a large cart and ran down the wet cobbles. It was strewn with rubbish and broken glass, a ditch overflowing down one side, and I picked up my skirt, hurling myself along the filthy passage, searching for a door with a new plank of wood.

It was right in the middle and I stopped to catch my breath, knowing I would have to be quiet. I lifted the latch, leaving the door half-open behind me. The kitchen was dark, exceptionally neat, the table scrubbed clean. A basket of clean laundry stood on the table, two newly baked loaves by its side. Ahead of me, a heavy curtain hung instead of a door and I peeped through a tiny gap at the side.

The horse doctor had spread out his medicines. His woollen gloves were open at the top, the tips of his fingers caressing the bottles. White hair fell to his shoulders, his long bushy beard moving as he spoke. A pair of heavy white eyebrows rose and fell above the thick iron frames of his glasses and even from behind the curtains, I recognized the exact bottles I had thrown into Lady Melville's fire, the exact same bottle I had taken out of Pierre de la Croix's hands.

'I believe I have everything you might need. Will you raise that shirt of yours, my wee man, and let me take a listen to your chest?' He reached for Joe's pulse at his neck, lifting Joe's chin with his long tapering fingers. He leaned closer and I watched him carefully. Something looked wrong. Beneath the thick black coat seemed too strong a frame for an old man — his shoulders were bent, he had a definite stoop, but they were broader than I would expect in a man with such white hair.

He had heavy lines on his face, his cheeks swollen, his upper lip covered by his bushy moustache, but he seemed to move with undue ease, showing no stiffness for a man who needed a cane. His voice was soft, persuasive, a definite Scottish accent.

'A rash like this . . . coupled with a wheeze . . . is not good, I'm afraid. The child has all the signs of worms, dear lady. Not worms in your stomach, but worms in his lungs. Has he been on a sea voyage? I usually only see this level of contagion in sailors.'

Sofia clasped her hands to her mouth, her eyes wide with terror. 'Oh, yes, Doctor. We've been at sea until quite recently, and for a very long time. Are you telling me there are worms in my beloved son's lungs? Can you cure him, Doctor? Can you rid him of them?'

The horse doctor kept his back to me as if he was watching the door. Mrs Oakley was clearly distressed, and Sofia rushed to take her hand. He turned to speak to them, and I saw his face clearly. His glasses looked familiar and I stared at the heavy rims, blood rushing from my head. I had seen those glasses before — those very glasses, just two nights ago.

The black coat leaned over the terrified boy. Joe was pulling back from him, but Sofia was smiling, nodding for him to let the doctor examine him further.

'Open your mouth for me, ye poor wee man. Oh yes . . . dearie me . . . it's definitely the contagion you get from the weevils in ship's biscuits. It's not safe what they give those poor men. They need limes and fruit, not insect-infested biscuits. They lay their eggs in the timbers of the ships and

453

when they hatch they have to find a body to infect. They're too small to see but they travel round your blood and once you've got them, they eat your organs and you just wither and die.'

'No!'

'But I have drops that will clear away these worms in no time — at very little cost to such a lovely lady and such a poor wee mite.' He reached for his bottle, pulling out the cork. 'Here now, let's see if these drops work. We usually tell straight away. Here . . . open your mouth, wee laddie.'

Sofia rushed forward, cradling Joe in her arms. 'Worms in his throat?'

Behind me, I heard the faintest noise and Luke slipped to my side. I did not speak but pointed to the other end of the curtain and he leaned forward to watch.

'Aye, it's worms all right, in the back of his throat. They're in that huge red lump, dangling there, as plain as plain. I've seen this time and time again, but I can put your mind at ease — I've just what he needs. And you, my poor wee lassie, you must have some too, because if your son's got the worms, you'll have the worms. Only it's easier and much better to get them *before* they cause this rash.'

'We'll buy the vial, Doctor — in fact, we'll take two. I can't thank you enough. But, here, let me give them to him — my Joe's a delicate boy and he gets frightened by strangers. Tell me, Doctor, have you anything I can take for my sore joints? I've terrible aches since the damp of the voyage

— burning joints, all the time. It's not the worms in my joints, is it?'

He put down the vial and held her wrist up to the light. 'Och, you poor wee lassie, it's as like as not. They lay their eggs in the joints. It gets so painful, I've seen grown men cry.'

I could do nothing but stare at his glasses. Nothing else was the same. His face looked fuller, the white hair must be a wig, the beard false, the bushy white eyebrows stuck on with glue. He was clearly a master of poisons, but why poison Mrs Oakley and her son? I put my hand on Luke's sleeve, pulling him back through the kitchen. Once outside in the filthy alley, I leaned against the bricks.

'It's Francis, Luke, I know it is, and he means to poison them. He got to Pierre before us — only Pierre was busy in the garden and he sold his poison to Mrs Hambley. I recognize the glasses. You saw them that night — they're the same, aren't they? That can't be a coincidence.'

Luke ran his hand across his mouth. 'Yes, I saw the glasses.

That's a young man's movements . . . it has to be him. He tried to kill Lady Melville and Mrs Alston with his poison, but you intervened and stopped them in time. I'll get James — and Major Trelawney. Stop Mrs Oakley from taking anything — they're not to have a single drop.'

'I've told her not to — she won't. And I told her to keep him talking but I don't know how much longer she can hold him.'

'Stay here. I'll be straight back. Why does he want to hurt them?'

'I don't know. Hurry, Luke — hurry.'

I stepped back into the dark kitchen, tiptoeing across the stone floor to the heavy curtain. Sofia had her skirt pulled up and was unrolling her stocking. 'And here, Doctor. See this horrible red bruise? I've had it as long as the journey. You're a doctor, so you won't mind me rolling down my stocking like this — showing it to you. Only with worms and such, could these be eggs as well?'

'Undoubtedly. They lay their eggs deep beneath your skin — and we don't want them crawling out' He sounded slightly more abrupt, glancing back at the door. 'Dear lady, I've other patients asking for my help and I can't stay much longer. Is it two vials you want? That's just four pence. That's two pence each — now that's nothing, is it, for a total cure of the worms?'

He knew she was delaying him, and she must have thought so too. She pulled up her stocking and reached for her bag. 'That's very kind. I'll start the drops as soon as I've paid. How many drops shall I give my son, and how many for myself?'

He was packing up his chest, his long thin fingers in their woollen gloves, smoothing down the remaining bottles, covering them with a velvet cloth. There was no sign of Major Trelawney or James Polcarrow. He was getting ready to leave. The door to the shop was still locked but I could see a new swiftness to his movements, no sign of stiffness, but a young, fit man looking round as if he knew he might need to run. I glanced at the back door. Should I lock it, or should I wait for Luke to come?

'Ten drops three times a day should suffice but keep taking the medicine until you finish the two vials. That's absolutely vital. Don't stop the treatment halfway, or it won't work.'

People were passing the window, a man riding by on a horse. A ship was leaving the quayside, men were shouting, coiling in the ropes. The sails were rising, a line of women waving. On the polished counter behind him, pieces of neatly cut leather lay ready to be sewn into a pair of gloves.

'It's been such a pleasure, Doctor, but before you go, my mother-in-law stitches gloves and she gets terrible sores on her fingers. Some get quite large and they have puss in them. Show him your fingers, Margaret — not that you've got the puss now — but perhaps the good doctor has something for when you do? Have you come across puss fingers before, Doctor?'

He looked angry now and I turned at the faint sound of shuffling. Luke and James were in the kitchen, behind them Major Trelawney, and I pointed to the curtain, standing back so they could get a glimpse of the man selling poison. He was examining Margaret Oakley's fingers.

'Och, they look fine to me. A few pinpricks and some certain reddening, but I have something for you that will ease this inflammation. It's best to get this sorted before the puss comes back. I've a tincture, but I think my lozenges will do better. Suck two or three a day, and that redness will go.' He opened the case, thrusting a bottle towards her. He shut the case and walked quickly across the shop. 'I'll not charge you for that, because I'm in a hurry now

457

. . . I've got a list of patients to get through.'

He reached the door, expecting to open it. He searched the keyhole for the key. 'Open this door! I'll not be held like this.' There was panic is his voice, his Scottish accent slipping. 'Give me the key.' He rushed back, his huge frame pushing Sofia to the floor. He flung open the curtain.

'We'll take that.' James wrenched the bag from his hand, holding tight to both wrists as the black-coated arms lashed out. The man twisted free, punching James in the face, making for the back door. 'No you don't.' James was on to him again, his arms reaching out as he flung himself across the floor to grab him round the thighs. He pulled him to the ground, pinning his arms behind his writhing back. Major Trelawney was ready with his handcuffs and clamped the clenched fists tight, followed by the frantically kicking ankles.

'Francis Bainbridge, I am arresting you for the murder of Lady Charlotte Melville and Mrs Annie Alston. For the attempted murder of Captain Pierre de la Croix and for the brutal murder of your half-brother Edmund Melville.' Henry Trelawney grabbed the white wig, pulling it from him, ripping off the long white beard and glasses, and I stared into the murderous eyes of Francis Bainbridge.

Sofia Oakley was in the doorway, rubbing her injured elbow. She gasped, staring in horror at the man with short dark hair and a scar above his upper lip. 'But it's Mr Daniel!' she cried. 'It's Philip Daniel. Why on earth do you want to poison us?'

50

Town House, Truro
Saturday 24th February 1798, 11 a.m.

Papa threw another log on the fire and resumed his seat. Major Trelawney and Sir James had just left.

'So Francis Bainbridge denies everything, does he? Well, he can't deny that the bottles he peddled contained laurel water — Luke and Dr Nankivell can both swear to that. He'll be found guilty, no question about it.'

'He needed to kill Sofia and Joe because they knew him as Philip Daniel. They were the *only* ones who could recognize him under that name.'

Mother was wearing her silk turquoise gown, copied from an exotic print of a Turkish lady. The skirt was divided into pantaloons but she had stopped short of the gold armlets and long veil, opting instead for a shorter one that fell to her shoulders.

'Indeed, my love. Captain Banyan was dead but Sofia and Joe could identify him as being on the ship from Sumatra. Another blow to his story — and when he read that Elizabeth was looking for a Mr Philip Daniel, it threw him into a panic. He had to find out who had recognized him.'

'But first, he needed to silence Pierre. He knew Pierre would know there was no prison hulk. That night — that rage we saw — was fear as well as anger. He couldn't hide it. He must have visited Mrs Hambley's just moments before we got there.'

Mother shook her head. 'It could have been a very different story. I shudder to think of it. And he hurried back in the stagecoach dressed in his doctor's disguise which is why no one saw him return. Thank goodness Pierre was busy and didn't take the medicine straight away. And then he went straight to find Sofia and young Joe. Do you know what chills me most?'

'That he could kill a mother and her child?'

'That apart. His deviousness — his ability to cover his tracks . . . like telling the innkeeper Philip Daniel was looking for him. That's so calculating.'

'He didn't see Pierre only because Mrs Hambley didn't want to disturb him. She bought the medicine because he persuaded her it would cure his rheumatism and only gave it to Pierre as we left. If we hadn't stopped him from taking it, he would have died.'

Mother shook her head. 'He's devious, and very clever. He must have arrived in England not long after Sofia and Joe — in November, not December. He had time to collect his disguise and gather up his poisons . . . I believe he probably wanted to poison his aunt back in December but something stopped him. Maybe you didn't leave the house, Connie? Either way, he must have hidden the disguise and potions and came back for them later.'

Constance was wearing a soft grey gown and Mother's burgundy shawl, her black hair falling around her shoulders, looped on both sides with a pair of Mother's pearl hairpins. She put down her book, *Marshall's Rural Economy of the West of England*.

'And he can't have been in London when he said he was. He might have written to Sir Alex from London, but then he must have hurried down to Bodmin . . . and hidden, watching the house, waiting until I'd gone to the village before he risked selling his poison to Annie.'

Papa swirled the globe again, his fingers trailing across the vast blue ocean. 'He was here in Cornwall . . . in November, but he had to wait for the right ship in Ireland. He hid the poisons, sailed to Ireland where he had to wait for an appropriate Portuguese trader. It might have taken him weeks . . . then he struck lucky. A storm brought the ship in . . . he got talking to the crew, learned everything he needed to know — where they'd traded, what they'd been carrying — and everything slotted into place.'

I knelt at his feet by the globe. 'James reckoned he probably went straight to Jamaica, then sailed for Sumatra . . . yes, that makes sense. He had over three years to get there and back — time enough to search out the merchant who'd swindled his father. He must have been planning to go there all the time.'

A wave of sorrow flooded my heart. Sir Richard *had* loved Edmund, yet for so long, Edmund believed otherwise. 'Sir Richard and Edmund were both at Francis's mercy,' I whispered. 'Do you think it was *Francis* who suggested to Sir Richard that they should go to

461

Sumatra in the first place? And Sir Richard didn't trust him with Edmund so he changed his mind?'

Papa traced the outline of Africa, stopping at the port of Mombasa. 'I think that very likely, under the circumstances. Do you think Francis poisoned the merchant, too?'

Mother shrugged. 'Who knows? I think he most likely *coerced* them into honouring the shipment. I imagine he intended to continue trading with them so he left them alive but in no doubt about what would happen if they cheated him again.'

Sunlight filtered through the windows, the room bright, the fire roaring. Not half an hour ago, Major Trelawney had stood by the fire and shocked us all with his thoughts — his absolute belief that Francis had swapped his uniform with one of his fallen comrades. He believed the bag Francis had taken from the ship was not full of explosives but clothes — clothes he said had been stolen from his trunk. How else had an officer been recorded as one of the fallen men?

A shiver ran down my spine: the thought of him holding me, almost forcing me to kiss him. I had felt such revulsion. Recoiling at the touch of a murderer, a man who would strip a comrade of his clothes and replace them with his own.

Connie was looking at me. 'Francis asked me if I had the key to Father's desk. He wasn't sure about how much I knew . . . or what I had access to. He had to know, because I would have seen the letter he claimed he found. He put that letter in Father's desk — the one about the spices. He had it all organized — he was going to claim the insurance and pay off the debts.'

Mother joined us at the globe. 'But what I can't understand is why he got off the ship in Lisbon. Why not wait for an escort? He posted Amelia's letter from there . . . he must have got someone to write it in Portuguese . . . but why didn't he get back on the ship? You don't think he saw someone he recognized on the quayside, do you? He couldn't risk a navy escort because he might be recognized?'

Papa's finger was on Lisbon now. 'Maybe the officer who came on board was from his old ship?'

My heart thumped. 'What if it was *Frederick*? HMS *Circe* is on escort duty in the Mediterranean. What if he saw Frederick?'

Constance looked almost at peace. Her cheeks had lost their gauntness, her frown and tight lips no longer there. Her eyes seemed softer, her smile quicker, reaching her eyes. 'I'm going to order a beautiful new tomb for Edmund. I'm going to place it where he used to love to sit. The view from there stretches right across the moor . . . you can see the sea in one direction and the peaks of the moors in the other. It's not among the other tombs . . . it's just by the orchard. I know he'll love it. He's at peace now.'

Mother glanced out of the window, her eyes following someone across the square. 'Amelia, my love. Fetch me some more paper from your father's study, would you? Only I'm running rather short.'

She must have seen the tears welling in my

463

eyes and I was glad to seek some solace. I could not help it. Connie's talk of Edmund's new tomb had moved me to tears. *He's at peace now.* Papa's study was warm, the fire blazing, and I picked up some paper for Mother. I had to put it down again and leaned onto the desk as another wave of sorrow swept through me. His death was so brutal and it felt so raw again. Only this time it was worse because I knew the truth. He had never deserted me, never stopped loving me. He even addressed me in his last letter as *wife*.

I reached into my pocket, his miniature trembling in my hands and I stared back into his haunted eyes. The door opened and Luke strode purposely into the room.

'Oh, forgive me . . . I didn't see you there . . . it's just . . . your mother sent me in for some writing paper.' He saw my tears and came slowly to my side, cupping his hand gently beneath mine as I held the miniature. I made to put it away, but he kept his hand firm.

'Don't ever feel you must put Edmund's portrait away in front of me. Never think I don't want to see it, nor see you grieve for him. Remember what I said — that I never sought to take his place but only sought to lodge beside him in your heart? There's room for both of us, Amelia. Don't hide him from me.'

His arm slipped round my shoulders, the other still holding my hand. Edmund was looking back at us and tears splashed my cheeks. 'I would have loved him as a friend, Amelia. Had I known him, I would have wanted his good opinion. And had you already been married, I would have admired you as *his* wife. Don't ever hide your grief from me. You must never forget him. We must never forget him.'

'I planted my herb garden because I needed somewhere to be alone with him. He's in every herb, every single drawing. I did it all to honour him.'

'Which is why you must dedicate your herbal to him — *In honour of Sir Edmund Melville, my beloved friend.*'

I glanced up. His blue eyes were searching mine, full of tenderness and understanding. Deep furrows etched his forehead, his eight long years of study and his patients' suffering taking their toll. His hair was freshly washed, worn short, receding at his temples, the auburn hints in his sideburns catching the firelight.

'Amelia, I vowed to Edmund a long time ago — to the departed soul of a man I had never met but who had loved you so very dearly — that I would look after you for him. That I would love you, honour you and cherish you, and that vow will stand for the rest of my life. I will do everything in my power to bring you the happiness he would have brought you.'

A sound of scuffling, followed by a breathless shout. 'Aunt Amelia . . . Aunt Amelia . . . Oh, *there* you are — we've been looking *all* over for you.'

Luke's arm dropped. 'Oh dear . . . here we go again!'

'Hello, Dr Bohenna. It's good you're here because Uncle Emerson is with us and you can talk your *doctors' talk.*' The two boys beamed

465

adoringly up at me. 'Did you know Uncle Emerson has *never, ever* slid down the banisters *in his whole life?*'

'What, never in his whole life? Are you certain about that?'

'Never, ever, ever.' They shook their heads. 'And he's *never, ever* climbed a tree!'

I shook my head back at them. 'That's terrible. Poor Uncle Emerson.'

William and Henry rushed to the window. 'Oh, here's Grandmother. She said she'd follow us here.'

I looked at Luke but turned quickly as Papa rushed into the room. 'Hurry, it's The Galleon, and she's in full sail,' he said, flinging himself behind his huge leather armchair. 'Quick, take cover. *Pilchards*, everyone.' He scrambled out again and ran back to the hall, shouting into the drawing room. 'PILCHARDS, Clarissa, Connie. Quick. PILCHARDS.' He came tumbling back into the room.

Luke grabbed my elbow and pulled me behind the red damask curtain.

'But that's where *we* usually *hide*,' insisted Henry.

Luke was adamant. 'Not today, boys — William take the other curtain; Henry, pop into that cupboard. Lord Carew, you're safe behind the chair. Ah, good day, Dr Polgas — I suggest you hide behind the door.'

'Whatever for?' came the shocked reply.

'*Pilchards*, old boy,' came a voice from behind the heavy armchair.

'Don't tell us you've *never* played *Pilchards*

either?' came a shocked voice from behind the other curtain. 'Just hide behind the door, Uncle Em, and we'll teach you properly later.'

Luke's arms closed round me and we stood behind the heavy curtain, trying not to laugh. 'Poor boys. They usually hide here.'

He laughed softly, as I knew he would. 'You honestly think I'd give up this chance? *Never, ever . . . not in my whole life.*'

He held me to him, his strong arms folding round me. He bent to kiss my hair and I leaned against his crisp white necktie, his physician's jacket and his simple white shirt. He smelled of soap, of all that was wholesome, of everything I loved.

Through the thick damask brocade we heard Lady Polgas striding from room to room. 'Of course they're here. They were just ahead of me, for goodness' sake. I stopped for *five* minutes, *ten* at the most. Where are they?' She must have been peering into the study as her voice got louder. 'They can't just disappear? Where are they?'

'I'm not sure, m'lady. I think they've been here but they're not here now . . . Shall I check the kitchens, m'lady?'

'The *kitchens*? Good God, man. Are you saying my grandsons might be in the *kitchens*? Go and fetch them at once.'

I pressed my finger against Luke's lips. 'Shhhh, she'll hear you. Don't laugh. Don't give us away.'

I heard a throat clear and I recognized Bethany's politest tone. 'They're not in the kitchens, Lady Polgas. I think maybe they arrived and found no one was at home, and so they didn't stay. Perhaps they've gone back to look for you? I shouldn't wonder that you'll find them back at your house. Shall I call for some refreshments . . . for while you wait? . . . Oh, you're going.'

The front door closed and the boys peeped out. 'Well done, Uncle Em. Well done, Grampa. Well done, Dr Bohenna. That was brilliant fun. Are you coming, Aunt Amelia?'

Papa eased himself out from behind his heavy leather armchair. 'Your aunt has just left — she and Dr Bohenna . . . Didn't you hear them go out?'

Mother must have been at the door. 'How about we make some more *biscotti di Saronno* for Uncle Emerson, boys?' she said quickly.

'Oh yes, please let's. Uncle Em *loved* them — he said they were just like ship's biscuits. Didn't you, Uncle Emerson?'

We heard an uncomfortable cough, the beginning of a terrible excuse. 'Umm, yes, what I meant was they're very like the *very best* ship's biscuits we used to . . . have sent to us . . . from . . . very expensive shops . . . '

'Splendid,' came Mother's joyous reply. 'But maybe we should make some Turkish delight, instead? Yes, I think we'll make that. And then, boys, you can teach Uncle Emerson how to slide down the banisters. I think Uncle Emerson would like that very much.' We heard footsteps, then a call across the hall. 'Connie, my love?'

'Yes, Lady Clarissa?'

'I'd like you to get ready to receive some visitors, my dear. I have invited two eminently suitable men for your approval — or disapproval — as the case may be. They'll be here soon. One might be a bit old, I grant you, but the other has a lot of rather splendid qualities and I believe he may make a very suitable match. No pressure, of course, but seeing you are going to inherit the house and estate . . . I feel a certain *obligation* to your dear mother. You understand, don't you, my dear?'

The door closed and we made no move, Luke's arms staying tightly around me. 'Thank heavens for *Pilchards*,' he whispered, 'and your wonderfully eccentric parents, who do nothing but think of ways to throw us together.' His lips brushed my hair, kissing my forehead. 'Amelia, it's too soon . . . I understand that. I can wait as long as you need.' He kissed my forehead again and I thought my heart would burst. I was in the arms of the man I was meant to be with, fate had decreed that many years ago, and I lifted my chin, looking deeply into the eyes of the man I adored.

'No, Luke,' I whispered. 'It's not too soon. It's not too soon at . . .'

Our lips touched and a flame burned my heart, the intensity of my love making my eyes water. Luke Bohenna, the kindest, most compassionate man I knew, with his serious studying and his wicked sense of humour. How I loved him. How I adored him.

His voice was hoarse, wrung with emotion. 'Dearest Amelia, will you do me the very great honour of becoming my wife?'

I reached up to kiss his lips. 'I'd love to Luke. There's nothing I'd love more.'

He began fumbling in his jacket, first the right pocket, then the left, then the inside lining. 'Ah! That's a bit of a nuisance,' he whispered. 'I may just have to run home . . .'

'No,' I whispered back. 'Don't leave . . . not now we're finally alone.'

We started laughing, softly at first, then louder, the two of us doubling up out of sheer joy. He drew me to him, holding me like he would never let me go. His lips brushed my hair. 'You haven't asked me about Joe's rash?' he whispered.

'Do you think it looked like Mrs Templeton's? And Mrs Jennings's? It follows the same treatment and it's the exact same timing.'

'That's precisely what I thought — the rash isn't contagious but it imitates a fever. It flares for two days and then it fades. Do you think it could be a reaction to the laudanum tincture? What is it? Why are you smiling?'

'Look,' I whispered, peering from behind the red damask curtain at the two men hurrying across the square; both were tall and slender, one with white hair beneath his tall hat, the other with rather distinctive red hair. Both were wearing dark black jackets and breeches, both with high foreheads and kind eyes. They stopped to adjust their neckties, which were still slightly askew. 'Mother's invited Reverened Kemp and Adam for tea. I hope Connie chooses to marry one of them — preferably the younger, although

I believe she loves the elder just as much. Shall we go and greet them?'

He closed the gap in the curtain, his smile filled with the mischief I loved so well.

'Maybe not . . . quite . . . yet . . . perhaps we may in a little while?' His lips closed over mine. 'Perhaps in . . . a . . . very . . . long . . . while.'

★ ★ ★

There is no herb, no balm, no decoction, no sedative, no purgative, nor hypnotic so effective for those who grieve than the passage of time and the tender shoots of a new beginning. With compassion, and the understanding of a true mind, broken hearts can once more beat in unison, nurtured and healed by the power of enduring love.

THE LADY HERBALIST

We do hope that you have enjoyed reading this large print book.

Did you know that all of our titles are available for purchase?

We publish a wide range of high quality large print books including:
Romances, Mysteries, Classics
General Fiction
Non Fiction and Westerns

Special interest titles available in large print are:
The Little Oxford Dictionary
Music Book
Song Book
Hymn Book
Service Book

Also available from us courtesy of Oxford University Press:
Young Readers' Dictionary
(large print edition)
Young Readers' Thesaurus
(large print edition)

For further information or a free brochure, please contact us at:
Ulverscroft Large Print Books Ltd.,
The Green, Bradgate Road, Anstey,
Leicester, LE7 7FU, England.
Tel: (00 44) 0116 236 4325
Fax: (00 44) 0116 234 0205

THE CORNISH LADY

Nicola Pryce

Educated, beautiful, and the daughter of a prosperous merchant, Angelica Lilly has been invited to spend the summer in high society. Her father's wealth is opening doors and attracting marriage proposals, but Angelica still feels like an imposter among the aristocrats of Cornwall. When her brother returns home, ill and under the influence of a dangerous man, Angelica's loyalties are tested to the limit. Her one hope lies with coachman Henry Trevelyan, a softly spoken educated man with kind eyes. But when Henry seemingly betrays Angelica, she has no one to turn to. Who is Henry, and what does he want? And can Angelica save her brother from a terrible plot that threatens to ruin her entire family?

THE CORNISH DRESSMAKER

Nicola Pryce

Cornwall, 1796: Seamstress Elowyn Liddicot's family believe they've secured the perfect future for her, in the arms of Nathan Cardew. But then one evening Elowyn helps to rescue a dying man from the sea, and everything changes. William Cotterell, wild and self-assured, refuses to leave her thoughts or her side — but surely she can't love someone so unlike herself? With Elowyn's dressmaking business suddenly under threat, her family's pressure to marry Nathan increasing, and her heart decidedly at odds with her head, Elowyn doesn't know who to trust anymore. And when William uncovers a sinister conspiracy that affects her whole world, can Elowyn find the courage to support the people she loves in the face of all opposition?